Spies Don't Fall for Their Rival: A Sweet Romantic Comedy

Interior Design by Mountain Heights Publishing

Author website: www.megeaston.com

ALSO BY MEG EASTON

Romancing the Spy romantic comedies

Spies Don't Fall for Their Asset

Spies Don't Fall for Their Rival

Spiced Chais and Secret Spies (coming 2024)

———

How to Not Fall romantic comedies

How to Not Fall for the Guy Next Door

How to Not Fall for the Wrong Guy

How to Not Fall for Your Best Friend

How to Not Fall for Your Ex

———

A Mountain Springs Christmas

The Christmas Pact

The Christmas Bet

The Christmas Clause

———

Nestled Hollow Romances

Coming Home to the Top of Main Street

Second Chance on the Corner of Main Street

Christmas at the End of Main Street

More than Friends in the Middle of Main Street

Love Again at the Heart of Main Street

More than Enemies on the Bridge of Main Street

————

Love Started Romances

It Started with a Sunset

It Started with a Note

It Started with a Glance

————

Silver Leaf Falls romance

Coming Home to Silver Leaf Falls

Spies Don't Fall for Their Rival

Spies Don't Fall for Their Rival

USA TODAY BESTSELLING AUTHOR

MEG EASTON

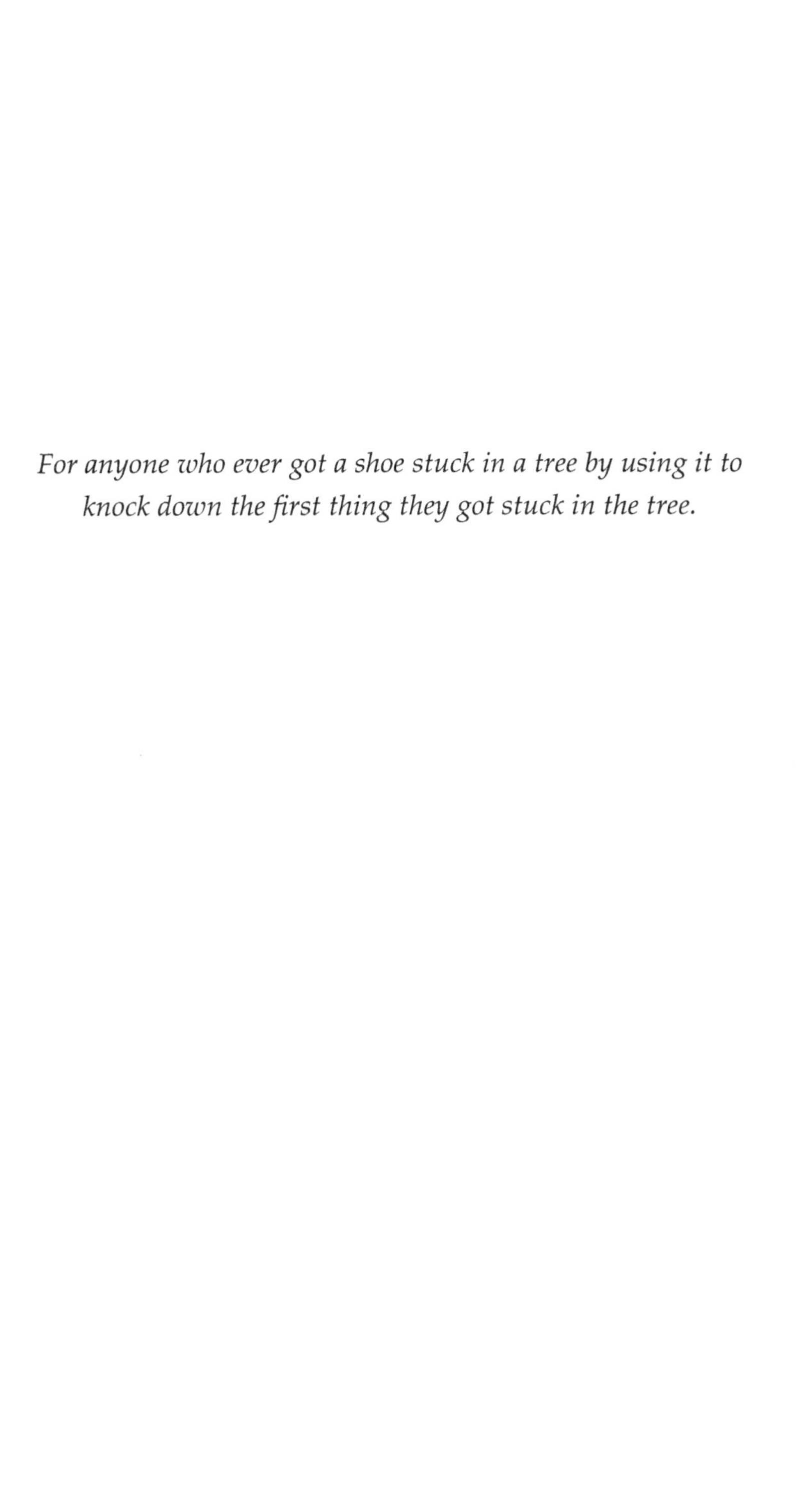

For anyone who ever got a shoe stuck in a tree by using it to knock down the first thing they got stuck in the tree.

CONTENTS

CONTENT NOTICE

This book is a lighthearted and fun romcom that is heavy on humor and light on spy/suspense/danger elements. If you appreciate trigger warnings, read on! If you see them as spoilers and don't need them, skip ahead to the swoony fun of this book.

Some possible triggers:

- Abandonment issues
- Child neglect (past)
- An anxiety attack
- Derogatory comments about stinky cheese

In case you'd like to know: Although one character gets injured in a non-life-threatening way, no one dies during the book. There is no sex, either— just several swoon-worthy kisses. And, like all Meg books, you'll get lots of witty banter, fun characters, and a happy ending.

CHAPTER 1
HOODIES AND HANDOFFS
LEDGER

get to travel to a lot of places as an intelligence operative, and I love it when my job brings me to Philadelphia. This place has soul. It's practically a playground for anyone with a sense of adventure.

I smile to myself as I cross the one-way street in the heart of Philadelphia, heading away from a giant mural on the side of a building toward the ancient building that holds the clothing shop where I'm meeting my asset. I nod at a couple of women seated at a small outdoor table in front of the sandwich shop next door as I pass by, and they both make flirty faces at me. I return it with a grin and a wink.

It's probably because of my scruff. My job requires that I be clean-shaven except while on assignment. Since it never hurts to have a disguise, I applied the stubble during part of the forty-six-minute helicopter ride here. I think it looks pretty good. Obviously, the two twenty-somethings think so, too.

Of course, they could be attracted to the muscles. My biceps do a little twitching flex. They look pretty good in this shirt, too.

I step into the shop and glance at the layout of the store like it's my first time in here— which is true— and I'm trying to figure out where to go to get what I'm looking for. Which isn't true— I spotted my contact the moment I opened the door. But there are a dozen or so others in this shop, so the act is for them.

Then I let my eyes fall to where my asset is fidgeting in front of a rack of designer hoodies, but his attempts at casual browsing are pretty unconvincing. I let my face light up in recognition as if I just spotted my long-lost friend somewhere unexpected. "Kolson!" There's an underlying tension between us because of our real purpose here, but I don't let it come out in my voice.

My asset jumps slightly, a clear sign of his frayed nerves, before schooling his features into a smile. It's strained and doesn't reach his eyes, which are currently darting around the shop as if expecting trouble to burst through the doors at any minute. It doesn't surprise me based on our phone call this morning. We shake hands, transitioning into the bro clasp— a bit too hastily on his part— which is how I know that his palms are clammy.

"How are you doing, my friend?" I ask, keeping my tone light, trying to ease Kolson's nerves. He's been invaluable over the past several weeks, but seeing him this rattled underscores the risks he's taken.

"Good. Just… shopping for a hoodie."

"Oh," I say. "I need a new one, too."

I start looking through the rack, and Kolson leans in and murmurs, "I found out that the handoff is going to be right in front of Paws & Reflect."

"A *'Whimsical Pet Parlor?'*" I say, remembering the tagline of that particular business. *"That's* where they chose?"

"It's over on Market Street, between third and fourth." He wipes his brow with the back of his hand. It's a quick gesture, as if he doesn't want me to notice that he's so nervous he's sweating.

I nod. "I know the area." At the Clandestine Services Agency, we've been tracking some stolen art pieces, and we believe that they're using the transporting of the art to move illegal arms. We think that the case Kolson called me about in a panic might contain smuggling routes or key contacts. "When?"

Kolson winces, abandoning the hoodie ruse entirely. "At one."

My eyes widen as I look at my watch. "That's in six minutes."

"I'm sorry. It's the best notice I could give. I worried that you wouldn't make it here in time at all."

Fifty-three minutes ago, I got a call from Kolson. He said he overheard an associate talking about a handoff for the "Abstract Exchange," the name he figured referred to the art thefts, and he said it sounded like it was going to happen soon. He planned to dig deeper while I traveled, and then meet me here to share what he found.

I was on a helicopter heading toward him from the Clandestine Services Agency building in Maryland seven minutes after his call. I'm not sure I could've made it any faster, but I really wish I could've shaved a minute or two off the time.

"You're the best," I say, patting him on his tense shoulder. "Thanks, man."

As I walk toward the back of the shop, I say in a low voice, "Did you catch the circus?"

In my earpiece, my handler, Kella, who is young, fun, and always exactly specific, says, "Caught the tightrope act, and I've got eyes on where the clowns are supposed to emerge from their tiny cars. The handoff will happen point five two miles from your current location. I'm searching for a cab in the area."

"There's no time. I'll run."

"What's your mile time?"

"Six minutes."

"Okay, so factoring the corners, both pedestrian and vehicle traffic, you could probably make it in three-and-a-half minutes."

"Any cameras out the back door?"

"Yes," Kella says, "but there's a blind spot against the building until you reach the cross street."

"Good enough." I'm not going to walk out the front door because when I grab this briefcase as it's handed off from one bad actor to another, at least one of them is going to hack into some CCTV cameras and backtrack to where I came from. And they can't see me walking out of a shop that my asset walked into not long before. I'm not about to burn him.

But this place does have a back room, so I pretend that I'm really drawn to some clothes near it. Just as I get to them, a woman pushes the door open with her body, her arms full of folded pants. Like a gentleman, I rush forward to hold it open for her, and then I slip inside as it closes.

I take two steps into the back room and see another shop worker, standing at a table, looking like she's been folding shirts all neat and crisp but is now frozen mid-fold, just staring at me.

"Do you have a back door out of here?" I ask. "I just saw that my ex-fiancée and her mean friend are sitting at one of the café tables out front. If I exit that way, they're going to start throwing things at me. I have a job interview in fifteen minutes, and I can't go there with shaved beef, onions, and Cheez-Whiz on my shirt."

I am currently wearing a fitted t-shirt and drawstring cotton pants with elastic at the ankle, and at the moment, I can't think of a job where this would be appropriate interview attire. Maybe I should get into the habit of wearing a suit on missions like my brothers Jace and Miles do. Except that would mean I'd have to stop doing the opposite of what Miles does, and I'm not willing to do that.

"Yes, of course," the woman says, and instead of just pointing toward the door, she actually rushes to it and opens it for me.

I give her a smile. "Thanks. You totally saved me."

Then I step out and take off all-out running, keeping

close to the buildings as the sound of the Liberty Bell echoes in the distance.

The trick to getting people to do what you want is to mention one bad thing that could happen to you— the ex-fiancée and mean friend throwing things at me. Don't let them think about it for too long before mentioning a second bad thing— not wanting to be embarrassed at a job interview. The person might not relate to the first thing, so the second thing has to be more universally relatable.

Saying something specific is important, too, like the Cheez Whiz on my shirt, because that gets the person picturing it. And once they picture it, it's as good as real. Inevitable. And once it's inevitable, people are always more than willing to help out.

Kella says, "Oh! I see you've already shot off like a bullet! So you'll get there in time, assuming the guys doing the handoff are the on-time sort."

As soon as I get to Sixth Street, I cut across the grassy area by the Liberty Bell, not slowing my pace at all. I ran track all through high school and college, and I still train as though I'm trying to win gold in the 800-meter run.

I weave in and out of tourists and leap over a dog lying in the grass next to its owner. A woman must've decided she forgot something and spins around unexpectedly. I dodge, but we still manage to brush shoulders enough that she nearly gets knocked off balance. I call out a "Sorry!" as I exit the park and turn onto Market Street, passing by a tour bus that looks more like a boat with wheels.

The sounds of the city surround me— people talking, cars, buses, and trucks running, dogs barking, construction sounds in the distance, occasional horns honking, and street vendors calling out to people. I try to tune it all out as I run. Just like I'm trying to tune out the way my lungs are burning and focus only on the adrenaline coursing through me.

In my ear, Kella says, "I'm looking at the cameras in front of Paws and Reflect and see clown number one leaning against his car— a black late-model Chevrolet Impala— so not a tiny car, after all. He's exhibiting classic shady character behavior: glancing around casually, but the nerves just below the surface are evident."

I'm on the wrong side of the road, and I don't have time to wait for cars to stop at a crosswalk, so I run between a gap in the cars. Only one honks at me, so I count it as a win.

"Well-played game of Frogger," Kella says. "Okay, clown number two just stepped out of the building, holding the case, and flanked by his personal fan club. He's headed toward Shady Clown and the black Impala."

"I see him." I'm only about two hundred and fifty feet away. I'm running like I'm just out for a jog, not running like my life depends on it, because people ignore joggers. Everyone notices run-for-your-life-ers. But really, my speed suggests that my life depends on it. It's all in the facial expressions. Mine are calm, like I run marathons in my sleep and this is just a light Sunday jog. And I will catch up to the man with the case before he reaches the man at the car.

"I bet you a coffee you can't snag it before he makes it twenty feet."

"You owe me so many coffees I could start my own café."

I'm picturing exactly how I'm going to do it as I run. The sidewalk is extra wide, so I move to the middle, looking like I'm not on a collision course with the case-holding man. At the last second, though, I'll veer toward him, go right between him and the man on his right, grabbing the case as I do. Then I really will run with life-depending speed around the corner and use evasive maneuvers until I've lost them. I can feel my body drawing in more oxygen, muscles tensed, already preparing for the burst of speed it will need.

A hundred feet from my target, the man with the case is a dozen feet from his target, and I spot the one thing I never wanted to see on this mission. The one thing guaranteed to throw a mammoth-sized monkey wrench into the system.

Zoe Steele.

Even though I am running fast, frustration and anger still manage to hit me hard as she steps out from the doorway that the man with the case just passed. Everyone on this street is dressed casually— jeans, t-shirts, shorts, sneakers. Even from this distance, I can see that Zoe's blonde hair is in a low ponytail, and she is wearing a deep purple top cut just low enough to bring the eyes up from her black leather pants. Do they not teach CIA operatives how to blend into a crowd?

Now, instead of my body preparing for the extra burst of speed it'll need, heat is building. And not heat in a "she is so hot" way, even though she is and once upon a time, I even made the mistake of falling for it.

No, it's heat more like blood boiling. She's closer to my target than I am. Zoe gives me a look of surprise, which I don't trust is genuine, and then her expression turns sly. Like she already knows she's won. Now I *do* summon that burst of even faster speed.

She's faster, though. She grabs the guy's case in exactly the same way I was about to, had I been closer, and she heads to the same corner I was going to head toward. She cannot be here collecting this case. It contains information *I* got from *my* asset. The one I've been developing for weeks.

I run past the men, who've barely had time to realize the case was ripped out of their hands, as I chase Zoe. I turn the corner to see that she's halfway up a two-story building she is scaling. She gets to the flat roof on top, turns and gives me a wink, then disappears across the rooftop and out of my view.

I want to go after her. To climb that building. To get to where she's going even faster than she can. I could easily beat her in a running race, and she knows it. Which is why she's on the rooftops where she's out of sight. But I don't chase after her, even though my body desperately wants to fight for this win. To chase her across this city, if I have to.

If she was the enemy, that's exactly what I would do. I would chase her across the world if needed. I would get that case out of her hands and into the hands of the CSA.

"Zoe is not the enemy. The CIA is not the enemy," I hear playing on a loop in my head, in the CSA director's voice,

of course, since she's the one who's said it to me countless times.

Right now, though, it feels like Zoe very much is. It makes me want to outdo her at every one of her missions. To claim every single win. To put every single tally mark in my column, not hers. I stand at the base of the building for a couple of seconds, breathing heavily. Zoe won.

I just don't know why she is playing the game.

Or how she even knew that this particular game was being played. To my knowledge, we haven't shared any intel about this mission with the CIA. They shouldn't even know it exists, let alone think they can put a player in the game.

There are cameras on the street. I know Kella saw exactly what happened in real time. So I skip an update and let my voice come out in the growl I'm feeling when I say, "Tell the director to call me."

"Will do," Kella responds, and I appreciate that she doesn't say another word.

The agency helicopter is on a helipad at a local hospital that's only about a block from where I originally met my contact, which makes it only about a half mile away. Or .62 miles, if you ask Kella. But I don't run back to it. In fact, I stomp back, not even caring how many cars I make honk at me.

I'm mad. I'm mad that after so long of working on this mission, building up my relationship with Kolson, shaking so many trees to see what fell out, and finally getting a big break, it gets stolen from under me. I'm furious that the CIA thinks they can just swoop in on our op.

And I'm mad that Zoe Steele bested me. She's probably sitting back in an agency copter right now, buffing her nails, reveling in her success.

I'm walking across the roof to my helicopter when a call from the director comes in on my secure line. The director is also my mom, but I never think of her like that when I'm working. I don't even say hello before asking, "Why is the CIA here? Why did Zoe show up? This is *our* op."

"It is," she says in a voice that is so much calmer than mine. "I've already spoken to the director of field operations in the Global Intelligence Division at the CIA. They are running a different op that just happens to overlap with ours. So he's going to share with us the information in the briefcase that pertains to our op the moment that Zoe gets back with it."

Our operation overlapping with another agency's isn't common overall, but it does occasionally happen. Sometimes with the CIA and sometimes with the FBI. Although "occasionally" is how often other operatives experience it, "frequent" is the word I'd use when it comes to my missions overlapping with Zoe's. Knowing that Zoe is working on an op that is different from mine— that she wasn't just trying to steal mine— helps a bit. I can't say I'm all zen right now, because I'm never okay with losing, but my anger is fading a fraction.

"This should still be counted as a win," I say. "We wouldn't be getting the information in that case if I hadn't secured the meet time and location from my asset and gone there to get it."

"We'll count it as a win," the director says.

"Good," I say before ending the call.

Not that it is *really* a win. Maybe one-third of a win. If even that. In this contest between me and Zoe, I know I lost. I don't like the feeling and it makes me determined to never take second place again. But I do like the director calling it a win. I like my job. It gives me everything I need — adventure, new places, new people— and it never hurts to show the agency that I'm indispensable.

Even if a certain building-scaling blonde is always trying to prove otherwise.

And this isn't the end. We'll get the information in that case— information that I'm sure is actionable. Then I'll secure whatever it is that the CSA needs, and I'll do it long before Zoe gets what she needs for whatever op the CIA is doing.

CHAPTER 2
A LESS-THAN-TYPICAL PEDESTRIAN
ZOE

cannot believe I got to the case before Ledger. I didn't expect that extra shot of excitement and satisfaction on this mission. Mostly because I didn't expect to see Ledger here at all. The man is rather nice to behold in any circumstance, but seeing him run is a glorious thing, and I will never be sad to witness that.

I'll also never be sad to witness the look on his face at the exact moment he realized that I was going to best him on this mission. Or the look of frustration on his face when I winked at him from the rooftop. I beat him in Cairo when we crossed paths there, but then he took home the prize when our missions took us to the same back alley warehouse in London not long after, so I'm glad I won this one. I can't let Ledger get two in a row.

Not that I can't handle him winning now and then. It's what keeps me sharp. A competition is only worthy of actually competing in when the opponent is on your level.

I am a little disappointed that Ledger isn't chasing after me, though. I kind of figured he would. Maybe not from the rooftops, but definitely from the ground. I make it a block and a half away from the acquisition site, across half a dozen connected— or close enough to jump— roofs, descend back down to the street, duck into an alcove, pull the super-thin and lightweight magenta jacket and teal bag from the pouch at my waist, put the jacket on, slip the case into the bag, let down my hair, and walk half a block before I realize he isn't tailing me.

Not that I would've let him catch up to me. I've worked hard to get all the information that led me to this case, and we need its contents. Some artwork was stolen, and we believe it's being sold to fund terrorist activity. This case likely contains the catalog of stolen art, along with their current location and potential buyers. I don't want this information in anyone else's hands. Not even Ledger's.

Especially not Ledger's.

So, I navigate this enemy territory with speed and agility. Normally, I wouldn't consider a city filled with normal people "enemy" territory, but between overly-enthusiastic tourists asking me to take pictures of them in front of the—admittedly, rather impressive— Masonic Library / Museum and the dive-bombing pigeons, it feels like it fits. But I do love Philadelphia. It's a city of revolutions and rebirths, which has pretty much been the theme of my life.

My evasive maneuvers aren't just for Ledger, of course. I don't want the guys I stole the case from or the one accepting the handoff to catch me, either, and I know they're out searching for me— I've nearly run into them twice.

Which is why I don't just stroll the nearly two miles up Market Street to my extraction point. I double back. I go around. I take a bus, a commuter train, and a *trolley*, of all things. I am as adept at evading obstacles in the field as I am at avoiding social commitments back home. And, of course, the entire way, I navigate construction detours, which take about the same level of tactical planning as evading capture. At least the orange cones are less intimidating than armed guards.

Luckily, Packston, the tech op in my ear is very good at seeing the overhead view and directing me to locations at precisely the right time, because I'm also in a big hurry to get back to Langley with the case. This is a big city, but the longer a game of cat-and-mouse goes on, the more likely the mouse is to get caught. And I never get caught.

I cross over the Schuylkill River the second time on foot, and as I approach the building with the private heliport, I tell Packston, "I've hit the extraction point."

"Roger that, Zoe. Initiating protocol 'Rooftop Rendezvous.' And just for the record, since our evasion pattern had more twists than a roller coaster factory, the subjects called off their pursuit of you. Harrison is on standby, rooftop level."

I drum the fingertips of my free hand against my leg as the elevator takes me up the six stories and onto the roof, where Harrison is, indeed, waiting for me in the chopper. Its blades are turning slowly like it's powering up in preparation to take off the moment I step aboard. The second the elevator doors are open enough for me to slip through, I run toward the helicopter.

Like quite a few flat rooftops in Philly, this one is grassed to help with stormwater runoff. Maybe because I was just traipsing through the city in less-than-typical pedestrian paths, or maybe because I'm in a hurry to get back, I channel my inner Pythagoras and run the hypotenuse, because I'm all about taking the shortest distance between two points—the straight line.

Which means I am cutting across the grass instead of walking on the sidewalk like a civilized pedestrian. Except it's not grass, it's more like a ground cover of succulents, and it seems that it rained last night. And, apparently, ground cover on a gravel roof is *very* squishy.

I barely slow my run, though, as my shoes are getting soaked through, and I'm almost to the helipad when my foot catches on a plant and I fall. In my pre-intelligence operative life, I might have fallen flat on my face. Instead, I execute a perfect tactical roll back to standing. Which means that instead of getting my entire front side soaked, I get my entire backside soaked. But I don't lose hold of the case— I keep my grip tight, at the expense of my hand.

I recently slacklined on a one-inch wide polyester webbing between the Petronas Twin Towers in Kuala Lumpur. It was 700 feet across, and I barely wobbled. And here, I fall on a soft, mostly flat surface? I am trained in a dozen different weapons, yet I am no match for succulents. (Which I already know, because Packston gave me a potted succulent to "personalize" my desk once. Apparently, they actually have limits on how long they can go without water.)

My face heats, and I am wondering if Packston or anyone else back at Langley witnessed my fall— they haven't exactly commandeered a satellite to watch my op, but there are probably cameras on this rooftop— when Packston says, "Interesting choice of escape route."

Sometimes it's difficult to tell when Packston is being serious or sarcastic, but I can hear the smile in his words. So I respond with, "Mission update: succulents are now classified as hostile entities. I'm proceeding with caution."

I look at my hand that held the case. I tore a fingernail down so far that it's bleeding. I shake it off and climb into the helicopter. My nails are in such sorry shape that it's not like it makes them look much worse.

Harrison glances back at me, and I don't need my expertise in reading body language to tell me that he saw the fall and that he's feeling a mix of amusement and pity for me. Whether it's for my injured nail, the embarrassment of falling, or the fact that the entire backside of my body is now soaking wet is anyone's guess. Whatever. I got the case, and that's what matters. "Just keeping up my skills in gracefully evading ground-based threats."

Harrison chuckles and goes back to piloting, lifting us off the building and back toward Langley.

The thirty-two minutes we are in the air isn't nearly enough time for my clothes to dry, but it's enough to make them not look like they're soaked. One of the benefits of wearing dark colors. I glance down at my utility belt and then at the bag at my feet that holds the case I acquired from the targets. I have, on my person, gadgets for every possible mission scenario. But I don't bring extra shoes? I'll have to start packing a thin, foldable pair for my next mission because my feet are feeling way more humid than feet should ever feel.

As I walk into the Global Intelligence Division in the CIA building at Langley, carrying the case I acquired, I really hope that the squishing I'm pretty sure my shoes are making with each step is all in my head. My eyes rove over the heads in the room and immediately find Packston's blond curls, and we give each other a nod before my eyes find Sullivan Reynolds, the director, on the opposite side.

I'm almost to Packston's desk, halfway to the director, when my co-worker, Troy, swaggers up to me, coffee in hand, trying to appear superior. It's too bad for him that our field records don't back that up.

"I heard you made quite the splash on your latest op," he says. "I didn't even know you had taken up diving, Steele, yet I heard you executed a perfect forward tuck." He pats me on the shoulder like he's "congratulating" me when I know it's to see how wet my back still is.

"The key word in that sentence is 'perfect.'"

He makes a show of drying his hand on his pant leg. "You know, I hadn't thought about wearing a wetsuit on a non-aquatic mission. That's an interesting touch."

"You should try it sometime," I say. "It might help you to stay cool under pressure."

I glance at Packston as Troy disappears back toward the bridge he lives under.

"Hey, in my defense," Packston says, holding up his

hands, "if I'd have had any indication you were going to get all acrobatic, I wouldn't have tapped into the rooftop cameras or put it on the big screens."

I cringe that my slip-up was on the big screens, but I feel the compliment behind Packston's words— I don't mess up, so he wouldn't have had any indication that I might. I'll take it.

Director Reynolds, who is also my case officer for this mission, stands straight from where he'd been leaning to look at one of my coworkers' computers, and he spots me before his eyes immediately go to the case in my hand and he smiles. He's always proud of me at the end of a successful mission. I kind of live for it.

When I reach him, I hold out the case, and the first words that come out of my mouth are, "Why was Ledger Lancaster there? We've worked really hard on this op— the CSA isn't just going to steal it from us, are they?" I am not whining. My voice is coming out as strong and unyielding as steel. Just like my last name.

He accepts the case. "They aren't going to steal it from us. Don't worry, it's still your operation."

"Good," I say, crossing my arms.

"But we are going to share the contents of the case with them."

"What?!" My shoulders immediately tense back up, which is funny, because the director's sag just a bit at my outburst.

"It appears that it also contains some intel from an operation of theirs."

I give him a wary look. It sounds like their way of trying to steal it from us.

"A *different* operation," he clarifies. "We'll know more after the contents are analyzed. For now, go home."

"I'm fine. If that case contains what we think it does, we'll need to act on it soon."

"Even if it does, the analysts will still need time with it first. There's nothing you can do right now. How long has it been since you last slept?"

"I'm fine."

Sully studies me in a way that makes me feel like he can see everything. "That fall on the lawn said otherwise."

I wince. Of course, he saw it.

"Zoe, you've been working this case too hard for too long. *Go home.* After how long you've been gone, I bet it'll be nice to sleep in your own bed again."

I'm actually exhausted. I know, because Sully's right— I never would've fallen on that rooftop if I wasn't. So I tell Packston I'm heading home, leave Langley, get takeout Chinese food because I've also realized how ravenously hungry I am, and head to the hotel I'm currently calling home.

This place is clean and although the walls are painted the yellow of a mostly healed bruise, they're better than the purple and orange plaid wallpaper of my previous hotel. Not that it matters. This is just the place I sleep and occasionally eat. I don't need more than this. It's not like I've ever really had a place to call home to compare it to— I only have vague recollections of the apartments I lived in with my mom before I started moving from house to house in foster care.

And now, I spend half my time in hotels around the world. A hotel might not be what most people call "home," but it's what's most familiar to me, and that's the same thing. It means I can feel "at home" when I'm at Langley or out of town.

I drop my go bag on the floor just inside the door, lock both locks, and take my Kung Pao Chicken to the desk, because it feels more like a kitchen table than my coffee table does. I'm partway through the container when I hear the sound of the *Friends* theme song coming from the TV in the room next to mine.

One of the bad parts about living in a hotel is being at the mercy of whoever is currently staying in the room next to mine. I watched an episode of *Friends* once. I could tell that it was a great show, but I hated it. At least it isn't quite as bad as the previous guests who stayed in that room and watched one episode of *Modern Family* after another. I don't like feeling melancholic. Or inadequate. And I definitely don't enjoy longing for a past— or a present— that I've never experienced. And I feel all three with those shows.

So I grab my headphones, open an app I have on my phone that plays brown noise, and I crank it up loudly enough to drown out the sounds of the TV. Then I eat my spicy chicken in peace and think about how great it is that I have this space to myself. In foster care, that wasn't a luxury that I ever enjoyed, so I always make sure to enjoy it now.

A few minutes later, I remove my headphones, close the box of Chinese food, unsure if I'm full or if I'm too tired to finish eating, and stick it in my mini fridge. Then I walk to my suitcase and stare at it. I'm too exhausted to change, but I'm not about to sleep in leather pants. So, as usual when exhausted, I still do whatever has to be done. I peel off my clothes, which are, in fact, dry now, pull on a nightshirt, and, as the director suggested, I crawl into "my own" bed.

It's not that all mattresses in all hotels are the same that makes this one my own. But the circumstances of my childhood gifted me with the ability to sleep anywhere. And traveling the world for the CIA and spending time in so many different time zones has gifted me with the ability to sleep at any *time*.

Which is good, because the clock on the nightstand reads 6:02 p.m. as I put a pillow over my head to drown out the sound of Ross's dinosaur lecture being met with Phoebe's quirky retort, and, like a pro, drift off to sleep within seconds.

CHAPTER 3
SIBLING REVELRY
LEDGER

The moment I open the front door to my mom's house for our weekly family dinner, I can hear sounds of everyone chatting coming from the kitchen and dining room at the other end of the long hall. And the sound of Blake's toddler daughter shouting "Wedgejo"— her best attempt at saying my name— as she runs toward me, hands up in the air.

"There's my favorite rocket ship!" I say as I scoop her up and swing her around to sit atop my shoulders. And, as is our custom, she raises her hands up so she can run them along the ceiling, making "rocket ship" sounds as we head down the hallway.

In the kitchen, my sister Charlie is showing my future sister-in-law, Mackenzie, something on her phone and they're both laughing. Jace is, of course, next to Mackenzie, my brothers Miles and Blake are talking to my mom. So everyone except Emerson is here.

I like that Mackenzie comes to all of our family dinners now. The more the merrier, if you ask me. As long as Jace doesn't go off and get all boring now that he's engaged. I mean, I do like that he's happier and less stodgy. I like the happier part because that means he's down to do more fun things. But I've seen friends get married, and it doesn't take long before their lives get boring. Like cry-into-your-tax-forms boring.

I am never going to let someone trap me and make me boring. I suppress a shudder. Tie me up and make me watch daytime talk shows, force me to fold endless laundry, and pluck out my nose hairs one by one if you want, but don't ever trap me in a boring life.

I walk over to my mom, put my free arm around her shoulders, and give her a hug. My mom gives me a squeeze back. Heidi wants in on the action, but I'm enough taller than my mom that Heidi can't reach her, even though she does try. Instead, she sticks a leg straight out, and my mom gives her foot a squeeze.

"Is Emerson coming?" I ask.

My mom shakes her head. "He's at work."

I grin because I can tell by the look in her eyes that it means Zoe is back with the case and that the CIA kept their word and shared with the CSA the info I'd worked so hard to get. So now it's time for Emerson's team to do their analyzing thing.

"Hey," Miles says, "I wasn't in the office to catch you adding another tally mark to Zoe's side of the board, but I heard you bit the dust so hard they had to scrape you off the floor."

If I didn't currently have Heidi on my shoulders, I might grab his baseball hat and hold it just out of reach, or do something equally childish and every bit as brotherly.

"Hey," Jace says, walking over from the table. "Save the smack talk for the court."

"Court?" I say, cocking my head at one of my favorite words.

Jace grins. "We thought that maybe you'd want to burn off a little steam after being trounced on earlier today."

I shoot him a look at the use of the word "trounced," but then he adds, "So we thought a little footvolley is in order. We can go to the sand court at Shadowridge park."

"Really?" Heidi starts squirming, so I reach up to lift her off my shoulders and set her back on the ground.

Miles nods and clasps Blake on the shoulder. "We even managed to talk this curmudgeon into joining us."

All thoughts of Zoe besting me flee my mind— okay, *most* of them do— and I grin as I say, "All right man." I hold out my fist for Blake to bump, but he just grumbles. "You think you can swing those legs of yours high enough to be any real competition?"

"You better hope so, because you and I are on a team."

I look to Jace and Miles. "You paired 'oldest and youngest' against 'middle children' again?" I definitely said "middle children" with a lot of sarcasm.

"We figure it's the fairest pairing," Miles says. "Experience and youth teamed against good looks and skill."

"*Youth?*"

Miles shrugs. "I was born on a different day, a different

month, *and* a different year, so you'll always be the 'youth,' bro. Even when we are eighty."

"You're older by *twelve minutes.*"

"Older is older."

I'm glad that we weren't born in the years 1999 and 2000 because if Miles could also claim being born in a different decade and a different century than me, he'd be unbearable. I can tell by the mischievous smile on his face that he's just saying it to get a rise out of me, so I'm not going to give it to him. Instead, I respond with, a very calm, "That's okay because we all know who got all the 'First Baby of the New Year' accolades."

"Yeah, but we were both in those pictures, and I'm the one who was the most photogenic."

I am still bitter about those pictures. I mean, they could've waited until I stopped wailing to take them. Since Heidi's no longer on my shoulders, I wrap my arm around Miles's neck in a fake choke hold. Which is easy, since I'm a good six inches taller than him.

"Boys," my mom says. "Are you ready to stop flexing? Because CarterQue Barbeque made a beef brisket that smells like heaven, and I'm hungry."

Blake goes to where it's warming in the oven and pulls it out, and my stomach immediately growls. It does smell like heaven. I drop my arm from around Miles and turn to Charlie. "Are you going to play?"

Charlie shakes her head. "Nope. Us girls," she says, motioning to our mom, Mackenzie, and Heidi, "have plans tonight. Mackenzie's friend Livi is coming over, and we are giving each other pedicures."

"Oh, fun," I say, not meaning it. I turn to Mackenzie. "Are you sure you're okay with us taking your man tonight?"

"Silly Ledger," Mackenzie says, wrapping her arm around Jace's waist and gazing up at him. "We can handle being apart." Then she puts on an exaggerated expression of fear. "We can, can't we?" And then they kiss.

Yeah, Jace is definitely on the path to becoming boring.

Not me. I'm going to eat that delicious brisket, mac and cheese, and baked beans, and then Blake and I are going to show Miles and Jace just how much trouncing "youth and experience" can do.

———

When we get to the park, the sun has set, but there are plenty of lamps lighting the area. The sand volleyball court is being used by a group of high schoolers, and not a single one of them is playing like they are trying to win. Such a waste of a good court.

But there is a pickleball court available and in a pinch… well, a court is a court.

"This will work," Blake says, assessing it.

Miles nodded. "You're just happy that you'll actually be able to get it over the net, old man."

"Just try to keep up, 'kid.' And try not to cry when you're eating our dust."

Footvolley is basically volleyball but uses soccer rules when it comes to touching the ball. So feet, legs, and heads only. Jace serves the ball, drop-kicking it over the net.

Blake takes it, using his head to bump it toward me, and I kick high, sending it back over the net. "If we're playing on a pickleball court, we can't just call this footvolley. What do we call it? Foot pickle?"

"No," Blake says, catching the ball with his hands, stopping its motion, which goes completely against the rules of this game. "We are not calling it that. I veto. We're still using a footvolley ball, anyway."

"Volleyfootpickle?" I say. "Pickle-volley-foot? Foot-pickle-volley."

"Just stop. Seriously."

"Footvolley for the height-challenged player?" Miles suggests.

"I've got it," Jace says. "Footvolley in a pickle."

"Footvolley for those with skills too low for a high net," I offer, mostly because our suggestions are annoying Blake.

"I don't know," Miles says. "I'm kind of a fan of PickleFoot."

Maybe to get us to stop with the bad jokes, Blake tosses the ball back to Jace to re-serve then says, "So, you were out in the field today, huh? Anywhere fun?"

"That's classified." And he knows it. "But I will say it was close enough to travel to by helicopter."

I don't think that Blake appreciates everyone in the family except him being in the know about cases we're working on at the CSA. But he's the one who chose to turn his back on the family business and become a dentist, of all things. He probably wouldn't like field work, but he's smart enough that he could've been an analyst, like Emerson, or a handler, like Charlie. Or he could've worked in any of the sub-levels. With his knowledge of facial anatomy and his precision skills, maybe he could be like Abraham and work with disguises.

Or maybe he just wishes he could travel to different locations at the drop of a hat like we do. But with Heidi, that isn't exactly possible.

Who am I kidding? Blake doesn't do anything without spending weeks planning it first. Even if he didn't hate the CSA, he would hate being an intelligence operative.

"If Zoe beat you to the objective," Blake says as he kicks the ball over the net, "does that mean you didn't finish the mission?"

A muscle in my neck twinges. "I don't think you get how this smack-talk thing works. You're supposed to be antagonizing *our competition*, not *your teammate*."

"I'm just trying to understand. You're okay just walking away from the mission, leaving it unfinished?"

Blake would never just walk away from something, leaving it unfinished, whether it was a root canal, a DIY home project, or a five-course meal.

"I'm not just leaving it unfinished," I say. "The mission is still moving forward, and right now, it's in Emerson's court." I do a twisting jump kick, sending the ball over the net and downward like a missile. Jace dives for it but doesn't get it before it hits the ground.

"How are you not calling him every five minutes to get an update?" Blake asks.

"First off," I say, not taking my eyes off Miles because Blake is going to serve to him, and he's wearing a pretty intense expression, "any info he discovers goes straight to the director—"

"To *Mom*," Blake interrupts.

"—to *Mom*, first, so he's not going to tell me. As of right now, I've already done my part of the job."

"If by his 'part of the job,'" Jace says as Blake serves the ball, "he means letting Zoe secure the objective before he does."

"See?" I say as I motion to Jace. "*That's* how you smack talk." Then I kick the ball that Miles sent my direction over the net, aiming straight at Jace's head. "Anyway, right now, it's Emerson's turn with the case. It's called working together as a team."

Miles and Jace work together— Jace bumps the ball to Miles using his head, Miles bumps it back to him using his knee, and Jace twists in the air as he sends the ball over the net and toward the ground. Blake goes for the ball but doesn't get there before it bounces off the pickleball court.

I hold out a hand to pull him up. "Something that you clearly know nothing about."

"I'm just saying that I wouldn't walk away with things not finished," Blake says, picking up the ball and throwing it back to the other side.

"When it's my turn again, I'll be there with bells on. In the meantime, I'm going to enjoy some family adventure. This moment right now is for blowing off steam. And the only thing I need to worry about is smack-talking and making sure we win."

CHAPTER 4
INFILTRATING THE SECRET LAIR
ZOE

Sully pulls up to the guard house at the gate of a huge mansion and hands the guard— a dark-haired man in his early forties named Moss, if his name tag is telling the truth— both of our IDs. "Director of Field Operations for the Global Intelligence Division of the CIA Sullivan Reynolds and Intelligence Operative Zoe Steele here to meet with Director Lancaster."

The man accepts our IDs without a word, bending over just enough to see me in the passenger seat and to glance in the back seat. Then he goes around to the back of our car, probably to check our license plate number, before he heads into the guard house. It wouldn't surprise me if we are stopped on top of some device that checks the bottom of our vehicle for explosive or tracking devices.

My focus goes from the sign on the gate that reads "Lancaster Business Solutions," which is apparently the Clandestine Services Agency's cover business, to the building at the end of a very long, curving, cobblestone drive with meticulously cared for grounds. The building is a giant mansion. A *mansion*! This place is supposed to be a top-secret government intelligence agency and it looks like this?

It probably has an indoor swimming pool and sauna. Likely a day spa, too. Definitely more bathrooms than bedrooms, and boasts a wine cellar, a home gym, and tennis courts out back. Is this a situation where a reclusive billionaire got bored and decided he wanted to hire a crime-fighting team? Are we going to find a Batmobile in the garage?

I am definitely not thrilled that we are having this meeting at the CSA instead of at the CIA. Especially because our lead analyst is apparently already at this building, so they must've been doing their work here. *I* am the one who recovered that case, not Ledger. That means it's ours, and we are just sharing. Director Reynolds should've fought for us to have the meeting on our home turf.

Moss comes back to the car and hands our IDs back. "Head down the drive and park in front of the building. Go to the front doors— the director is expecting you."

Sully thanks him and raises his window as the gate opens. As soon as he starts driving toward the building, he says, "Now I don't want to see too many sparks flying between you and Ledger Lancaster in here."

He knows that Ledger and I are rivals, so he's saying it like he's being funny and sarcastic, expecting a laugh from me. But I wonder if he's actually prodding for information about the two of us. I've kind of suspected that Sully has a sixth sense about which missions are likely going to have CSA crossover, guesses when the CSA is likely to send Ledger, and then sends me on those same missions. Almost like he's some kind of matchmaker. His comment makes me suspect it even more. I need to make sure he understands that anything between Ledger and me is never going to happen. "Women like me don't fall in love."

"Women like you?" he asks, giving me an opportunity to elaborate. I don't. After a beat, he provides his own guesses. "Do you mean women who are intelligence operatives? Or women who were abandoned as a child?"

I wince. If that comment came from anyone on this planet other than Sully, I'd probably deck them. But never Sully. So I say, "Take your pick." He could've also added "Or women who are professional loners? Or women who have never actually been in a relationship before because they know they would be terrible at it? Or women who have no chance of getting a guy to hang around?" Instead of saying any of that out loud, though, I just say, "But especially when it comes to Ledger."

There was a time a year and a half ago when I completely underestimated Ledger's impressive ability to make people feel like he truly cares about them, which made me forget about all those reasons for a minute. And forgetting led to things ending poorly. And by "poorly," I mean akin to a pyromaniac wielding a flame thrower in a field of fireworks. There's no way that true sparks between us will ever happen again.

Sully glances in the rearview mirror. "Okay, well, play

nice in here." It's something he's already told me, but apparently feels the need to reiterate.

I nod. "But if we go knock on the door and a butler answers, leads us past an indoor bowling alley on our way to a briefing room that doubles as the owner's home theater, and then sits us down in those padded reclining chairs with cup holders, I'm out of there."

He chuckles. "As much as it might look like it, this isn't a billionaire's house. And although it's a fraction of the size of Langley, it's much larger than it looks."

My head whips in his direction. "You've been here before?"

"No. But a long time ago— back when I was a field operative and so was Director Lancaster— right after she moved from the CIA to the CSA, I was on a joint mission with her. She mentioned that there are multiple sub-levels, and that the part underground is much bigger."

I turn my focus back at the building, considering it, as I run my finger and thumb along the chain of my necklace. Sully pulls into one of only five parking stalls. The other four are empty. I get out of the car and we walk up to the front door as I ask, "Are we supposed to ring the bell? Knock?"

But Sully just opens the door. A valid choice, even if it doesn't feel like it at a place like this.

The lobby is large, cold, and has sharp angles everywhere. There's a single massive desk in the middle near the back wall, with a few uncomfortable-looking chairs to our right, tucked into a corner. This place is meant to look intimidating.

As is the receptionist behind the desk. Her hair is in a tight bun, and her black suit is as angled as this room. "May I help you?"

Sully repeats our names to her and says that we are here to meet Director Lancaster, and the woman picks up a phone. Her posture is rigid, her voice professional, and her facial expressions neutral. But from where we're standing now, I can see her feet. They're crossed at the ankles—something she would never do if she wasn't comfortable, and the foot on top is bouncing up, which tells me she's happy. The incongruousness between the more obvious body language that she's trying to control above the desk and the subtler body language below the desk that she isn't, the intimidation is all for show. I respect that. She's doing a masterful job.

A moment later, a door to our right opens, and Director Lancaster walks in. She's wearing a knee-length dark gray pencil skirt with a light blue blousy shirt tucked into it. Her hair is pulled into a loose bun that isn't nearly as severe as the receptionist's but still looks professional. The woman has to be in her late fifties now, and she still looks amazing.

She greets Director Reynolds first, saying "Hello, Sully. It's so wonderful to see you again." Instead of just shaking his hand, she gives him a hug that's somehow both friendly and professional, and I can't take my eyes off the two of them. From how their feet are both pointing toward one another, to the way their eyes opened more upon seeing each other, to the way their torsos are slightly leaning in toward one another, there is nothing discordant.

Both of them genuinely have a lot of respect and admiration for one another.

Then *the* Evelyn Lancaster, director of the Clandestine Services Agency, turns to me and shakes my hand, placing her left hand on the outside of my hand as she does. "Zoe Steele. I've heard so much about you. It's great to finally meet you in person."

What I want to do is stare at her in awe. Ask her all the questions I've had about her over the years. Tell her that even though she doesn't know it, she's been my mentor. Blurt out facts about my favorite missions of hers. Get all tongue-tied about the fact that she knows my name— that she's heard "so much" about me.

What I manage to do— even though her welcome gives me goose bumps and makes my heart feel like it's got a helium balloon tied to it, lifting it— is stay professional and say, "It's great to meet you in person, too. Thank you for welcoming us here." Because I'm nothing if not a consummate professional.

But a big part of me really wants to just ask her to tell me everything. About her entire career.

I was eight years old when I decided that when I grew up, I was going to be an intelligence operative. One of the few times I went to a movie theater as a child, we saw one about a female intelligence operative. She did so many impressive things in the show, and she was so skilled. Everyone in the theater was *oohi*ng and *ahhi*ng as much as I was.

And when we left, I heard the reactions of everyone around me as they talked about how awesome the main character was. I hadn't known that being an intelligence operative was a career until then, and I decided at that moment that I wanted it. I wanted to be impressive just like her. I wanted people to *ooh* and *ahh* over my skills.

I was first made aware of Evelyn Lancaster when I started my training at the Farm. In one of my classes, they told us about how, as an intelligence operative for the CIA, she single-handedly extracted vital intel from a compromised safe house when everyone else thought it was lost. I realized that she was the kind of operative that I had been picturing myself being since I was a kid.

That evening, I looked up everything I could about the woman. The legend. She quickly became my idol. Throughout my career, every time my clearance level increased, I checked her file to see what more I could learn about her. She is the kind of operative that I aspire to be.

And I hate that Ledger can call her "Mom." Does he even understand how lucky he is? When I was a kid, every night, I would lay in my crappy bed in whatever foster home I currently lived in and dream of a different life. And I always dreamed I had a mom who worked for the CIA and would teach me everything I needed to know to follow in her footsteps.

Ledger had that handed to him.

Director Lancaster leads us through the doorway into a hall where we pass through a scanner that I know checks for weapons, listening devices, trackers, chemical agents, and a host of other dangerous things. At the end of the hall, everything opens up into a large room not that dissimilar from our department at the CIA. Huh. So it really isn't just a billionaire's lair. There are… twenty-nine people at desks or walking from one desk to another, so about the same size as the Global Intelligence Division.

What surprises me the most, though, is how unhappy or uneasy all of the operatives, officers, and analysts appear at our being present in their space. Like we are intruders. I lock eyes with Ledger, who is standing in the opposite corner of the large space from where we are, his stance wide, his arms crossed. Ledger looks the least happy of all of them.

A smile spreads across my face. I'd considered the fact that our meeting taking place at his agency was a win for Ledger, but it's clear from the expression on his face that I was wrong. This is a win in my column.

I may never get this particular "win" again, so I take in every detail as Director Lancaster leads us past several glass-front conference rooms at the back of the space and Ledger heads toward us. Just before we reach the last conference room, I notice a whiteboard on the wall closer to where Ledger stood when we first walked in. It's split in half vertically, with tally marks on each side. At the top of one side, it reads *Ledger* and the other side reads *ZOE in the CIA*.

He's keeping a tally of which one of us wins missions. That's adorable, actually. It shows how much he cares about our rivalry. And I have no doubt I wasn't meant to see it. Director Lancaster opens the door to the conference room, but I take a step past it to meet Ledger head-on. Even though that tally board shows me as up by one point currently, his stride and posture still show confidence. I like confidence in a man. It lets me know that I don't have to dial things back.

And I love that smirk on his lips. His narrowed eyes are betraying his irritation at my presence in his domain, though. But I kind of like that, too. I am grinning, and my own body language must show that I like seeing this exclusive peek into the CSA offices.

"Enjoying yourself?" Ledger asks, motioning vaguely to the room as if he's asking about me enjoying simply being on his turf.

He crosses his arms, but my smile widens. "Oh, immensely. I rather enjoy seeing you squirm when I best you on a mission. It's not often I get the distinct pleasure of watching you squirm simply at my presence in your top-secret lair."

He scoffs. "Please, Steele. You wish you could get under my skin that easily."

I shrug. "I don't know. It looks like I do a pretty good job." I cut my gaze ever so quickly to the tally board toward the front of the space before my eyes are back on his. It's a slight motion, but I know he's a good enough spy to pick up on what I'm referring to even without turning to look at it.

I am rewarded by a small flex in his jaw. Just enough to show me that he's a bit irritated that I noticed the chart, and it makes me smile. So I add, "And it's not just about a battle, is it? It's about who wins the war. And let's be honest— we both know who that's going to be."

Ledger leans forward just a bit, his gray-blue eyes boring into mine with an intensity that I have to admit is rather attractive. Real sparks may never fly between us, but there is a heat here that I always enjoy. "It's not over until it's over. And trust me: it's far from over."

If I was the type of woman who fell in love, Ledger would check all the boxes. He's insanely attractive, from that sandy blonde hair that's just the perfect amount of unruly, to those big strong shoulders, to those legs I'm sure are rather sculpted that can easily run or scale the side of a building. He is an impressive intelligence operative, too, which makes him the best kind of attractive.

But since I'm not, and since something between us could never happen, we can only be one of two things—rivals or enemies. Sometimes, he's fun competition. Other times, he gets under my skin and we are definitely enemies.

"You're a worthy adversary, Ledger, and I hope that we get to keep battling it out in the field for years to come. This mission, though? This battle? I think you're going to have to put another tally mark in my column. I suspect that we're having this meeting here because when the analysts went through the case that I recovered, they only found info relating to my mission. Our directors decided to let this meeting happen here to soften the blow of us taking its contents."

"I don't know how you generally do things in the CIA, but at the CSA, we aren't in the business of 'softening the blow.' The meeting is here because the contents of that case belong *right here*." His eyes burn into me for a moment before he adds, "And why were you even on that mission? Philadelphia isn't exactly foreign soil."

"Except you know that in a lot of cases, my division can operate on U.S. soil, too."

He shifts his weight from one foot to the other. The motion is slight, almost imperceptible. "Oh," I say, dragging out the word. "That's part of why you compete against me— you feel like I'm encroaching on your territory. That's part of our rivalry, isn't it?"

I can't believe I haven't picked up on that before. The CSA's purpose is to cover the gap between what the CIA's and the FBI's responsibilities are, but my division of the CIA has a lot of gray area that overlaps the CSA's responsibilities. Which is why Ledger and I have found ourselves on so many of the same missions.

The way Ledger moves his arms in front of his torso to adjust his watch tells me that the blow I just aimed at him landed.

"Zoe and Ledger, would you care to join us?"

My face heats at the sound of Evelyn Lancaster's voice. I assumed she had gone into the room, not stayed directly behind me, listening to our bantering. It's the kind of mistake I never make. It must just be Ledger's presence that threw me off. I quickly turn to face her and give a respectful nod. "Of course."

CHAPTER 5
THE ART OF TRUST
ZOE

irector Lancaster leads me and Ledger into the conference room behind Director Reynolds, where Kenneth, the lead analyst for my division, is standing next to a guy who I'm guessing is his CSA counterpart— a man in his late twenties with dark hair who doesn't wear glasses but looks like he'd be at home in them. Our analyst is probably twice the CSA analyst's age, but they have an eerily similar look and vibe. Like I'm seeing the younger and older versions of the same man.

"Thank you all for coming. Some quick introductions before we get started," Director Lancaster says, motioning to the two men behind the oval table, who have the case I recovered open on the table in front of them. "This is Kenneth, the lead analyst for the Global Intelligence Division, and this is Emerson, the lead analyst here at the Clandestine Services Agency."

Director Reynolds told me on the drive over that both

Kenneth's team and the CSA's team have been working on the contents of the case through the night and all morning long. Based on how haggard the two men look, I believe it. When I first turned the case over to Sully and he said we were going to give the information in the case to the CSA that was part of their operation, I had stupidly thought that we'd open the case, take out our stuff, then turn the CSA's stuff over to them.

But I've been on enough missions to know that recovered intelligence isn't that cut and dried, and that information doesn't just easily divide up. Everything is connected. So I should've guessed that both teams would need to analyze all the information and that we'd be meeting together for this briefing because it contains information we both need.

Director Lancaster closes the door, picks up a remote from the table, and presses a button that darkens the glass wall and door. We can still see out, but I have no doubt that others can't see into the room. The two analysts stay standing, but once the two directors, Ledger, and I are all seated, Director Lancaster says, "I know you're anxious to learn what the two teams of analysts found in the case, so we won't keep any of you waiting. Emerson and Kenneth, would you like to share what you've discovered?"

Emerson, the CSA's analyst, says, "Before Operative Steele recovered this case, based on the intelligence my team found, we thought that the case might contain smuggling routes or key contacts, believing that the stolen art was being used as a cover to move illegal arms."

"And my team," Kenneth says, "believed that the art

was being sold to fund terrorist activities and that the case might contain a record of the stolen artwork's location and potential buyers."

"What neither of our teams guessed," Emerson said, "is that it would contain one of the stolen pieces of art." He pulls out a sculpture of entwined metal and glass, and I suck in a breath. The sculpture is of two figures leaning into each other, supported by each other, and based on everything I've found so far, I'm sure it was recently stolen. I glance over at Ledger, who is also sitting up straighter, and I know he's thinking the same thing I am.

Kenneth picks up a tablet, taps a few things, and the screen on the wall behind them changes to show the five art pieces that we already know are stolen— an abstract painting, a necklace, a mixed media piece with paper, fabric, and pictures, a realistic painting, and a relief carving in wood.

"We were stumped at first," Kenneth says. "No, we were *clueless* at first that the thefts of these pieces were related at all, since they are all different styles, media, and genres, even after we discovered that it is the same group of people who have stolen all five."

"But last night," Emerson says, "We discovered—"

"*Emerson* discovered," Kenneth interrupts. "This part was all him."

"—that the pieces themselves are all connected." Emerson is talking faster and faster as he gets further into the explanation. "Each of them was created by an artist who was living at the same art colony in the Netherlands in the late eighteen-hundreds. None of the artists are Rembrandts, but they all did pretty well. Their pieces generally sell for hundreds of thousands, up to five million dollars."

Kenneth nods and continues the fast pace. "One day while the artists were sitting around the campfire, singing Kumbaya, or whatever artists did back then, they decided that they were each going to do an art piece in their own style, all with the theme of 'Trust.' The group didn't publicize the theme at all. In fact, it took a lot of digging to find out that little detail."

"You can see in this piece," Emerson says, picking up the sculpture, "by the way that the two figures are leaning into each other that it represents how trust involves reliance and vulnerability between individuals." He points at the abstract painting on the screen behind him, a piece that has a chaotic mix of colors that slowly forms a clear path leading from one corner to the other. "This one represents the idea that trust can guide you through the chaos and uncertainty of life. And in this necklace, which actually has interlocking pieces—"

"Emerson," Ledger says, more than a little impatience coloring his voice. "They have a theme. Got it. We don't need an art history lesson. Let's get to the 'Why it matters' part."

"Right. Okay, well, the art colony connection itself wouldn't have given us too much, but in studying this piece, Kenneth found that it contains a computer chip." He squints down at where the metal attaches to the base. "It's teeny, was very well hidden, and could've easily been overlooked. But we got it, gave it to the tech team, and found that it contains a number."

My eyebrows draw together. "Like what? A membership number? A ticket number? An access code? A serial number?" And I'm really starting to wonder just how connected Ledger's mission is with mine. If it really is just one big operation, then one agency is going to try to claim ownership of it. And it better be the CIA doing the claiming, because I've been working my tail off for this. I look over at Ledger and see the same hunger to pull off a successful mission that I have.

No, Ledger. This one is *mine*.

Kenneth shakes his head. "Just a single digit. A six, specifically."

It hits me that both analysts are excitedly sharing their information, which means that this isn't just one case that's going to one agency only. They aren't the ones who get to make that decision, of course, but they've seen where the info is taking them and can guess. I bet they've found where the two operations separate, and we're about to hear it. And no matter which half of this big operation the CIA gets, I'm going to complete my missions faster than Ledger completes the half that the CSA gets.

"One digit?" Ledger asks. "That helps us *how*?" For as much as Ledger and I are usually on opposite sides of, well, everything, we both seem equally baffled at where this minuscule clue is going.

"It only helps when combined with some chatter we've collected online about this man." Emerson taps the tablet, and a photograph comes up on the screen. The man in the picture has strong facial features, a neatly trimmed beard and dark hair that's graying at the temples, devious eyes, and a mischievous smile. The man has always seemed equal parts dangerous criminal mastermind and jovial strategist to me.

"Callid Aragundi," Ledger growls.

It's a name we all know because he's on the Most Wanted list of pretty much every agency in the world. A lot of lives lost can be attributed to him.

Emerson nods. "Callid Aragundi. It seems he's thinking of retirement and wants to pass his fortune along to a person or a group who is 'worthy' of not only the cash but also of his vast criminal network. Which means that the chaos and terror he's caused will be able to continue.

"From what we've been tracking, he may have found a candidate and is now testing his possible successor with a bit of a scavenger hunt-like task, hiding a number in each of these art pieces so they have to steal all of them to get the full number."

I roll my eyes. "Oh, he's a literal bored billionaire, but rather than getting his own crime-fighting team, he has his own crime-causing team."

"So instead of being Batman," Ledger says, "Aragundi is The Riddler."

I glance at Ledger. Okay, points to the man for thinking of Batman, just like I had been earlier.

"If you combine The Riddler with The Godfather, then yes," Kenneth says. He brings up a screen that shows various works of art. "There are ten Trust pieces in total. Our best guess, based on what we know of Aragundi, is that the ten numbers combine to make GPS coordinates leading the possible successor to a location where they have to find something that allows them to continue.

"Now, his possible successor is going to want all ten. Just to give you an idea as to why— and this estimate could change, based on several factors, like how close to the equator the location is— if they get all ten numbers, it will lead them to an area roughly the size of a baseball diamond. If they get eight, the area they'll have to search for whatever Aragundi has hidden will be closer to the size of Disneyland. With six, it's more like a small town. With four, we're talking about them having to search an area the size of a large metropolis. They've already recovered five."

He picks up the sculpture. "And we have one, but we don't know if they were able to get the number from it before attempting to hand it off yesterday— all we know is that the chip is still in it. They're *really* going to want the other four."

"And you're sure the numbers are GPS coordinates?" I ask. I don't know what chatter the analysts have seen, but from what I've seen, that's a big leap. It's their job to see so much more than I ever could, though.

Kenneth shakes his head. "It could be part of an international account number."

"Same concept, though," Emerson says. "If they have nine of the ten numbers, they've got a one in ten chance of guessing the missing number. If two are missing, it's a one-in-one-hundred chance. Three missing? One in a thousand."

Kenneth spreads his arms, palms up. "Or it could be a social security number of a target. A Library of Congress number. A CIA asset tag. An encoded message. A patent number. The point is, they're going to want to recover all four of the remaining art pieces, or their chances of winning Aragundi's challenge are small. Especially because there's something else on each of the computer chips. We haven't been able to make any sense of it yet, but we suspect that when all ten chips are together, it'll give information that none of them would give separately."

Sully says, "But just keeping them from getting the art pieces— and therefore, the numbers— isn't enough. We want to be able to send in a team to take down the organization itself and make the world a safer place. Which means installing a tracker and letting them continue to steal the pieces."

"The good thing is," Emerson says as he brings a new image up on the screen with four art pieces, "we know where the other four pieces are, and we have a decent guess as to the order the thieves will try to steal them. First up is this tapestry in Dublin, then this ceramic sculpture in Belgrade. Then this stained glass window in Venice, and finishing with this charcoal drawing in Ankara."

"We've reached out to the governments where each of the four pieces reside and gotten their cooperation," Sully says. "Cooperation from individual art owners is a different story. The ones in Dublin and Ankara are fully on board with our plan. We know enough about the owner in Serbia to know not to contact him, and the fourth, the one in Venice, we haven't been able to contact at all yet. Those last two will likely require some covert ops."

I nod, already itching to leave. It looks like I have a good amount of travel ahead of me, which is no problem. I've never been to Ireland, so that'll be fun. And I'm a big fan of Venice. "This better be our op," I say, partly to Sully, but partly to everyone in the room. "It was ours first."

"No," Ledger says, "it was *ours* first. It's *our* operation. You can't just come and steal it because you want the credit. We are taking it."

"Both agencies want it," Sully says. "And trust me when I say that 'calling dibs' or claiming ownership in this room isn't taken into consideration. This was a decision already made in a room with the Director of National Intelligence, my boss, Director Lancaster, and myself, after looking at it from all angles. After much discussion, we came to an agreement that it's an op best served as a joint mission between the CIA and the CSA. End of story."

I lean back in my chair and cross my arms. Fine. So they'll divide up the locations between our agencies. Two for Ledger, two for me. Of course, the two I'll pick if I have the choice immediately come to mind— Ireland and Italy. But both directors have turned to face me and Ledger with looks on their faces like maybe it's already been decided.

After a long, slow breath, Director Lancaster says, "Director Sullivan and I discussed who we should send on this operation, and we decided that we want the two of you to team up."

Ledger and I simultaneously let out a disbelieving "What?" like we can't believe anyone could ever think that's a good idea. I manage to stay seated, though, whereas Ledger immediately stands, sending his rolling chair backward. I'm happy to see that he appears just as shocked and horrified as I am.

I shake my head. "You mean the two of us going to the same locations? We can't do that." I enjoy competing *against* Ledger. I cannot work *with* Ledger. That was what we were doing a year and a half ago when everything went disastrously.

I cannot be with this man twenty-four hours a day for an undetermined amount of time. Every mission in our past, our current rivalry— it all makes me feel connected to Ledger in a way I rarely feel with anyone. I crave that connection, even though the glimpse it gives me into what I can never have is a physical pain. And if I've got the choice, I prefer to stay far, far away from pain.

Plus, I know myself well. I've got strong opinions, I am a lone wolf, and I do not work well with others. Most of all, I do not work well with Ledger Lancaster.

Sully says, "The two of you are not only the operatives with the greatest knowledge of the ins and outs of this case, since you've been the primary two working on it for quite some time now, but you're also the most qualified for this particular mission. You, Ledger, because of your fearlessness and ability to befriend assets—"

"You mean his recklessness and unreliability?" I cut in.

"—and you, Zoe, because of your expertise in reading body language and ability to strategize."

"Oh," Ledger says, "you mean her ability to convincingly lie and be inflexible?"

Sully continues, as if neither I nor Ledger interrupted, "And because you both have an innate need to win at any cost. And *everyone* really needs us to get this win."

I meet my director's eyes, feeling a bit betrayed that he didn't warn me during our hour-long drive here that he and Director Lancaster had made plans to put me and Ledger on a mission together. All he told me was that both teams of analysts had been working together all through the night and that we were coming to hear about it. I gave him my best "we're going to have words later" look.

Director Lancaster turns to the two analyst team leaders and says, "Can you give us a minute?"

Emerson places his tablet on the table, and he and Kenneth both walk out the door, shutting it behind them. Ledger takes a deep breath, grabs his chair from where it had rolled near the wall, and sits in it again.

Then Director Lancaster says, "Ledger, do you agree that you're perfect for this mission?"

"You better believe I am. But—"

Then she turns to me. "Zoe, do you agree that you're perfect for this mission?"

"Absolutely." And I do believe it. Still, though, hearing Evelyn Lancaster insinuating that I'm perfect for this mission sends a thrill through me like nothing else.

"We're each perfect for this job on our own," Ledger says. "We're less so together. It'll be disastrous."

I know he's thinking of that mission we were on together a year and a half ago. "Disastrous" is the same word I use whenever I think of it. Glad to see we're on the same page about it. And at least we're on the same page for wanting it to never happen again. We hadn't crossed paths before that mission, and it was our first time working and spending every hour together. A few sparks might have ignited between us then— whether they were real or not didn't change the fact that those sparks then scorched the earth.

Then Director Lancaster says to Ledger, "So you're saying that I should choose a different intelligence operative for this mission? One who is less perfect for the mission but who can better work with Operative Steele?"

Ledger crosses his arms, which, I have to admit, shows off his impressive muscles. He must get that it isn't a question that she needs to have him answer because he keeps his mouth shut.

Then Sully says to me, "Should I choose a different operative who can work better with Operative Lancaster?"

I don't answer, either, but when Ledger stands again and takes a step to the corner of the conference room, turning away from us a bit, I suggest, "Why don't you just split us up? Have us each take two art pieces."

Director Lancaster pulls her eyes from Ledger's back to meet mine and shakes her head. "That might be doable for the first art piece, but the other three can't be done solo. Besides, neither agency is willing to give up point on this mission, so it has to be a joint mission. The preferences of either of you to not work together isn't going to change that." She glances at Ledger. "Please excuse me for a moment." She stands and walks over to him.

I take the moment to say in a low voice to Sully, "This

is a bad idea. After last time, he's never going to trust me again."

He studies me for a long moment, and then he says, "But isn't that a specialty of yours? We'll just have to make one of your objectives for this mission be to get Ledger Lancaster to trust you."

CHAPTER 6
INSIDER INFORMATION
LEDGER

don't trust her," I say to the director. I keep my voice quiet enough that Director Reynolds and Zoe shouldn't be able to hear. Not that I'm unwilling to say it to Zoe directly, but it doesn't feel right to say it in front of her boss.

"That is what's at the root of this?"

I nod. "And don't give me some line like, 'You don't have to trust her to work with her.' Have you ever had a successful mission with a partner you didn't trust? It's kind of a requirement."

"I'm not going to tell you that you don't need to trust her. But I am going to tell you that it's never too late to build trust. I think the two of you can get there."

I disagree, but it doesn't seem like that really matters, so I breathe through my frustration until the heat of it dissipates, and then I step back to the table and sit down.

My director takes her seat, too. I lean against the back of my chair, my arms crossed. "So how would this work?"

"Well, you're in luck," Director Reynolds says, "because the first art piece is in Dublin, and the Irish Ambassador to the United States just happens to be traveling home to Ireland today for his daughter's wedding. He's been read in on the part of your mission that is need-to-know. Since he would like to keep organized crime and terrorism out of his country— especially anything having to do with Callid Aragundi— he's willing to let you hitch a ride with him. So you'll get to fly there on a luxury business jet."

I smile. We'll get a private plane with nice seats instead of flying coach, where these legs of mine don't exactly fit into the designated "leg room" area. My would-be fellow seatmates and would-be flight attendants would rejoice right now if they knew I wouldn't be joining them on their flight. At least one thing is going right.

"Your flight leaves at six p.m. from Washington Dulles," my mom says, and both Zoe and I immediately look at our watches. It's almost three now, and it's a good hour's drive to the airport, without traffic. There's a lot here I'll have to do to prepare for the mission, and then I'll need to go home and pack before making the drive.

"The plane will be in the air for roughly seven hours, and Dublin is five hours ahead of us, so you'll arrive at about six a.m. You'll need to be at the Éireann Expressions Gallery at nine, which means that tired or not, you'll need to sleep on the plane."

It might sound like we'll be taking the redeye flight, we'll actually be in the air from six p.m. until one a.m. our time, which is really not my standard sleeping hours. I can fall asleep anytime, anywhere, as needed. It's waking up at odd times when I haven't gotten enough sleep that I struggle with.

I glance over at Zoe, and she's wearing an expression of confidence like she has no problem at all with the sleeping constraints. Of course, she doesn't.

"The owner of the gallery in Dublin has been briefed and is willing to let you plant the tracker," Director Reynolds says. "Apparently, finding out that your prized piece will be stolen makes a person not only more willing to up their security but more than willing to have a tracker placed so that they can recover it if it does get stolen.

"That shouldn't take too long, so you won't need to stay the night in Dublin— we've got a flight lined up for you tomorrow at three p.m. that will take you to Belgrade, Serbia. That's a five-hour flight, and with the one-hour time difference, that will put you pulling up to your hotel by ten p.m."

"The leg of the mission taking place in Serbia won't be as easy," Director Lancaster says. "Especially because the owner, Zoran Savović, is a highly distrusting individual, and he is especially distrustful of foreign governments. So we can't partner with him to place the tracking device— you'll have to sneak it in. Both agencies will be working on a recommended plan while you're traveling and placing the tracking device on the art piece in Ireland."

Zoe leans forward, tapping a finger on the conference table. "The hotel in Belgrade— you got *two separate rooms,* correct?"

That gets my attention, and I sit up straighter. "Yeah," I say, making my voice firm and commanding. "None of this business where there's 'only one bed available' so we have to share or one of us sleeps on the floor." Zoe is one attractive woman who is impressive in nearly every way, and every single guy everywhere would probably kill for the chance to share a room with her. But I've experienced it. I've experienced how she can lead you to believe that she feels one way about you, then go out and prove just the opposite. Once was more than enough for a lifetime.

"We wouldn't dream of it," Director Reynolds says. "We've got two rooms reserved for you tomorrow."

Zoe nods. "Which of us is in charge? Because—"

"—It better be me," both of us say at the same time.

"Neither of you are in charge," Director Lancaster says. "You're partners. Equals."

I narrow my eyes. "Yes, but when we disagree, who gets to make the final decision?" Because we *will* disagree. Often and vehemently.

"You'll have to figure out how to work together to come to a final decision."

Zoe rolls her eyes and leans back in her chair, arms crossed. "That's impossible."

Director Reynolds raises an eyebrow in challenge. "Impossible? I didn't know that word was in your vocabulary."

Apparently, we are done discussing details because my

mom opens the door and welcomes Emerson and Kenneth back in. "You both likely have a lot to do to prepare in a short amount of time, so we'll let you get to it. We will send you both a secure file with all the details by the time you board your flight. Emerson, will you please show our CIA guests out? And let Charlie and Kella know that I need five minutes."

Emerson nods, and I watch— mostly Zoe— as the four of them leave, shutting the door behind them.

Then it's just the director and me, with all of her focus on me. "Why don't you want to do this mission?"

"I *do* want to do this mission."

"Okay, correction: why don't you want to do it with Zoe? Beyond the trust factor."

"Because she thinks her way is the right way— the *only* way— even if things in the field change. Because things always go bad when we work together. Because she tries to do everything in the most boring way possible. Because she would sell her firstborn to complete a mission. Because she forgets that sabotage should never be used on someone who's on the same side as you. Do you want me to go on? Because I could go on."

She studies me for a long moment. "You've had a lot of experience working with very difficult people, and you always manage to work with them to accomplish your objectives. I mean, you convinced a street artist in Berlin to use their graffiti to send coded messages to one of our operatives when communications went down. And you talked a very skeptical cat lady in Bogota into attaching cameras to her cats' collars so you could use her feline network as a surveillance system."

"It's different with Zoe. She's an intelligence operative, so I can't exactly promise her exclusive spray paint from a rare collection or guarantee the safety of her beloved pets with state-of-the-art tracking devices to get her on my side."

She takes off her lanyard with her CSA credentials and places it on the table, signaling that she's switching from being my director to being my mom. "Ledger. You're the kid who always looked out for the boy on the playground at recess who had no one to play with. You were the kid with a great group of friends who planned fun activities, and would still always invite others outside that group of friends to join in so they could make new friends, too. The kid who always accepted people exactly as they were."

"It's not the same, Mom. Zoe and I just can't work together."

"But you've never actually worked together— only *against* each other. Sure, you both fight for the same cause — making the world a better place. But you've done it from opposing sides, working as competitors."

No, there was one time that we worked together. Or at least I *thought* we were working together. It wasn't a joint mission like this one. It was just a matter of the case she was working on and the case I was working on overlapping unexpectedly. It's embarrassing how easily Zoe was able to betray me without me even seeing it coming. Embarrassing enough that I haven't told a soul about it. I'm for sure not going to tell my mom/director about it.

She sighs, puts her lanyard back over her head, and straightens it as she stands up. "Well, I didn't want to do this, but I'm going to have to combine my knowledge of being your mom and my knowledge of being your boss." She takes a deep breath and lets it out slowly. "I don't think you can pull off a successful mission with Zoe."

I cross my arms and meet her eyes, shaking my head slightly. She's not saying she's about to switch me out for another operative, and she's not saying she's going to go back to Director Sullivan and say she's changed her mind. No, I know exactly what she's doing— she's using reverse psychology on me— and it's not going to work. I'm not going to suddenly want to pull off a successful mission with Zoe just because my mom/director said I can't.

I mean, I *could* pull off a successful mission with Zoe if I *wanted* to. But I don't want to. I don't want to work with her at all. But we are both some of the best at what we do, and we can prove it. *I* can prove it. I may not want to work with Zoe, but I can work with her and pull off a mission. Even a mission that is really four missions, like this one is. I can work with someone impossible to work with, and I can still be successful. I'll prove it.

The director has a hand on the doorknob, about to open it, but then glances back at me. She's trying to hide a smile that tells me she knows the journey my mind just went on, and that her reverse psychology did, in fact, work, even though I knew she was doing it. I grind my teeth.

She opens the door, and says, "Charlie? Kella? You can join us now." Then, to me, she says, "We've got some news to share about your handler."

Oh?

Charlie and Kella come in, but they leave the door open. For as different as my sister and my handler are, they are alike in some ways. For one thing, their hair is about the same length— almost touching their shoulders. Charlie's is light brown, wavy, and a tiny bit chaotic.

Kella's is dark brown— almost black— and is sleek and straight as can be. But underneath all the dark hair on top is a vibrant teal fading into purple. If you see her from the back, her hair looks professional and a little boring. If you see her from the front, the teal and purple practically frame her face. It's kind of like a mullet, but instead of the party being in the back, it's hiding underneath.

They are alike in their enthusiasm level when they are excited. And right now, they are very excited. From the moment they walk into the room, I can't help but feel the same, and all frustration about my latest assignment falls away.

The director says to Kella, "Do you want to tell him the news or have me do it?"

"I want to tell him. Okay, you know how I have always wanted to be a field operative?"

"Yeah?" I say.

She seems so excited that she's ready to burst. "I finally talked to Director Lancaster about it." Her voice is rising in octave and speed as she talks. "She gave me her blessing to fill out all the application paperwork so they can start the vetting process and I can start on the testing."

"Right on," I say, giving Kella a fist bump. "Congratulations! It's the best job. You're going to love it."

"Thanks," she says, grinning widely.

"So what does this mean?" I ask.

"Right now," the director says, "it shouldn't make much of a difference for you. There could be a time here and there when Charlie will need to take over as your handler if she has to be away for a test when something goes down. Charlie might just have to pull double-duty for a bit now and then."

I grin at my sister. "Just like good old times." Charlie has been my handler quite a few times over the four years I've been here. But we both know I'm referring to our childhood, when she was on the other side of our walkie-talkies, directing me and Miles as we spied on our neighbors from the treehouse. "So when are you going to apply to be a field operative?"

Charlie's eyes go wide and fill with a terror that's so over-the-top, it's comical and makes me laugh. Charlie has always preferred running things behind the scenes and never stepping a single toe into the spotlight.

"Just kidding, sis. You're too good at what you do. We'd all be lost without you on the other side of our comms."

"If you'll excuse me," the director says, "I need to get to a meeting. Don't hold him up too long— he has a mission to prepare for." She gives me a look like she did when I was a kid, supposedly doing homework, when she walked in to find me laughing with friends in a group video call.

As the director is leaving the room, Abraham walks in. He was an intelligence operative a million years ago, like at the same time my dad was. He's too old to be a spy now, but I don't think he ever wants to leave the spy life behind. I don't blame him. "I just came by to see what kinds of disguises you might need for your mission. Oh, and to wish you good luck, have fun, and don't die."

"Thanks, Abraham," I say.

I'm about to talk with him about disguise needs, but then Kella asks, "So, you're preparing for a mission with Zoe, huh?" Even though I know she knows the answer to that.

Then Charlie says, "Oh! Maybe this mission will be the second act of your enemies-to-lovers arc."

"My… *What?*" My eyebrows pull together in confusion, but I'm also pretty sure I don't want either of them to un-confuse me.

"You know, a romance trope," Abraham says, surprising me. "You two start off as enemies and then you turn into love interests."

"No," I say as firmly as I can to all three of them. "Absolutely not. If anything, it's the opposite of that."

Now both Charlie and Kella look confused. Abraham just pulls up a chair, looking rather entertained.

Then Charlie makes things so much worse by talking through her confusion. "Opposites? The opposite of enemies to lovers would be lov…" Then she full-on gasps. Hand over her lips and everything, like she just heard the most scandalous thing ever. "You two—"

"No!" I practically shout. "Not exactly. Not that at all. But no, we are *not* doing an enemies-to-lovers thing. This mission will be more of an enemies-to-*worse-enemies* thing.

It won't surprise me if only one of us comes home on that plane."

All three of them are quiet for a moment, then, like a true sister, Charlie says, "If it's Zoe, can I have your prized spyglass that Portugal's Director of Maritime Trade gifted you?"

And now I'm back to grinding my teeth.

CHAPTER 7
SKY-HIGH RIVALRY
LEDGER

This is my first time flying on a private luxury jet, and boy, could I get used to this. It uses a separate terminal with private lounges— not that I have time to sit down in one, but they are nice to walk past. Security screening is easier than finding a Starbucks in Seattle, and a private shuttle just dropped me off on the tarmac in front of the waiting plane.

I'm not even all the way up the stairs with my bag before I hear talking and laughing. As soon as I step through the door to the plane, I see that Zoe has beat me here, which makes my eyelid twitch a little.

She's chatting up a gentleman in I'm guessing his late fifties, who is wearing a navy suit and looking rather entertained. He's standing like he's used to commanding attention, yet there are plenty of laugh lines around his eyes that seem at odds with his posture. Based on the green tie and pocket square with a Celtic knot design on the fabric, the pin of an Irish harp on his lapel, and his chestnut hair streaked with silver, I'm guessing he is the Irish Ambassador to the U.S. who offered to let us ride with him.

A man in his thirties is standing next to him, looking equally Irish but nowhere near as commanding of a presence. But he does look every bit as entertained as the Ambassador. Which doesn't surprise me, since Zoe is chatting with them. As usual, she's morphed into the perfect conversationalist for this situation. It's a skill that is rather impressive and useful for a spy to have. I respect it— as long as she doesn't use it on me again. *That* I can't stand.

She's dressed in dark gray slacks and a light purple blouse, and she looks amazing. When I first laid eyes on Zoe at a café in Moldova when our missions overlapped, I was so awestruck that I forgot my cover name and story. I almost forgot my actual name. Before that point in my life, I hadn't really thought about what the "perfect woman" looked like. Seeing her was all I needed to know that she was exactly it. From her honey-colored hair to her lean muscles, right down to the way her ankles looked when she was wearing heels. Yep, I even noticed the ankles.

And that is part of what makes Zoe Steele so maddeningly dangerous. Because a part of me always whispers, *but she's just what I want.* Physically, she is. She also has a job and a set of skills and interests that are so in line with mine. Nearly everything about her is, on paper, exactly what I most want in a woman.

But I've been around her enough to know that I can be attracted to her, yet also want nothing to do with her. Getting your heart targeted by a precision strike only to be left in the blast radius of a bomb can do that to you. Now, all I have to do is divert my mind anytime I'm accidentally attracted to her. I'm not normally around her for such a long period of time, though. I'm going to have to be very vigilant on this mission.

As I walk over to Zoe, the ambassador, and the other man, Zoe smiles welcomingly and says, "Oh, Ledger. I'm glad you're joining us."

No, she isn't.

"The ambassador was just telling me about a sport they have in Ireland called hurling. It sounds like it's a mix between football and soccer—and maybe hockey?" she says, glancing at the ambassador for confirmation— "but played with a ball the size of a baseball. Oh, and all the players on the field have bats."

The ambassador gives a hearty laugh at her description. "You're funny. I like you."

I'm sad I didn't arrive earlier so I could've heard all about this glorious sport. "Wow. Is that for real? And they all have bats? How many players are on the field at once?"

"Fifteen for each team," the younger man says.

"That sounds like my kind of game. Hi, I'm Ledger Lancaster." I hold out my hand to the older gentleman first, and he shakes it.

"Nice to meet you, Ledger. I'm Odhrán Connolly, Irish Ambassador to the United States." He doesn't have much of an accent, but he's still unmistakably Irish. He motions to the younger man and then the three other people on the plane. "This is my aide, Evan O'Brien. And that's our flight attendant, Saoirse, and our security officers, Ronan and Patrick."

I nod to each person as he says them, committing their names to memory.

Evan asks me, "How long are you going to be in Dublin?" and after hearing the ambassador speak, I'm surprised at how strong his aide's accent is. I don't think I've ever seen a TV show or movie with an Irish character who sounds so… Irish. It makes me wonder if TV got it wrong or if Evan is the exception.

"Less than twelve hours."

"That's minus craic," Evan says. "It's my pet hate to go somewhere new and not be able to check it out. We're mostly up to ninety here for six days, what with the wedding and a host of meetings, then we'll be back in the States. When you've got some free time and it isn't manky out, give me a ring or a text." He holds out a business card, and I take it. "We'll gather some fellas and get a game of hurling together."

There were a lot of words in there I didn't understand. But calling the embassy to get together for a game of hurling I *do* understand, and a smile spreads across my face. "I will for sure take you up on that." And I will. Maybe I'll even talk my brothers into joining us.

"Congratulations on your daughter's upcoming marriage," Zoe says. "That's very exciting."

The ambassador smiles widely. "It is. She's my youngest. I've got my kilt all ready to go."

"Wait," I say, not entirely sure whether he's telling the

truth or trying to pull something over on me. "Are you really wearing a kilt at the wedding?"

"I never miss a chance to show off these legs."

As we are all laughing, I'm thinking about how glad I am that we are hitching a ride with someone easygoing and with a sense of humor instead of someone pretentious or stuffy. And I'm extra glad that I'm not currently trying to squeeze my knees into a coach space as an attendant pushes a cart down the aisle. So I give him a very genuine thank you, especially since he didn't have to offer.

"This will be my first time in Ireland," Zoe says, "and I think it will be for Ledger, too. Do you have any advice for us?"

That's a good question— I wish I would've asked it. Not only because it's a good way to get some great advice, but also because it's one people love to answer. Evan's face immediately lights up. "I do. Don't be a chancer and get your takeaway at a kip. Find yourself a deadly chipper and have some craic."

I swear the man is speaking English, yet I have zero idea what he said, and judging by the look Zoe gives me, she doesn't, either. In a stage whisper, she says, "Craic? Is that some kind of food? A *deadly* food? I'm guessing it's crispy lamb tongue."

I stage-whisper back, "Or goat kidneys."

The ambassador does that hearty laugh again, and Evan chuckles as well. Neither of them seem to have any clue how much Zoe and I don't actually want to be standing next to each other, let alone being on the same plane. Or in the same state. So kudos to us for being able to fake it so well.

"He's saying to not take a risk and get your takeout at a dive," the Ambassador says. "Find yourself a fantastic restaurant and have some fun."

Evan nods. "Oh, but if you really want a treat, try black and white pudding."

See? Sometimes you get great advice when you ask for it.

We continue to chat with the group until the attendant announces that we are ready for takeoff, which is about the time that both Zoe's and my secure phones ping with the mission briefing. The ambassador says that they need to have a thirty-minute meeting and will have it at the front of the plane, and that he knows that Zoe and I need to meet also, and that we can do it at the back of the plane.

The flight attendant shows us to our area as the plane starts slowly taxiing toward the runway. She tells us that the plane is used most often for flights overseas during the night, so the seats can transform fully into beds, and that she will be back with bedding after our meeting.

She also says that there are dividers that close off our two seats from the rest of the plane, and she closes them as she leaves. I vow to make friends with every single ambassador to the United States who flies on a private jet so I can increase my chances of traveling like this again.

The plane engines get louder as they pick up speed, and we take a seat. Before long, the plane's wheels lift off the runway, and the noise quiets soon after. There is a small table between our two chairs, and Zoe pulls a tablet from her bag, sets it on the table, and says, "Do you want to look at this instead of our phones?"

A mental image fills my mind of the two of us leaning in as we look at the same tablet, our faces close, heat building between us at our proximity, and I immediately divert my thoughts. I pull out a tablet from my bag and hold it up, giving it a little shake. "Nope. I've got my own."

We both connect through our secure phone lines and pull up the briefing. Zoe, in her need to always be fifty steps ahead, scrolls through the briefing, and says, "It looks like I'll be impersonating an international art appraiser when we get to Belgrade. Eliza Cholmondeley, code name 'Mona Liza.' She's going to be appraising the entire collection at the fortress where the sculpture is. When she flies in, the CIA will delay her in customs so we can show up in her place."

I glance at Zoe. She's holding the locket of the necklace she always wears between her thumb and finger. I noticed she tends to do that when she's reading or thinking, and it draws my eyes to the little dip at the base of her neck. She's always had a great neck.

A moment later, she says, "Apparently, Eliza is well-known in name, but rarely in photos. She and the owner of the mansion have never met, so all I have to do is wear a wig and they think I'll pass for her. Except I don't speak Serbian... Oh! Perfect. Neither does she. She's from the UK and will be speaking English. And it looks like there's a Serbian native who's a CIA operative who will be meeting us on the ground."

She also says things like "I bet we can pull off a secret art exchange during the Venice Biennale," and "Looks like we'll be in the historic part of Ankara." What I'm concerned with is the mission we are going to be doing *tomorrow morning*. As in half a day from now. Everything else can wait.

To get Zoe back on track, I say, "It looks like the gallery owner in Dublin who is on board with us planting a tracker is out of the country right now. And she really doesn't want her employees to know we are planting the tracker because they are quote, 'talkers,' and she doesn't want her employees to have information that the suspects will want to extract from them if they come by to steal it. She says the less they know, the better. Good choice on her part."

"So we'll have to plant the tracker covertly." Zoe quietly scrolls on her tablet for a moment while I keep reading.

"Okay," I say. "There are security cameras in the room, but the gallery owner has access to those from where she'll be, so we don't need to worry about disabling them. She'll pull the footage just in case her employees suspect anything and go back to look at it."

Zoe nods. "The gallery opens at nine, with the first group tour at nine-fifteen. What do you say we join the tour? Then we can just be stragglers and get the tracker planted."

I check the address of the gallery to see how long it'll take to get there from the airport and what our transportation options are. "Okay, we can take a taxi or— Oh, they even have Ubers. Or we can take the shuttle that will get us pretty close. There's one that leaves every fifteen minutes. It looks like whichever we choose, we'll need to plan forty-five minutes or so to get from the airport to the gallery. Nine-fifteen should work and still give us plenty of time to get breakfast from the Blarney Bean Café that overlooks the gallery."

Zoe rolls her eyes.

"Hey," I say and pat my stomach. "This body needs fuel regularly. Speaking of which, do you think the flight attendant is bringing us dinner? Snacks?" Maybe I should've picked up food on my way to the airport.

"Okay, I'm buying gallery tickets." Her fingers fly across her tablet for a bit, then she pauses. "So, what's our cover?"

I say, "Not spouses," at the same time Zoe says "Not a married couple." Good.

"Siblings?" I suggest. "One of us can be visiting from out of town."

Zoe nods. "That works. Siblings annoy each other, right?" She works her way through the form, mumbling things as she enters them. "Two tickets… Person one's name: Shauna Glazier."

"Shauna? *Shauna*?"

Zoe looks up at me, eyes narrowed. "That's my cover name. What's wrong with Shauna?"

"Nothing. Shauna's great. But generally, operatives choose something closer to their actual name. Like, I don't know, Zora or Zuri or… Oh, Chloe rhymes with Zoe. Do you know what? 'Zero Chill' rhymes with Zoe Steele. *Shauna* does not."

Zoe narrows her eyes at me like she's telling me I don't get to have an opinion about her cover name. And she's right— I don't. "I'm Zoe all the time," she says. "Sometimes, I just want to be Shauna."

"Fair enough."

She starts typing. "I'm putting you in as Linus Lightweight."

"Now see? An insult only works if it hits home." I flex my biceps. "'Lightweight' doesn't really do it for me. It's the equivalent of me saying that I don't like your purple hair. You don't have purple hair, so it doesn't work as an insult."

"You're right. You're now 'Lenny Laggard.' Because when it comes to which of us wins, you are always lagging behind."

"Ouch. That hurt."

She licks her fingertip and then draws an invisible tally mark in the air. "I'll take that as another win for me."

There's a knock on the divider between our small area and the rest of the plane, and I quickly turn off the screen of my tablet before Saoirse slides the divider open, her arms laden with bedding. "Are you ready for me to set things up for you?"

I nod and put my tablet in my bag. "Yeah, I think we're all finished up here."

As the flight attendant is unfolding the chairs into beds and putting on bedding, Zoe says, "You know, this winning streak is just really fueling me. I think I'm going to keep it going by falling asleep first."

I shake my head. "I'm a twin and I have three older brothers, so I learned to fall asleep in even the most chaotic of situations. You're not going to continue that streak—I've been training for this since birth."

"You're a twin?" There's something in the way Zoe asks it that I can't quite put my finger on.

"Yep." Somehow, I've never mentioned that to her.

"Identical?"

"Miles wishes. No. Not even close." I turn to Saoirse. "Which of us do you think will fall asleep first?"

She stops spreading the blanket over Zoe's bed and studies both of us, a finger tapping her lip. Looking at Zoe, she asks, "Siblings?" When Zoe shakes her head, Saoirse says, "I have three kids. When the oldest was an only child, he fell asleep for naps the fastest, hands down. My youngest, though? He was the one who could fall asleep anywhere. So this early in the day, while on an airplane?" She holds her hand out flat and tips it in both directions. "It could go either way."

She places a pillow on each bed, then says, "Okay, I think you're all set," as she's lowering the window covers. "The dimmer's on that wall, and there's a bathroom right there and it's big enough to change in if you'd like. Do you need anything before I go?"

"Snacks?" I ask.

"Something he can eat in bed," Zoe says. "Preferably something that makes a lot of crumbs."

Saoirse leaves to get snacks, and I motion to the bathroom. "Are you going to change? Ladies first."

"Ledger, we are on a plane with people we don't know, and I'm sharing a room with *you*. No, I am not going to change." She pulls a small bag from her duffel. "I am going to brush my teeth, though."

Ten minutes later, the lights are out, and Zoe and I are both in our beds. Compared to normal beds, they aren't the most comfortable things ever. Compared to the seats on a regular airplane, they're downright glorious. The space is dark enough to be the middle of the night, even though I know the sun won't set for a while.

I do what I normally do when I need to fall asleep. I clear my mind, breathe slowly, and focus on lowering my heart rate. Before long, I'm turning over in the narrow bed, trying to get comfortable. Adjusting my pillow. Staring up at the dark ceiling. Letting my mind wander to a million different things.

If I had known last night that I would have to go to sleep before seven p.m., I would've woken up earlier today. Yes, I can fall asleep anytime, anyplace, but generally, that happens after having been in the field enough to be exhausted. Last night, after our footvolley-pickleball game, I got into bed before midnight and I woke up on my own ten minutes before my seven a.m. alarm went off. So I'm a little *too* well-rested.

It doesn't help to know that Zoe Steele is just three feet away. Close enough that I can hear her breathing. Almost see her silhouette as she lays on her side. The rise and fall of her chest. Feel her nearness. It doesn't make for optimal sleeping conditions.

After a bit, Zoe asks in a quiet voice, "Are you awake?"

"No."

"Same here. I'm fast asleep."

My normal reaction, and the reaction I'd have if it was anyone else in this space with me would be to say, "I have a deck of cards, do you want to play a game of Gin Rummy or Golf?" Or maybe see if anyone else in the other compartment is awake and wants to play Hearts or Poker or Euchre.

But, put your hand on a hot stove and get burnt once, you know not to put your hand on the stove again. So I stay quiet. The competition is still on, and I'm going to fall asleep first.

CHAPTER 8
TRUST ME, IT'S PUDDING
ZOE

I look diagonally across the street toward the Éireann Expressions Gallery from where we are seated at an outdoor table at the Blarney Bean Café, and sip my cup of tea. We've already scouted the building as much as we can. It seems pretty straightforward.

Ledger ordered a full Irish breakfast, and the massive plate in front of him has bacon, sausages, black and white pudding, baked beans, eggs, mushrooms, grilled tomatoes, soda bread, *and* toast with marmalade. I can't imagine one human being able to eat that much food in one meal.

"I thought they said black and white pudding is included." Ledger glances back toward the doors. "I think they forgot it. Since Evan suggested it, I want to be sure to try it."

I try to hold back a smile. "They didn't forget it." I point first at the dark disk that looks like a speckled hockey puck, and then I point at the tan one. "Black pudding, white pudding."

Ledger pokes at it with his fork. "That is *not* pudding."

I shrug.

"What is it?"

"A spicy but somewhat sweet sausage with oatmeal. That one's 'black' because it also contains pig's blood."

For as big, tough, and commanding as Ledger's presence is, he's looking awfully green right now, and those eyes are comically wide.

"You knew it wasn't just chocolate and vanilla pudding together in a bowl? Thanks for the warning."

"If I warned you, I would've missed out on seeing that look on your face."

He blinks a few times like he's simultaneously feeling deceived and like he absolutely should've expected it. I smile as I take a sip of my tea.

Ledger eyes me as he cuts into an egg. "I thought you hadn't been to Ireland before."

"I haven't, but I have been to England."

"They eat it there, too?"

"Yep," I say, and pull my phone from my backpack so I can go over the details in the briefing again. Since we aren't checking into a hotel, we left our bags in a storage locker. There are plenty of things that no covert operative would leave behind, and all of those are in the backpack at my feet. But our clothes, shoes, and non-sensitive equipment? We really didn't want to lug them around with us.

I rub my finger on the locket of my necklace as I read through the part again about what security measures the gallery owner said that the tapestry has, the dossier about the employees who will be working, and the details about the tracker. I check my backpack to make sure the tiny piece of technology is right where I expect it to be. The reason most of my missions go off without a hitch is because of my preparedness.

Of course, my partner here is the King of Improvisation. The guy who likes to go in with a half-baked plan and just "figure it out" as he goes along. If we were both metaphorically on a high cliff and someone came along and dropped two bags with paragliding equipment, one at my feet and the other at Ledger's, and then told us we have ten minutes to jump off the cliff and get to a specific point in the distance, we would act very differently.

I would strap on my harness, making sure it's secure, and put on my gloves and helmet. Then I'd survey all the areas I could see between the cliff and the target location, check the wind speed and direction, and determine the best spot to land in order to make it to the target. Since I wouldn't be able to find out the wind information closer to the target, I'd also make contingency plans. I'd lay out my canopy perfectly, connect it to my harness, and be ready and waiting to go at the sound of the whistle.

Ledger, on the other hand, would spend the entire ten minutes talking with whoever was also up on that cliff, about stuff that wasn't even mission-related, until the very moment the whistle blew. Then he would whoop loud enough to echo off the surrounding cliffs as he ran toward the edge, paragliding equipment bag in hand, and leap off the cliff with nothing more than a hope that he could get strapped into his harness as he fell, put on his helmet and gloves, and open and attach his paragliding canopy in time for the wind to catch it before he plummeted to his death.

Sometimes, I admire his adaptability. I wish I could just go with the flow more easily. But most of the time? Let's just say that this job requires planning to be successful.

I glance over at the man— he is already three-fourths of the way through scarfing down his breakfast. "This black 'pudding' isn't half bad. Want a bite?"

"I'm not really a breakfast eater."

"Not a breakfast eater, or just afraid to try it?"

I meet his eyes, take his fork from his hand, cut off a big piece, put it in my mouth, and chew, all without taking my eyes off him. He actually looks a little impressed, which I take to mean one more tally mark for me. Do I like black pudding? *No.* Am I going to let Ledger know that I don't? *Absolutely not.*

"By the way," I say after I swallow, "before we head back to the airport, we are stopping at a restaurant that serves cheese."

"Cheese?"

I nod.

"Why cheese?"

"It's just something I do when I'm in another country, and I'm not going to skip the cheese just because you're on this mission, too."

"But why *cheese*? I mean, I like cheese as much as the next guy, but—"

"But not as much as the next girl," I say, pointing to myself. "And I won't be leaving this country without trying its cheese."

I am skilled enough at reading body language that I can tell when someone's checking me out, even discreetly, and if they like what they see. I've caught it from enough people to feel fairly confident about my looks. There's something about Ledger checking me out and liking what he sees, though, that feels different. I don't know why, but I do like it.

I just really hope that my skill in hiding any of my own body language is greater than Ledger's skill in reading body language, because I really don't want him picking up on how often I've checked him out. Try as I might, I've never been able to control my pupil's dilation. And if Ledger is paying attention, I'm sure he can see plain as day that my pupils widen every time my eyes glide over his shoulders or take in how beautiful his face is.

People have started walking into the gallery, so I send a secure message to Packston, my tech op, letting him know that we are about to start, and then I put in my earpiece. I see Ledger doing the same, even though we likely won't need our tech ops at all for this mission.

"Good morning," Packston says. It's four a.m. in Langley, and Packston's voice sounds like he either hasn't been awake long or hasn't talked at all since he woke.

"Sorry to wake you so early," I say so he knows my comms are working.

"I don't know what you're talking about. I'm always up this early."

"Of course you are," I say, even though we both know it's not true.

I'm not sure he even heard me, though, because at the same time, Ledger is saying, "Heyyy, Kella! Good morning! Nothing like rising before the sun, huh?" Then Ledger turns to me and says, "Let's go make history."

I know from working with Ledger a year and a half ago that it's what he says before embarking on any mission. I smile at him, knowing that I'll be the one winning this particular mission, and it's always the winner who writes the history. So I say, "I'll bring the pen."

I tell Packston that I'm going radio silent as we put on our backpacks and cross the street to the gallery. We step into a small lobby where nine people are standing, already waiting for the tour. Six are obvious tourists, plus a mom with two small children who look local. A tall man with light brown skin and natural curls that are long and sticking out in every direction points at Ledger and me with both hands. "You here for the tour?"

We nod, and he says, "Our printer is on the fritz, so if I could get you to come up and write your names on your name tag, we'll get started soon."

I'm closer, so I walk up to the counter where a package of peel-and-stick name tags sits next to a black Sharpie. I write *Shauna* on one of them and stick it to my shirt. Then I write *Account* on the other one, peel off the back, then go over to Ledger and stick it to his shirt. I pat his very firm chest twice, then say, "If anyone asks, tell them your last name is *Book*." Ledger can drive me nuts at times, but he's also rather fun to mess with.

"Haha. 'Account Book,' because my name is Ledger. *So* clever." He walks over to the desk with the name badges, and I figure he's making himself a new one. Probably with the name Lincoln, since I'm pretty sure that's his favorite cover name. But when he turns around with a name badge in his hand, he sticks it on my shirt, covering *Shauna*. I look down to see he's scrawled *Stainless* on it.

"If anyone asks, don't tell them your last name is 'Steele' or you'll blow your cover."

I don't have time to say any kind of comeback before the man with the wild curls starts talking. "Welcome, everyone. I'm Kieran, and I'll be your tour guide today. It looks like we've got a fun group. We've got," and he starts reading off the names of everyone in the group, having to squint or cock his head with a couple of them to decipher their handwriting. Then he gets to me and Ledger and says, "And here, we've got... 'Account' and 'Stainless?'" He glances at our faces like he's trying to confirm that he read them right.

"Yeah, our parents are a little weird," Ledger says.

I nod. "I mean, they'd have to be to have two kids who are so vastly"— I motion between me and Ledger— "different from each other."

"Well, it was really only one of our parents who was weird." He puts a hand beside his mouth like he's attempting to be discreet, then mouths in about as exaggerated of a way as possible, *Our dad.* Then he puts his arm around my shoulders and gives me a brotherly one-armed hug. "And Stainless, here, is the spitting image of our dad.

No one can look at her without saying, 'I know exactly who your daddy is.'"

I bristle and shrug his arm off my shoulder. Then I take a slow, deep breath. What was that he said yesterday about an insult only working if it is a direct hit? This one hits the bull's eye, and he doesn't even have the slightest clue that he aimed at a target.

Keiran leads us all into the first room, which has paintings on all the walls. It's the "Impressionist Instagram" room, as our tour guide refers to it. Ledger motions at a painting of a woman sitting by a table, looking like she's either really bored or just disappointed about the way her life has gone. "Oh, look— there's a painting of you!" Before I've had a chance to give either a courtesy laugh or a retort, his eyes have landed on me and he sees whatever expression resides on my face after his comment about my "dad." He leans in and asks in a quiet voice, "Is everything okay?" His head is tilted to the side a bit and his eyebrows are drawn together.

I nod. "Just fine." Then in a voice loud enough for everyone to hear, I ask "Did Monet get royalties for inventing the original filter?" Not the greatest question, I know, but I couldn't think of another quickly enough, and it seems like one our tour guide would appreciate.

I try to ignore Ledger's gaze on me as Keiran says, "Unfortunately, no. But he's definitely rolling in 'exposure' currency, which is worth exactly zero at the bank. Legend has it, though, that he's still collecting likes in the afterlife."

I pretend to look around while trying to keep my mind on how, exactly, I'm going to disable security on the tapestry and how uncomfortable it feels to see a genuinely concerned look on Ledger's face when I know the look is because of me. That's not how we interact. But it still manages to take me back to that small moment in time a year and a half ago when it was how we interacted. We know from experience, though, that spies can't date spies. It doesn't work for so many reasons.

It especially doesn't work for me. No relationships ever do.

Then Kieran leads us into the "Sculpture Selfie" room, where we all gaze at a bunch of marble "influencers" frozen in time.

Packston hasn't said a word in my ear since we started our mission. Not that he needs to, but he usually likes doing a running commentary. I'm about to check to see if my earpiece is actually working, but then I hear something that I'm pretty sure is soft snoring.

"And this is the Tapestry Room," Kieran says as we all file into the next area. "Also known as the 'Threaded Views' Room, as I like to call it. Take a look around, and you'll see ones from Greece to Greenland, from the Renaissance 'like and subscribe' period all the way up to nineteen ninety-nine. We'd appreciate it if you didn't touch any of them because their historical updates are still buffering."

Kieran walks just beside the tapestry that we are here for, and my heart rate picks up. It's about two feet wide by five feet long, and it's mounted on the wall inside a clear case. He motions to it and says, "This piece is called *Threads of Accord*, and I bet you're wondering why you couldn't touch it if you wanted to. It's the most expensive piece in the whole gallery. Worth two-point-five million Euros." He emphasizes each word, then pauses to give everyone a moment to gasp at its worth before he continues.

"The clear case it's in keeps it protected from the elements. Like light, air pollution, and *your hands*. See those fingerprints all over your cell phone? Yeah, we don't want those on our tapestries. So this one is all safe and locked up inside its little home. It also has an alarm that will go off if it tries to leave home, which is pretty much just like it was for me when I left for college. In fact, there are rumors that the gallery went to my mamma and recorded her wail to use as the alarm sound. So I'd appreciate it if you didn't bump it or do anything to set it off." He gives an exaggerated shudder.

"This is the pièce de résistance of our *Trust Me, I'm a Tapestry* collection. What you're looking at, ladies and gentlemen, is not just a piece of fabric, but a historical group chat between two rival factions who decided to swipe right on peace. Observe the intricate patterns—each thread is a message, each color a status update, showing how their lives got so entangled that they could no longer even remember what the feud was about in the first place.

"Now, the centerpiece of it, this handshake here, is the original 'no hard feelings' emoji. And if you squint and cock your head just right, you might see the fine print in the corner that says, 'Terms and conditions may apply, including but not limited to, annual potluck dinners and mandatory trust falls at team-building retreats.' Truly, this tapestry teaches us that trust is the foundation of any great reconciliation."

Ledger shifts his weight uncomfortably, and I know he's thinking about the lost trust between us. Right now, though, my mind is one hundred percent on getting past the security on that box so I can place the tracker.

As the last few people exit the room to follow Keiran to the "Cubist Clickbait" room, I take off my backpack and say to Ledger, "Okay, you guard the door and I'll disable the security."

"No," he says, taking off his own backpack, "*you* guard the door and *I'll* disable it."

I put my backpack on the floor and crouch to start pulling my tools from it. "I'm faster at it." Plus, I can guarantee that the steps to disable it haven't been running through his mind on repeat since reading the briefing on the plane last night, as it has for me.

He shakes his head. "No, *I* am."

I try to let out a slow, calming breath, which isn't exactly slow and sounds more like a huff since my active mission adrenaline just kicked in. "When we were in Egypt, you know you couldn't have opened that safe as fast as I did. And what about in Algiers?" I can tell by the look on his face that he knows I'm right. "You're really good at making friends and talking your way out of things, right? That's your specialty; go do your specialty."

"Fine," he huffs— apparently his active mission adrenaline kicked in, too— and goes into the hall just out of view of the room.

I start by waving at the security camera in the corner,

just to acknowledge to the owner of this gallery that I know she's watching. She was sent pictures of both Ledger and me, so even without the wave, she should know we're not the thieves and that we are placing the tracker, but it feels polite.

"Packston? You awake?"

"Um, yeah," I hear his scratchy voice through my headpiece. "Yeah. Of course, I am."

"Of course. Will you let the gallery owner know that we are working on placing the tracker right now so she can pull the footage?"

The clear case holding the tapestry might be five feet tall and a couple of feet wide, but it's only about three inches deep, and the locking mechanism is on the side, toward the bottom. It has an electronic component and a key component, so I first pull out my jammer to temporarily disable the electronic part before using my picks to get it unlocked. There are tiny sensors between the back of the case and the front, so I slip a thin, transparent film over them to mimic the case's closed state so I can trick the sensors into thinking it hasn't been opened.

I swing open the front of the case, then pull the tracker from the side pocket of my backpack. It's small— about the size of the tip of a pencil— and has a short, stiff wire-like thread attached to it that allows me to kind of weave it up into the tapestry just a bit.

Ledger pokes his head into the room. "Don't set off the alarm. We don't want to cause Kieran any PTS."

"And based on his shudder," I say, "I really don't want to hear his mom's wail."

I don't look at Ledger, but I hear his soft chuckle from just outside the room.

When I get the tracker mostly into place, I peel off the backing to reveal the sticky part that is strong enough to hold it in place without damaging the tapestry or leaving residue, and then I maneuver it behind a thread so it's completely hidden.

I pull up the tracking software on my phone, activate it, make sure it's receiving the signal, and smile. The signal is nice and strong. I swing the front of the case closed, slide the film off the sensors, and am just using my picks to relock the case when I hear Kieran's voice coming down the hall toward us.

"Oh, there you are, Account. You're about to miss the Abstract Algorithms room."

"I was just heading back to you. That tapestry with the llamas really caught my attention and I had to look at it longer." Ledger is doing a good job of keeping Keiran from coming close enough to see into the room.

"That's one of my favorites, too. Where is Stainless?"

I get the case locked and disable my jammer. "Packston?" I say in a low voice. "All finished. The tapestry is secure again."

"She wasn't with the group?" I hear Ledger say from just outside the room. "She did mention how much she was drawn to the painting with the woman sitting at the table, looking serious, like she doesn't even have the ability to have fun. Maybe she went back to that room. I'll go look with you."

Ledger can't see me, but I still roll my eyes as I put

everything back into my backpack. I peek around the doorway and see their retreating backs as they head back to the Impressionist room. I walk in the opposite direction — the direction the group had headed after leaving the tapestry room, and when I'm about halfway there, I turn around and head back.

My timing is perfect. Ledger and Kieran turn the corner to my hall after not finding me in the Impressionist room. "Oh, there you are, Account!" I hook my thumb behind me. "I stayed in the Cubist room a bit longer, then I couldn't find you with the group."

"I've spent quite a bit of time in that room myself. Let's get back to the others, though. You're in for a real treat as we head into the Gothic GIFs room."

Ledger raises an eyebrow in my direction as we walk, and I give him a small smile, confirming that the mission was a success. I catch his smile even though he's not directing it at me. But I can tell that it's a smile of admiration at a job well done, which is my favorite kind of smile. Then I smile to myself even bigger because I think it's safe to say that I won this mission.

A few hours later, we've grabbed our stashed luggage from the lockers, have gone through security at the main terminal, with Ledger lamenting the fact that we aren't heading back to the private terminal, and are sitting down to eat lunch before our flight to Belgrade.

I'm eating boxty with smoked salmon and a nice wedge of coolea, a Dutch-style Gouda cheese that has a bit of a caramel-like flavor, while Ledger eats a corned beef sandwich. The cheese is good and I savor every second it's in my mouth, but I'm the one lamenting not having the time to eat at one of Dublin's amazing restaurants.

"You know," Ledger says as he finishes a bite, "if we keep finishing missions as fast as we finished today's, we'll be back home by the end of the week."

"And then we can leave the memory of a joint mission behind us."

He lifts his rhubarb and ginger Irish soda and I lift my elderflower one. "Here's to finishing quickly," he says, and we bump our bottles together.

He comes in a little hot, though, and our bottles don't bump so much as they smash, causing a bit of a carbonation explosion that covers our table and what was left of our food in soda.

I'm choosing *not* to see it as a bad omen for this mission.

CHAPTER 9

JUNGLE GYM IN THE AIR, TURBULENCE ON THE GROUND

LEDGER

Sometimes, intelligence operatives get invited to nice events at nice places. And by "invited," I mean we forge invitations or get assets to hook us up. Except for my brother, Miles. He seems to get legitimate invites to the fancy events all on his own.

Most of the time, though, we stay in sketchy hotels and meet people in alleyways and abandoned buildings. Sometimes, we fly by helicopter, on government aircraft, or on diplomatic flights. But usually, we fly on commercial flights because it's the most inconspicuous way to travel. Especially when we've got impeccable false IDs and a good cover story.

And because intelligence almost always has to be acted on quickly, flights are often nearly full, and the only available seats are the middle seats in coach.

I'm a tall guy. I've got broad shoulders, too, and sometimes that causes an issue, but it's my legs that are the bigger problem— they don't exactly fit within the confines of the middle seat.

Usually, I try to fold my legs up against the seat in front of me. Then, I make friends with the person in the aisle seat, and within five minutes, they offer to swap seats with me out of pity. On this flight, though, the guy in the aisle seat, a man with a broad forehead yet narrow-set eyes, doesn't want to chat. And doesn't offer to swap seats. He mostly just seems annoyed and keeps muttering something in Serbian that I am pretty sure means, "Maybe you should've booked your flight sooner if you didn't want a middle seat."

Which, fair enough. He probably booked his early to make sure he got that aisle seat. So I just sit with my knees folded like an origami crane against the seat in front of me, praying that the person sitting there won't lean their seat back. I angle my shoulders so I won't hit the annoyed man in the aisle seat or the man in the window seat who apparently can fall asleep in four seconds flat.

Zoe is in a seat somewhere closer to the front of the plane. She's probably between two yoga instructors who take up no space, whisper motivational quotes during the flight, and offer to share the extra lavender-scented neck pillows they brought.

Ten minutes after takeoff, I'm wondering how I'm ever possibly going to make it through a five-hour flight when someone in the aisle seat one row up, on the opposite side of the aisle, gets up to head to the restroom. We make eye contact, and I give her a big smile. As soon as she sees my predicament, she offers to trade seats. I thank her profusely and swap.

What she failed to mention before swapping is that her seat is next to a toddler with an unrelenting runny nose and a mom in the window seat who is fast asleep. The toddler is either hopped up on sugar or secretly downed his mom's coffee, and for four hours and fifty minutes, I get to be his jungle gym. Which wouldn't be so bad if it weren't for the runny nose and the kid's Goldfish cracker obsession, which he never stops attempting to hook me on.

But at least my knees can be in the aisle. Where they beg to be hit by the drink cart. And sometimes the flight attendants. And every passenger heading to the restroom. One flight attendant seems personally offended that my legs are the length they are and is targeting them. I consider asking if she is single so I can hook her up with Annoyed Guy a row back. I think they'll get along well.

The longer the flight goes on, the more tiredness settles on me. It's after midnight my time, and with the rough night of sleep on the flight to Ireland, I am exhausted. I manage to fall asleep and get in a solid ninety seconds before the toddler tries to push a sticky Goldfish cracker up my nose.

We finally land, and I hobble off the plane to find that Zoe is looking bright-eyed, beautiful, and refreshed. Of course, she is.

Luckily, we have an English-speaking, Serbian-native CIA operative, Damjan Petrović, pick us up so we don't have to get a rental car. For being a covert intelligence operative, the man has no problem giving us all the information about himself that intelligence operatives normally hold tight to.

Within the first five minutes of the drive toward our hotel, we learn that he grew up in a suburb of Belgrade, went to the U.S. for college, has a photographic memory, was recruited by the CIA, and has been stationed in Belgrade ever since graduating. He's got three sisters, two of which are married to guys who are "buldala"s, which I'm pretty sure means idiots. The other sister is married to a guy who's been his best friend for years. Oh, and his favorite color is olive, like the long-sleeved polo he is wearing, and he's obsessed with retro video games.

All in five minutes. The guy is an open book. I could probably even ask him for his passwords and he'd give them to me. I wonder how he's survived as a covert operative.

He's also terrible at driving, which he doesn't need to tell us, since we've figured that one out all on our own. He'll suddenly turn onto a street when all clues point to him going straight, announcing that he's taking a shortcut. Either "shortcut" doesn't mean the same thing here, or it's his way of avoiding surveillance. I'm hoping it's the latter.

The back seat is small, so Zoe and I aren't sitting very far apart. But still, when Damjan suddenly turns right very unexpectedly, the momentum sends Zoe hurtling in my direction. With the grace of a startled cat, her arms fly out to stop herself, and her elbow finds a highly uncomfortable landing spot in my ribs. I wish she wouldn't have tried stopping herself because I could've handled her falling into me just fine. Then I remember I'm trying to divert my mind from thoughts like that.

She's opening her mouth, possibly to apologize, possibly to tell me that it's payback for comparing her to the woman in the painting at the gallery, when Damjan takes a quick left, sending me toward Zoe. I manage to put one hand on the back window and the other on the front seat, keeping me from falling into Zoe. In my head, I'm putting a win tally mark in my column for that one.

Zoe and I share a look. It's like Damjan learned how to drive inside a pinball machine.

"And here's your hotel," Damjan says as he screeches to a stop in front of a building with sand-colored stone, windows framed in dark wood, and a broad archway leading to the front doors. "I told you I'd get you here in one piece." He looks at his watch. "And before ten p.m., just like I promised. Here's the spare set of keys. I'll get the car parked in the garage so it'll be waiting for you in the morning. Keep me updated— I'm here to help with whatever you need."

We grab our bags and get out of the car. As we are walking into the building, Zoe looks at me with wide eyes and an expression that says she was left a little traumatized and a bit nauseous by that drive. I just grin. "It's all part of the adventure, right?"

"Like riding a roller coaster." Then she adds, "The day before they condemn it and tear it down."

I laugh as we head into the lobby. It's pretty big. There's a café that takes up a good portion of the space, and it looks like they serve coffee and pastries, with plenty of round tables to sit at. Even though it's late, there are still a few guests chatting over drinks. Traditional Serbian textiles and artwork— maybe even by local artists— are displayed on the walls. And all of the signage is not just in Serbian, it's also in English and German.

We walk up to the counter to check in before it occurs to me that maybe we should've asked Damjan to come translate for us. Serbian is a teeny bit like Russian, which I can speak fine, but it's not close enough for me to know actual words. The guy behind the counter has a long nose, dark hair peppered with gray, and is wearing a tailored suit and an air of confidence. He says something, and I open Google translate and fumble over the words, "Morato de se prijavimo," which I don't even get remotely right, based on the guy's expression.

I turn to Zoe. "I can speak Arabic, Farsi, French, and Russian, but not Serbian. What have you got?"

"Arabic, Farsi, Mandarin, Czech, and Hindi."

Of course, she can speak five. She always has to win.

The guy hears us speaking to each other, though, and says, "You speak English? I speak English."

I let out a relieved breath and tell him that we need to check in. I get out the words, "It should be under the name…" before it hits me that I didn't read this part of the mission briefing to know whether it's under my name or not.

Zoe cuts in and says, "Kaila Sonnenschein."

I raise an eyebrow at her and she just shrugs in a way that makes me imagine her saying, "What? I like the name Kaila. Sometimes I just want to be Kaila." At least

Sonnenschein starts with an S, just like Zoe's actual last name.

Based on how things don't seem to be where the guy checking us in thinks they should be and the way his eyes rove around as if he's trying to keep track of everything going on in the hotel, I'm guessing he's the manager and doesn't usually check guests in. Our cover story is that we are in Belgrade on business for our restaurant chain, so I start up a conversation with him, commiserating over employees calling in sick or just not even showing up. Or, worst of all, quitting over text. And how it leaves all their work to be covered by the manager.

It must be a sore spot for the man and he was in desperate need of an understanding ear because he fires right up. And then he says he's giving us a great room. We chat for a bit, and he asks what we are in town for. I tell him that Kaila and I are scouting restaurant locations.

"Oh, what is your restaurant chain called?"

"Bite Nite Burgers," I tell him. It's a cover business I've used often— it has come in very handy over the years. It's verifiable, too, complete with pocket litter. "It's a vampire-themed burger joint."

As the man activates our room key cards, he says, "Please tell me that you serve your burgers with a big toothpick in the top, like a stake in the heart."

I smile. "That we do."

"And do you have one with a garlic aioli sauce?" he asks, looking hopeful and more than a bit excited. "You know, to keep the vampires away."

"The Count Chuck-ula Burger."

He claps his hands. "And do you serve it with fang-tastic fries and ketchup?"

"We just call them fries." I turn to Zoe. "We should suggest a change, don't you think?"

She looks like she's annoyed that we are just standing here, chatting, but she nods. Then the man says to her, "What is your favorite menu item?"

"It has to be the Nosfera-Tots," Zoe says. "They're bite-sized potato tots that are delicious." Okay, I'm impressed that she came up with that on the spot. The woman is definitely quick on her feet.

"Oh! Because Nosferatu slept in dirt, and potatoes grow in the dirt! Brilliant! Maybe you can put one of your restaurants across the street. The grill there is *awful*. They always overcook their meat because they're too busy bickering over who chooses the best music. For the record: it's none of them. They're all just as bad at choosing music as they are at grilling."

I tell him that we'll check it out, and I give him my business card, which has one of my cover names, Lincoln Lombardi, on it, along with the Bite Nite Burgers logo, website, and a phone number that redirects to Kella. Then he gives us our keys and tells us where our room is.

As we step into the elevator with our luggage and the doors start to close, Zoe hisses, "That legendary friendliness of yours? You're supposed to use it to turn assets. When checking into a hotel, you want to *not* be memorable. Not get the manager of the place to weave you a friendship bracelet. Do you know nothing about being a covert operative?"

I glance over at her. She looks mad, like I just compromised our mission or something. But I shake my head. "I disagree. It's good to have friends everywhere. You never know when it'll make a difference." And sometimes, it's enough if that "difference" is simply the amusement of connecting with someone six time zones away from home over vampire-themed burgers and flaky employees after a really long, very tiring day.

The elevator doors open, and Zoe leaves first, apparently not too tired to angrily speed walk down the hall with her bag over her shoulder. "The room's this way," I say, trying to hide the smile in my voice, and she stops in her tracks. I see her shoulders rise and fall from her deep breath before she turns and heads back toward me. I open the door to our suite and she goes inside.

The place is nice. It has a large living room with a couch and a couple of padded chairs, a coffee table, end tables, two desks, a kitchenette area with a mini fridge and microwave, and a small table. There are doors on opposite sides of the room that presumably lead to each of our bedrooms.

It's a little strange to share a common area like this with Zoe. Except for the one mission a year and a half ago where we spent the bulk of the time staking out an abandoned building, our missions that crossover usually go something like this: I work hard on gathering intel, find a lead on a piece of information I need, and go on a mission to get it. Then, either I get there first and grab it before Zoe shows up and I flaunt that I got it first, or she gets there first and flaunts that she has it.

But staying in a place like this that resembles a home? It's just so *domestic*. And we don't do domestic. I don't know how to be in this space with her. How do I act? How do I feel? I have no idea. But with the arm not holding my bag, I motion to the room. "See what making friends gets you?"

Zoe drops her bag. "We don't need nice rooms; we need a successful mission."

"We'll get the successful mission." Because I'm not about to be unsuccessful on a mission, and I know Zoe isn't, either. "Tomorrow, you'll dress up as Eliza..." I can see the last name Cholmondeley in my head, but I can't remember how it's pronounced. "Chumley" comes to mind, but surely, it's not that. So I skip it and go for her code name instead "...'Mona Liza' in *nice rooms* instead of a hovel, and we'll place the tracker like the pros that we are."

I've barely finished saying the sentence when my secure phone rings. It's my mom. Even before I press to answer it, I pull my RF detector from my bag as Zoe is pulling an NLJD from hers and we both start sweeping for bugs with the equipment and with well-trained eyes. I press answer. "Hello?"

"Hi. Did your flight go well?"

"Well enough. But hold on because we just got to the room and haven't finished sweeping it yet..." I glance at my watch. It's about 4:30 p.m. for her. "Okay, the sweep is done. We're all clear."

My mom's voice had initially been chatty, but with the "all clear" news, she instantly switches into CSA Director mode, and her voice matches the role. "I've got mission news, so if Zoe is there with you and you're alone, you can put me on speaker."

I do, and Zoe steps closer so I don't have to turn the volume up any higher than needed. There's a buzz between us that's always there when we are close, and it does something to my chest. So, like I always do, I divert my thoughts to the mission, which is pretty easy to do with the director on the phone talking about it.

"We got word tonight that… Mona Liza didn't get on her flight." The way my mom paused before saying the code name for the appraiser tells me she's not entirely comfortable with the name "Mona Liza." I'm now one hundred percent convinced that Charlie must've given the appraiser that nickname early on and it stuck. "She was supposed to travel on the red-eye from England to Belgrade, and we were going to delay her in customs until you completed your mission in the morning."

I turn to face Zoe, and we both just look at each other, knowing that the plan we'd had for this mission as we walked into the room is no longer going to be the plan.

"Both Emerson's and Kenneth's teams have been searching online chatter and they've caught wind of a by-invitation-only auction in Belgrade, and we think it's at the same mansion that the Trust art piece is at. Mona Liza was previously in Austria, so we believe that instead of heading home to the UK for a few days before flying to Belgrade, she just took an overnight train straight from Austria to Belgrade to give her extra time to prepare for the auction."

"So no more impersonating Mona Liza," Zoe says.

"No. We were relying on Zoran Savović, the owner of the mansion, having not met Mona Liza in person, but we believe she arrived at his place three days ago, so you no longer will look similar enough to pull off the impersonation."

I ask, "When is the auction?"

"In five days."

Zoe nods. "That might be when the team trying to steal the art pieces will act. So we'll need to come up with a new plan to get to the art piece and plant the tracker before then."

"Yes," the director says. "There is word that the collectors who they invited can request a private viewing before the auction. But the only way to get a private viewing is to be on the guest list."

"So we need to get our names on that guest list," I say.

"Agreed. But I know you've both had a long day and likely have jet lag, so I'll let you head to bed. Keep me updated."

As soon as I end the call, Zoe says, "All right, so we should brainstorm a plan to get us on that list."

"In the morning," I say, picking up my bag and walking toward the door on the right since it's closer.

"No, *tonight*."

I turn to face her. "You slept on the plane, didn't you?"

She stretches like she just woke up. "Yes, and it was glorious. *So* restful. Now let's plan."

I actually can't tell if she's being serious or not. She would've claimed the win for a restful flight even if she hadn't slept a wink. "You can never stop working, can you?"

"*Hello*. We are on a mission. It's kind of how these things work. We have to always be on top of our game."

"Which we will be only if we get sleep," I tell her. It's been a long day in a different time zone. "We'll come up with a better plan in the morning when we've got fresh minds than we ever could tonight. How about we get together right after my run?" I know that adding in a run is going to frustrate her, but I can't help it. It's just too easy. Plus, I really like starting the day with a run.

"You are infuriating! I *care* about the success of this mission."

"Oh, I know you do." If nothing else, I admire her passion. The way she can get so fired up about things is actually very impressive. And, okay, she's really good at being an operative. She's also unbelievably attractive. I could write an entire sonnet just about her looks. Me. The guy who came this close to taking a C in English Lit my sophomore year, nearly destroying my perfect GPA, because I refused to write one.

Even standing there in her soft pants and matching tee, underhandedly accusing me of not caring about this mission, I have to admire her ability to achieve her objectives, even if I don't admire the lengths she will go to do it. But I will never let her know how much I admire her ever again.

Nope. Now, if I'm forced to work with her, I just have to find joy in needling her.

"What is that supposed to mean?" she asks.

"That you'll succeed at *any* cost."

"And that's a bad thing?"

Bag still in hand, I cross my arms. "It depends on the cost." She succeeded at the cost of me once. She probably doesn't even have a line she won't cross. No cost is too high for her.

"Meanwhile, you only care about succeeding if it seems fun. Or if it doesn't interrupt your ability to have fun. Do you even care about completing this mission?"

My eyes narrow at Zoe. I care about winning *a lot*. Just like I didn't take that C in English Lit back then, I don't settle for mediocre now. I want a win in my column *every single time*. But I do have a line I won't cross. And I could argue my points all night. But, instead of saying something I might regret in the morning, I just say, "Goodnight, Zoe."

Then I turn and walk into my room.

CHAPTER 10
TALES FROM THE SPY SIDE
ZOE

"Have you ever disarmed a bomb in a moving vehicle?" I ask Ledger.

He nods. "On the Autobahn in a sports car. The bomb's timer was linked to the speedometer, so I had to keep it above one hundred kilometers per hour while figuring out how to disarm it. You?"

I nod, too. "On the Tokyo Bullet Train, weaving through passengers while deciphering a foreign language manual."

"That was you?" Ledger asks with enough awe in his voice that it makes me smile.

Maybe I was in need of sleep last night, too, because I definitely woke up this morning in a better mood than I went to bed. I was still annoyed that Ledger went for a run first thing when we had a mission to plan, though. But I did take the opportunity to pound out a couple of miles on the hotel's treadmill while he was gone and still got showered and ready to go before he returned.

From the research we got from both of our agencies and our own brainstorming, we decide that getting ourselves onto the guest list is going to be nearly impossible.

So instead, we decide that we need to find an employee of Savović's who we can turn into an asset. And then we need to get that asset to do one of two things: either shut off the security system long enough for us to place a tracker on the sculpture, or get us a copy of who's on that guest list already so we can schedule a private showing in their name before they arrive in Belgrade. Either way, we need to turn an employee.

The place is a fortress, though, so we are currently sitting in the car that Damjan got for us, staking out the back entrance where the day shift employees are likely to exit from, trying to pass the time.

From the backseat, Damjan says, "I've got one I bet neither of you have done. Have you ever posed as a circus performer to surveil a target?"

Ledger grins. "I juggled fire in Rio's Carnival while keeping tabs on a diplomat."

Okay, that's pretty good. I'm smiling, too, but inside, I'm smiling way bigger. "I went undercover in Cirque du Soleil in Vegas."

"You've got to be lying," Damjan says. "There's no way."

I shake my head. "Very much *not* lying. I had to plant listening devices, and because of an incident at a craps table between a Spiderman from a superhero convention and a Klingon from a Star Trek convention that turned into an all-out brawl, I couldn't get there before the show started. So I dressed in costume, then tightrope-walked and swung across the stage and audience while planting the bugs. Not a soul suspected the high-flying operative among them."

"Is there anything you two haven't done?" Damjan asks. "Oh! I've got it. How about swimming through shark-infested waters to complete a mission?"

"Off the coast of Cuba," Ledger says.

"I'm calling bull," Damjan says. And I have to admit, I'm pretty impressed, too. "Aren't there tons of sharks in those waters?"

"Nearly twenty percent of the world's shark species," I say. "How did you stay safe?"

"Who says I stayed safe?" Ledger chuckles. "But I did have homemade shark repellent and a flare gun for company."

In the rearview mirror, I can see Damjan's eyes narrow. "Homemade repellent?"

"From Julia Childs herself, before she became a culinary icon."

"You're making this up," Damjan says.

But I'm intrigued. "Copper acetate mixed with black dye, right?" I ask.

Ledger looks surprised and maybe a bit impressed that I know. He nods.

"Did it work?"

He shrugs. "Maybe. And you?"

"I swam the English Channel, *in winter*, mostly

avoiding not just the sharks but hypothermia, and still managed to deliver the documents I had acquired."

This time, it's not Damjan who's looking skeptical— it's Ledger. "There aren't sharks in the English Channel."

"There are." I pull up my skirt enough to show the shark teeth scar on my thigh. "It was a tope shark that did this. It wasn't any longer than me, but it still had a nasty bite."

"Ouch!" Damjan says.

Ledger lifts his shirt and shows me a similar scar on his torso, and I just can't stop staring at the silverish-white scars on his very muscular abdomen. "It was a smaller shark, too— a seven-foot blacktip— that got me."

"So the repellent didn't work?" I finally ask, with my eyes still on the scar. And his abs.

He lifts a shoulder in a shrug. "Maybe it was what saved me from a much bigger Hammerhead or Great White."

He lowers his shirt, and it's the only thing that gets my eyes to go from his abs back to his face. For a long moment, I just look at him. Staring at his gray-blue eyes while he stares back at me. I don't know what he's thinking, but I'm suddenly having thoughts I shouldn't allow myself to have and wondering if maybe we have more in common than I thought.

Ledger is looking like he's having some of those same thoughts. I'm catching things in his look that I don't get from others. Things that go beyond checking me out and liking what they see.

But why? Why would Ledger be looking at me like he

is attracted to more of me than what's on the surface? I've seen that look between couples before, but I've never had it directed at me. Ledger is a very skilled operative, but I'm still impressed at how good he is at manipulating his body language. He's master-level good. I just can't guess his motive behind showing me that he's interested in me.

And fake or not, the fireworks show currently going on in my chest and my gut feels real.

After a moment— I'm not even sure how long— Damjan says, "Whoo is it getting hot in here! Say, have you two ever..." And then he points back and forth between us, raising a meaningful eyebrow.

Oh, we are *so* not taking the conversation in that direction. And I can't even *think* in that direction again. I mean, what was I doing letting my mind go there? It isn't like a person can judge whether or not they have a lot in common with someone based on whether or not they have matching shark bite scars.

Besides, what does having something in common have to do with anything? Two parallel rivers can still clash when they merge. Two alpha wolves in the same pack would definitely clash. And that's what we are. Two alpha wolves.

I look toward the mansion and say in a very obvious subject change— for both the conversation going on in the car and the one going on in my head— "Hey, Ledger, did you catch a vibe between our directors at our briefing?"

Ledger looks at me warily. "I mean, they know each other. They worked together back when my mom was an agent in the CIA. They're colleagues and counterparts."

I shake my head. "I think there was something more between them."

"Hey," Ledger says, his voice rising, "that's my mom you're talking about. You know, *the woman who was married to my dad until he died?*"

I had poked Ledger to get him fired up and get my mind off thoughts of his abs. I hadn't guessed it would further endear him to me to see him get all fired up in defense of his mom. My plan has maybe failed a bit. But still, I push, because surely he's thought of this. "What? Just because your parents were married until one passed away, your mom can't ever date again? She might want someone by her side as she eventually becomes a grandma and grows old."

And maybe seeing something happen between our directors is just hopefulness on my part. I would love it if Sully and Evelyn Lancaster fell in love and got married. Especially if it meant that she would stop by his work every now and then and come to our holiday party. Then I could ask her all the questions I want. Maybe she would even take me under her wing and tell me all her secrets.

Ledger doesn't say a word for a moment, and I don't know if it's because he doesn't want to respond, or if he just really hasn't imagined his mom ever dating again. Finally, he says, "No. She can date people. But it's not like the Director of the Clandestine Services Agency and the Director of Field Operations for the Global Intelligence Division of the CIA can just submit the proper paperwork about their intention to date."

"Yeah, I can't really see that getting approved," I say

and try to not make my sigh audible as I squint toward the back gate where I see movement. "I think the employees are leaving."

All three of us sit up straighter. The gate opens, and five women walk out together, laughing and bumping into one another like they know each other well and are probably friends. It's just after five p.m., so the sun isn't even close to setting yet, making it easy to see them. They all look fairly young, maybe lower- to mid-twenties. Two are wearing light blue uniforms with aprons and sensible shoes— maids if I have to guess. One is wearing dark slacks and a pink blouse with a satchel over her shoulder. One is in a black cotton shirt and black pants, and another is in a colorful dress.

We'd decided against placing a listening device and we are too far away to hear, so I narrate what is going on based on the women's body language so Ledger and Damjan can keep their heads down and not appear as suspicious. We are just parked on the side of the road a bit away from the gate and near the place where the few employees who own cars park them.

"Okay, Woman in Black is pulling out car keys. The other four are heading for the street, so I'm guessing it's public transportation for them. Okay, the car owner is holding her keys up, shaking them while she's saying something. I'm pretty sure she's asking the others if they want to join her maybe to go get dinner or go to a bar?

"Oh! Both maids and Colorful Dress are all very much in. That took zero persuasion. The professional one in the pink shirt is telling them no as she keeps walking away, but her feet and torso are saying she wants to go with them. She must have other responsibilities pulling at her.

"And," I say, dragging out the word as I watch, "the others sense her desire to join them, and they are gathering around her and— oh! Looks like they were persuasive enough. Pink Shirt is joining them."

Ledger starts the car and drives about a block down the street before making a U-turn so that he's headed in the same direction as the woman's car when they pull out of the parking lot just in front of him.

They're headed toward the waterfront where preparations for the Belgrade Waterfront Summer Fest are in full swing. Banners and flags line the streets, and off to our left, we can see parts of the waterfront area where workers are stringing lights and putting up illuminating art installations, stages, interactive displays, tents, and pavilions. A few street vendors seem to already be selling merchandise, too.

The woman's car pulls into a parking spot by a pub, and we park along the street nearby, then we all put in our earpieces. Instead of connecting to our tech ops, though, Damjan is our tech op for this mission. Ledger hands him the car keys, and Damjan says he's going to get us items that we need.

Once we are inside the pub, we are seated at a round table with four chairs. We take the two seats facing the pool table, where the five women are all standing, chatting, and playing. The place is loud, though.

The walls of the pub are decorated with signs, and Ledger gets up and meanders near the women under the guise of seeing one of the signs more closely. When he sits back down, he says, "They're all speaking Serbian. I heard Savović's name, so I'm sure they're talking about work. Maybe we can ask for a closer table, and then Damjan can translate for us."

I shake my head. "We can figure out who might be willing and able to get us that list without knowing what they're saying. Sometimes words can get in the way of reading actions. Always trust the body language over the words."

Ledger's body language right now says that he doesn't believe that even a little bit. "Just watch them," I say. Then I snap a picture of the menu and send it to Damjan, asking if anything on the menu has cheese. With missions like these, you never know when you're going to suddenly be leaving, so it's best to get cheese as soon as possible. Besides, if we're not eating or drinking, we're going to look suspicious, so really, the cheese is for authenticity.

Ten minutes later, I am savoring a cheese platter with fruits, nuts, and breads, along with Pirot cheese, which is hard and sharp, and Trappista cheese, which is smooth and mild and absolutely delicious. Ledger is trying out Ćevapi, which are small, grilled minced meat sausages that he, of course, loves. It continually amazes me how much food this guy can eat.

"So what's the deal with you and cheese?" he asks, our eyes as inconspicuously on the women as possible. "Is that the only thing you eat?"

"Nah, but I do get it wherever I go. It's a food that nearly every country has, so trying it everywhere showcases how different each country's is." I spear a cube of Trappista with a toothpick and hold it up, studying it. "Cheese is like a story passed down through generations in an area. It gives me a connection to the people and helps me understand where I am, beyond the sights and sounds. Like I'm using another sense— taste— to connect in a way that's universal."

I believe what I said fully, but I'm laying it on thicker than I normally would, allowing Ledger to make fun of it so I can push back. Instead of pushing back, though, he looks thoughtful and then nods. "I feel the same way about joining in a sport with locals in a park or street or court. It connects me with the people and place."

I realize that my mouth has dropped open in surprise at his understanding, so I stick a piece of cheese in it so Ledger won't notice.

When I finish chewing and swallowing, I say, "Come in for a selfie."

Ledger scoots his chair closer to me and puts his arm around the back of my chair. For some stupid reason, it makes my heart rate kick up and some kind of fluttering thing happens in my gut. I even get goosebumps spreading along the back of my neck at his touch.

Stop it, I tell myself. Just because he understood about the cheese is a ridiculous excuse for letting my body react.

We lean our faces closer and smile at my phone, but I haven't turned the camera toward us— I aim it at the women playing pool and eating appetizers, getting a picture of each of them when they're facing the camera. Part of me itches, though, to flip the camera toward us and take a picture. Not that I want one. Just because I'm curious as to how the two of us look side by side.

I don't, though. Aragundi is poised to pass along his empire to the men trying to steal the art piece from Savović — assuming their thieving is successful— so he can ensure that chaos and devastation can be spread across the world by an all-new generation. And I can't let that happen.

So instead, I send each of the pictures to Packston and ask him to run a search on them. We can't try to turn anyone into an asset without knowing if they have any reason to be in our database first. Then I say to Ledger, "So, which woman do you think we should try to turn into an asset?"

He looks back at the five of them. "Pink Shirt— she's dressed like she might be in a position to have access to a lot of things, but doesn't hold herself like she has power. A personal assistant, maybe? She might be a little too timid to do something like sneak us information, though. Or maybe the maid with the top half of her hair in a bun— maids have access to a lot. But I'd probably choose the woman in the pink shirt."

"I agree about Pink Shirt. Not about Bun Maid."

"Why not the maid? They both seem disgruntled and therefore easy to turn."

"Tell me," I say, "why did you say you'd choose Pink Shirt over Bun Maid?"

"I don't know. My gut just said she is the one."

I nod. "Bun Maid's body language doesn't match her face when she's complaining, and the face is the easiest part of the body to consciously manipulate when it comes to showing emotion. When Pink Shirt complains about work, her shoulders sag. Like she is re-living it just by telling it, and it exhausts her. She also does a lot of behaviors that are meant to comfort her— touching the base of her neck, playing with her hair, holding her upper arm with her other hand, like she's giving herself a hug.

"When Bun Maid complains about work, she still has happy feet. Her arms still move a lot, instead of being more rigid at her sides. The more the others buy the story she is telling, she becomes proud of herself for pulling it off so well. So a smile leaks through at a time when it shouldn't, or she'll put her hands on the side of the pool table, spread wide, in a show of confidence. Did you see how she put her tongue between her front teeth a couple of times, the tip of it sticking out a bit? That means she feels like she pulled one over on them."

"So, she doesn't hate her job?"

I shake my head. "She likes their sympathy. I suspect that the reason she's working so hard at convincing them is not for the sympathy, though— it's because she's hiding a secret."

Ledger's attention whips back to Bun Maid. "She's sleeping with someone."

I nod. "My guess is her boss. Maybe Savović himself."

His eyes go wide, like it's hitting him how bad it would be if we approached her to try to make her an asset. Her loyalty is likely with Savović, so it would've backfired and possibly compromised the whole mission.

I decide to throw the guy a bone. "Your gut instincts have always been good, Ledger. Just like how they told you that Pink Shirt is the right choice. Listen to what your instincts say— they'll tell you what your brain missed."

"Did you just give me a compliment?"

"Well, I did also say that your brain missed it."

"How'd you get so good at body language?"

"That's need-to-know."

Ledger rolls his eyes just as a text comes in.

Packston: All five are clear.

Hearing from Packston makes me realize that we haven't heard much from Damjan. For as chatty as the guy is in person, I figured he'd be non-stop talking in our ears the whole time. But since he told us what to order, we haven't heard a peep. Pink Shirt is clearly saying goodbye to everyone, and while she's saying something, she hikes a thumb toward the restroom before hugging another of her friends.

"I'm going to go talk to her in the restroom," I tell Ledger as I put my napkin on the table.

"How? She speaks Serbian."

"Most young people here also speak English, so I'm crossing my fingers that she does."

I make it to the restroom before Pink Shirt does. It's always good to make it seem like they're following you, not the other way around. As soon as I hear the door open-ing, I say, "Ugg! Not right now!" I'm standing at a sink, leaning my hip against it, looking down at my phone, my other hand on my forehead.

Pink Shirt hesitates a moment, then asks, "Are you

okay?" Her accent is very thick, but she speaks English well.

"Yeah," I say. "My boss is just the worst. He thinks he can ask me to do anything anytime, and doesn't even care that I'm on a date."

"You, too, ay?"

Score one for me on reading her body language well as she was complaining to her friends. "Let me guess— you are a personal assistant, too?"

Pink Shirt nods. I hold out my hand. "Hi, I'm Shauna."

The woman shakes my hand. "Milena. But people call me Mila." She looks younger up close. If I had to guess her age, I'd guess twenty-one or twenty-two.

"Does your boss make you do seventy-five percent of the work, too?"

"Da," my new friend, Mila says. "I come up with the best ideas, but she takes credit. She knows this job is important to me, so she threatens it to make me do all the work."

"It sounds like your boss is in finance like mine is."

"My boss, Petra, is over…" Mila pauses for a moment like she's trying to recall the right word, "events for a man who deals with art. And probably more things, but art is what he wants people to know about him."

"Ugh," I say. "I've been to plenty of art events with my bosses— art people are every bit as snooty as finance people."

"They're the worst! We are planning an event for even more snooty art people, so I will be surrounded by them."

I sympathize with Mila and we chat a bit more, all

while I'm silently cheering that we found the perfect asset. Then I say "Sorry, I just need to get an Uber on its way so I can go help my boss," loving that Uber is virtually everywhere.

I look like I'm going into an app, but really, I'm counting on Damjan to do the Uber scheduling for me. In my earpiece, he says, "I'm on it!"

"Oh!" Mila says. "I forgot I'm in a hurry!" She looks down at her watch, and then pulls out her phone and starts tapping on it as she says, "I live with my sister. She works at our house, but she doesn't start until I'm there to watch my niece and nephew. I'm supposed to be there already, and…" Her shoulders drop. "I just missed a bus, so now I have to wait another twenty minutes for the next one. My sister will be so mad."

"What direction are you headed?" I ask.

"We live in Zemun, not too far from Gardoš Tower."

"Oh, I am headed to that same area— maybe half a kilometer past the tower! My Uber will be here soon—"

"Six minutes," Damjan says in my earpiece.

"—so you should just ride with me. I can drop you off on my way. It'll be faster than the bus, and you won't have to wait the extra twenty minutes, either."

The woman looks so grateful that I could probably ask her for anything and she'd say yes. But I know enough about turning an asset who works for the opposition into one who secretly works for us to know that within a few minutes of meeting them isn't the time to make big asks unless you have no other choice. So we both head out of the restroom, and I go over to say goodbye to my "date."

CHAPTER 11
SOCCER, SECRETS, AND STROLLERS
LEDGER

've experienced a lot of things as an intelligence operative. I have to say that this is the first time I've listened to a conversation via my earpiece of two women in a public restroom, where one is an intelligence operative and the other is a potential asset. It isn't my first time, though, hearing Zoe become exactly who she needs to be for the situation. She does it masterfully, which both impresses me— when I see it in action, and frustrates me— when I experience it used on me.

The two women walk out of the bathroom, and through my earpiece, I hear Zoe say to Mila, "Let me just say goodbye to my date." Then Zoe walks up to where I'm still sitting at our table and leans in as if she's kissing the space right in front of my ear. Her breath is warm, and it tingles as if that's actually what she's doing. The tingle goes right up my spine and neck, too, and makes my breathing kick up a notch, even though it has no business doing either.

Instead of kissing me, though, she breathes in a low voice, "Follow us at a respectable distance. After I drop her off, we'll regroup." Then she pulls back, gives me a smile, and reaches for my hand, which she then squeezes. I manage to come out of my stupor in time to remember our cover story and say, "It's okay. We'll catch up later. Good luck with work stuff."

The bar's windows are a little grimy and partially covered with signs and blocked by furniture, but I can see the women standing out front, waiting for their Uber. I say, "Damjan, you're back, right?"

"Yep." I hear what I'm guessing is the trunk closing. "Ready to go."

"Get in the passenger's seat and let me know when their Uber arrives." I don't want Damjan driving for two reasons— one, Damjan's driving isn't exactly discreet. And two—I just ate a bunch of sausages, onions, and bread, and I'm not entirely sure that my stomach can handle his driving.

They drive on the right side of the road here, and except for some streets at odd angles, their roads aren't too different from roads in the United States. Their stoplights are even similar to ours. The buildings are a mix of single-story and multiple-story structures and range everywhere from run-down and graffitied to newer and well-cared-for.

I follow Zoe's Uber across the river and along streets that are lined with trees and grass and nice buildings. The closer we get to Mila's home, though, the narrower and more cracked the streets get and the smaller and closer together the homes are.

I keep further back as Zoe's and Mila's Uber driver drops Mila off at her small house on a street barely wide enough for one car, in a neighborhood filled with run-down houses and pavement. Not a yard— or even a patch of dirt— is anywhere.

As soon as Zoe's Uber is out of sight of Mila's home, Zoe has the driver let her out on a slightly wider road. When the driver leaves, I pull off the road, park near Zoe, and get out of the car. It's still plenty light outside and warm without being too hot. About seventy-five degrees, if I have to guess.

As soon as both Damjan and I are out of the car, Zoe says, "I think we can turn her." She sends a message to Packston, her tech op, and loops him in, and a moment later, I have Kella looped in, too, so the five of us are together on comms. "Packston, what have you got on Mila?"

"A few things that I've also forwarded to Kella. Her full name is Milena Nikolić. She is twenty-one years old and currently lives with her sister, Maja Nikolić, and her sister's two kids— a five-year-old boy named Andrej and an almost two-year-old girl named Anja. She attended the University of Belgrade for a year and a half, studying busi-ness administration, and living on campus. She was doing quite well, too. I'm looking at her transcripts, and she got nines and tens in everything. Well, except for Public Speaking, where she got a six, so barely passing.

"Then her brother-in-law, Bodgan, died about a year

and a half ago in a work-related accident at a chemical manufacturing plant. Mila's sister, Maja, couldn't work and take care of the kids, so Mila left school and moved in with her sister to help out. Mila got a job working for Zoran Savović as an administrative assistant to Savović's event planner, Petra, and works during the day, then watches her niece and nephew after so her sister can work."

"And from what I got in speaking with her," Zoe says, "she does a lot of the grunt work at Savović's. She's a smart girl, but she never gets the chance to really shine."

"All right," I say. "So what should we use to motivate her? We've got the standard money, ideology, coercion, or ego." I gesture back toward her street. "Clearly, they could use money."

Zoe nods slowly. "She didn't once complain about her pay or their living conditions, though. That doesn't mean it isn't an issue, of course, but it wasn't on her mind enough to bring it up during the short time we've had to chat. She mostly talked about how bad it is working for her boss, Petra."

"Petra Popović," Kella says. "It says that she's over events and special occasions at Savović's mansion. Mila is the only employee under Petra. There's a picture of Petra. Yeesh. If she were a librarian, she'd probably shush you for breathing too loudly. And then make you write an essay on the importance of following the posted rules, right before claiming it as her own work."

"So," Packston says in our earpieces, "maybe you can

convince her to help you by saying if she does, it'll stick it to her job. Help her to get revenge."

"Except her helping us wouldn't actually stick it to her job," I say. "In fact, it'll help them, since they'll be more likely to get the piece back after Aragundi's wanna-be's steal it with our tracker in it."

"She doesn't seem like the vengeful type anyway," Zoe says. "Besides, she doesn't have an issue with Savović—only with Petra." Zoe starts tapping her bottom lip with her finger and I'm having a hard time not getting distracted by it. Maybe it wouldn't be so distracting if I hadn't kissed those lips a year and a half ago and know exactly how they feel on mine. To know how it feels to hold her close while those lips are on mine.

Head. In. The. Game, I tell myself.

In our earpieces, Kella says, "And it sounds like anything that made things worse for Petra would just be pushed onto Mila anyway, so that direction in general is a bust."

"What about finding a way for her to leave that job?" I turn to Damjan. "What's the job market here like? Is offering that a possibility? If she hasn't gotten a chance to shine, a new position might give her that chance."

Damjan nods. "Yeah, I think it's a real possibility. I have some contacts I could check in with."

Zoe is nodding, too, and everyone else is silent for a moment. Sometimes when we discuss what kind of motivation will convince an asset to spy for us, we come up with an idea that seems perfect. It doesn't feel like we've hit "perfect" for Mila, but with the time we have to turn her, we don't have access to the kind of information that will get us to perfect.

"I say go for that," Kella says. "As a backup plan, Packston and I will get with our directors to see what kind of a compensation package they'll approve if you end up needing to offer money. What's the timeline?"

Zoe hikes a thumb to the northeast. "She is going with her nephew and niece to a soccer— or 'fudbal'— field about two blocks away for her nephew's practice at seven. It'd be good to approach her there."

We all look down at our watches. That's in fifteen minutes.

"We'll go work on that now," Packston says. "We'll check back in with you before seven."

Damjan claps his hands together. "Okay, let's talk about the approach itself." He aims his clapped hands in my direction. "Because you, my giant friend, are intimidating, and you're going to scare her."

My head pulls back in surprise. "What? I am not."

"Hey, listen. *I* know you're just a big fun-loving guy. First impressions, though?" He winces.

"I saw the way Mila flinched when I said goodbye to my 'date,'" Zoe says. "He's right. We need to make you softer."

"Softer?"

"Don't worry, I've got you," Damjan says as he goes around to the back of the car and opens the trunk. The guy spent a good amount of time in the United States, but his accent is still plenty Serbian. He pronounces all his vowels clearly, rolls his R's, stresses the first syllable of his words, and rises in pitch at the end of sentences, but his English is perfect, including slang. "Just think of you as James Bond and me as your own personal Q."

Zoe lights up. "Ooo. Do you have gadgets for us?"

"Something like that. When you guys were in the bar, I left. I found a little girl with one of those baby dolls that looks and feels like a realistic baby." He lifts the doll from the trunk and holds it up by one arm. "Check it out—doesn't it look like the real thing?"

"And you just took this from a little girl?" Zoe asks.

"What kind of a monster do you think I am? No! The girl was holding the doll by its ankle while gazing long-ingly at a group of kids riding bikes, looking for all the world that she drew the short stick. So I bought a bike and traded her. Made her entire year."

"And a baby doll is going to help us... how?" I know the look I'm giving Damjan right now isn't a generous one, but I can't help it.

Damjan pushes the doll into my chest, and when I grab hold, he reaches into the trunk and pulls out a very pink stroller. As he's opening it, he says, "Because you are going to be a dad when you go talk to her."

"And that'll make me 'softer?'"

"You bet it will. Mark my words— with that woman, Mila, in particular, if you show up like you are, you won't even get through your pitch to turn her before you've scared her off. *If* she'll even talk to you at all. If you have a baby with you, she'll relax enough to hear you out. You might even be able to convince her to help you."

"Fine," I say. Luckily, the doll came with a couple of baby blankets— also pink— which is good, because just tossing the doll in the stroller isn't going to convince anyone. I spread one of the blankets out in the trunk, place the doll so its head is by one of the corners, and then wrap the blanket so it's swaddling the doll, just like I did with Blake's daughter Heidi when she was a baby. Then I put the baby in the stroller and arrange the second blanket around her.

When I stand back up again, Damjan is appraising me with his arms folded and nods. "Yep, that'll work just fine."

Zoe and I walk to the soccer field with me pushing the pink stroller like we are a cute little family out for an evening walk.

Yeah, like that could ever happen. A year and a half ago, I'd thought maybe it could. I had tracked a rogue scientist to an abandoned research station in the dense forests near Moldova's eastern border. Zoe and I crossed paths and discovered that there had been some sort of inter-agency miscommunication, and the CIA had sent her to do what was essentially the same mission as mine. At the time, I'd only heard of Zoe— we hadn't met. I'd known her name and who she worked for, but not much else.

We'd teamed up to complete the mission, and for three days, we'd worked together to stay warm, shared stories of our pasts, flirted, became a little vulnerable, took turns standing watch, shared some life-altering kisses, and built what I thought was trust. She was the most incredible woman I'd ever met, and like a fool, I'd fallen for her completely.

So completely that I'd already started imagining a life with her. Not a traditional life, of course, but one that would work for who we are. One where we would be open with each other like that all the time. Discuss crazy things going on in the world that few people knew about over breakfast. Compare daring feats we'd done while snuggling under the covers at night. Go sky diving, snowboarding, or river rafting together on the weekends. Maybe even go on a few missions together.

I'd *thought* she felt the same. I hadn't even suspected it was all an act until it was too late. And by then, she'd not only taken my trust but she'd also taken my heart. I'm not about to give her either again.

Just as we reach the fence, Kella says in my earpiece, "I just sent you the approved amount you can offer Mila."

I pull out my phone and take a look. If we can't get her to help us by offering to get her a new job, the money should do it. We spot Mila through the chain-link fence. She's standing on the sidelines, a toddler on her hip, cheering for the five-year-olds playing soccer on the field.

She doesn't see us as we get the stroller through the gate and head up the sideline toward her. We've seen a few other soccer fields in the city that were much nicer than this one. This is mostly a fenced-in yard with dirt and weeds on the sidelines, a grassy field with lines painted on it, and an old building that looks like it houses restrooms on one side.

It isn't until Zoe puts a hand on Mila's shoulder that she turns her attention away from her nephew on the field or her niece who's now sitting at her feet, playing with a dandelion. She turns and sees Zoe, and confusion washes over her. "Shauna?" She glances from Zoe to me to the pink stroller. "What are you doing here?"

"Can we talk to you for a moment?"

Mila looks toward her nephew, then her niece. "Um, sure." She picks up her niece and places her on her hip again as the little girl tries to pull each seed individually from the white dandelion. We walk a dozen feet away so we aren't by any other people as we talk. But even if we were, we aren't speaking Serbian, so probably most wouldn't know what we are saying.

Mila's not just confused now— she's also a bit alarmed. I realize that having the stroller near us isn't enough, so I turn to the baby like it's fussing and coo at it, reaching in to give its little hand a gentle squeeze.

"I don't actually work at a financial firm," Zoe says. "I work for the Central Intelligence Agency in the United States, and this is my coworker, Lincoln. We could really use your help."

I'm glad she just went with "coworker" for my description instead of bringing up the CSA or fumbling over what to call me.

Mila is full-on alarmed now, and she keeps eyeing us like we're about to tell her that she's arrested and needs to come with us or something. So I reach into the stroller, lift out the swaddled baby doll, and put her against my shoulder, making sure the blanket covers the back of her head. Then I start patting her on the back. Mila instantly releases her tense shoulders and relaxes her stressed expression. Wow. It actually worked. Score one for Damjan.

She is watching me curiously, though. As if she hadn't pictured me as a dad when she saw me in the pub and is now wondering if I stopped at the daycare to pick up my child after I left.

Zoe and I go back and forth, almost like we've practiced this, explaining that one of Savović's art pieces is going to get stolen by bad people who are going to use it for bad purposes, leaving out the specifics. We tell her that we need to place a tracking device on the art piece so that we can find it— and the thieves—once they steal it. We say we've heard that the only way to even get close enough to the sculpture to place that tracker is if she can turn off the security system at a time when we can sneak in, or by Zoe and I scheduling a private viewing to see the piece.

And the only way to get a private viewing is if we impersonate someone who is already on the guest list for the auction. Preferably *before* the auction takes place, since we think that the men plan to steal it then. And we tell it to her all while the little girl she's holding is trying to put dandelion seeds up her nose. What is it with toddlers and noses?

At one point when Mila isn't even looking at me, I realize I'm bouncing the baby, but only when I catch a look on Zoe's face that I can't quite decipher. An expression I've never seen on her before. I stop bouncing and place the baby back in the stroller, arranging the blankets so her face can't be seen.

"I can't turn off the security system," Mila says in her thick accent, setting her squirming niece back on the grass. "I'm not even sure the head of security can. Mr. Savović is very distrustful."

Zoe and I give each other a look. So much for doing things the easy way. Then I ask Mila, "Do you have access to the list of people who will be coming for the auction? Can you get it for us?"

"You want me to steal the list from my work for you? I could get fired for that!"

"Just a *copy* of the list," Zoe says. "We know that it is risky and that you could get caught. But these are very bad men who want to steal that art piece, and by helping us, you could also help to save a lot of innocent lives. We also know that you don't love your job, so as a thank you, we will get you a new job."

"You're going to make me leave my job?"

Zoe and I both shake our heads, and Zoe says, "No. Just help you get one where your contributions will be recognized and you'll really be able to shine. And, as a bonus, you won't even have to deal with art people."

"Listen," she says, putting both hands up like she's trying to stop this conversation and stop anything from moving forward that we've suggested. "I know I complained about my job, and my boss is not nice, but I like the work. And I made friends. I hope someday it will help me get a position I really want."

Okay, so we were far from coming up with the perfect

motivation for Mila. Zoe gives me a look that says, *Well, do you want to offer the money, then?* And I'm about to open my mouth to do it when another idea hits me. One I can't believe we didn't come up with when we were all brainstorming ideas.

"Mila, would going back to school help you to get that position you really want?"

"Da," she says, but she shakes her head. "But that's no longer possible."

"What if it was?"

Her eyes are on me, and I've got every bit of her attention.

"You did *really* well in school, so I'm guessing you liked it. I'm also guessing the reason you stopped going was because you needed a full-time job to help your sister after your brother-in-law died?"

Her eyes are wide like she's surprised we know all this about her, but she doesn't say a word— she just nods.

"What if we could get you back in school, and for the two years you'll be in school until you graduate, we pay you the same amount per month that you'd be earning at your job?"

Tears literally start falling down her cheeks as she looks between me and Zoe. "You would do that? You will help me go back to school?" Her eyes finish on Zoe. She already heard it from me— she's looking for confirmation.

"We will," Zoe says. "That's how much we need your help."

Then she hugs us both. All right. That's not something I usually get when asking someone to put themselves at risk. I might have to start taking a baby to all my asset negotiations.

We give her a secure phone, tell her she can call if she has any problems, and she says she'll get a copy of the list for us at work tomorrow. She's leaving work a bit earlier to go to her nephew's fudbal tournament that is part of the city's Summer Fest, so she'll be back on this field at three. We tell her that we can't meet her again in the same location without raising suspicions, so we'll need her to do a dead drop that we pick up later.

Zoe points to a small, run-down structure made of cinderblock and adorned with graffiti at the edge of the field. "Are those restrooms?"

Mila nods.

"Just go in sometime during your nephew's game and leave it in the garbage can."

"But make sure it's well hidden," I tell her. "We won't be able to come immediately inside after you leave it, and we don't want someone else to spot it first."

"Okay."

"And don't worry," Zoe says. "You won't be able to spot us, but we'll be watching, so we'll see when you do the drop."

Mila nods at Zoe, then reaches down to pick up her niece who has found a new dandelion that has gone to seed. Mila's eyes flick between the two of us, and as if she's giving a fierce rallying cry at a volume that no one outside of the four of us (five, if you count my fake baby) can hear, she says, "I won't let you down." I am sure she won't.

I am also sure that her niece is about to fully get a dandelion seed into Mila's nose without Mila even seeing it coming. As Zoe and I walk away, me pushing the stroller, I hear Mila sneeze, then say, "Anja!"

Yep. The niece succeeded.

CHAPTER 12

FROM SUITE TO CELLAR

ZOE

Ledger and I have been hanging out in the common area of our suite all morning with our earpieces in, getting updates from Packston and Charlie, who is Ledger's handler today. Apparently, his normal handler, Kella, is away at some kind of appointment. We've heard updates on other efforts to find the men stealing the art pieces, as well as more details about the art auction at the mansion that is now only three days away.

My missions are virtually always solo missions, and always with Packston in my ear. If there's ever anyone else, it's Sully, just popping in on Packston's comms to tell me something. Having Ledger's handler in my ear, too, has been quite the adjustment.

We sign off at the end of the meeting and, just like it has all morning— and, okay, all during the night, too— my mind goes back to Ledger at the fudbal field yesterday. I just can't seem to stop thinking about him holding that baby doll. He was just so sweet with it. He swaddled it and placed it in the stroller so carefully. He crouched down next to the stroller so he was closer to its height to coo at it. He cradled it as he put it up to his shoulder and patted its back.

And when he started bouncing the baby, even though Mila's eyes weren't on him, I nearly forgot everything, including what country we were in.

The thing about reading body language is that you can usually tell when someone's being deceptive. Not because of telltale things, like how fast they are blinking or whether they're making eye contact. It affects everything. Your words, the way you hold your body, your movements—both type and amount, everything. I've been around Ledger enough to know what is normal for him, so it's much easier to tell when something doesn't line up. All I have to do is watch to see if another emotion peeks out somewhere because it's impossible to manage all of your body language when there is something else going on in your head. Your body knows whether what you're trying to show is authentic or not, and it'll tattle on you.

And it was all authentic. He was that authentically sweet with a *doll*. I can't seem to stop thinking about how he would be with a real baby. It surprises me that it has affected me so much. Maybe because I never knew my dad? Whoever he is, he doesn't even know I exist. I never experienced having a dad gently pick me up and cradle me.

A year and a half ago, when Ledger and I did a mission together at a run-down cabin in Moldova, we got to know each other pretty well. He did an impressive job of faking interest in me so that he could try to catch me off guard and get the prize himself. To the point that I even had a hard time finding any discordance at all in his body language— he's that masterful at it.

And I had gone along with it because even though I knew it was a lie, it felt nice to have someone acting like they cared so much. I didn't think that I'd be left with real feelings when it was over— feelings that have been impossible to shake.

Now, Ledger doesn't try to hide his negative feelings about me. It really helps to remind me to keep my distance. But since seeing him with that baby yesterday, I'm having a bit of trouble with that. My heart was reminded of how it felt to be loved by Ledger, even if it wasn't real, and it's craving that again, which is so dangerous. Why didn't I fight harder to *not* come on this mission with him?

Even though I want to distance myself from him now, I still have to know more. So I say, "Yesterday, when we met with Mila, you seemed pretty experienced with that baby doll."

He's reviewing the mission stuff on his tablet that we just talked about, which is what I should be doing, and he looks up. "Oh, it's because I've got a niece. Heidi. She's two, and she's the coolest little kid."

"Your brother has a kid? Is he married?" I realize that I don't actually know much about his siblings. Back in Moldova, we talked about a lot of things, but mostly about our time as operatives, a few random things about childhood, our moms, and his dad who died.

"Not married. The stork just dropped her on his doorstep."

I roll my eyes. "Is he an intelligence operative?" I can't help my curiosity. It's not that we can't have kids— or marriages, for that matter; it's just that most of us don't.

"Blake? No. He has no love for the CSA."

In our ears, Charlie chuckles and says, "If you ever want to get Blake all riled up, just ask him why he doesn't work for the CSA. Or just ask him if anyone should work for any intelligence agency."

I startle at her voice. I didn't realize she was on comms still. "You know Blake?"

"I mean, yeah. He's my brother."

I mouth to Ledger, *Charlie's your sister?*

A knock on our hotel room door makes us both stand up quickly, darkening the screens of our tablets. I make it to the door first and peek through the hole. "It's the hotel manager," I say quietly, and Ledger opens the door.

We both smile widely and say hello. When we'd checked in, the man had looked a little stressed and annoyed. Right now, though, the way he's wringing his hands and ducking his head is showing nervousness and regret.

"I, uh, noticed that you haven't checked out yet. I'm guessing you were hoping to stay longer?"

"Oh!" Ledger says, which is probably what would've come out of my mouth if he hadn't beat me to it. "We hadn't even thought about that. We do need to stay longer. Is this room still available?"

"I wish it was, but so many people are coming in for the Waterfront Summer Fest, and this room is already booked."

"Oh, butternuts," Charlie says. "We only thought you'd need to be in Belgrade for a day. Booking the second day was overkill just in case. And then with Kella being gone for her physical and switching with me, we completely missed it!"

"Do you have another room we can switch to?" I ask. Hopefully, it's another double room.

The poor guy looks like he just ruined Christmas or just broke his grandmother's favorite vase. "We are fully booked. I am so sorry."

"No problem," Ledger says. "We'll just find another one."

"I am on it," Charlie says in our earpieces.

But the manager grimaces. "I don't know if you will. Since it's you," he says, holding out both hands, palms up, toward us, "I called around to see if I could find a room at another hotel for you. I really didn't want to have to show up to tell you I don't have a room for you without another option in hand, but there aren't any. This is a big festival, and lots of people come to town for it."

"Uh," Charlie said, "I don't know how to tell you this, but I can't find any, either. Everywhere I'm clicking is full."

"I don't want to send you away with nothing, though," the man says. "We have a room we use for emergencies. It's not much, and it's not meant for guests— it's for employees who have to work late and can't get home for some reason. But it's got clean bedding and is a place to stay. Of course, if you have somewhere else to go, that's fine," he's quick to add. "And if it was anyone else, I wouldn't offer, but I would like to offer it to you."

"Thanks for having our backs," Ledger says. "We really appreciate it." And then the two guys do some kind of handshake thing that only dudes who are friends do that somehow they both know even though they live half a world away from each other.

The guy gives us a keycard and tells us how to find the room. Then, as he goes to leave, he turns back and says, "Have you made any progress on finding new locations for Bite Nite Burgers? Because if you choose the location across the street, I'll let you stay here whenever you want." Then he adds. "Oh, and I have an idea for a new menu item for you. The 'Twilight Vegetarian Burger.' It can be one of those meatless ones. You know, for people who like their burgers as mysterious and vegan as teenage vampire romances."

Apparently, it's not just bro handshakes that are known around the world. *Twilight* is, too.

After we thank the man and tell him goodbye, Ledger shuts the door behind him and says, "See? It's helpful to make friends everywhere. We've got ourselves a room we wouldn't have had otherwise."

When we get our stuff packed up, we head down to the room, and it doesn't take long to realize that there is a reason why they never rent it out. It's down a dark, uncarpeted hall that feels like it might lead to a dungeon. Which,

I guess, is somewhat fitting because the room has cement floors without a single rug. Two of the walls are cement, too, and the one window the room does have is teeny and up near the low ceiling. If there was a fire and we had to escape through it, I'm not sure that Ledger's shoulders could even fit.

I'm pretty sure it was never meant to be a room at all. There are three commercial-sized water heaters along one wall and a big furnace in a corner. A single queen-sized bed sits against an unpainted sheetrocked wall, but it does have the same bedding on it that our other rooms had. The room does have a bathroom, although its size suggests it belongs in an RV. Beside the bathroom is a small rod to hang clothes on that's suspended from the ceiling by two metal wires.

We both stand just inside the doorway, staring at it, not saying a word. Then Ledger pulls out his phone and calls Damjan, putting it on speaker.

When we tell him that we lost our hotel room, Damjan says, "You didn't have a room booked? During the festival? Yeah, you're not going to find anything else. Unless the CSA has a safe house here?"

"We don't," Charlie says through our earpieces, which Ledger relays to Damjan. "Does the CIA have one?"

"I mean, we do," Damjan says, and for a small second, hope starts to rise, then he adds, "but it's small. Just a single twin bed, and the last time I was there, it was infested with rats. And cats. You'd think the cats would take care of the rat problem, but no. They've gone all biblical and are living in peace."

"So, we've got the option of living in the CIA's Cozy Critter Condo, or the Utility Room Cellar we've got here." Ledger runs a hand over his face, thanks Damjan, and hangs up.

"Well," I say, "at least this room is better than that cabin in the forests of Moldova that we stayed in."

"True. But I have to say that the CSA has better safe houses."

"Better than your non-existent one here?"

"No, this is perfect," Charlie says through our comms. "It's the classic 'one bed' trope. This mission just got a whole lot more interesting! Play nice, you two."

Ledger grinds his teeth, turns off his comms, then removes his earpiece and tosses it onto the bed.

CHAPTER 13
TRASH TALK
ZOE

"You should see the CSA safe house in Zurich," Ledger says. "It has a wine cellar. There isn't actually wine in it, but it's there."

"Oh yeah?" I say. "We've got a rooftop garden at the CIA's safe house in Paris. Well, it's mostly roof access with a couple of potted plants, but a garden nonetheless."

"How is that 'safe'?"

We are still comparing safe houses when we get to the fudbal field to stake out Mila's dead drop. Which is worlds better than discussing the one bed back at our hotel room.

"Our safe house in Sydney might as well be a vacation home," Ledger says. "It even has an ocean view."

"It wouldn't stand up to the CIA's in Tokyo. That place has a jetted tub big enough for two."

We are sitting in our car that's in the parking lot of a restaurant next to the fudbal field. The lot is mostly bordered by trees, but there's a gap in the trees that gives us a view of the side of the field's restrooms with the doors.

Even if the hotel manager hadn't told us that the festival started today, we'd know it, even though we aren't even near the Waterfront. The streets are so much busier, and there's a celebratory vibe running through the city itself. Yesterday, there weren't many people at the fudbal field, but today, they barely all fit on the sidelines.

"She's going in," I say, and we watch as Mila walks into the restroom holding her niece's hand, a bag slung over one shoulder. Two other people go in after her and then come back out before Mila and her niece exit. When she walks back through the door, she glances around, trying to act like she's not being suspicious and failing miserably, but she never even looks in our direction. She does give a subtle thumbs-up, though, even though it's obvious she doesn't know which direction to aim it for us to see.

One of the hardest parts of intelligence gathering is the waiting. Especially when what you need is so close. But if any of the parents of Mila's nephew's teammates saw us talking with Mila on the sidelines yesterday, and then saw us go into the restrooms right after she went in, it would look mighty suspect. So we wait.

Fifteen minutes go by, and we are both itching to get out of the car and go retrieve the list when a guy who had walked into the men's restroom comes out carrying a big garbage bag tied at the top. He sets it against the wall of the building and heads for the women's restroom.

Ledger and I both hurry out of the car and race over to catch the man before he goes into the women's restroom and also removes the garbage bag containing our list. As we near him, Ledger calls out, "Wait!" The man stops in his tracks and turns to look at us.

"Will you give us a minute before emptying the garbage in the women's restroom?" I ask him. "I think I threw away my retainer in that garbage." *My retainer?* I'm an intelligence operative highly trained in the art of deception and very practiced in coming up with lies on the fly, and I say that *I lost my retainer?*

Maybe it was because when I was in ninth grade, my friend Naty and I raced after the school janitor when she'd taken out her retainer to eat lunch, then left it on her lunch tray when she dumped its contents in the trash. But I'm not a teenager and this is a restroom, not a lunchroom.

The man says something to us in Serbian that I'm pretty sure means "I have no idea what in the world you are saying," which, in this instance, I'm grateful for.

Ledger pulls out his phone, I'm sure to bring up a translation app so he can explain to the man that he can take the garbage from the men's side, but we need to search the garbage on the women's side first. I don't waste any time going inside the women's restroom to find that list while the two of them chat outside of it.

The place has a vague prison cell feel to it with its cinderblock walls, cracked cement floors, a single fluorescent bulb, and a questionable-looking puddle of water near one corner. The stall partitions have seen better days, too.

The mostly-full garbage bin is three feet tall and stands next to one of two cracked sinks. Knowing that Mila would be leaving the list in the garbage, we thankfully brought disposable gloves. I put mine on and start moving the top few used tissues and paper towels aside, looking for a paper that might have a list. I assume she would've crumpled it up.

Ninety seconds later, Ledger walks in, holding a garbage liner, and looks around. "I've been in prison cells cozier than this."

I smile.

"The man outside says he's got other things to do. If we want to search the garbage, we'll need to take it out when we're done." Then he starts helping me search. "Find any lost retainers yet?"

I throw him a look, and he says, "What? You might not be the only one who accidentally threw theirs away."

We search for a minute, but the bin isn't too wide, so we can't search deep down very easily. We pour the bin's contents onto the floor, sorting through everything quickly because we've seen how often this restroom is used.

We are both crouched on the floor, grabbing pieces of trash and moving them aside as we confirm each item is not the list, when an older woman walks in with a young child. I am opening my mouth to explain what we are doing and why Ledger is in the women's restroom with me. Lost contact lens? Research project? Public health study? Environmental audit? Something way better than my retainer story. But the woman already has her hands on the kid's shoulders, steering him in a wide arc around us, looking like she very much does *not* want to know the details. So we just keep working.

We've found plenty of used paper towels, some empty

plastic bottles, wrappers from snacks, soda cans, wet wipes, a dozen bandages, which feels like a lot but I'm guessing is par for a restroom at a sports field, a couple of receipts, three dirty diapers, and four empty coffee cups. But zero lists. Zero writing of any kind that isn't on a printed package.

The woman comes out of the stall with the child, looks toward the sinks, then must decide that going around us to get to them is a more questionable action than walking out with dirty hands, and they scurry to the door.

"Mila came in," I say. "She gave us the thumbs-up when she left. It *has* to be here." Ledger and I look at each other without saying a word for a long moment. Then, almost simultaneously, both of our eyes go to the diapers.

"No," Ledger says. "It can't be in one of those."

"Well, you did tell her to hide it well so no one else would see it."

He groans.

We scoop all the garbage except for the three diapers back into the bin and stand it back upright. Then we take the diapers to the pull-down changing station on the wall.

"Which one should we start with?"

Ledger bites his lip, looking less comfortable with opening used diapers than he was with cradling a baby doll. Understandable, yet still makes my mind go right back to picturing him acting all dad-like. Then he points at one. "That one's it."

"All right. Let's do this." I open the first one, and we immediately turn away, gagging. How can opening the diaper release so much more smell? It is a very foul diaper, but there is no hint of a list.

A woman in her thirties walks in and her eyes immediately land on me and Ledger as we stand at a changing station with no kid to change in sight, looking at a dirty diaper. Her steps halt a bit.

"I'm sorry I'm in the women's restroom," Ledger says. "But our toddler swallowed my wife's wedding ring. We forgot to tell the sitter, and she said she changed his diaper here."

That's a decent story. Way better than a retainer. Whether the woman speaks English or not, we had to give an explanation and hope for the best. Luckily, she both speaks English and has kids and therefore apparently understands.

"Oh, I know that feeling all too well," the woman says, her accent thick. "My son swallowed one of those little Lego people once. Doc told me to watch his poop for it. It took a week of searching through every dirty diaper before it showed up!"

She goes into one of the stalls, and Ledger and I look at each other with wide eyes. In a quiet voice, he says, "I'm glad we aren't looking for something that small," and wraps the diaper back up. "You pick next."

So I do, and he opens this one. It's just wet, thank heavens, but it also doesn't contain a list. I grab the last one and open it. Unfortunately, it is not just wet. And it packs its own pungent smell. But sitting right on top of the poop is a list inside a sandwich-sized Ziploc bag. We both let out a breath that is half relief, half shuddering.

Ledger carefully pulls apart the bag's seal. I pull off one of my latex gloves, turning it inside out as I do, and reach with two clean fingers inside the bag to pull out the list just as we hear a toilet flush. I push it into my pocket without looking at it first, and Ledger is wrapping the diaper back up when the woman comes out of her stall.

"Did you find it?"

"No," Ledger says with a sigh. "I guess we have more searching in our future."

"Good luck! There's nothing quite like parenting, is there?"

I have no idea how parents do it.

We both throw our gloves and the diapers into the trash, tie it up, put in the new liner, and wash our hands. Ledger grabs the trash bag and we both head outside, him heading straight toward the Dumpster at the opposite edge of the field. He passes by a group of kids who all look about ten or so and probably have younger siblings on the field. They are playing something that looks like hacky sack, but with a soccer ball.

I want to pull the list out of my pocket and see if any of the names on it are familiar to me. I won't do that out here, in the open, but I am dying to get somewhere secure so that we can get this list to our tech ops and start researching the names. Then we can come up with a plan of who to impersonate and how to keep them from coming into town early. I glance toward the area where we met Mila yesterday, curious to see if I can spot her. But there are too many people to see.

I glance back in the direction of the Dumpster, since

Ledger should've made it back to me by now, and see that he's playing with the kids! He's bouncing a ball on his knees, his ankles, and his head, and bouncing it back and forth between him and them. I am instantly fuming. We don't have time for this!

We are in the middle of a mission, and I, for one, care about that mission. For a lot of reasons. Not only is it important in the grand scheme of things, but I want to report good things back to Sully. Not only is he my director, but since I'm the top operative, he's quite often my case officer. He's also the closest thing I've ever had to a father. So it matters to me that I impress him. And that I keep being the top operative.

I walk halfway over to Ledger and stand with my hands on my hips in a place where he has to see me. It takes a full minute of him bouncing the ball from his knee to his opposite ankle to his other knee to his head then to another kid before his eyes fall on me. He gives each of the half-dozen or so kids a high-five before he walks over to me.

We turn and start walking back toward the restrooms. When we get around to the backside, where there are no people, I hiss, "What are you doing?"

"Hey," he says, stopping, so I stop, too. "I didn't get to play hurling in Ireland, yet you got cheese in both locations. Let me connect with Belgrade!"

"Focus," I say. "We've got a mission going on here! And not just a mission in general— we've got a specific piece of intel that we need to get passed along ASAP."

"It doesn't need to get passed along so urgently that I can't take five minutes to play with some kids."

"If we don't place that tracker, we won't find that team, so they'll get the fortune, and they'll do very bad things with it. Lives are at stake. I know you don't take your job seriously, Ledger, but I do. "

The muscles in his jaw flex. He does *not* like me insinuating that he's slacking in any way. "I know you do. You'd sell out your own child for a successful mission."

I narrow my eyes at him and study him for a moment. "You aren't still mad about that mission in Moldova, are you?"

"Oh, you mean the one where you sold *me* out?"

"I didn't 'sell you out.' I just took the win. You would've done the same thing if I had been the one sleeping when the scientist showed up with that case."

His gaze burns into me for a painfully long moment. I'm waiting for him to fight back. To argue. But then, he simply asks, "Would I have?"

Then he turns and walks back to the car, leaving me rooted to the ground, completely bewildered. His question, the way he asked it, that look on his face— it all feels enormous. Too much to process.

He would have done the same thing I did, right? That had been his entire goal and what he'd been working toward while we'd been in that hovel in the forest. The reason why he got close to me. The reason we cozied up together for three days, swapping stories about our pasts.

Right?

I watch his backside until it disappears behind the trees

and shrubs, then I hear a car door open and close. I can't seem to get my feet to move. I don't know what to do with this information. Is it possible that I've been so wrong about him all this time?

This is too big. It's more than I can take in.

CHAPTER 14
CONCRETE CRITIQUES AND CHEESEBURGER CHATS
LEDGER

f you ever want to keep your self-esteem intact, I strongly advise against having your handler, your intelligence operative partner, and your partner's tech op ever discuss how your body matches up against others. Especially if they're doing it as if you can't hear every word they say. It's like standing in front of a jury, wearing nothing but a unitard, and having your physical traits up for discussion.

Oh, and do it in a room where the walls are cement, the lighting is harsh, and the only mirror is warped and makes you look like a funhouse attraction.

The list of art enthusiasts who are invited to Savović's private auction that we got from Mila contains sixteen names. Right off the bat, we eliminate eleven names because their body type is too different from mine, because their faces are too well-known, because Savović or Mona

Liza are close to them, or because they only speak Serbian, and I do not. For the other five, I get to hear Packston and Kella in my earpiece and Zoe in real life as they look at pictures of the men on the list and give their opinions of who I should impersonate in order to get a private showing.

Opinions like, "I think we could fake the tattoo sleeves, but Ledger doesn't exactly have the build of an ultra marathoner." And "I don't think so. Look at that picture of the man rock climbing. If Ledger tried to impersonate him, he'd look like he was smuggling boulders under his climbing shirt." And "The guy's a former ballet dancer— I don't think Ledger can pull off being that graceful."

I exhale loudly. "Do I really need to be present for this conversation?"

After a little *too* much discussion, we settle on Tobias Rennert who, according to Kella, is a "hyper-animated tech mogul turned art investor from Toronto, Canada." He live-streams art experiences, which makes impersonating him both easier and more difficult.

From what I've seen of his videos and other intel they've gathered about the man, he talks at breakneck speed about the convergence of technology and art, is always sporting (and can't stop talking about) his high-tech accessories, like smart glasses, he visits the gym often, and almost always wears a blazer over a t-shirt with some kind of tech joke.

And, from all the info we were able to gather, he and Mona Liza haven't been in the same location, so my cover won't be blown. The guy is single, too, so we won't have to explain why he's showing up with his administrative assistant instead of his wife.

His personality is a bit much, which is good because then impersonating him will help take the focus off Zoe so she can place the tracker. Which we need since she's the kind of woman who grabs people's attention. She grabbed mine. She still grabs it every day, even when I'm vigilant in distracting myself from thinking about her. Even though I know she fakes feelings about people. About me.

We work with the CSA and CIA to come up with a plan to stall the real Tobias Rennert from entering Serbia before I finish pretending to be him. We settle on creating a situation where he'll need to stop in Berlin, Germany on his way from Toronto to Belgrade to fix a manufacturing problem with an interactive art installation that uses his company's technology. The issue is happening on the eve of its unveiling, much to the consternation of the panicked organizers. And by "panicked organizers," I mean Packston embracing a role he "was born for."

We let Packston and our agencies do their thing while we go gather everything I'll need to impersonate Tobias. But as charming as I am on the phone with Mona Liza, I can't get a private showing at the mansion scheduled until tomorrow morning.

Since there isn't anything more we can do to prepare, Zoe and I actually have time to sit and wait. And I hate sitting and waiting. Spending five minutes playing with a soccer ball with the local kids when the next step is ready to be taken is one thing. But being held back from doing the next step is frustrating.

So, instead of sneaking into the mansion, disguised as someone else, and completing this leg of the mission, we order room service. Pljeskavica for me, which I've never had but from what they tell me, is a Serbian burger made of spiced pork, beef, and lamb. And a mushroom risotto for Zoe, along with Sjenica cheese.

We both sit on the bed to eat in our budget dungeon suite with the cement walls and floors because the only other place to sit in the room is on the cot they brought in for me. And honestly, I don't think it'll hold both of us and stay in one piece. And since we are eating in bed, I made the request to room service that Zoe's food be "Something that makes a lot of crumbs," just like she requested for me on the plane. So they sent the cheese with very crumbly crackers.

I tipped them extra.

Zoe unwraps the cheese, and immediately, a very assertive, earthy, pungent smell fills the space. I put a knuckle under my nose. "I can't believe you brought that into our room."

Zoe just smiles, cupping the cheese in the palms of her hands, like it's precious, and smells it, breathing in deeply. "It's an art, Ledger. The stinkier the cheese, the deeper the flavor, the richer the experience. Want to try it? You've been missing out on a whole world of taste."

"Missing out?" I raise an eyebrow. "I prefer my food not to assault my senses before I eat it. It smells like you've marinated gym socks in vinegar, put them in a gym bag, then left it in a hot car for a week."

"That 'assault,'" she says, breaking a piece of the white cheese off and looking at it like it's a rare gem, "is a symphony of history, culture, and a meticulous aging process. It's not just cheese; it's a story in every bite." She places the piece of cheese in her mouth and closes her eyes, moaning at how good it is.

I cross my arms. "And 'the story' is a suspense thriller where the plot twist is that everyone's noses are the victims." This is the Zoe I fell for back in Moldova, and I'm feeling drawn to her in the same way right now that I did then. My brain keeps sounding the alarm that shouts *Divert your thoughts!* And I should. I know I should. But I'm also having fun.

We are sitting on the bed like the comforter is a picnic blanket, and Zoe laughs and breaks off another piece, holding it out toward me like she wants to place it right in my mouth. "Come on, try it. Live dangerously. Who knows, you might just find that your taste buds are more adventurous than you've given them credit for."

Even though, smell aside, it looks rather tempting between Zoe's fingers and part of me really wants to lean in toward it, to lean into her, I eye it like it's a live grenade. "I don't have a HAZMAT suit with me, so I don't think I'll survive the first bite. I'll just stick with this adventure," I say, picking up my burger which actually looks rather tasty. It probably *smells* tasty, too, but it's hard to tell over the stench of the cheese. I take a bite— it's definitely tasty.

Zoe pops the cheese into her mouth. "You don't know

what you're missing, Lancaster. But I'm happy that it means there's more for me."

I lift my burger, and just before I take a bite, I say, "When you find the right guy, you'll make sure to warn him about your stinky cheese obsession before you get to the 'I do's, right?" I cannot believe I just said that. As far as I know, marriage hadn't even been on my brain. It had to have been the baby carriage that planted the thought. It was still working in my subconscious. I blame it all on that. But I'm also surprised that I actually planted the mental image of Zoe being with anyone else. I don't like that image at all.

Zoe's initial reaction is a shocked look that I can't quite read before it's gone, and then she scoffs. "I am *not* getting married."

"Ever?" I ask. I'm both surprised and not surprised at the same time. And, strangely, a teeny bit disappointed.

"Oh, come on," she says. "As if I'd have any idea how to be married. No Dad, remember? And it wasn't like most of the foster homes I lived in were shining examples of marriage. Most of the time, they just fought."

She reaches up and touches the locket at her neck before picking up her fork and moving it around her risotto. "There was one family I stayed with that *was* a shining example, though. My first one. I was five— in the middle of my Kindergarten year. It was the one place that showed me that life could be different. I could live a life I never knew existed."

It's been a long time since Zoe shared anything personal with me. At least not anything like this. I'm holding my breath, like I'll be able to keep from spooking her into stopping, but she's stopped anyway. So I give a little nudge. "How long were you there?"

"Five months, then I went back to live with my mom. I've often wondered what my life would be like if I had been able to just stay with them, though. If I'd never gone back with my mom and then into different foster homes. Maybe I could've eventually been adopted by them. If I had been, then maybe I would understand how to be married."

She gives an almost imperceptible shake of her head as if she just realized that she got so personal and is pulling herself out of it. "How about you? Do you think you'll get married?"

"Sure. At some point." Huh. My initial thought wasn't my usual *Heck no. I'm not about to give up my freedom!* My mom would be so proud if she knew. Only Charlie is younger than me and none of my older siblings are married, so I doubt she's been worried that I'm twenty-six and still not married. But I'm betting it has crossed her mind that I might not ever want to be.

Honestly, I'm also pretty surprised at my line of thinking. I've had a couple of previous relationships that made me feel trapped and that's the worst feeling.

"I guess that makes sense," Zoe says. "You grew up in a house with a pretty good example of marriage, right? Your parents were at least married long enough to have... how many kids?

"Six. And yeah, my parents were married all the way up until my dad died."

"Six?!" I didn't see Zoe take a bite of her risotto, but it seems like she's almost choking on it. "How did this never come up in Moldova?"

I shrug. "I guess it's because we spent all our time talking about being intelligence operatives. And what we wanted in our futures."

"And about our moms."

I nod.

"But apparently not about siblings. Okay," she says, holding up one finger, "so I've met Jace in the field a couple of times, and I did know then that he's your brother."

"He just got engaged while we were both on that mission in Cairo, so I'll get a sister-in-law soon, too."

"And apparently your handler—"

"My substitute handler—"

"— Charlie is your sister. And then there's your brother who's the dad of your niece… Blake, right?"

"Yep, he's the oldest. Then you know Emerson."

"I do?" A moment of confusion crosses her face before she gasps. "Emerson? As in the lead analyst that teamed up with Kenneth? He's your *brother*?"

It hadn't occurred to me that she didn't know. She's still gaping at me in stunned silence when I say, "And then there's my twin, Miles. I don't know if you saw him when you came in for the mission briefing."

"Miles is your brother, too? I know *of* him but haven't met him. Ledger, does your entire family work for the CSA?"

"Not Blake."

"Oh, of course. Not Blake. The black sheep. Because you live in some insane world where *not* being an intelligence operative would make someone the black sheep of the family." She rolls her eyes. "It's a good thing you've got the CSA because that kind of nepotism would never fly at the CIA."

"Hey," I say, feeling heat rise right along with the need to defend my family. "It's not because of nepotism that so many of my siblings work at the CSA."

"Yeah, sure it isn't." She pops a piece of cheese in her mouth.

I take a deep, somewhat calming breath. "Who is the best intelligence operative in all of the CIA? If you were judging without bias."

"With or without bias, the answer is the same. It's me."

I nod my agreement. "And we've gone up against each other…"

"Eight times," Zoe finishes, and I'm impressed that she knows the exact number. It looks like I'm not the only one keeping track.

"And you're currently ahead on 'missions won' by one. Do you know how many of those eight times I've been up by one?"

"The same as me. Okay, so fine. You're almost as good as me. But that doesn't say anything about your siblings. Are you the best intelligence operative when competing against them?"

"I don't compete against my siblings."

I can tell by the look on her face that she's running through her mind the couple of interactions she's had with

Jace. And I can see the moment it dawns on her that I might not even be the best in my family. Not that I would ever admit to any of my siblings that they are better than me. But I like that Zoe is wondering about it. "Let me ask you this: Who is the best intelligence operative that the CIA has ever had?"

Objectively, we both know it's my mom. We talked enough about her in Moldova a year and a half ago for me to know that she idolizes my mom. Her eyes stay on me, and she bites her bottom lip, which is extremely distracting. She doesn't answer. She doesn't need to.

"And that's just *one* of the parents who raised me and my siblings and taught us everything they know. The other parent— my dad— is legendary at the CSA."

She puts her fork down and crosses her arms. "Fine. The CIA would probably name an entire division after the Lancasters. They'd let your whole family work there."

"Except for Blake."

She waves a hand. "Except for Blake." Then she picks up a piece of cheese and punctuates the air with it. "But they'd let him if he wanted to."

I try to hide my grin. I believe that is one point for me. But I didn't tell her all that so I can claim a win for getting her to change her mind about something. I did it because, crazy as it seems, I apparently really want her to like my family.

Now what I really want is to hear more about hers. "How about you? Do you have any siblings?" I don't think she does, but I guess we don't know each other as well as we thought we did.

"Nope. Only child here. But I was in a foster home once for almost a year and a half when I was fourteen. Two boys were in the same foster home— actual brothers— one was a year older than me and one a year younger. They felt like what I imagine brothers feel like. I still talk to them once a year or so."

I've never known what it's like to not have a bunch of siblings, and I can't imagine how lonely it must've been to be an only child in foster care. Back in Moldova, she told me about her mom. Things hadn't exactly been stable at home with her. She'd gone into foster care permanently when she was six. Her mom passed away at some point. Even though she hadn't been living with her, she'd told me how hard that was. It meant she wasn't only a foster kid— she was also an orphan.

So I had gathered that her dad wasn't in the picture, but I've never actually asked her about him. "And your dad?"

I'm not even sure she'll answer. But after a moment, she takes her tray of food and twists to set it on the nightstand. When she turns back, she says, "My mom wasn't ever really a get-their-last-name kind of person. So when I asked about my dad, she didn't have much to tell me, except the first names of four possibilities. For one, she couldn't remember whether it was Brian or Ryan. For another, she said the name he gave her was likely a nickname. None of the four ever found out that they might be my dad— she didn't have a clue how to even find them."

She's quiet for a moment, then chuckles softly. "So, of course, I became obsessed with people's last names. I learned how to read pretty well during Kindergarten, and especially while I was in that first foster home. When I was back home after that, every time my mom brought a guy back to our place, I would catch him before he left the next morning and ask him for his full name. Then I would write it down so if I ever got a sibling, we would know who their dad was."

"But you never got a sibling."

"No. But other than my necklace, that little notebook was the one thing I carried with me to each foster home." She smiles. "I read back through it once as an adult. I'd thought I was so good at reading at the time, but those were about the most creative spellings of names I've ever seen."

I chuckle softly, too. Then I close my eyes and rub my forehead, thinking back to the comment I made at the gallery when explaining our names "Account" and "Stainless." I'd said something along the lines of no one being able to look at her without saying "I know exactly who your daddy is." I hadn't figured it out at the time, but it was the comment I had made right before she started acting like something was wrong.

I meet her eyes. "I'm sorry for the comment I made about your dad at the gallery."

"You were making it about Account's and Stainless's fictional dad."

"Still. I am sorry."

She gives me a smile that's sad but also something else. I'm not quite sure what. Then she looks at her watch and says, "We should probably get to bed."

I nod and take both of our food trays out to the hall for pickup. Then I head into the bathroom that's almost big enough to fit my shoulders and arms as I'm pulling off a shirt and change into a tee and shorts. Once I come out, Zoe heads in to change.

I'm getting the blankets situated on the cot when she comes out, wearing an oversized nightshirt. I swallow, look up at the ceiling, and grasp for anything to think of to divert my mind, coming up blank. I can't be feeling so close to Zoe emotionally right now and also let in thoughts about her legs.

I look down at the blanket on my cot. Wrinkles in the bedding. I can focus on smoothing them.

"Ledger, you can have the bed."

"Nope, it's yours."

"You're not going to fit on that thing."

I meet her eyes and repeat with more conviction, "The bed is yours."

She looks like she's going to argue, and I'm already thinking of what my responses could be, but for some reason, she just sighs, gets into bed, and turns off the light. "Goodnight, Ledger."

"Goodnight, Zoe."

She's right. I really don't fit on this cot. And I'm a little nervous about turning over in the thing— I'm pretty sure it'll either break or dump me on the floor if I do. Even though this isn't the critter-filled CIA safe house, the thought of lying on the cement floor makes me think of dozens of rats and cats all over it, living in peace. So I mostly stay still.

Several long minutes go by and I'm nowhere closer to being asleep when Zoe says, "Ledger?"

"Yeah?"

It's quiet for a moment before she says, "I'm sorry about Moldova."

CHAPTER 15
THE ART OF DECEPTION
ZOE

All morning as we got ready in our small room and during the drive to Savović's castle, Ledger has been listening to the live streams that Tobias Rennert, the man that he will be impersonating, has posted on social media. He'll listen to a part, then repeat it back, trying to nail the speech patterns and cadence of Tobias. He has gotten pretty good. I might give him grief for not taking missions seriously enough, but I have to give the man credit— he puts in the hard work it takes to convincingly impersonate someone.

The mansion's grounds are bordered by an eight-foot-tall fence. The bottom five feet are stone with cement pillars, and the top three feet are wrought iron. But just along the inside of the fence are enough trees and shrubs that it makes seeing the mansion itself nearly impossible.

Unlike last time, when we parked by the rear entrance, I drive to the front gate. As soon as it opens, we go up the curving cobblestone drive flanked by lush green grass and park in front of the mansion.

I can tell that Ledger is still sore from sleeping on the cot by the way he gets out of the car. He was looking especially sore as soon as he rolled out of bed this morning, but he hasn't been willing to admit it. He just tries to cover it and says he slept great. But, expert in body language here, so it's not like I'm fooled. And, I realize, I've become quite the expert in Ledger himself.

He was hoping to wear a t-shirt that said something like *Hackers Gonna Hack*. Or *The Data Whisperer*. Or *I have connections*, with the ends of HDMI, USB, and Lightning cables. Or something like *Home is where the WiFi connects automatically*. But since we are in Belgrade, all the local stores only had t-shirts with words written in Serbian. And since Tobias is from Canada, he opted for a medium-toned olive gray t-shirt with an artistic interpretation of a computer chip in gold. I think it fits today's art theme better, anyway.

He's wearing a navy blazer over the shirt, slim-fit charcoal gray pants, modern and expensive-looking leather loafers, and an ultra-stylized smart watch. He's also wearing a pair of state-of-the-art smart glasses, and I have to admit that he looks rather attractive in them.

"Before we head back to The Six," Ledger says as we walk toward the front doors, "stopping to drop a toonie or two for a double-double would be good, eh?"

I roll my eyes and try to hide a smile as we step up onto the intricately patterned marble tiles of the porch, where stone columns rising to an arch that covers the porch area lead to the heavy oak doors. Potted ferns and exotic flowers sit on either side of the door, adding a bit of softness. "Before I knock, do you have any other Toronto-isms you need to get out of your system so you don't hit them over the head with them?"

"Just one more." Ledger closes his eyes and tips his head up as he breathes in deeply. Then he opens his eyes and says, "Now *this* is patio weather."

I raise my hand to knock, but look over at him first. "Are we good now?"

He gives a nod and says, "Let's go make history."

I knock.

A moment later, Mila answers the door. Her face is welcoming at first and then shows a flash of surprise at seeing us before she puts her mask of hospitality back on. Ledger holds out a hand and she shakes it. "Hello. I'm Tobias Rennert, and this is my administrative assistant, Kaila Sonnenschein."

"Hi. I'm Mila," she says in her Serbian accent and then shakes my hand. "It's nice to meet you both. Come in. You are here to meet Eliza Cholmondeley for your private showing, yes? Follow me."

She leads us down a long hallway and through a doorway to a big gallery with paintings on the walls and four-foot-tall pedestals spread throughout that each hold a piece of art. My eyes immediately find the Trust piece on one of them— it's a ceramic sculpture with seven figures, each holding up the next in a circle, creating a self-supporting structure.

I recognize the forty-something-year-old woman walking across the gallery toward us as Eliza, code name "Mona Liza," from her picture in our briefing. From what I read, she has a military background, and it shows in the way she holds herself with refined authority and in her outfit choice. She's wearing a navy blazer with embellished brass buttons, a cream-colored silk blouse, and tailored trousers with polished oxford shoes. Her medium brown hair is in a sleek, low bun, and she has a lightweight scarf in an abstract art print draped elegantly around her neck.

Mila says, "Mr. Tobias Rennert is here, and his administrative assistant, Ms. Kaila Sonnenschein." She trips over both the words "administrative" and Kaila's last name, but otherwise is pretty amazing at speaking a language that is not her own. And then she turns to leave us alone with Eliza.

"Tobias!" Eliza says in a British accent as she places her hand in his for a gentle handshake. "It's so good to see you again."

I give Ledger a glance. We didn't know they'd seen each other before. I suddenly wonder if this is going to go south. Ledger and the real Tobias look similar, but it's not like they look like twins or even brothers.

"It has to be what? Ten or twelve years since I last laid eyes on you?"

Okay, so long enough ago that she probably assumes that he looks different. Maybe she doesn't remember him exactly. Or maybe they were just in the same room together but didn't really get to know each other at all.

"It feels like a lifetime ago," Ledger says, totally nailing Tobias's cadence. "You are looking radiant, as always."

Eliza takes a step back to take him in. "And you are looking beefier than I remember. Have you been hitting the gym?"

"Every day. I'm trying to make sure I'm more sculpted than the pieces I bid on."

She laughs and playfully swats at his arm. "Well, it is definitely working for you." I am surreptitiously looking around the room and at the Trust piece, deciding on my plan of action for placing the tracker, when Eliza holds out a hand and says, "I'd like to introduce you to Mr. Savović's head of security, Flynn."

I turn to see that a man has come up behind us without me even hearing him. It's pretty impressive. Most people hire heads of security that are bald, look like tanks, and dress in black suits. This guy, though, is anything other than what I expected. He's got light brown hair in unruly curls and is wearing a khaki sleeveless jacket over a long-sleeved polo shirt, cargo pants, and scuffed but sturdy boots. He doesn't look like he can squash me like a bug, either— he's only maybe an inch taller than me and is relatively thin.

"Well, should we take a look at the art, then?" Eliza says, and she and Ledger start to walk toward the first piece.

Most people will place security guards around a room or at the exits when the room is filled with this many valuable things. It's not always the most effective method, but in a lot of ways, it works. I like it because it's easy to use distraction, smooth motions, and body language to my advantage, which is what I had planned to do. But this head of security apparently knows more than your run-of-the-mill heads of security, and he sticks to me like glue as Ledger is with Mona Liza.

I stop and take a look at a painting on the wall, and he stops next to me. I happen to glance down at his right arm, which seems to be missing a hand and has the sleeve pinned up. Flynn notices me notice it and says, "I used to be in wildlife conservation," he says in an Australian accent— also something I hadn't expected to encounter here. "This here is a reminder not to get too friendly with crocodiles or they'll eat you for brekky."

I wince. "I'm sorry."

"No worries, mate."

"Huh," I say. "Going from wildlife conservation to head of security doesn't seem like it'd be the typical job progression."

He laughs. "It might not seem like it, but I think the animals are what trained me to be good at this job. They can be sneaky, cunning, adaptive, and have mastered the element of surprise."

I walk to the next piece, really hoping he won't follow so I can make my way to the Trust piece and place the tracker, but he follows me like an attentive puppy. I glance at him from the corner of my eye. "Which animals taught you the most?"

"You mean besides the crocodile?"

This time, I'm the one to laugh.

"Because he taught me about patience and timing.

Crocs can stay still, nearly invisible in the water for hours, just waiting for the right moment to strike. He also taught me about the importance of a good grip and never letting go once you've got hold of something. Dingos, though— they teach you all about stealth and adaptability. I saw one evade a trap for weeks on end. She knew how to change her route, timing, everything— she always stayed one step ahead."

Based on the way he snuck up on me, it looks like the dingos taught him well. "It sounds like wildlife conservation should be required training for heads of security."

"I've been saying that for years."

We chat as I move around to look at different pieces because everywhere I go, he goes. But I keep watching for an opportunity to get away from him enough to go to the Trust sculpture that's on a pedestal in the middle of the room and place the tracker.

And every chance I get, I also sneak a peek at Ledger and Mona Liza, making it look like I'm admiring a piece of art when I'm really admiring Ledger. It's amazing how easily he connects with people. I have to admit that it draws me to him, too. He has even convinced Eliza Cholmondeley, the woman who we had trouble finding any pictures of online, to pose with him for a selfie in front of an abstract art painting so he can post it on social media.

I have been seeing him so differently the last couple of days, and not only because of the baby doll in the stroller thing. Partly because his comment at the fudbal field made me realize that maybe he wouldn't have actually taken the win in Moldova. I still haven't fully absorbed that bit of news or figured out what it means for the two of us. What I do know is that I rather enjoy watching him work. It's fun to watch someone who is an elite spy. It's a thing of beauty.

And it's partly because of the conversation we had last night. In some ways, hanging out with him as we ate and chatted on the bed reminded me of Moldova— of the Ledger I knew then. The one I had laughed with and joked with and shared things with that I hadn't shared with anyone. The easy Ledger, not the one I'm in competition with.

But it also wasn't the same as Moldova. Our connection feels different. Maybe because in Moldova, we had just barely met. We were getting to know one another in that cabin for the first time, and neither of us knew how good the other person was at being an intelligence operative. Now, after bumping into each other on missions eight times, we know exactly how good the other person is. So, now as we talk, it comes with an additional layer of admiration and respect.

Of course, it also comes with several layers of mistrust and rivalry that have been building for a year and a half. Plus, back then, I hadn't thought through any implications of a relationship with Ledger. Now I have. So whenever I start feeling all warm and fuzzy about Ledger, I remind myself that getting attached to someone is a good way to make them step out of your life.

And I remind myself that he is an intelligence operative. I am an intelligence operative. Even if only one of those two things were true, we wouldn't work. But with two? It's an impossibility. Partly because feelings can't be trusted. Mine or his. We are too good at faking.

Just like Ledger right now with Mona Liza. He sees that she's responding to his flirting, so he's giving her more of it. I know Ledger well enough now to spot his tells when he's lying. Every spy has a tell that appears when they are telling part of a cover story. Manipulating the situation. It's different for everyone, it's subtle enough that operatives don't usually pick up on the tells of other operatives, and usually, the operatives themselves don't even realize they are doing it.

But if you study an operative well enough, you can spot it. Sometimes, it's rubbing their chin, licking their lips, playing with a watch, straightening a tie, brushing lint off their shirt. For Ledger, it's scratching his left cheek with the back of his middle finger on his right hand.

"So," Flynn says in a quiet voice as we both stand next to a pedestal, studying an abstract sculpture of a spiral staircase that seems to ascend into infinity, "how long have you been in love with your boss?"

"What?" I say, pulling back from Flynn a bit. There is no way he picked up on my changing thoughts about Ledger.

"I've seen the way you look at him when you're pretending to look at the art."

I am an intelligence operative. I am sneaky for a living. Was I really obvious enough in my surveillance of Ledger for Flynn to notice? I guess observing animals for a living can make someone really good at noticing details. I choose to respond by ducking my chin a bit as if I'm embarrassed that he knows. "It's new, actually. Was it obvious?"

"Not at all. Does he know?"

I shake my head.

"Ahh. Secret love."

The fact that Flynn noticed me look at Ledger also makes me realize that he's much too observant to not catch me sneaking a tracker onto the piece. I don't even go near the Trust sculpture because I don't want Flynn to think of me in relation to it later, like after Aragundi's men steal it. But I do want to know more about the security features protecting it.

We step up to a creation on a pedestal that looks like shattered pieces of colored glass were arranged to form a cityscape. It's resting on the same kind of pedestal that the Trust sculpture is, so I'm checking it out fully. I admire it from one direction, and then from another, looking to see how the light catches it and casts shadows in different colors. Then I reach a hand out, like it's just drawing me to it and I can't help but touch it. I plan to just give it a teeny bump. Not enough to move it, but enough to tell me how sensitive the security on it is.

Before my hand can touch it, though, Flynn blocks my attempt and gently moves my hand away. "Careful, Kaila. Every move is recorded, and each of these pieces is rigged with a state-of-the-art security system. Even the slightest shift in pressure will trigger an alarm. It's not just a loud bell, either. It'll immediately lock down the gallery. It's how we can keep it easy to view without it having a physical barrier."

I thank him for stopping me from doing something really embarrassing, but really, I'm thanking him for letting me know what I'll need to do when I come back.

We shift to the other side of the gallery— the side where Ledger and Eliza started— and look at several pieces there when I sense that Ledger is about finished. I turn to Flynn and thank him for being so attentive and showing me around.

He leans in close and says, "By the way, I've been watching how your boss gazes at you when you aren't looking. I don't think you're the only one who is secretly in love."

My eyes flash to Flynn. Ledger was gazing at me as if he's in love? Why? There isn't anyone here that we need to fool. It'll buy us nothing for Eliza or Flynn to believe we are an item. I look over at Ledger, seeing if he is trying to tell me anything or send some kind of covert message. It doesn't appear that he is, though. It doesn't make sense.

Maybe Flynn was just noticing Ledger's feet. I was noticing them, too. Wherever Ledger was in the room, he always had one foot pointed toward me. But that doesn't mean he's interested in me— or *in love* with me— it's probably because I'm his partner and I'm the one who's been trying to plant the tracker that will allow us to complete this part of the mission.

"It's been a pleasure, Ms…"

"Sonnenschein," I tell him.

"Ms. Sonnenschein. I hope to see you again at the auction."

As Ledger and I head toward the doorway, Mila is bringing another couple in for a private showing. We walk through the door as Eliza and Flynn greet them. Instead of going left, toward the front door, I steer Ledger right. We go further down the hall and down to a little alcove. I pull a makeup compact from my bag that is really a device that essentially takes our words and turns them into white noise so we can't be overheard, and I activate it.

Ledger leans against the wall, and I get very close to

him because I do want him to be able to hear me. I try to ignore how being this close to him is making my heart rate raise, my breathing quicken, and all of my nerve ends stand at attention, begging for any kind of touch from Ledger. A brush of a fingertip along my arm. An accidental bump of a shoulder. Anything. "I couldn't place the tracker," I say. I hid the frustration well while we were in the gallery, but I'm feeling it now.

"I know," he breathes in a low voice. "I looked over at you several times and saw that the security guy wasn't giving you an inch."

Oh. I suddenly get it. He was looking at me to see if I was able to complete the mission. He covered it by appearing like he was in love with me so that Flynn wouldn't be suspicious. Smart.

"The auction is in two-and-a-half days," I say. "We have to get the tracker placed before then, because Aragundi's men are sure to find a way to be at that auction, and we don't want to contend with them as well."

"Especially because it might tip them off to the tracking devices."

I nod. "And we need to finish here quickly so we can get to the other pieces before they do. But I got Flynn talking about the security on the piece enough to know that it's a PX-three-twenty-six-H."

"Whoo," Ledger says in a release of his breath. "The guy is serious about security. So our only option is to purposely set off the alarm, then."

I take a deep breath. It really is the only way. We could break in during the dead of night to do it, but we'd still set off the alarm and could get caught. So we need to have someone set it off who won't arouse suspicion, and the only person who can do that is Mona Liza. It'll be extra tough since Mona Liza has been in the mansion for a week. People here know her and her mannerisms well. I nod. "I'll need to impersonate Mona Liza."

From my peripherals, I see someone coming down the hall. I don't look directly at them, but I can tell by the man's gait and speed that he is security. I lean even closer into Ledger and breathe into his ear, "Don't look, but someone is coming." I don't look, either, but I can tell by the sound of the man's footfalls that he's about to ask why we are here when we shouldn't be.

Ledger can sense it, too. He says, "Kiss me."

It's a great way to deflect suspicion, so I do. I press my lips against Ledger's, and for good measure, I press my body into his, too, since I'm already so close, anyway. He wraps an arm around my waist, holding me close.

Oh, my.

I forgot how incredible it feels to kiss Ledger Lancaster. How it feels to be so close to him. To have him holding me tight. To share the same air. To feel the gentle caress of his lips against mine. Even though I'm leaning into him and he's holding me tight and security is almost to us, his kiss is still so soft and tender, like I'm a rare, undiscovered gem, showing he's so perfectly in control of the situation.

I've got my hand on the wall he's leaning against, and I just really want to run the fingers of my other hand through his hair. I want to stand here and fake kiss Ledger all day long. To feel his heartbeat next to mine. Connect with him in a way that doesn't require a single word. Everything is taking me right back to Moldova, and I can't believe I ever managed to repress how incredible his kisses are. How did I ever get past the craving of wanting this every moment?

The security guard clears his throat loudly, and I pull back, acting surprised that he is there, looking around dazed, as if I forgot I was even there. It isn't a hard reaction to fake.

He says something in Serbian, and I show confusion before saying in a hopeful voice, "English?"

"You're not supposed to be back here," the man repeats, this time in English.

"I'm so sorry," I say, fanning my shirt to cool myself. "As if looking at art isn't enough, hearing this guy talk about it just makes me unable to wait a second longer before planting my lips on him." The guy looks unimpressed, so I add, "We'll go, though."

I'm not saying the words with my own personality, so Ledger knows it's all a show, but in reality, I'm feeling the words deeply. I felt the kiss deeply. I reach up and squeeze the locket of my necklace as if it can somehow ground me and help me force my head back into the mission. "Oh, and I left my handbag with a young woman in dark slacks and a light blue blouse. She told us her name... Um, Mila, I think? Mika? Where can I find her?"

"Head straight down this hall," the guard says, emphasizing the word "straight," in case we were thinking of going somewhere else we shouldn't. "You'll either find her in an office on your right just before you get to the lobby, or she'll be in the lobby itself."

I thank him, and Ledger and I start walking down the hall. Ledger glances over at me, and I know he's probably trying to assess whether the kiss was as real for me as I'm sure it seemed while we were kissing, and suddenly everything feels awkward. I've kissed people while undercover before, and it's never been a big deal. Ever.

But I shouldn't ever kiss Ledger. It makes me desperately want things I can never have. Plus, we are partners on this mission, so having one of us get our feelings tied up in things is very much *not* helpful. I need to shake myself out of this. Is that even possible? I let out a breath that comes out as a huff of a humorless laugh. Now I remember why I repressed what kissing Ledger feels like. Because it's hard to work with the man when I fully remember.

I need to figure out how repressing works again.

I start by reminding myself that it isn't real. Just because Ledger is a great kisser and can make it *feel* like there is a lot of emotion being poured into a kiss, doesn't mean that there actually is. He's an intelligence operative. He fakes things as part of his job. And he's really good at his job.

So I just look at Ledger with what I hope is an expression of pure focus on the mission and not any lingering kissing bliss, and I mouth to him, *That was close.*

He clears his throat and then nods.

Yeah, the awkwardness is still there.

As we near the office on the right just before the lobby,

a woman's voice carries through the open door. She's speaking Serbian, but it isn't hard to tell by the tone of her voice that she's berating someone. My guess is it's Petra, and the someone is Mila. No wonder Mila hates her boss— Petra keeps going on, relentless about chiding Mila for whatever she feels she did wrong.

We reach the door, and Ledger knocks on the frame to get the attention of the two women. Mila sees us and immediately hurries over, looking embarrassed that we heard whatever her boss was saying. "I'm sorry," she says. "Let me go get your bag."

When we reach the lobby, Ledger glances back in the direction of the office. "I don't speak Serbian, so I don't know what your boss was saying, but I can see why she's no fun to work with."

Mila looks a little relieved at the reminder that we couldn't understand her boss even though we heard her words, and she just nods. "It's okay." But the girl does look rattled, and I hate that she's exposed to that daily. I'm glad that we'll be able to help her.

"Mila," I say, "do you have access to Eliza's schedule? Or can you get access to it?" If I'm going to impersonate her in a place where everyone knows her face well, I'm going to need to have her face.

"I know it well since I'm the one doing all the work around here." She glances back toward the office.

"Do you know what her schedule is today?" Ledger asks.

"She has private showings all morning, then she's

meeting a..." she searches for the word, "collector for lunch at two at Kafe na Reci, near the waterfront."

"And do you know what hotel she's staying in?" I ask.

She does. It's the hotel directly across from ours— the same one that houses the grill with the overcooked meat and bad music where our hotel's manager wants us to put a Bite Nite Burgers location.

I give Mila a grin. "Thanks, Mila. You're amazing. Don't believe Petra if she tries to tell you otherwise."

Mila smiles back, and I tell her that we'll be in touch with her soon.

As we exit the mansion, Ledger pulls out his phone. "I guess I need to call Damjan to see if he has a contact who can print some 3-D facial appliances for us."

CHAPTER 17
WHEN IN DOUBT, ADD MORE FLOWERS
LEDGER

should've known better than to tell Zoe to kiss me. We could have done something different to cast off suspicion. *Anything* different. Gotten into an argument. Looked like we just got worrisome news. Zoe could've started crying about something and I could've comforted her. Yet I chose the terrible option of her kissing me.

Because kissing Zoe just reminds me how it felt to kiss her a year and a half ago in Moldova. Back when it was real. Or at least when I *thought* it was real. It turned out to be fake then, just like it is now. During the kiss, though, it felt anything but fake. It felt like a glass of cool water after a year in the desert. It felt like longing and surprise and apprehension and exhilaration. And it wasn't just coming from me. It seemed that Zoe was mirroring my emotions.

But then the look on her face after told me that it was just as fake as I should've known it was.

Still, though, I'm beginning to see a side of her that I

haven't seen before. Like when she apologized last night about taking the win in Moldova. That one line from her hasn't really addressed the bigger picture, of course, but I got the sense that she wasn't ready to address more yet. And that's okay.

It does make a tiny, hopeful part of me wonder if the look she gave me that says *"it wasn't real"* is actually the part she's faking. Maybe the kiss was real. Maybe she is feeling everything I'm feeling.

Of course, I tell myself to quit being so hopeful. Because, really, what is it that I am hoping for? A relationship with an intelligence operative? Round One with the two of us should've been enough to convince me how bad of an idea that is.

Besides, it's not like I'm looking for *any* relationship. Spy or not. I love my freedom.

But I am spending a lot more time thinking about Zoe than I ever have. Including Moldova.

While Damjan meets with his contact about doing a 3-D face overlay for us, Zoe and I scout the location where Mona Liza will be meeting a collector for a late lunch. It's an outdoor café near the waterfront, and because of the Waterfront Summer Fest going on, there is a lot of action around it. A whole line of street vendors has been set up in every free space around. Under a canopy right next to the café is a flower shop that seems ideal for our needs.

Because Eliza just saw us both, and because there are so many vendors in the area, Zoe and I take the opportunity to shop all along the waterfront to find disguises. We both get exaggerated floral-print outfits and oversized hats.

Pretty much everyone— the outdoor vendors and everyone shopping in this area— is wearing sunglasses, so we both get sunglasses, too. That'll help.

Then we head back to our cozy concrete chamber at the hotel. I dig through all the disguise options that Abraham hooked me up with, and Zoe goes through her stash. I put on an absurdly large mustache and Zoe pulls her blond hair into a wig cap and puts on a wig with straight, black hair that barely brushes her shoulders. Then we put the new outfits we bought on over the clothes we wore to the private showing at the mansion.

"We look ridiculous," Zoe says as we both stare into the warped mirror in our room.

I grin. "And nothing at all like ourselves."

I feel the buzz of a text and pull out my phone.

> Charlie: Just wanted to check in to see how your enemies-to-lovers arc is coming along.

I darken the screen and shove the phone back into my pocket as quickly as I can, then run a hand over my face. Zoe's looking at me, curious, so I smile and say, "It's nothing. Just my sister being a sister."

We pick up Damjan, who now has the laser scanner we need to use to make a mask overlay of Eliza's face to affix to Zoe's face, and we all head back to the waterfront. We scan Zoe's face since Damjan's contact needs both. But, I don't think that Eliza will let me just walk up to her and say, "Hey, can I scan your face? No particular reason— I just want to." We think we can hide the scanner in a bouquet of flowers, though, and get her to smell them long enough to scan her face.

Damjan goes to find a lookout spot, and Zoe and I, in our very floral disguises, go to the pop-up flower shop to talk the owner into letting us take over for thirty minutes or so. The owner doesn't speak English, but he does speak Czech, so he and Zoe have that in common. Zoe talks to him while I stand there like an idiot, not having a clue what they are saying.

Their discussion goes on for a bit, with much gesturing by both of them. Then Zoe slips him a stack of bills and both he and his assistant take off their aprons and hand them over to us. He says a few more things that I'm sure are instructions, then he leaves.

As I put my apron on, I ask, "What did you tell him?"

Zoe ties hers on, too. "That we are part of the Security Information Service in the Czech Republic, that we are trying to track down a gem thief, and that we think that the people running the booth next to us are trying to sell the gems to a buyer through the jewelry they are making. I told him we needed to be close so we could investigate undercover. He seemed kind of excited by the idea of his shop being so close to some action."

I look over at the jewelry vendors next to us— a mom, a dad, and a kid who is about ten— and I can't imagine a group looking less like international gem thieves.

Zoe works on getting the laser scanner situated in a bouquet of flowers while I talk to customers. And by "talk to them," I mean I alternate between saying, "Ne govorim srpski," which I'm pretty sure I butcher every time, and "English?" in a hopeful voice.

This would be so much easier if one of us spoke Serbian. Or if Damjan could man the shop with one of us while the other keeps watch, but since we can't use him in an active mission because the CIA worries his cover will be blown, he's on comms and it's all up to Zoe and me.

I do make a few sales, though, and I'm feeling pretty proud of myself.

A customer who responded with a "Yes" to my English question has been eying some sunflower starts on one of the shelves. She turns to me and asks, "Do these require special soil pH levels? I've heard they do."

Yeah, I have no idea about soil pH levels. "These aren't your average sunflowers," I say. "They prefer a pH balance that's equivalent to a light gourmet coffee. Just sprinkle coffee grounds around them every now and then— they love the caffeine boost, especially just as the sun is rising."

She nods slowly as if she's trying to decide if I know what I'm talking about or not. Apparently, she decides on *not*, because she walks out of the booth without buying them.

Zoe turns to me holding a giant bouquet of flowers, with a paper thing wrapped around the outside of them. "What do you think?"

"Ten out of ten. I like that you skipped colors that traditionally look 'pretty' together and instead went for the bold choice of combining very conflicting reds, purples, and bright oranges. It makes it… festive."

Zoe rolls her eyes. "I chose based on which were the

most scented ones since we want her to smell them. Come on; give it a test."

I take the flowers, lean in, and breathe deeply through my nose. The combination of the three "most scented" ones isn't horrible. Of course, it isn't exactly pleasing, either. But it is interesting. Enough to take a second sniff.

"Got it," Zoe says, looking at an app on her phone. "Hmmm. One of the flowers got in the way and kept it from scanning the bottom right quarter of your face."

She rearranges it, then has me try it again between customers.

This time, it works.

"Did you see the scanner when you were smelling them?"

I shake my head. "It was the red light that I mostly saw."

Zoe bites her lip, which takes my attention right to them, and I try not to think about earlier today when those lips were on mine. Or last night, when I felt so connected to her in an entirely different way. "Well, then, I guess we're going to have to get her to smell them with her eyes closed."

"Head's up," Damjan says in our earpieces. "Mona Liza is on her way to you. She's about five booths away."

"I think she'll respond better to you," Zoe says and puts the bouquet in my hands.

I pull back. "Wait. Are you saying that you think I am going to be better at this than you would be?"

She nearly takes the flowers back, but I turn away. "Nope. I'm doing it because I agree that I'd be best at it." I know what kind of flirting Eliza responded to earlier, so I can do it again. Just not with the same voice.

I go to the front of the booth and hold out the bouquet, offering to let people smell it as they walk past. From my peripherals, I see Eliza nearing. She's ditched the navy blazer but is still wearing the cream blouse and dark pants from earlier.

I run my finger and thumb down the two sides of my big handlebar mustache to make sure it's stuck well. One of the languages I speak best is Russian, and I've got the accent down pat, so I'll use that accent to keep Eliza from recognizing my voice.

As she reaches our booth, Zoe goes out and around me, like she's trying to get to the other side, nearly knocking into Eliza. She apologizes, and I take the moment with Eliza halted to say, "You are a beautiful lady. You're the first person whose beauty matches the beauty of this scent. I'd be honored if you would stop to smell."

I suddenly don't think she's going to say yes. She doesn't seem like the type of person to stop and smell the flowers often.

"Oh, thank you." She looks toward the café, then glances at her watch and nods. "Okay, I think I've got a tick."

I think it's my voice that got her to say yes. My accent is very different from the accent I use as Tobias, but something in the sound of my voice seems to enthrall her in the same way. It's too bad it's not a universal thing for everyone I run across. It sure would make life easier.

Just as she's leaning in to smell, I pull the flowers back

and say, "Wait. I need to set the scene. Okay, now close your eyes. I want you to picture yourself standing in the middle of a meadow."

She looks wary for a moment but then I guess she decides to throw caution to the wind because she closes her eyes. I continue, trying to make my voice extra… whatever it is this woman likes about it. "You're standing with your arms out, eyes closed, tilting your face toward the sun." I hold the flowers up to her, and I can see Zoe on Eliza's other side, pressing the button in the app to start the scanner. "Now breathe in deeply," I say as the red line moves across her face from top to bottom, "taking in the scent of all the flowers that surround you."

She does, keeping her eyes closed. And then just as the laser is crossing her bottom lip toward her chin, she inhales three breaths in quick succession then sneezes, loud and big. I barely pull the flowers back before the gale hits them.

"Oh! I apologize. That's a bit whiffy," she says, pressing a knuckle under her nose. "I wasn't expecting that. Um, if you'll excuse me, I've got to get to a lunch date."

I turn to Zoe, who is looking down at her phone. She lifts a shoulder in a shrug. "It's not perfect, but it's probably enough." She meets my eyes. "You did good." She takes the bouquet to the back of the booth, reaches into the middle of the bouquet, pulls out the scanner, and then slips it into her bag, all while I'm in shock at the compliment.

I'm in the middle of selling a woman some flowers when the owner comes back. He apparently doesn't agree with the amount of money the woman is offering— and I'm accepting— and starts to say something in Serbian, but then he sees the bouquet that Zoe made, and he seems even more upset about that. And a little overdramatic.

If I had to guess the translation of his words, it would be along the lines of, "Why would you put those flowers together? Are you trying to make people's noses sad? Make their eyes want to cry? I cannot occupy this space for one more second with such a travesty in my midst!" He takes off the paper thing wrapped around the bouquet and starts putting each of the stems back where they go. Once they're all back, he calms, like the world was made right again.

Then he seems to remember that we don't speak Serbian and talks to Zoe in Czech, glancing over at his jewelry-making neighbors. I'm guessing that she's telling him that they weren't the gem thieves we thought they might be. He nods a few times, and when the people look over, obviously sensing that they're being talked about, he smiles big and waves. But when he looks back at Zoe, he seems disappointed that he wasn't part of some big dramatic thing. She pats him twice on the shoulder before we leave.

We head over to Damjan and hand him the scanner. He's going to take it back to his contact, the contact is going to make the mask, and Damjan will get it to us later tonight.

As we walk away, Zoe says, "We are going to have a difficult time finding something for me to wear as I imper-sonate Mona Liza. She has a distinctive style that we aren't going to find just anywhere. I think that if we want to be successful in the morning, we need to break into her hotel room and borrow an outfit. We already know where she's staying."

"True," I say. "Do you have a plan for how to break in?"

Zoe grins as she pulls a keycard from her bag and holds it up. "I swiped it from her purse when I bumped into her. We'll just need to find a hotel employee to cozy up to so we can get them to give us her room number."

CHAPTER 18
THE SPY WHO STOLE MY HEART
LEDGER

like sneaking around with Zoe. It's actually pretty enjoyable when we have the same objectives and are working toward the same goal. It's making me feel connected to her in a way that I haven't felt for a long time. Probably because I've purposely stayed away from situations where I could, but it's nice.

As we walk toward our car, Damjan says through our earpieces, "If you two are going to sneak into Mona Liza's hotel, I'll stay here for a bit and keep an eye on her."

I thank Damjan, then tap the back side of my button mic, which mutes me so that Zoe doesn't have to hear me double as we drive. She does the same. Mona Liza's hotel is only a seven-minute drive away. And since it is just across the street from ours, we park at our own hotel and leave the outlandish clothes we'd put on over ours in the car, along with the hats and sunglasses. Then we head across the street to Mona Liza's hotel.

The hotel lobby is much bigger and more open than ours. It has high ceilings, ornate plaster work, vintage tiles, and classical sculptures along with more contemporary furniture. Not only does it have several restaurants on the ground floor, but it also has quite a few shops. Based on how many employees are manning the check-in desk alone, this place has enough rooms that we can't exactly just try the key at several rooms to find the right one.

"Okay," I say. "I figure I can go up to one of the check-in clerks and convince them that we were just called in to fix an urgent computer issue and that we need to install some virus software ASAP. I can probably throw in that we got word of a credible threat to their network and have to act quickly."

Zoe shakes her head. "I'll go up to an employee who speaks English and seems susceptible to charm. I'll tell him that I'm Eliza's assistant and that I'm supposed to go to her room to take her some headache medicine, but I forgot her room number and that she's not answering her phone or responding to texts. I'll show that she gave me her room key, and say that she's probably not responding because she's lying down. I'll prey on his desire to help by saying that I really don't want to get into trouble by not getting the medicine to her because she has an important meeting this afternoon."

"Or we can go with the computer virus idea," I say. She's not the only one with good ideas here.

Zoe glances toward the clerks and, without looking back at me, says, "Act like you don't know me." And then she walks toward them.

Okay, we're doing it her way. I amble over to a rack of sunglasses that's sitting just outside a little shop next to registration and start trying some on, pretending to check how they look on me in the little mirror. I'm really just watching how things are going with Zoe, though.

She's standing just outside of the check-in area but in full view of the six employees helping guests, looking like she's typing something into her phone. Then she moves the phone from hand to hand like she's impatiently waiting for a response, as she glances from the elevators in front of her to the doors behind her.

After a moment, she does something on her phone again before putting it up to her ear. My guess is that she's eavesdropping on the employees checking in guests, listening for any of them to speak English. Maybe trying to judge which one seems more likely to bend rules. It's impressive— it doesn't look like she's paying any attention to them at all.

She acts like she's hanging up her phone, bites her lip, looks down at her watch, paces a little bit, and then pulls the keycard out of her purse as if she's looking it over to see if there is a room number on it that she didn't notice before.

She must've found a good target because she turns to look at the check-in desk like it suddenly occurred to her that they might be able to help. She goes right up to a man in his lower twenties with his dark hair in purposefully unruly curls. It's obvious that he finds her attractive by the way his entire expression changes when he sees her coming to his check-in area. I wish I had thought to ask her to turn her mic back on so that I could hear their conversation.

They chat for a moment, clearly both flirting. They even laugh a bit. Zoe puts her hand on his arm a total of three times, and each time, I'm pretty sure the guy is so taken by her that he's forgotten the name of the hotel. She has worked quite the spell on him, and he is appreciating every moment of it.

She holds up the keycard and glances in the direction of the elevators, looking worried. I don't need to be able to hear what either of them is saying to know that the guy has bought in to everything she has said, and he is very invested in her plight.

This is why I can't ever fall for Zoe again even though every part of me is so drawn to her. Not at all because she's flirting with a guy to get information in order to do her job well. But because she's so good at it that I can't tell that she's faking. Since she knows so much about reading body language, she knows exactly what to show to make everything seem authentic. No one looking at this exchange would think it is anything but genuine.

If I didn't know any better, I wouldn't be able to tell that it's all an act. And if I wouldn't be able to tell that she was faking interest in a complete stranger, how could I ever tell if she's faking interest in me?

It looks like Zoe is at the thanking-him-profusely stage, moving into the I-owe-you-a-drink-for-coming-to-my-rescue stage. Then she turns and heads in my direction, a big smile on her face.

I let Zoe get completely out of view of the employees at

the check-in desk before I leave my sunglasses shopping to join up with her. As soon as I do, she says, "Got it. Fifth floor."

Before I even get a chance to respond, Damjan comes through our earpieces, saying, "Eliza's lunch date never showed, so she left and hopped into an Uber. I am following her. I thought she was heading back to the mansion, but it looks like she's not— she's heading to her hotel. You've got maybe two or three minutes to get in and get out."

I turn my mic back on and say, "Copy." My eyes meet Zoe's. It's going to be tight to get up to the fifth floor, get to her room, go through her things, find a complete outfit that Eliza won't miss, do a quick search for anything else we might need, and get back out. We pick up the pace as we head toward the elevators.

"That's not enough time," Zoe says. "We could probably get to Eliza's room and find what we need, but chances are too great that we'd cross paths with her after while carrying an armful of her clothes. Unless you stay down here and distract her long enough for me to get clear."

"Agreed," I say, and stop walking. Getting caught by Eliza is a much worse outcome than not getting what we need from her room.

Just before Zoe reaches the elevators, though, there's a little girl. She's maybe five years old, hiding behind a potted fern, and she looks scared. Zoe immediately hesitates. Then she looks back at me, her eyes pleading for understanding.

Then she turns all of her focus to the little girl. I walk closer, needing to hear what Zoe says to her.

When I was eight years old, my siblings and I were hooked on a reality TV show about becoming a superhero, where the aspiring superheroes had to go through a bunch of challenges to show how worthy they were of the title. A challenge in a public area outdoors in the very first episode stood out to me more than all the others. One at a time, when summoned, each contestant had to find somewhere inconspicuous to change into their superhero costume. Then they had to run as fast as they could to get from there to the finish line. Whoever finished the challenge in true superhero fashion with the fastest time won.

What the contestants didn't know was that there was a little girl placed near the finish line who was crying, saying she was lost, asking for help in finding her mom. Whether or not the would-be heroes stopped to help the little girl, thereby risking their fast finishing time, was the actual point of the challenge.

Maybe my siblings and I loved the show so much because we all wanted to be superheroes ourselves. Or maybe it was because we knew that our parents had both been intelligence operatives. I didn't know at the time just how elite of operatives they had been, but I did know that my dad's job title was Director of the Clandestine Services Agency and that my mom's was Head of Counterintelligence at the CSA, so we grew up knowing there were real superheroes in the world.

But maybe it was because, at the time, it had only been three years since my little sister had been kidnapped. And so when I saw that little girl crying for her mom, I saw Charlie. Maybe we all saw Charlie. Maybe Charlie even saw herself there.

Regardless of what reason made us love the show, we were all obsessed. So, of course, we rooted for every super-hero who stopped to help the little girl and compromised their ability to finish as quickly (risking elimination from the competition) by doing so.

And just like eight-year-old me rooted for those super-heroes, I'm rooting for Zoe as she goes up to the little girl and crouches down to her height.

Zoe asks her what is wrong, and thankfully, the little girl speaks English. She says she lost her mom. So Zoe asks her what she and her mom were doing the last time she saw her before she realized she'd lost her. The little girl says that her mom was shopping for some earrings but that she stopped following her mom so she could look at some stuffed monkeys.

"I'll help you find her," Zoe says. "Do you want me to hold your hand, or carry you, or do you want to just walk beside me?"

I love that Zoe gives her a choice instead of choosing for her. The little girl thinks for a moment, and then says, "Hold your hand." Zoe takes the girl's hand, and the two of them head off toward the shop most likely to have both earrings and stuffed animals.

This. This is why I'm falling for Zoe all over again. Maybe I never stopped falling for her. She may intimidate, track, engage, and neutralize bad guys, navigate danger zones fearlessly, and break into high-security installations with the best of them. She might also be difficult to trust and always thinks her way is best. But we've crossed paths a lot— enough for me to know that she will always look out for the underdog, the vulnerable, the forgotten, the overlooked.

I realize that I was wrong. Zoe isn't willing to sacrifice anything for a mission. We may work for different agencies and we may compete in the field, but she has dedicated her life to the same thing I've dedicated mine to.

As I watch Zoe walk away with the little girl, I realize that I'm seeing Zoe differently than I used to. And maybe I've slowly been seeing her differently the whole time we've been on this mission.

In my earpiece, Damjan says, "Mona Liza is heading into the hotel lobby right now. Are you guys out? If not, get out now."

I suck in a breath. This lobby is huge, but that means she's behind me. I suddenly remember that I'm still wearing my handlebar mustache. Without the crazy outfit, the hat, and the sunglasses, it'll be an easy guess for her to figure out it was "Tobias" at that flower shop. Especially since I'm still wearing the t-shirt with the computer chip design and the dark gray pants.

I hurry to pull the mustache off, and as I'm shoving it into my pocket, Zoe comes walking out of the shop she'd taken the little girl into with a huge grin on her face. Of course, she's still wearing the black wig. I give her a discrete head shake and she immediately pivots and heads back into the shop.

I turn to look at yet another carousel of sunglasses in

front of a different shop— apparently, lots of people either forget or lose their sunglasses— and try to re-summon the accent, cadence, and inflections of Tobias's voice.

About five seconds later, I hear Mona Liza say, "Tobias!" I turn, surprise on my face, as she asks, "Are you staying in this hotel, too?"

"Eliza," I say as I take her hands in mine, just like Tobias Rennert would. "So good to see you again! No, actually, I'm staying across the street, but I lost my sunglasses and heard there are some here, so I'm checking out the place." I'm not wearing the blazer anymore— an outfit staple for Tobias in every video— but apparently Eliza doesn't find that odd.

"Oh," Eliza says, reaching a hand halfway up to my face before halting. "You've got a bit of redness around your mouth. Is that an allergic reaction?"

My eyes close for a second as I realize it's from pulling my mustache off so quickly. "I don't know if it was an allergic reaction or something else," I lean in and cup a hand at the side of my mouth, whispering conspiratorially, "but I would maybe stay away from the grill here. And not just because of this. They also overcook their meat because they're too busy bickering over who chooses the best music." I feel bad throwing the grill under the bus since it was the manager at my hotel's experience, not my own, but I do need to maintain my cover.

"I'll bear that in mind," Mona Liza says. "I do wish I could stay and chat, but I've got to dash up to my room to do some paperwork before heading back to Savović's." She gives me a look like she doesn't really want to leave. "See you at the auction?"

"Of course," I say, and she waves goodbye before hurrying toward the elevators. As soon as the elevator doors close, I let out a breath of relief, then head into the shop to find Zoe.

CHAPTER 19

SECRETS, SWEETS, AND SILHOUETTES

ZOE

know I keep giving Ledger strange looks, but I am having the hardest time figuring him out. It's something that doesn't happen with many people. If at all. Back at Mona Liza's hotel, right after I reunited the little girl with her mom, I started noticing a change in Ledger's expressions. His face muscles are more relaxed, he's tilted his head to the side a bit more than once, and his eyes— and pupils!— widen when he looks at me.

His expressions aren't vastly different from what he used to flirt with Mona Liza so her attention would be off me during our private showing. But not once has he scratched his cheek with the back of his middle finger around me like he did around her. As he does anytime he's not being entirely truthful.

And I don't understand. Getting rid of a tell isn't easy, and if you get rid of one, a new one usually pops up. Not showing a tell at all is possible— it just isn't probable. Did

Ledger really figure out how to stop showing tells just since we were last at the mansion? Or maybe I'm simply missing his new tell.

And maybe this is part of the reason why I love competing with Ledger so much— he's not so easy to figure out. He's like a coded message without a cipher. Every time I think I've cracked him, I find another layer. And this layer feels like decoding a transmission by using only half the alphabet.

After talking with Mona Liza at her hotel, he came into the little tourist shop to find me, and when he spotted me, his eyebrows went up and a smile spread across his face. It's relatively easy to lie with your face. But people have micro-expressions that flash on their faces for a fraction of a second before they have a chance to school their face into what they want to show. Those micro-expressions are nearly impossible to fake. Ledger's looked a lot like being elated to see me.

Yes, it could've just been relief that we hadn't blown our cover, but it still did something to my heart. Why, Ledger, do you have to go making my heart want things it can't have?

After we left the hotel, we went shopping for the clothes I'll need to impersonate Eliza. We settled on a tailored charcoal-gray dress with an asymmetrical slit and a fitted bodice that seems to strike a balance between professional and artistic flare, like Eliza's normal outfits. We also got a colorful scarf and bold, geometric earrings. The pieces we got aren't as authentic as if we'd been able to secure an actual outfit of Eliza's, but since we'll be at a location where they expect Eliza to be, hopefully, it'll be enough.

We got an early dinner while we were out. Through it all, Ledger and I bantered. Teased each other. Disagreed on several things. But the whole time, Ledger just kept looking at me differently.

Maybe we should go back to being enemies. Because this is feeling like friendship— and not just a surface friendship but the kind where you deeply care about the other person— and my heart can't take it. Intelligence operatives don't get this. We don't get to care deeply about anyone. We wouldn't even know how.

When we get back to our Broom Closet with a Dumpster View, Damjan stops by with the mask overlay that I'll wear. We go through all the details of our mission tomorrow once again, making sure everything is in place. Today has been exhausting, and tomorrow will be, too, so Ledger insists that we have a bit of down time to relax. He thinks we'll be more on top of our game tomorrow if tonight, we think about, talk about, or work on anything *other than* the mission.

I am about to argue all the reasons why the mission is *all* we should think about, talk about, or work on if we want to be successful tomorrow, but then he suggests that we relax with room service dessert and reads the menu out loud.

What can I say? I'm a sucker for Jaffa cakes.

I sit cross-legged on the bed, and Ledger stretches out on the bed facing me, lying on his side and propped up on one elbow, his krempita on the bed in front of him. He gets a fork full of the layered pastry filled with vanilla custard, and grinning, says, "Hey. I finally got my pudding."

"It's too bad it's just the 'white' part of the black and white pudding you thought you were getting."

Ledger moans a bit as he takes the bite. "I wouldn't say it's 'too bad.' This is amazing." I can feel his eyes on me as I slide my fork into the little sponge cake in my lap with orange jelly and a layer of chocolate and then take a bite. I haven't had this particular dessert in probably two years, and it's just as I remember it. Totally worth giving up a debate with Ledger over.

Ledger cuts another piece of his dessert, but only lifts the fork half way and looks at it, like studying it is more interesting than eating it. I can't help but notice the muscles in the shoulder supporting his weight and then in the other shoulder as it flexes and moves. He is one very fit man, and looking at him makes me suddenly want to scale the side of a building with him. See who gets to the top first.

And also, I kind of want to reach out and run my fingertips along those shoulder muscles and down his arms. To skim my fingertips along his jaw, where stubble from a long day is just starting to appear. To tangle my fingers in his hair as we reenact that kiss from earlier. I reach up and play with my necklace as I picture it.

Zoe, what are you doing? You know you can't fall for this man. Or any man, really. Intelligence operatives just can't. *I* can't. And I especially can't fall for Ledger. I started to once before, and it sucked me in so fully that it actually made me lose sight of the mission for a moment.

Was it blissful for that moment? Absolutely. But, I knew that Ledger was just working the mission. I knew it the whole time. Still, though, it shook my heart more deeply than I care to admit. I don't want to have to face that again.

His eyes cut to mine for a moment, and then he says, "So, earlier today, you stopped our mission to help a little girl."

"I need to apologize for that. It won't happen again."

"What made you do it?"

"I…" I start, trying to figure out what I was thinking at the time. "I guess I just saw myself in that little girl, and it reminded me how grateful I was for every bit of help I got along the way."

"Did you usually get the help you needed?" he asks, then eats a bite of his dessert, not taking his eyes off me.

I shrug and push my fork down into my Jaffa cakes. "A lot of times. Just not always in ways that I wanted." I can tell by the look in his eyes that he wants me to continue, so I do. "Like, sometimes, what I really wanted was for a mom to wrap me in a hug and protect me and tell me everything was going to be okay, and what I got was a lot of experience in reading body language or learning how to listen closely which, as it turns out, helps with learning languages.

"When you move around homes and have different guardians and different foster kids in the home, you don't really get the chance to get used to someone enough to anticipate what they're going to do. You have to watch for more universal body language in order to anticipate and act or react in the right way."

"Is that how you got to be so good at it?"

I take a bite of my dessert, looking up at the ceiling as I ponder my answer. "It's one of probably three reasons I'm good at it. So the first was necessity. If I hadn't read body language while I was in foster care, I wouldn't have known when to do an extra something nice for one of my guardians, when to just be quiet, keep my head down, and do chores or homework, and when it was best to just get out of there quickly. But really, I needed those skills in my original home, long before foster care. I might not have learned them, though, if I hadn't had ample need for them.

"Second," I raise my shoulders in a shrug, "I'm just naturally gifted at it." I'm not bragging. I didn't earn it—it's just part of me. "I realized it was a talent when I tried over and over to teach foster siblings what I had learned. They had the same need for it that I did, but no matter how much I practiced with them and pointed things out, they never got as good at it as I did.

"And the third thing is training. Once I realized I had a skill for it, I decided I should get as much training as possible. I wanted to master it. To be the best."

Ledger grins at me. "Of course, you wanted to be the best."

"Well, yeah," I say. "Did you think I didn't start wanting that until we met?" I take a bite of my dessert, reveling in the taste of chocolate and orange mixed. I've had packaged Jaffa cakes before, and they're nowhere near the experience of having the real thing.

He chuckles. "Not for a second." He takes a bite of his dessert, too, then asks, "So, the CIA trained you?"

"Well, yes. But I was talking about college."

"Let me guess. Just like colleges send scouts to high schools to find students good at sports, a spy college sent out a scout to find high school students good at reading body language and offered you a scholarship."

He's chuckling, and I laugh, too. "That would've been a much easier way. But no, I tend to do things the hard way. I grew up in Quicksand, Oregon, but the moment I turned eighteen and graduated from high school— which happened two weeks apart— I was out of there. I got a bunch of crappy jobs and lived in crappy apartments, starting out in Colorado and moving my way eastward. With each new place, I tried to become a new version of myself. A better version."

"Ahh. An emotional runner, I see."

"One of the best."

"I'd expect nothing less."

"So, one day, I'm working at a hole-in-the-wall restaurant in northern Ohio with my awful boss, when he asks, 'Why aren't you in college?' in his deep, rattling voice. He said, 'You're a smart girl. Someone in your situation can get into college and get a scholarship. Maybe even a grant. Do it. Don't spend your life working in dung heaps like this.'

"And, okay, he wasn't so much awful a boss that day, because it hadn't even occurred to me before that it was even remotely a possibility. But I looked into it, and I decided to go all in. To become a new person. A *college* person. My boss wasn't wrong— I was a smart girl. And I'd always wanted to be an intelligence operative when I grew up. I just didn't know how to get there.

"Anyway, I had taken the SAT during my junior year of high school and had gotten a great score, so I applied and got a full scholarship to the University of Michigan, including housing and a food plan. It helped that my income was minuscule and as a foster kid, there were no parents' incomes to consider when it came to scholarships and grants. The food plan only covered one meal a day, but I made it work."

"Let me guess: you put an extra apple, orange, or banana on your tray, then pocketed it for later."

I nod. "A carton of milk is a good one, too."

"And then Ziplocks for the squishier stuff so you won't get your pockets dirty."

I smile just picturing this man in college. "And going to every club, lecture, and social event that promised food, even if you're not interested in the topic."

He nods. "You got it down."

"Yeah, it was nice. It was the first time in my life when I could focus on improving myself, instead of just surviving."

He's giving me a look that's baffling me. I'm not quite sure how to interpret it, which makes me as uncomfortable as the look does. So I barrel on. "And I did really well in school."

Ledger holds out a fist and says, "Competitive natures for the win."

I bump his fist but say, "I bet school was easy for you.

You just sailed right through it, even though you were focused on friends and fun, right? I had to work so freaking hard."

"Hey," Ledger says, a bit defensively, "I might have made sure to squeeze in fun, but I worked hard, too. I have three older brothers who were already being all kinds of impressive *and* I have a twin who was actively trying to best me in everything. That piles on all kinds of pressure."

Maybe I don't give him enough credit. I kind of always assume that fun is the number one priority for him, but maybe it isn't. Huh. Things just keep rearranging in my head to make room for new information about this intriguing man.

I am studying him, wondering how many other things about him I got wrong, when he says, "Wait. The CIA doesn't recruit from the University of Michigan. How did they find you?"

"Oh," I say. "I didn't stay there. Toward the beginning of my sophomore year, my mom passed away. I hadn't seen or talked to her in a lot of years, but I don't know. It still hit me hard. Things got tough, and I thought about dropping out." I give him a little smile. "I guess the emotional runner in me activated. Luckily, I had an academic advisor who saw through the story I was telling her, saw the kinds of grades I was getting, and suggested that I change colleges instead of dropping out.

"She helped me do everything to get accepted as a transfer student to the University of Virginia. I think that's where I needed to be. Plus, it *is* a college the CIA recruits from. I thrived there, and it was life-changing for me.

Especially when I took Nonverbal Communication and Body Language. My professor was a recruiter for the CIA, and I was his star student. He turned in my name, and the CIA approached me while I was still in college."

Ledger smiles at me. "And I'm guessing that being an intelligence operative has given the emotional runner in you exactly what you need. You can be a different person and run to different places, yet still come back home each time."

I nod slowly, so impressed that he gets it. No one ever gets it. And the thing is, Ledger doesn't only understand things that he's experienced— I doubt he's an emotional runner himself— he just seems to keep listening and asking questions until he understands. But the most amazing part is that I don't feel judged by him for any of it. He just accepts me.

Maybe what made me fall for him before was exactly this— how well he listens. Even if I'm sharing something with deep emotions, he listens as if he cares about every single word. Like he wouldn't rather be anywhere else.

I know he's an attentive listener who always seems to care, so I can't believe I just told him a story that would showcase that side of him, putting me in danger of falling for him all over again. I had enough trouble trying to get over him last time.

This is why Ledger is the worst. Spies can't fall in love. Ledger would never fall for me, and I can't fall for him. Yet he just goes ahead and makes me *want* to. Like it's nothing.

"We've got an early day tomorrow," Ledger says as

he's getting up off the bed, grabbing both of our plates and forks. "We should probably sleep."

I nod, and when he meets my eyes, I say, "Thank you." I don't say what for, but he seems to understand.

We both get ready for bed, and I can tell by the way that he walks from the bathroom to the cot that his body is hurting again just thinking about sleeping on it, even though he's trying to hide it. I grab my pillow from the bed and say, "Don't even think about taking the cot. It's mine tonight."

He takes my pillow and tosses it back onto the bed. "You're not sleeping on the cot. Take the bed, Zoe."

Yep. He's *the worst*. "No, you took the cot last night and I had the bed. It's only right to swap tonight. A guy your size should not be on that cot."

Ledger puts his hands on his hips, elbows out. "I am not taking the bed."

I step close to him, mirroring his pose. "Why." It comes out more as a demand than a question.

He's quiet for a moment before he says, "Because there is no way I'll be able to sleep at all if I know you're on the cot." I open my mouth to say something about it being cruel and unusual punishment to the cot to have him sleep on it two nights in a row, but before I can say anything, he adds, "And I really need to sleep tonight if I want to be at the top of my game tomorrow."

We are barely a foot apart in a silent standoff with both of our hands on our hips. I search his eyes as I try to think of the argument I can pose to get him to agree to take the bed, but all I see in them is pure resolve. A determination for me to not sleep on the cot.

Eventually, I realize he's not going to give in no matter how solid my reasoning is, so I say, "Fine. I won't sleep on the cot. But neither are you. This is a big bed— no reason why that side of it should go unused while you break your back on the cot." He doesn't immediately shoot down the idea, so I've at least got him to pause and think about it. To help sell it, I add, "We can roll up the blanket from the cot and put it down the middle as a barrier if you'd like."

I keep my hands on my hips, standing at my full height, as he searches my face. I hope he sees the same level of resolve and determination in me that I see in him. That he understands his choice is either for me to take the cot or for both of us to take the bed.

After a bit, he says, "Fine. But I'm taking the side closest to the door."

Spoken like a true protector. "Fine," I say back, and we both crawl into bed for what will likely be our final night in these cinderblock chic quarters.

Each of us turns off the light on our nightstands, and we both lie on our backs.

Sleeping in the same room as Ledger last night was one thing. We were in two separate beds at two very different heights. Ledger's cot was near the foot of the bed, so I couldn't even see him when I was lying down.

Sleeping— or trying to sleep— in the same bed as him tonight is something else entirely. It hits me that on the plane, we were probably as far apart from each other as we are now. But this feels different. I could reach out and easily touch him now. Especially because neither of us actually placed the rolled blanket barrier.

Even though I slept in the same room as Ledger last night, I still fell asleep relatively easily. But a lot has changed today. We kissed, even if it wasn't for real, Ledger is looking at me differently, my feelings have been growing and changing all day, I opened up to him in a way I never open up to anyone, and I have come to know a side of Ledger that I didn't know existed. Not in Moldova, not over the past year and a half of crossing paths with him.

I may be able to fall asleep virtually anywhere and anytime, but I can't fall asleep on my back— I have to start out on my side. So I roll to my right side, just like I always do. Our one window doesn't have great blinds, but it's also not very big. It does let in just enough light that, now my eyes are adjusted to the dark, I can see the silhouette of Ledger.

He is so close. So touchably close. He only has the blanket pulled up to his mid-torso, so I can see the outline of his chest and shoulders. The soft rise and fall of his chest with every breath. The silver light from the moon as it catches his cheekbone.

I desperately want a life with this in it. I want to be near Ledger. I want to be the kind of woman who can fall fully and completely in love with him. Get married. Fall asleep every night next to the man she loves. Sleep in the same bed as him and actually reach out and touch him. And I want to be the kind of woman who deserves every bit of the love he has for her.

But I am not her. I wish I was because it is so painful right now to not be her.

Ledger turns his head toward me. "Just so I know what to expect, I'd love to know— are you planning to stare at me all night?"

Of course, he felt my gaze on him. I shrug with the shoulder not pressed into the bed. "Undecided. I might."

"You are not going to make this easy, are you?"

"I don't know how you do things," I say, echoing his statement from our briefing meeting at the CSA but with much more of a teasing tone, "but I'm not in the business of making things easy."

He lets out a soft growl, then rolls to his side, facing away from me. But good golly, his back is pretty great to look at, too.

His voice is quiet, but I'm pretty sure he mumbles, "If you only knew how easily you can get under my skin."

I smile, remembering what I said after he made a similar comment at that same meeting— *I don't know. It looks like I do a pretty good job.* I guess I'd been right. I would claim this victory, revel in the fact that I can get under this man's skin. If only I could be the kind of woman who is capable of it all.

You are not her, I hear echoing through my thoughts.

I don't think this night is going to be easy for either of us.

CHAPTER 20
UNDERCOVER ALARM BELLS
LEDGER

am dreaming. It's sometime in the future because Zoe and I are married. Either we aren't on missions right now or we both are on the same one, because in the dream, I am waking up with her in my arms. I know it's not real, because we aren't arguing and because Zoe herself said she isn't the marrying type. She doesn't believe that intelligence operatives even *can* get married. I don't think that's true at all, but maybe things are different for CIA operatives.

I want to stay in the dream for as long as I can because it feels so good to wake up with her in my arms. This dream just feels so real. Almost as if I can feel her head on my shoulder, her hair against my arm, her skin under my fingertips.

The dream starts to fade, and I reach for it, trying to pull it back. My own thoughts swirl in and out with the dream as I think of yesterday. I had been meandering on and off the path of falling for Zoe this whole mission. When she stopped to help the little girl yesterday instead of completing our objective, I felt like I'd stepped solidly on the path of falling for her.

Now, though, as I lie with her in my arms, I realize that I've fully fallen for her. All the way. Completely.

Much too soon, sleep starts to flee, and I'm being pulled from the dream world to the real world. But just like in my dream, I still feel her in my arms.

My eyes fly open, and I must jerk as they do because hers fly open at almost the same time. Our faces are only inches apart, her head on my shoulder, my arm around her.

We each let out a sound somewhere between a yelp and a squeal, and we both jerk back, putting some space between us. Zoe is staring at me with her eyes wide, breathing heavy, a look of shock on her face that I'm sure mirrors my own. It takes a moment for our breathing to calm, our heart rates to slow, and for our recently asleep brains to register that there is no danger here, only awkwardness.

I guess I should be grateful that at least she didn't reach for a weapon.

The awkwardness is fully present, though. I may have had some realizations, but I am not ready to voice those. Not when we have a mission to complete in just a couple of hours.

After a beat, Zoe says, "So… we pretend this never happened?"

"Nothing happened," I say, throwing the blanket off me. "I'm going to get in the shower."

I head into the bathroom quickly, mostly so that I can have a moment alone to process that dream and the feeling of waking up with Zoe in my arms. I'm not sure it helps, though, because ten minutes later, I finish showering and head back into our shared room, having figured out nothing more than I knew when I walked in. All I know is that I liked it. I like the thought of us being together. And that I'm quite possibly in love with Zoe. And by "quite possibly," I mean "definitely."

But also, I'm fairly certain it can't happen.

As we move about the space, we are both eyeing each other, and I figure she's trying to guess how I feel as much as I am trying to guess how she feels. Things have been changing while we've been here. I know we'll need to talk about it at some point, but I don't feel like I should push it yet because it might just make her run.

After talking with Zoe last night, it occurred to me that she might not have much experience with feeling loved. Maybe like with most new things, it's hard at first. Or scary. Or, I don't know, uncomfortable, I guess.

And maybe she's not interested at all, but I get the sense that she is. And if she is interested in both me and a relationship— which are big *ifs*— she'll likely want to move slowly. That's okay. I realize that she's the only woman I've truly been dreaming about ever since Moldova. I'm not going anywhere. I can wait as long as she needs.

We spend the early morning preparing for the mission.

Zoe does a lot of practicing saying things in Mona Liza's voice and British accent, trying to get it just right. Trying to get a voice right on your own is hard because your voice always sounds different to you than it does to the people around you. So usually, when I'm alone, I do a lot of recording my voice and playing it back until I get it right. But since I've spent a good amount of time with Eliza and Zoe can practice on me, the process goes so much more quickly.

Zoe applies the facial pieces that make her face the same shape as Eliza's, and then she gets to work on the makeup. The selfie I took yesterday with Eliza is a big help in getting it right. Then Zoe practices Eliza's walk until I swear that it's actually Eliza in the room with me.

"Okay, I think we're ready," I say as I put on the blazer that is the finishing touches of my Tobias Rennert outfit. "Let's go make history."

We pack up the rest of our things because one way or another, we have to be done with this leg of our mission today. We grab our bags, and as we are about to head out the door, Zoe pauses and turns back to the room. "Are you ready to leave our Fortress of Solitude on a Budget?"

I chuckle and look at the space, too. "Without a doubt. It's amazing how much can happen in a room that feels like a secret agent's fallout shelter."

Damjan drives us to Savović's mansion, drops me off out front, then drives Zoe around to the back employees's entrance. He'll go off to hide on a nearby street where he won't be noticed and wait. He's on comms with both me and Zoe, along with Packston and Kella, but I suspect it'll mostly be Zoe, Damjan, and me doing any talking.

I knock on the front door, a bag holding my tablet over my shoulder, and Mila lets me in. She has been invaluable throughout this mission. We told her we needed to arrive at a time when there weren't any last-minute private showings going on before the auction tomorrow since we'll need to be in that room. She also let us know when Eliza would be in a meeting with Savović to discuss the final details for the auction. We can't exactly have two Elizas running into each other.

Mila leads me to a small room toward the back of the mansion where I can hardline connect to their network and, with the help of Kella, who is remotely accessing the system, I tap into the security feeds so I can keep watch for anything not going according to plan.

I'm just getting connected when there's a knock at the back door, and Mila says, "That's probably Shauna. Excuse me," before leaving me alone.

Through my comms, I hear Mila open the back door, and Zoe says in Eliza's voice, "Sorry to have you come back to let me in, but I seem to have misplaced my security pass."

"Oh, it's no problem. Would you like me to scan my badge to let you into the art gallery?"

"You're an absolute star. Thank you. You must feel like a doorman lately."

"You have no idea." Then, in a whisper, I hear Mila say, "You look and sound so much like Eliza!"

And I'm into the feed. I've got access to more than a

dozen cameras, and I move the streams around so I can see the art gallery, the hallway leading to it, the hallways outside my room, the foyer, and the hallway leading to security. The security feeds don't have audio, but I can hear Zoe through my comms.

Mila lets Zoe into the art gallery. When we approached Mila with this plan, she was actually excited about it, even if it does come with risks. Mila said that if things went poorly and she was questioned, she'd simply say that she thought it was the real Eliza asking for help. I have no doubt that she'll be fine if that does happen, but I really hope nothing falls back on her at all and makes her job any more miserable until she leaves to go back to school.

Mila heads back up to the lobby, so my attention goes straight to Zoe in the gallery. Flynn, their Australian head of security, is already in the room. We figured someone from security would be in there— it just means that Zoe will have to be more convincing since it's him.

"Thought you were in a meeting with Mr. Savović," Flynn says.

Zoe's walking around the room, stopping to inspect each piece of art. She gives him a glance as if she's so focused on her work that she's barely noticing him. "He got an urgent call and asked for some privacy to take it. That gives me a free ten minutes, so I thought I'd quickly check that everything's in order."

Flynn seems to buy it. But then he says, "Oi, weren't you in that teal blouse with the paint swirls, cashmere shawl, and wide-legged trousers?"

"I *was*, yes. Until I was grabbing a drink of water and

Petra came around the corner and bumped right into me. Got soaked. Luckily, I had this spare outfit in my bag. But it's not my favorite and I'll be changing back the moment my other one's dry."

Nice on-the-fly explanation, Zoe. And she is nailing Eliza's tone and cadence. I watch through the cameras in the room as she walks with Eliza's gait and holds her body the same way Eliza does. Even though it can compromise a mission quickly, most operatives either miss little details like that, or they just don't get them quite right. But not Zoe. She seems to catch every detail of every person's body language and every detail about not only their voice and accent but down to their word choices and cadence.

Yep. She's good at faking.

I ignore the voice and reframe the thought. *She is a pro.* And I have to admit that it is rather attractive. I get so lost admiring the master at work that I forget to check the other cameras until my periphery vision is drawn to movement on one of them.

The lobby camera shows Mila answering the front door again— this time, it looks like it's the caterer, bringing something for tomorrow, I'm sure. Mila is leading her back in my direction where they go inside a room that's not in my security feeds. After a moment, Mila and the woman head out of the room just as I can see that Zoe has walked over to the Trust sculpture.

"Biscuit crumbs?" Zoe says with both disbelief and extreme disappointment in her voice. "You must be having a laugh right now." Flynn has barely had a chance to take a step away from the wall he's standing by when Zoe lifts up the Trust piece and brushes the "crumbs" off the pedestal.

Just as we had planned, the alarm starts to blare, the room locks down, and three security personnel in other locations head toward the gallery just as Flynn shouts, "Eliza! What are you doing?"

From my vantage point through the security cameras, and I'm sure from Flynn's perspective, Zoe is so smooth that there isn't the slightest clue that she placed the tracker.

"I'm sorting out an issue that shouldn't have arisen in the first place," Zoe says in Eliza's British voice. "Have your staff been letting people in here *with food*?" She sounds equal parts disgusted and accusatory. She puts the Trust sculpture back in its spot on the pedestal. "If you don't want alarms going off, keep people with crumbs away from these."

I am scouring the footage from the halls, especially toward the security room, and I see what has to be every member of the security team either heading toward the room or watching the exits. Flynn is making sure the piece is just how it should be and is giving instructions to his security team that has just poured into the room when I get a phone call from a very panicked Mila.

"Tobias Rennert is here! The *real* Tobias Rennert."

Oh, no.

"When I was back in the kitchen with the caterer, Petra let him in. She said he wanted to see Eliza, so Petra messaged Eliza, and Eliza said she'll be down from her meeting to greet him in two minutes!"

"Delay that meeting," I say, my voice as urgent as it can

be without being loud enough to be heard outside the room.

"How?"

"Distract him. Get him somewhere else so he's not in the lobby when she comes down. She can't see him until we are gone."

"Okay, um…" Mila says. "Oh! The bathrooms. The one by the library is all black from ceiling to floor. People always think it's weird. I'll show it to him like it's an attraction."

"That's perfect," I say and end the call. Then through the comms, I say, "Damjan, stand by for extraction. Zoe, we need to wrap this up ASAP."

From the screens, I see that Zoe is heading toward the gallery door and I'm about to disconnect my tablet so we can make a quick exit, but then I see Eliza coming down the hallway toward my room. But before she makes it to me, she'll reach the small hallway that Mila just took the real Tobias down. So I say, "Hold that. Slight hiccup here— stay in the gallery if you can."

Then I disconnect the tablet, shove it into my bag, and head out into the hallway.

"Tobias!" Eliza says when she sees me, all smiles. "What are you doing here? We didn't have an appointment, did we?"

"Eliza," I say as if I'm enchanted to be in her presence. "No appointment— I was hoping I could see you and didn't want to wait until tomorrow. Are you possibly free to go get a drink?"

"Oh, aren't you just a charmer." She reaches out and

gives the lapel of my blazer a little tug, like maybe she's thinking about yesterday when she saw me not wearing it and wants it off again. The woman has a bit of a cougar in her. Sure, the real Tobias is only six years younger than her, but I'm a full fifteen. Then she meets my eyes and I can see regret in them. "As much as I'd love to, I can't today— every moment's already accounted for. But I'd love to sometime after the auction tomorrow."

"Of course," I say then lift her hand and place a kiss on the back of it.

She lets out a sound that is suspiciously like a giggle. This military-esque woman just giggled. I really hope the real Tobias flirts with her, too.

"I must dash and finish my meeting with Mr. Savović. It was lovely to see you."

"You, too," I say, then watch her with what I hope is a look of longing, just in case she turns to look back at me. The moment she's out of sight, I say into my comms, "Okay, the coast is clear. Meet me by the back door."

"And I'm in the back lot now," Damjan says.

I round the corner to the back hall just as Zoe is doing the same from the opposite end. We both get close to the door when we hear something and I spin to look behind me. Mila is coming around the corner, and she has the real Tobias with her.

I don't catch more than a glimpse of him before Mila says, "Oops! Wrong way," and turns to push him in the other direction. Then she pokes her head back around the corner, mouths *Stay*, and leads the real Tobias up to the lobby. I wish I could've gotten a full glimpse of Tobias—

since pretending to be him, I feel an odd sort of kinship with the man.

I lead Zoe to an area in the hall with a weird bend that I noticed isn't covered by the security cameras. "Mission accomplished?" I ask.

Zoe grins and nods. "We don't set alarms off on purpose nearly enough."

Mila rushes back into the hall and I wave her over to us and away from the cameras. "So sorry— Flynn was the other direction, so I led Tobias the long way around. Now he is up front waiting for Eliza." She grins. "That'll be fun when Eliza finds that the Tobias she's been talking to isn't the real Tobias. I thought of a great story to tell them about what might have happened."

"Oh, yeah?" I ask.

"Da. Don't worry. I've got this. Were you good? Did you win?"

"We were," Zoe says. "You have been amazing, Mila."

"We couldn't have done this without you," I tell her. Because we really couldn't have.

Mila is grinning, and she has a look on her face like she enjoyed being part of it. I don't blame her. There's a reason why I chose this job.

"You've been accepted back into college," Zoe says, "and the rest of your education is paid for."

"We just need your bank account number, and we'll deposit the amount you've been making here until you graduate. Do you know your number?" She nods and says it out loud. "Did you get that, Kella?"

"I did," I hear her say through my comms.

I nod. "Classes start in six weeks. Are you excited?"

She nods and then hugs us both. I'm not sure I'll ever get used to an asset hugging me, but it's nice. It feels good that she loves this like I do.

Zoe smiles at her. "We've got to run before Eliza or Flynn reappears. Thanks for everything— you saved us many times."

Then we rush out of the building and into the back seat of the waiting car. Like the maniac driver that he is, Damjan takes off like the mission was a failure and everyone is after us.

"You can relax," Zoe says. "We aren't being chased."

Damjan looks at us, confused, then lets off the gas a bit. "Sorry— didn't realize I was speeding."

"Congrats on a successful operation," Kella says through our earpieces, but something is off in her voice.

"What is it, Kella?" I ask.

"Well, it looks like we didn't guess the right order that Aragundi's team would steal the art pieces. We just got word that the Trust piece in Venice— the stained glass window— has been stolen."

"Oh, no," Zoe says.

"So that only leaves the one in Ankara?"

"Yes," Kella says. "And we don't know if the thieves-slash-bad-guys-vying-for-top-place-in-the-world-destruc-tion-and-domination-game are going there or to Savović's mansion next. We assume they'll go to the Trust piece you just placed the tracker on since the auction is in two days."

Zoe meets my eyes, hers wide with concern. "But if

they are heading to Turkey next, we are going to have to get out of here quickly to get there first."

"You definitely will," Packston says in our comms, "because the chase is on. Unfortunately, there are no available flights direct to Ankara until tomorrow, but we did get you booked on a flight to Istanbul, and from there, we got you tickets on their high-speed train that will take you the rest of the way to Ankara."

"When does it leave?"

"You need to be boarded in fifty-three minutes."

"See?" Damjan says. "I should've been speeding all along!"

I put one hand on the ceiling, just above the door, and Zoe does the same on her side. Then we link arms and hold on tight.

CHAPTER 21
HIGH-SPEED STAKES
ZOE

urkey knows how to make trains. In this car, one side of the aisle has two seats side by side, but on our side, there is only one. Half of the car is facing the front of the train and the other half is facing the back of the train. Most seats have a pull-down tray table, but Ledger and I have seats in the center of the car, facing each other, so there is a small table between us.

Our mics are off but our earpieces are in, and not long into our trip, Packston's voice comes on in our comms. "We split up the task of combing through all the footage at the locations that have had Trust pieces stolen— both official security feeds and unofficial ones, where available— between a team here at the CIA and a team at the CSA. And we've found them!"

I've used some impressive pieces of technology as an operative. Still, though, I'm amazed that while traveling 160 miles per hour, a tiny object that can slide in my ear and be nearly imperceptible can allow me to hear our handlers' voices loud and clear.

I tap my mic, which is in my earring, to turn it on and say, "The thieves?" I'm saying it to Packston, but I act like I'm just continuing the conversation I've been having on and off with Ledger all along. But I do try to not use too many words when talking about mission things.

"Yep! It's the Barno Brothers. Do you know of them?"

"A little," Ledger says. "Aren't they relatively small-time?"

"Not anymore," Packston says. "Apparently they've managed to stay concealed while growing their own little terrorist empire."

"And," Kella says, "Director Lancaster has been working with both the Turkish government and the Serbian government to use our facial recognition software on the footage they have from their surveillance systems at airports and train and bus stations. If they land at either, we'll know and keep you updated."

"We're going to get these guys," Packston says.

I grin at Ledger. We are. I'm already imagining the look that's going to be on Sully's face when we get back and he tells me how proud of me he is.

We know from the mission briefing that the charcoal drawing that's part of the Trust collection is on display at the Ankara Citadel. Between travel— via airplane, taxi, and high-speed train— and the hour we lost to the time zone change, we won't arrive in Ankara until after ten p.m. The Citadel and its surrounding shops will be long since closed, so Packston and Kella worked it out with the management of the castle to meet us at 8 a.m. to place the tracker— well before they open at ten.

Ledger and I can't talk about the mission much here because there are too many people who could overhear. Most people on this train likely speak Turkish, but Kella helpfully let us know that in the touristy parts of Turkey, about seventeen percent of the population also speak English, so we can't just trust that we won't be understood. But less than two percent speak Arabic, and even fewer speak Farsi. Both are languages that Ledger and I speak, so if we have to say anything, Farsi is our secret code.

But mostly, we keep the mission talk to a minimum and play games with the deck of cards that Ledger pulled out of his bag. I'm not sure why he thought that a deck of cards was mission-critical gear, but I'm glad for it. Because without it, the only thing I would have to occupy me is studying Ledger's body language, and I've been doing more than enough of that, even with the cards.

I can't see his feet or legs because of the table, which is too bad, since they are the most honest parts of the body. But I've seen them enough to know that his feet often point toward me. Every once in a while, he'll stretch his legs out, slightly into the aisle, and I can see that they are crossed at the ankle. It's a sign that he's comfortable here with me. But more telling, the toes of his feet keep bouncing up, which tells me that he's also happy.

He's facing me directly, not turning his torso at all. His arms aren't blocking his torso at all, even when holding his cards. He's staying open to me. And when he smiles, it's the kind of smile that moves his whole face— lifts his cheeks, causes the skin at the sides of his eyes to lift. And man, that smile is great. Its appearance makes my smile appear, too.

What gets me the most, though, is his body language whenever I'm talking. It can be about the most random thing, but his eyes will be on me, and often, his head tilts to the side. Tilting your head to the side feels very unnatural if you don't genuinely like the other person. His interest and admiration seem completely genuine.

All signs point to one fact: he likes me. Maybe even loves me.

If I had seen all of Ledger's body language that has been related directly to me— including all the ones leading up to this train ride— and they were aimed at someone else, I'd believe the authenticity, no question. But they're aimed at *me*. I don't even know what to do with this knowledge.

I'm realizing that he had so much of this same body language back in Moldova. I'd noticed it then, but I had taken it to mean that he was trying to manipulate me so that he could distract me long enough to complete the mission on his own.

But he told me that he wouldn't have taken the win on that mission, and I believe him. Would he have let me take the win if I hadn't taken it for myself? Would he have had us share the accolades? I might not ever know.

And suddenly, I'm wondering... if he wasn't lying about how he wouldn't have taken the win, was he also not lying about his feelings for me back then?

No. It's not possible. We'd barely known each other. If

he had known me better, he would've known that we'd never work out, so it couldn't be that. He was just extremely skilled at making his body language show what he wanted it to show.

But what could be his motivation for making me believe that he's falling for me now? It's not so he can take the win. If we don't "win" together, it'll cause friction between our agencies. And both of us are much too competitive to risk earning the disapproval of our directors.

Maybe I should just question him about it. Interrogating a trained operative isn't easy, but I just happen to be pretty good at interrogating people. I could get him to tell me what his angle is, and then tell him to stop it.

Because every time he looks at me like he's looking at me now, my stomach flutters and I start thinking of all the ways it would be nice to date Ledger. To be special to him. When his hand brushes against mine as we both reach for a card, causing tingles to shoot all the way up my arm, I imagine him reaching out to hold my hand. When his eyes crinkle as he laughs softly, I imagine us curled up on a couch somewhere, sharing a private joke. When he leans in close, I want to feel his warm breath against my ear.

And I've had plenty of experience wanting something I can't have— enough to have learned that not only does it not get me any closer to getting it, but it hurts. And not in an *I stubbed my toe* kind of way. In an *I tore my ACL* kind of way. The kind of hurt that is long-lasting.

Since we are facing each other, it means I've got three-

and-a-half hours of Ledger bombarding me with body language that he might not even be aware that he's giving off. Body language that's projecting all kinds of emotions that I don't know how to deal with.

Even when we play the most competitive game of Gin Rummy that I've ever played, smack-talking the whole time and not holding back on being competitive, his body language still shows positive thoughts toward me. Even when I win. When he wins, his arms raise. In the middle of a round, his arms are often on the table. Never restricted, never down by his side. He's leaning toward me, too, instead of resting his back against his chair. I realize I'm doing the same thing.

To give myself a break, I turn to look out the window at the scenery. I try to focus on the lush and scenic green landscapes lit by the setting sun, the beautiful blue waters with occasional glimpses of shipyards, and the storm clouds that are gathering, making the sunset the most vibrant oranges, reds, and blues and in the most dramatic shapes. The small amount of rain that is falling on the streets warmed by the summer sun in the distance seems to steam up almost instantly.

But as impressive as the scene is, my attention keeps getting pulled back to the man across the table from me and all the confusion swirling around my head and heart.

Eventually, we reach the Ankara train station in an all-out downpour. We are almost to the front of the line to get our rental car when Kella's voice sounds through in our comms, her breathing heavy as if she was just running. "We caught them on airport security footage."

Ledger taps his mic on and asks, "In Belgrade?"

"No," Kella says. "In Ankara. They aren't going in the order we thought they would at all."

Ledger and I look at each other, eyes wide.

"The information is delayed, of course, because we can't search the footage until after it's taken."

"How long ago did they leave the airport?" I ask. I don't know what languages Kella speaks, but it feels like a safe enough question to ask in English. I pull the hooded jacket from my bag and put it on, tuck my necklace into my shirt, and zip it up. Ledger does the same with his jacket.

"Five minutes ago. We are currently searching street cams for them."

"We're going to have to place the tracker tonight," Ledger says.

I don't know why, but I'm suddenly panicked about this mission. I *never* panic about missions. I blame it on Ledger. Because now I care about him so much more, and I really don't want anything to happen to him. I also really care about this mission. And I really want to show our directors that the two of us can be successful on a joint mission.

"We have to win this mission, Ledger."

His eyes are on the person standing at the rental counter ahead of us. "I know."

"No matter what," I stress. And then in Farsi, I add, "We can't let Aragundi pass on his empire to a new generation to wreak havoc all over the world."

"We'll get them," he says with enough conviction that

it actually manages to calm my nerves. We *will* get them.

I've had some long days in the field. Literal long days where I was awake for all twenty-four hours of it. But even considering that, it's strange to think that today is still today. This morning, we placed a tracking device on a very valuable ceramic sculpture in Serbia. By lunch, we were sitting on an airplane. By late afternoon, we'd boarded a train in Istanbul. And now, we are about to traipse our way to an ancient castle in Ankara that was built in the seventh century.

"Sonraki!" the attendant calls out, and we move up to the counter.

We are trying to quickly sign the documents to rent the car, but the language barrier is slowing things down. The pre-mission adrenaline is kicking in, and I need to move. We finally get the keys and are racing out to the car when Packston's voice sounds in our ears.

"Found them! I hoped they'd go to their hotel first, but nope— it looks like they are headed straight for the Citadel. You need to get there quickly."

That adrenaline is kicking into high gear.

"The good news is," Kella says, "the airport is further away from the Citadel than the train station is, so they've got a longer drive than you. A nineteen-minute longer drive, specifically. But they have a ten-minute head start on you. We are trying to contact the curator at the Citadel, the manager, or anyone who can meet you there and open the castle for you."

"You can't let the Barno Brothers see you, though," Packston adds. "If they find out that you are trying to get the same thing they are, they'll suspect sabotage and will for sure search all the pieces for a tracker. Then all this will be for naught."

"Which means we can't call in the cavalry," Kella says. "Or the local police."

"Got it," I say. I was quicker at grabbing the keys from the counter than Ledger was, so I slide into the driver's seat, start the car, and take off as Ledger is closing his door.

Ledger immediately brings up navigation and directs me along the tree-lined freeway, through narrow roads with too many cars parked on the sides, and then onto hilly and winding cobblestone streets lined with flower pots. The vendor shops all along the street are closed up, their goods taken inside, and no one is out walking, which is good, because the rain is coming down so hard that it's making it difficult to see. It's running down the streets, too, and a couple of times, our car loses traction.

"They are driving *way* too fast for the conditions," Kella says in our ears. "I hope they bought the extra insurance on their rental car. If they keep going at their same pace and don't wreck, they'll arrive six minutes or so after you."

"The charcoal drawing is in the private museum just southwest of the Ottoman building," Packston adds. "We finally got hold of someone at the museum, but they are twenty minutes away. If you can't place the tracker on it in time, you'll have to remove the Trust piece from the collection before the Barno Brothers arrive. Procuring this piece will get them too close, and we can't risk them choosing not to steal the two pieces you already placed trackers on."

"We'll get it," Ledger says, looking down at the navigation on his phone. "We can't pull right up to the building, or they'll see us go inside. Turn onto this next street. There will only be one row of buildings between us and the museum. "

I make the turn. These buildings look residential— this street is not one that tourists travel on, and its width shows it. It's barely wide enough for our car, and there is nowhere to park. I stop right in the street since that's the only place to go and pull my hood over my head, cinching it tight.

"Ack!" Kella says. "They are pulling onto the street you just turned off! Don't head out that way or they'll see you in about ninety seconds."

We get out of the car and both scan the area. The houses here— white, with terra cotta roofs and trim to match, with rivulets of water pouring off them and onto the streets— are mostly connected, even though everything is in layers of differing heights. The road we turned on winds in the opposite direction we are headed.

Ledger nods at a ridge on one house about four feet off the ground. "How do you feel about scaling some walls and taking to the roofs?"

I grin at him. "Let the adventure begin."

Ledger locks his fingers together and holds his hands down low. I step onto his hands, and he gives me a boost. I grab hold of the roof and pull myself up, then lay flat on it to give Ledger a hand. Once he's up, we take off across the roofs. For as much as the roofs all have the same look, they are at vastly different heights. If it wasn't raining, I would be racing across these rooftops as quickly as running on the road. I'd be having more fun up here, of course.

But the curved roof tiles aren't the easiest to get traction on with this much rain pouring down, and it is slowing our progress a bit. Every once in a while, we come across one that doesn't quite connect to the others and have to jump across the small space.

From up here, we can see the Barno Brothers' car pass by. We can also see the building containing the charcoal drawing, but they don't stop in front of it. Maybe they are looking for a place to park that won't block the narrow road and possibly get unwanted attention on them. Whatever their reason, I'm grateful for the extra few moments it gives us to reach the building and get out of sight. Maybe even make a plan of how to break in before they reach it.

There's a gap of a couple of feet between this building and the next, and then we can climb down from this house, scale the stone wall, cross the narrow street, and then jump the wrought iron fence that leads to the back of the museum.

We're going to get there. We're going to find a way inside that building and either place the tracker or stop the Barno Brothers from entering and taking the piece. As I do for motivation with every mission, I picture Sully's proud expression when I walk back into the CIA.

Ledger jumps across the gap, then his eyes flit to the museum, too, probably imagining how we are going to get inside. He turns back to me, sets his feet, and holds out a hand. I am moving as quickly as I can across the roof, set my foot, and leap toward Ledger.

Except instead of my foot staying set in place, it slips

on the rain pouring across the surface of the tiles, taking my leg out from under me just as my body's trajectory propels me toward Ledger.

The second my foot leaves the roof, I know things are bad. Very, very bad. I know it even before I see the look of horror on Ledger's face as he reaches for me, and I fall between the two buildings.

CHAPTER 22
OPERATION: SAVE ZOE
LEDGER

reach for Zoe. Her slipping foot changes her trajectory so quickly and drastically, though, that my hand only catches air as I watch her fall into the small space between the buildings, hitting the coupling of an exposed pipe on the way. And then, as she hits the ground, I hear a crunch I know can only come from a broken bone. The rain is coming down hard onto the roofs all around me, yet I can still hear my heart hammering in my ears and panic flooding my vision.

I slide from the roof into the small alley, trying to fit my body in the narrow space between the two buildings and maneuver my feet so that I can get to Zoe. The hood of her jacket has fallen off her head, and her eyes squint open enough to see me. She says the words, "Finish the mission," before she passes out.

I'm sure from the way she fell and landed that she doesn't have a spinal cord injury. And she didn't hit her head, so I know she isn't passing out from a concussion. It must be from the pain. I manage to get a foot on one side of her and a knee on the other.

Just as I'm bending over to pick her up, I see something shine in the water pooling beside her. It's her necklace. It must've caught on the coupling and broke. I know how important it is to her, so I grab it and shove it into my pocket, then work to pick her up.

The space is so small that I can't turn my shoulders fully, so lifting her body when I'm not sure what, exactly, is injured and when every part of mine seems to be an obstacle isn't easy.

I get her onto my shoulder, being extra careful with her legs and ankles, since I know one of them is likely broken. I can't turn around, so I have to back my way out of the small space. Once we are free of the buildings, I hurry to the car as quickly as I can without bouncing her and causing her more pain.

The nearest hospital is close, and within five minutes, I've pulled into the parking lot and am carrying her, soaking wet, into an area that looks like their emergency room. The intake nurse doesn't speak English or any of the other languages I speak, so I have to mime what happened.

They roll a bed out to us, and I lay Zoe gently on it, slip the comms unit out of her ear, and place a gentle kiss on her forehead. I whisper, "You'll be okay. Please, be okay." I know she's unconscious, but I'm hoping she still takes it in. I can't lose her.

I pace the waiting room. Update Packston and Kella as

much as I can. Leave a trail of water everywhere I walk. Talk to both my director and hers. Pace some more.

Finally, a doctor comes out. He doesn't speak English, but I use my translation app and it picks up enough to tell me that she has some bruised ribs, one cracked. I'm guessing it was from hitting the joint in the pipe on the way down that also pulled off her necklace. And she has a broken fibula that will need surgery. There aren't any signs of internal bleeding.

The waiting is agonizing. I've been around injuries before. I've been injured. I know from what the doctor said that Zoe's injury isn't life-threatening, but I won't be convinced that there isn't anything that they missed until I can hear her voice and see for myself that she is okay.

I don't even realize that I'm shivering from being in soaking-wet clothes until someone brings me a blanket. When I warm up a bit, I think to pull out my phone and bring up the contact information that Evan O'Brien, the aide to the Irish Ambassador to the United States, gave me so I could contact him for a game of hurling. I shoot him a text, explain that I need to ask the Ambassador for help, and see if he'll relay the message.

By the time a nurse comes back, my shirt is dry and my pants are only damp by the pockets and waist band. My shoes and socks have a long way to go. But, gloriously, the nurse, a dark-haired woman in her thirties named Nehir, is one of the only people in this hospital who speaks a bit of English, and she tells me that I can see Zoe.

She leads me to a room where Zoe is unconscious on a rolling bed. An IV bag hangs from a pole beside her, and a lot of bandaging wraps around her right leg. Seeing her like this causes a stabbing pain in my chest. Another nurse is at Zoe's side, marking something in her chart. "She's asleep, from…" the nurse pauses, can't seem to remember how to say the words to the next part, so she mimes giving Zoe a shot.

I nod to let her know I understand. "How long will she be asleep?"

The nurse shrugs. "It's different for everyone."

I pull the chair up close to Zoe's bed and take a seat. Everything looks fine with her hand, so I hold it in mine and wait as both nurses do their thing, going in and out of the room. It takes longer than I guessed it would for Zoe to come out of anesthesia— the room is already lightening from the rising sun— but both nurses are present when her eyes finally flutter open. I let out a huge breath of relief, and say, "I've never been happier to see someone open their eyes."

But then Zoe grabs the first nurse's wrist and says, "Something is wrong." My relief flees as quickly as it came.

Nehir hurries to Zoe's other side and runs her hand down Zoe's hair, over and over, and says, "Shh. It's okay."

But then Zoe grabs her wrist, too, and repeats, "Something is wrong."

"This is normal," Nehir says. "Your, um… body. It knows something happen. Your brain was…" She can't seem to come up with the English word to use, so she puts her fist at her head, miming being knocked out, then puts a hand out flat and lays her head on it, closing her eyes. "It wasn't there, so it doesn't know something happen. It tells you something is wrong. But you're good." She gives Zoe two thumbs up, which is kind of awkward with her right thumb since her wrist is still being held by Zoe.

Zoe doesn't look very comforted, though, so I move to where she can better see me and wave. Her eyes fly to the movement, land on my face, and she smiles. It's beautiful. She's injured and she just went through surgery, but that smile is everything. And I love that it was my presence that made it appear.

She looks relieved and a bit more relaxed, too… except for the death grip she's got on both nurses' wrists. The scene looks like a three-person arm wrestling match where everyone is stuck in a stalemate. Maybe the wrist grabbing is a common enough reaction, because neither nurse seems fazed by it, and they both continue to do their work of checking Zoe out with their one free hand.

About the time the nurses finish up, Zoe decides she can relinquish their wrists. The first nurse leaves immediately. "You need me," Nehir says as she's showing me a control panel on the bed, but then she can't seem to remember how to say the words she means to say, so she says, "Bzzzzzz, ding, ding! And there's water." I look to where she gestured and see two cups of water with lids and straws on a small rolling table.

"Where am I?" Zoe asks, her voice groggy and scratchy.

I grab a water cup and bend the straw, holding it so she can take a drink as I say, "A five-star hotel, where everyone will wait on you and bring you anything you need."

"Looks like a hospital."

"Well, some people call it that. How do you feel?"

"Heavy. Am I restrained?"

"No. Are you in pain?" I know she's on pain medication and was very recently under general anesthesia, but I still need to know that she's okay. "Can you feel anything? You've got bruised ribs, and one's broken, and you just had surgery on your lower right leg. Does anywhere else hurt?"

She shakes her head, then looks at the water again, so I give her another drink. Then she looks at me very intently, her eyes roving around my face, before she says, "You're so pretty."

I try to hold back a smile. "Am I?"

"Uh-huh. I like your face. It's so… face-shaped. The perfect face." She holds out the word "perfect," but not like she meant to— more like it was just a difficult word to say. All her words are groggy and not formed well, and I know she's just feeling the effects of the anesthesia, but I'm still really digging the compliment.

"I like the rest of you, too."

"*All* of the rest of me?"

She nods. "Like your shoulders. And your arms. You've got good arms." She reaches out and puts a hand on my forearm, which sends warmth all the way up it, even though her skin is cooler than mine. "You got good everything. But your hair is…" She makes a face.

I put a hand on my hair. Between the rainstorm and how many times I've run my hands through it in worry over the past few hours, it feels a bit, well, *big*. "I guess I can't have everything."

A moment later, she says, "I like competing with you."

"Oh, yeah? Why's that?"

"I don't know." She says it like it's all one big, slurred word. "Because it makes me feel like you see me."

"I definitely see you," I say, knowing that I'm "seeing" her more now than I ever have. Since we first met, there hasn't been a time when I haven't. But now, I feel like I understand her in a way I haven't before. I'm seeing all the sides of her that are beautiful and perfect.

"You have the most…" her sentence drifts off, and it's like she's coming out of the anesthesia just a hair more. Not fully, or even close to it, but more than she was. Enough to make her expression turn from blissful ignorance to something that looks a lot like frustration. In an accusatory voice, she says, "You gave me sowdeuhm thio… thiowe pentol?"

All her words have been coming out mumbled and slurred, but I've been able to make them out just fine until this one. It takes a moment before I realize she's maybe asking about sodium thiopental, and I chuckle. "You think I gave you *truth serum*?"

"I know they combine it with… sleep deprivation? Or being nearly asleep? And oxy, oxy, oxytose… I can't think of it. Bad guys followed me to Vladivostok once and captured me. They gave it to me, so I know how it feels. They try to make you believe that you're talking to someone you love and trust so you'll give up information."

She tries to sit up, but winces and decides to just pin me with an intense glare instead. "So who are you? Who's your boss? Who captured me?" Each question comes out like a single, slurred word. "I withstood it once before and I'm going to withstood… *withstood?* With*stand* it now."

"No one gave you 'truth serum.' You had surgery on your fibula, and now you're coming out of anesthesia. That's all it is. The effects should wear off soon."

She shakes her head. "No, you're lying. 'Cuz, I never would've said 'I like your face' to Ledger's face. You're not him. You gave me sodium thiopen…something. And now you're pretending to be someone I love so that you can get me to give up classified info."

I can't help the smile that crosses my face. "You love me?" Sodium thiopental is used by almost no one in the world for a lot of reasons, one being the fact that it doesn't actually work. Maybe the real 'truth serum' is general anesthesia.

I want to hear what else Zoe has to say. But not only does Nehir come in, but my phone rings. By the country code, I know it's the Irish Ambassador to the United States, and I know it's very early, especially in Ireland. I step out into the hall to take the call.

"Ambassador Connolly," I say after I answer the call. "Thank you for returning my call."

"Oh, of course. I was surprised to wake up to see that calling you was on my list of tasks for the day. Evan must've added it sometime during the night."

Had I even realized that it was the middle of the night

when I texted Evan? "How was your daughter's wedding?"

"Absolutely perfect. She was such a beautiful bride."

I can hear Nehir talking to Zoe in the room. Using the English words she is familiar with, she says, "That hamburger man. He a good one."

"Hamburger man?" Zoe asks, rightly confused, even without the recent anesthesia.

"No, no, um…" There's a pause, and I'm fairly certain that the nurse is trying to explain with gestures.

"Oh! Beefy!"

I'm really trying not to get distracted by their conversation, but then Nehir says, "Yes! That beefy man is good. He kept a constant virgin at your side."

"He kept *what* at my side?"

I run a hand over my face, mute the phone, and call out, "Vigil! I kept a constant *vigil* at your side." Then I unmute the phone and ask the ambassador, "Did you get lots of women ogling your legs while wearing your kilt?"

"You know, I was too busy fawning over my family and enjoying that we were all together in one place to notice, but afterward, my wife told me that there was plenty of ogling."

I laugh genuinely.

"And what about you? Did you try black and white pudding while you were in my country?"

"I did."

"And?"

"It… wasn't what I was expecting at all, for sure.

Honestly, I was a little afraid to try it, but it was pretty good!"

He chuckles. "We like to keep visitors on their toes. Next time we'll have you try the pickled herring. But, I'm guessing you didn't ask for a call so we could chat about the wedding and food."

"I didn't. I want to talk to you about your flight. When are you heading back to the States?"

"This evening. Why?"

"What is the possibility of you taking a detour to Ankara on your way?"

The ambassador and I chat for a couple of minutes before we end the call. When I get back into the room, I can tell just by looking at Zoe that she has come out of the anesthesia fully. Nehir is telling her, "You're in good square, so you'll heal fast," and Zoe is looking super confused. The nurse looks up, her eyes moving back and forth quickly as she thinks as if the answer is written on the top of the wall. "Square, circle, square….shap…Shape! You're strong. In good shape. You'll heal fast."

"You do really well with your English," I say to her. "Where did you learn?"

The woman beams at the compliment. "Thank you! I'm much better at Arabic and German. I learn those from Duolingo. You know it?" I nod, impressed that she knows at least four languages, and she says, grinning, "But I learn English from watching Grey's Anatomy."

"Impressive!" I say, and hold up a hand to give her a high-five. It amazes me when someone can learn a language by watching a TV show. And especially to be able to communicate as well as she is.

"Thanks. I owe my English to McDreamy." She sighs. "He keeps me coming back. That, and Cristina's and Meredith's…" She makes hand gestures as she searches for the word she needs, but I can't tell what they mean.

"Friendship?" Zoe says.

"Yes! That."

Nehir checks Zoe's blood pressure one more time, then says she'll be back to check on us later. Zoe's eyes stay on the nurse as she walks out the door.

The moment it closes behind her, Zoe's eyes fly to mine. "Did you finish the mission?"

I pull back my head in surprise at the question. I thought our surroundings and her injuries kind of told the story itself. "No. You got hurt."

"Ledger, you weren't supposed to sacrifice the mission for me!"

"So, what? You expected me to just leave you on the ground in the dark, during a downpour, passed out from the pain, and just go finish the mission?"

"Yes! That's exactly what I expected!"

I shake my head. "That was never going to happen. I would choose to save you every time."

"Before we got there, you agreed to finish the mission no matter what."

"Zoe, I didn't even know how bad your injuries were. Or if you had internal bleeding. Luckily you didn't, but you could have. And even if I *knew* you didn't have internal bleeding, there isn't a chance I would've left you there in so much pain that you weren't even conscious."

I can't fathom why this would make her so upset. Does she worry that her director won't be okay with us not being successful? "Listen," I say, "I talked to both of our directors while you were in surgery, and all they care about is your safety. They care about that *so* much more than the mission."

"Those men trying to be heirs to Aragundi's network and resources are bad guys. Stopping them is more important than my safety."

I flinch. Because as much as I want to stop them, I'm having a hard time right now thinking anything could be more important than her.

In a quieter voice, almost a whisper, she asks, "Was the Trust piece stolen?"

I pause a beat, wishing I could give her a different answer. "Yeah, it was."

She crosses her arms over her chest, and I catch the wince she tries to hide. The motion has to hurt with that broken rib and the bruised ones around it, but she seems too mad to care. She grits her teeth and looks away. She's breathing heavily, too, which makes one of the machines hooked up to her start to make a loud noise.

"Zoe," I say, "the operation isn't lost. It didn't all hinge on this one piece. We still have the trackers on the Trust pieces in Dublin and in Belgrade. Eventually, the Barno Brothers will steal them, and when they do, we'll catch them."

She gives a curt nod, still gazing at the wall, as Nehir comes back in to see why Zoe's heart rate spiked.

I've known Zoe long enough to know that she'll finish a mission at any cost. Part of the reason, of course, will always be because we don't get missions unless a lot is riding on their successful completion.

I've always known that there's more to it than that for Zoe, though, and I had assumed that it's because she's so competitive and wants the win. But if she is this upset that I didn't finish it even without her, then maybe I don't understand her motivations as much as I thought I did.

CHAPTER 23
TENDERNESS AND TURBULENCE
ZOE

The hospital made me leave in a wheelchair. I tell Ledger that if he values our partnership, this mission, and all of his limbs, he better not try to make me board the plane in a wheelchair. He suggests crutches. It's only been fifteen hours since my surgery, and I'm still feeling every bit of that fall. I know my leg is bad, but I can tell without even trying the crutches that it will be disastrous. My hurt ribs won't be able to take it.

Besides, the boot has my leg pretty protected. My body is exhausted, though, so when the attendant who drove us across the tarmac offers to take both mine and Ledger's bags up the ramp and into the plane, I'm grateful.

I'm also grateful for Ledger's careful and steadying arms as I struggle to make it up the ramp. My body is too weak for this, and I keep wondering why I turned down the stupid wheelchair. It's not like stopping twice on the way up to catch my breath is making me look any less frail.

When we step onto the plane, Ambassador Connolly and Evan O'Brien turn to greet us. I must look terrible because I catch the micro-expression of shock that crosses the ambassador's face before he schools it into a pleasant smile and welcomes us aboard.

"Thank you so much for coming out of your way to get us," Ledger says. "If you are ever in a position where I can possibly repay your kindness in any way, please reach out."

I think back to how I pictured each of us would react if someone gave us both paragliding equipment, a target landing point in the distance, and ten minutes before jumping off a cliff. I figured Ledger would spend that ten minutes making friends with whoever else was on the cliff instead of preparing to jump.

I have to admit that maybe his method isn't all bad.

O'Brien is saying something about hurling that I can't focus on when Ambassador Connolly interrupts to say, "But we can catch up later. I think we better get Ms. Steele to a seat before she collapses."

I give him a grateful smile, even if I'm embarrassed to be seen looking so incapable. I can't put any weight on my leg with the boot, and honestly, I'm struggling to keep my other knee from buckling.

The nurse at the hospital said that even though I'd be able to leave the hospital sometime tomorrow, it would be at least a week before I could travel on a commercial flight, and the CIA couldn't get a jet to us anytime soon. I'm sure

Ledger would've had to fly back long before then. Apparently, he wasn't okay leaving me injured, in need of care, and alone in an unfamiliar city where I don't speak the language. He takes the maxim "leave no one behind" very seriously.

We head back to the same room that closes off from the rest of the plane that we traveled in on our way to Dublin, and Ledger helps me to get situated in the seat. I am so tired, but my stomach starts grumbling loudly. I don't even remember when I last ate. Was it that vending machine bag of nuts while on the train?

Ledger hears my stomach, too, and *grins*. He leaves for a moment, then comes back with our bags. He puts his on his seat, opens it, and pulls out a brown paper box before putting his bag on the floor. Then he put the box on the small table between us and opens it out wide, flattening it.

"I didn't want you to leave Turkey without having Turkish cheese." He glances at the window behind me. "And we haven't taken off yet, so we are still in Turkey."

He got me cheese? I am too injured, too tired, and too hungry to handle all of the emotions welling up in my chest. It's even making my eyes well up.

"This," he says, holding up a small container, "is Lor. It's kind of crumbly, but it's got some herbs mixed in. It's high in protein and low in fat, so I figured it's perfect for eating post-surgery.

"And this," he says, unwrapping a white cheese that is sliced, "is Beyaz Peynir from Ezine. I wanted to get you some Dive Obruk Peyniri— it ripens for up to a year in a cave, *while sewn into a dried goatskin.*" He shivers. "It smelled like the floor of a barn, so you would've loved it, but I didn't think bringing that stench onto the plane would be the best way to thank the Ambassador for his generosity."

"It definitely would've been offensive to bring something so tasty on board if you didn't offer him any."

Ledger gasps in mock horror. "But I *like* the ambassador. Oh, and I also got some berries, some nuts, and these cracker things that are supposed to be high in fiber. All are supposed to help you recover."

He leaves for a moment to go get us some sparkling water from Saoirse, and I just gaze at the spread. This is not the meal Ledger would have chosen for himself, I am sure of it. He chose every item here with me in mind. I dab at my lower lid with my knuckle. This is one of the most thoughtful things anyone has ever done for me, and I don't know how to respond.

Ledger returns with two bottles, and says, "You must be starving. Let's dig in!"

So I do. I try the crumbly, herby Lor cheese and revel at the taste and texture. It's mild, yet so full of flavor. As if the herbs brought out all its best qualities. Then I try the Beyaz Peynir. It's so deliciously creamy and has such a rich flavor that I moan eating it. I try each of the two cheeses with the crackers, each with berries. Each with nuts. And I try them together. Somehow, they taste so different yet so perfect every way I try them.

I notice that Ledger is doing more watching me than he is eating cheese. "It's just so good," I say. "Eat some more."

Eventually, my stomach is no longer growling, and I sit back, feeling more content than I have in a while.

"How are you feeling?" Ledger asks.

"Everything still hurts, but it hurts less with a belly full of delicious cheese."

He laughs, and it's such a good laugh. "You look tired. Do you need to sleep?"

I nod, and say, "I expect you to have eaten the rest of that cheese by the time I wake up."

Ledger gets up, helps me to get my seat turned and reclined perfectly, and then arranges the pillows that Saoirse brought in under my leg, under my head, and at the sides of my hurt ribs. He takes off my one shoe, and then spreads a blanket over me, making sure I'm covered. He's so careful and tender about every bit of it that it's almost more than I can take.

"Thank you," I whisper.

He nods. "Let me know if you need anything. Even if I'm asleep. I've set my alarm to go off when it's time for you to take medicine. I don't know how you respond to someone waking you up in the middle of the night, but remember it's just me. Don't assume I'm a thief breaking in or something, because I don't think either of us will fare well if you attack me."

I chuckle, even though it hurts my ribs, and nod.

He tosses a pillow and blanket on his seat, then closes the window shades and turns off the lights before getting in his own seat and reclining it.

I shift a bit to get more comfortable. Between those two close buildings by the citadel, that pipe, and the cobblestone ground, I've got bruises all over, including— I found out before I left— on my spleen. I couldn't have told you where my spleen was located in my body before today, but now, I'm acutely aware. Especially because the pain radiates to my left shoulder and chest.

I reach a hand up to grab hold of the pendant on my necklace, like I always do for comfort, but it's not there. It's probably the fifth time since waking up from surgery and realizing it's gone that I've reached for it, and I feel the pang of its loss every time.

I hear Ledger getting situated in his seat, but it's too dark in here to see him. Still, though, I keep looking in his direction, marveling at how much he's shown he cares for me. The thing about being so good at reading body language is that it's easy to guess how people feel about you. I can tell when someone looks at me and appreciates what they see. I can tell when someone is awed by my skills.

Right now, I've got neither of those things going for me. I look like I fell off a building in the pouring rain, got all bruised and broken, had surgery, left the hospital early, and then got on a plane. And I can't do a single impressive thing right now. I can't even walk up a ramp on my own.

Yet every bit of body language that Ledger is showing is confirmed by every other bit. There is no deception— the feelings he's showing are genuine. It's… unsettling. I don't understand it. I just keep looking in his direction in the darkness, trying to figure out what might be going on in his head, until my eyelids are too heavy to stay open, and I let myself fall asleep.

CHAPTER 24
A BOOT, A BAG, AND A BUNCH OF FLOWERS
ZOE

pparently, when your body commandeers all available resources for healing, it also commands brainpower. Because I don't realize until we are off the plane that my car is in the parking lot and I can't exactly drive it with this boot on my right leg. I guess I'll have to call an Uber, have the driver meet me at my car, get my bigger suitcase out of the trunk, then drive me to a hotel near Langley. Then I'll just pay for however many days of extra airport parking it takes before I'm healed enough to get an Uber to bring me back to my car.

As we are walking out, I'm feeling... I'm not sure, exactly. A sad longing? Ledger and I have spent so much time together over so many days, and I got used to being around him all the time. And now, we won't be. We will still have to finish this mission at some point, and then I guess we'll go back to seeing each other every now and then when our missions accidentally overlap. I didn't think that would make me sad. I thought I'd be thrilled at this point, actually. But I'm very much not.

"Did you drive here?"

Ledger nods. "Did you?"

"Yep. Which way is your car?"

Ledger motions off to the left, so I say, "Okay, mine is this way, so I guess this is where we part ways until our debriefing."

"Wait, no," Ledger says. "You can't drive."

"I was going to call an Uber."

"No, I've got you. Give me your keys and point me in the general direction. You're going to sit on that bench until I get your car over here, then I'm going to drive you home."

"What about your car?"

"I'll come back and get it later."

I'd argue the point, but I really do just need to sit. I wasn't sure I was going to make it to my car. A few minutes later, Ledger pulls up and hops out to put both our bags in my trunk alongside my suitcase that was already there. I hadn't decided where, exactly, I was going to stay when I got back, but the hotel I was in before we left is as good as any, so I direct him there.

The entire drive home, I'm mad. Mad that I need so much help. Mad at myself for making such a rookie mistake. I should've known better than to do something as stupid as falling off a roof. I've traveled across roofs in all kinds of weather before just fine. Was I just distracted by Ledger this time?

And I'm mad that I lost my necklace. It's a small thing from a lifetime ago, and it shouldn't matter, but it does.

When we arrive at the hotel, I feel curiosity coming from Ledger that I led him to a hotel and not an apartment, but he doesn't say anything about it. He just gets my bag and my luggage and goes with me inside to check in.

I think he'll leave then, but he doesn't. He takes my luggage all the way up to my room. Asks if I want help unpacking. (I don't.) Asks me what I want to eat. Orders it for me. Helps me take off the boot so I can change into yoga pants. Helps me to put it back on, his hands carefully positioning my leg and arranging my pants before strapping it back on. He even stays and eats lunch with me.

He can tell when my body is getting too tired to stay awake, and he bows out, making sure I know that it's okay to call him for anything at any time. He even makes sure my phone is near me so I don't have to get up to call him. Then I ease my way onto the bed and under the covers, and I sleep.

I wake disoriented and sore, and I have no idea what day it is, only that it's light outside. I grab my phone off the night stand. It's ten a.m., which makes no sense because I'm pretty sure I started my nap at around one p.m. Then my eyes fly up to the date, and I sit up straight, then wince at the pain in my ribs. It's Wednesday? Did I seriously just sleep for twenty-one hours straight? Based on how many messages I've missed from Sully, Packston, and Ledger, I'm guessing yes.

I down two Tylenol before I even get out of bed, and then I hobble into the bathroom. I can't believe I slept for nearly a full day! I don't think I've ever been this unproductive in my life, and I've slacked on my responsibilities right during an active operation. I have got to get myself going. I'm not supposed to get my wound wet yet, but I desperately need a shower.

Then I remember that when Ledger got us lunch, it was sub sandwiches. He got a footlong one, and it was in a plastic bag. I hobble out to the main room and dig through the garbage until I find it. After shaking out the crumbs, I flop my injured leg up onto the bed, carefully remove the boot, and slide my foot into the bag, pulling it up over my incision. Then I grab a hair tie that has been stretched out way too far and slide it up my leg, holding the top of the bag tight.

Then I get into the shower. It's one of the most difficult things I've done, but I'm determined to do it. I wash my hair first since that's what's bugging me the worst, even though the motion hurts my ribs even more than I guessed it would.

It's a quick shower, my leg is almost numb from the hair tie being a little too snug, and it leaves me so exhausted that I have to lay back down on my bed for thirty minutes just to recover, but I am clean. And that makes it all worth it.

It takes another two hours to get ready for work, summon an Uber, and travel there, but I walk in with my head held high, looking like I'm ready to take on the world. In a boot. And with a limp. And an occasional wince. But ready, nonetheless.

And then, before I've even made eye contact with

Packston or Sully, Troy, the office troll, comes up and walks alongside me, matching my slow pace. "Hey, congratulations on such successful missions in Dublin and Belgrade!"

It sounds like a compliment, but I know he's really just setting things up for the dig.

"Especially having to do it with someone from the CSA. I think I heard somewhere that he's like your rival, right? So good job being so successful in those conditions."

I don't give him the satisfaction of saying "Thanks," even though he pauses so I can. But I know he's not done talking yet, so I just keep walking.

"You came so close to pulling off the perfect mission, too! Then at the last moment, you managed to pull off the seemingly impossible and seized defeat from the jaws of victory."

And there it is. The worst part is, it actually hits a nerve. Usually I can brush off everything Troy says, but this one hurts. I'm not about to let him know that he hit a home run, though, so I say, "It really was a tough one. How was work while I was gone? Have things at your desk been going well?"

I had heard that he got put on desk duty after he lost a secure comms device on his last mission. Based on the fact that he stops walking, I guess I hit a nerve, too.

"Zoe!" Packston notices me and runs over and gives me a hug so gentle that it feels like I'm being hugged by a cloud. "I didn't think you would be in today. Did you get the flowers we sent? How are you feeling? Did they say you could come back already?"

"I don't know," I admit. "I haven't seen my doctor here yet, and I don't remember if the nurse said anything about that when I was in Ankara." I suddenly wonder if Ledger got instructions that I missed. "I just need to talk to the director."

Packston tells me that he's in his office, so I turn to head that way, but he calls out, "And Zoe?" I turn to look at him. "We've all been pulling for you here. All of us."

I give him a smile. "Thank you. That means a lot."

Sully is just finishing a phone call when I get to his office, and he waves me in. I collapse into one of his padded chairs, because walking like you can take on the world when you can really only take on maybe one square foot of it is rather exhausting.

"It's good to see you, Zoe!" Sully says. "Ledger Lancaster has done a good job of keeping me updated on your condition. I was glad to hear that the surgery went well." He pauses a moment, then says, "But last I heard, you weren't doing well enough to walk more than a dozen feet. Why are you here?"

Not exactly the "I'm so proud of you" that I was hoping for at the end of this mission. "Because I can't just lay in bed all day and do nothing."

"But that's exactly what you should be doing."

Apparently, being injured brings out the teenager in me, because I want to reply with "You're not my dad," but I kind of wish he was. Instead, as I'm lifting one corner of my mouth in a smile, I say, "You're not my doctor."

He comes around and partially sits on his desk, facing me. "No, but I am your director, and I want you to get back to full health. Coming into work isn't going to facilitate that."

"I'm really sorry that Ledger didn't finish the mission," I blurt out. "I thought he would— I told him to— but he decided to take me to the hospital instead."

"I would've told him to do exactly that if I was there."

I run my hands over my face in frustration. "Why? I am not okay with that! That wasn't what I wanted, and I'm mad that I didn't get a say in it at all."

"Why are you not okay with that?"

"Because it's a black mark against *me*. I now have an unsuccessful mission in the books." And that goes directly against my "Be the best spy ever" plan that I've had my entire life. Getting injured so that I can't do a mission at all goes against the plan in a colossal way.

"There's no 'black mark' against you. No spy is ever successful at one hundred percent of the missions, and I don't expect you to be. It's impossible to have a perfect record unless you're only taking on the easy missions. You aren't built for easy missions, Zoe, so you're going to have some that don't end with a success."

I shake my head, not accepting that at all. "No, I need to be the best."

Instead of reassuring me that I am still the best, he says, "Why?" It isn't so much a question as a demand for an answer.

I shake my head. "You wouldn't understand."

"Try me."

I can't because maybe I don't fully understand myself.

It's just a feeling inside. A drive. It's not something I can explain, so I just stay silent.

"Okay, then, let me take a shot at it. Is it because if you're not going to open yourself up to being loved, you crave the next best thing— admiration? And you figure that being the best will get you that?"

I narrow my eyes at him as I'm grinding my teeth.

Sully raises his hands. "I pushed too far. I apologize."

"You didn't push too far. It just isn't true." What is pushing too far right now is my pain level. It's taking so much of my focus just keeping it under control.

"Okay, okay," he says, trying to placate me, even though I know he still believes it. He twists to grab some papers off his desk. "I got your medical report from the field. Broken fibula. Broken rib. Bruised spleen. Marked bruising on ribs, legs, and back. There are several recommendations listed. Here's one: recommend rest for one to two weeks before light office work."

He looks from the papers back to me. "That is dated Monday afternoon. Those kinds of injuries take time to heal, and they aren't going to heal very quickly here. Go home, Zoe. Give your body the rest it needs. *That's* your mission right now. I'll see you here next Tuesday, if you're feeling up for it then. If you're not, take another week."

I have to stop to rest halfway between my office in the Global Intelligence Division and the front door, where my Uber driver is picking me up. When I get back in my hotel room, I sit on my bed, take off my stupid boot, and chuck it at the floor. I hate the thing. I glare at it, like it's the embodiment of everything that's stopping me from doing what I need to do. And if I can't do what I need to do— the one thing I excel at— what am I even good for?

I flop back onto my bed, my good leg still on the floor, and stare up at the ceiling, not really seeing it. An hour later, I haven't moved an inch when I hear a light knock on my door before Ledger opens it with the keycard I gave him yesterday. He's juggling the keycard, a big vase of happy-looking flowers in each arm, and a bag with dinner in it. Seeing him is like a light is turned on when I've been in darkness. It makes my whole insides happy.

"The front desk said these came for you. I think this one is from your work," he says as he sets the first one on the small table, "and this one is from the CSA." He sets the second one down, and then looks down at where my boot landed on the floor. "I see you two had an argument."

I nod. "It's unclear who won."

"Looks like you put up a good fight, though." He sets the bag with dinner on my desk. "Are you ready to kiss and make up with it? Because I brought Thai."

I sit up. "Really? For Thai, I can make peace with the boot."

He picks the cursed boot up, then once again, gently gets my foot strapped into it before taking my hand and pulling me up from my despondency bed so I can walk to the table.

I watch the way he does everything. Takes care of me. Gets the food set out. Asks about my day as we eat. If I had to analyze his body language through it all, I would say,

"That man loves that woman." I see it in everything he does.

But he shouldn't love me. I'm not everything that he must think that I am. If he knew the real me, he'd see that I'm not worthy of it. My mom knew it. My foster parents all knew it.

They say that love is blind, so maybe that's what's going on here— love is just making him blind. But that blindness won't stick around forever. It's wonderful, and I'm soaking every bit of it in. Seeing him when I thought I wouldn't feels like getting a surprise gift.

Before long, though, he'll realize that I'm just... *me*.

But I'll give the guy points for consistency because he also stops by to bring me dinner the next night. And on Friday and Saturday, too.

Every day that he's here in my hotel room, I find that we touch more and more. A brush of hands as we are both reaching for the same thing. An arm offered when I get off balance. Help stretching my cramping leg. A rub of my calves through the ache.

On Sunday, he comes over in the early afternoon. We play card games and seated basketball with my trash bin and crumpled up papers. We sit on my bed and watch romcoms while eating ice cream. And instead of giving each other space, like we did in Belgrade when eating on the same bed, we sit side by side, close enough that our upper arms are touching. When I get tired and lean into him, he wraps an arm around me, supporting me. And when we need real food, he orders chicken parmesan and has it delivered.

We are touching more and more, and less and less of it is just accidental. But he never tries to kiss me. Part of me is relieved because I know the kind of longing that Ledger's kisses cause in me. But part of me wants it so badly that I no longer care whether it might be painful for future me or not. I just want this man's lips on mine.

Love is blind, and I am very grateful for that. As much as I resisted help at the beginning, I really love having someone look out for me like this. To have my back when it's impossible to do many of these things myself. It feels healing. And not just to my body, which is getting stronger every day, but to my soul. I want to hold on to it as tight as I can while I have it. To soak every bit of it in.

"My family gets together for dinner on Monday nights," Ledger says before he leaves. "What do you think about coming with me tomorrow?"

"I don't know. I'm injured— I don't want anyone to see me like this." I especially don't want Evelyn Lancaster to see me like this. Not that she doesn't already know that I messed up on the mission and got injured.

"We're all operatives. We've all been injured. Everyone gets it."

Spending every day with Ledger is one thing. Meeting the family is something else, and it feels huge. I pride myself on not being afraid of anything, but this feels… scary. It's a little thing, though. I should not be afraid of something as small as meeting someone's family.

Even if they are a family of operatives, and even if one of them is my idol and the person I've fashioned my career after.

You can do this, Zoe.

I repeat it until I somewhat believe it. And because I want to hold on to every bit of this thing with Ledger, I nod and say, "Okay, I'll join you."

CHAPTER 25
BBQ, BONDING, AND A BIT OF SPYCRAFT
LEDGER

have wanted to kiss Zoe so many times over the past week and a half. Right now, for instance. We're stopped at a stop light, and I'd love to reach over, cup her cheek in my hand, and press a kiss on her lips.

But I was the one to initiate our first kiss back in Moldova. I didn't know it, but things hadn't even been real for Zoe then. This time, it feels like everything is different. And this time, I'm going to let her make the first move when it comes to kissing. I'm not going to make the same mistakes as last time. I only want this relationship to move forward if she wants it to move forward, too.

And I think she does. But until she's ready, I will patiently wait for her, no matter how long it takes, and no matter how much I just want to grab her and kiss her.

Zoe was looking out her window, and then she turns her focus to me. "It feels weird to be out doing normal stuff while we have an active mission."

I flex my jaw. There are plenty of moments as an intelligence operative that are spent waiting. But this does feel different. Probably because we've got so many resources dedicated to finding the men who've been stealing the Trust pieces, yet so far, we've come up with nothing. No leads at all to where they might be or where they are headed next. It's almost as if they've disappeared.

All we know is that they haven't attempted to get the Trust pieces in either Dublin or Belgrade. And that the Trust piece we placed a tracker on in Belgrade is still in Savović's mansion, so it either didn't sell in the auction or wasn't put up for sale.

And because we know so little, it's worrying me and everyone else at the CSA. Enough that we've started to come up with alternate plans.

None of that needs to taint tonight, though. I paste on a smile, which helps me to feel it, and say, "Agreed. But since we don't have any actionable intel…" I shrug.

When we get out of the car at my mom's house, I try to not walk next to Zoe as if I'm constantly ready to reach out and help if she stumbles. She's gotten so much stronger over the past week since her injury so she needs it so much less. And I know she won't appreciate me acting as though she's weak or incapable. She'll want to walk like everything is normal and she isn't struggling, and I respect that.

Even if I didn't already know that everyone is out back, I would know it from the sounds of something fun going on. So I lead Zoe around to the side of the house. Before I open the gate that leads into the backyard, I stop and look at Zoe. "Are you sure you're feeling up to this?"

"Ledger," she says, "don't baby me. I'm good. Fastest healer in the, well, east."

Her healing has gone remarkably fast, just like Nehir, the nurse in Ankara, guessed it would. But she's still human, and I know she still hurts. And I know the boot is still awkward and that she hates it. But I grin, nod, and say, "Okay, then, let's do this." Then, I open the gate and lead her into the backyard I played in for most of my childhood.

Jace, Mackenzie, Miles, and Charlie are throwing a football on the grassy area, and Jace yells, "Heads up!" as he tosses it to me.

I catch the ball and tuck it under one arm. I point at Jace and say to Zoe, "I'm pretty sure you've run into my older brother, Jace, a time or two in the field. That's his fiancée, Mackenzie, over there." I gesture up at the deck. "That's my oldest brother, Blake, at the grill, and, of course, my second oldest brother, Emerson, and my mom at the table with my two-year-old niece, Heidi."

From my blind spot, I'm suddenly tackled. About the time my backside hits the grass, I realize it's Miles. I can't believe he caught me so off guard. Enough off-guard that I'm not only on the ground, but he also stole the football from my arm.

He bounces right up, football tucked under one arm, and shakes Zoe's hand with the other. "Hi. I don't think we've had the pleasure of meeting. I'm Ledger's older brother, Miles. I was born the year before him."

I get up and steal the football right back. Then I clap

him on the shoulder enough that it nearly knocks him off balance, too. "He was born twelve minutes before me."

"Yes, but in the previous year."

Zoe's eyebrows raise. "December thirty-first baby?"

"I was," Miles says, putting a hand on his chest before putting the hand on my shoulder. "Little brother here was a January first baby."

"And guess who can beat who in a race?"

Miles is saved from having to admit that I can sail past him in a race any time any day when Charlie, Mackenzie, and Jace reach us.

"Hi, I'm Charlie," my sister says, skipping the hand shaking and going straight for a hug that she, thankfully, remembers to give a little more gently than her normal. "It's so great to meet you in person! Especially after talking to you over comms. Plus, I've been hearing so much about you for, what?" She glances at me. "A year and a half?"

I catch the smile that Zoe tries to hide. She has to know I've talked about her— I know she saw the white board in the office that shows how many missions each of us has won. And since we got back from Turkey, every moment I haven't been working, I've spent with her at her hotel. Of course I've talked about her. Non-stop. I'm not embarrassed by it.

Jace and Mackenzie both shake Zoe's hand, and Jace says, "It's good to see you again when we aren't trading intel or evading capture."

We start heading toward the deck to say hi to the others, when Zoe says in a low voice, "You have so much family."

"Just how I like it."

She nods as we walk up the stairs. I know the boot is awkward, so I try to go a little slower than normal. "It's nice. Um…" She pauses a moment, so I glance at her. Her brows are drawn together in confusion. "I'm surprised you don't live like operatives. You're all… living normal lives."

"Yep. Which proves it's possible."

"But when you're a field operative, having people you're close to makes you vulnerable."

"I disagree," I want to say more, but we're already at the grill, so I say, "And this is Blake. Blake, I'd like you to meet Zoe."

He sets down the spatula to shake her hand and say, "I'm glad to meet the woman who enchanted my brother and has him smiling like a fool."

Okay, I might be a little embarrassed about that. I grab the spatula and peek under one of the burgers. "You're burning them."

In one swift move, Blake has the spatula in his hand and my arm pinned behind my back, which just shows that he can disarm an opponent as easily as any of us. No CSA experience needed. He releases my arm and we give each other playful shoves. "The grill: not part of your mission, bro."

I turn to Zoe, and in a stage whisper, say, "And you thought I didn't like my mission being encroached on." Before I turn around, Heidi stands up on the bench where she was sitting, coloring at the table, and leaps onto my back. I grab hold of her legs and turn so that she and Zoe can see each other. "And this is my niece, Monkey."

"Silly Uncle Ledger," Heidi says, completely butchering her L's and her R's in a way that I never knew could be adorable until she came along. "My name is Heidi!"

"Right," I say. "Heidi Monkey Lancaster."

She giggles and slides down from my back onto the bench again, then goes back to coloring.

"And of course, you've met my mom, Evelyn, and my brother, Emerson."

"Yes," Zoe says as she shakes my brother's hand. "I just didn't know you were Ledger's brother at the time."

My mom sits down with Zoe on the bench at the table and says, "I've been trying to let you rest and not have to think about work, so I haven't gotten a chance to thank you in person for all your work on the mission with Ledger. I'm sorry you got injured. Ledger says you're going back into work tomorrow. Are you feeling up to it?"

"I've never felt more up for anything. A week is a long time to be off work."

"And your injuries?"

"The doc says I'll have to keep wearing the boot for several weeks, but the ribs and spleen are healing quite well."

I know it's been so hard for Zoe to stay away from work. I get it. I would be going stir-crazy if I were her, too.

Blake announces that the burgers are ready, and we all bring the sides and condiments from the fridge in the house to the outside table. Everyone is chatting, like normal, and Zoe is joining in, for the most part. I know she grew up in several foster homes where there were multiple kids, but she's been out of the system for eight years. So she's been the only one in her "family" for that long. I can tell that this is very much not what she's used to.

Mackenzie is looking at the potato salad on Jace's plate that he's covered in mustard like she's equal parts curious and repulsed by it, so Jace gets a fork full and holds it out for Mackenzie to try. She gives in and takes a bite, then actually looks surprised that she likes it and gives Jace a kiss. Charlie has an elbow up on the table, her chin in her hand, watching them all wistfully.

Then she says to everyone, "So, who do you think will be the next of us to get married?"

"The twins," Emerson says.

Blake grunts. "Like that will happen. Miles is a player and Ledger won't ever give up his freedom."

Charlie says, "I don't know. Ledger is in the middle of his enemies-to—" I kick her under the table, so she finishes with "in the middle of his *Zoe* era, so you never know."

"And," Mackenzie says, with her burger halfway to her mouth, "Ledger is the only other person here who brought a date, so…"

"Even though he's the oldest," I say, "I think Blake will be the last because he is just going to growl at anyone who might potentially want to date him."

"Nope," Heidi pipes in. "He's going to be sooo nice 'cause I want a mom and he said he'll find me one."

Everyone looks at Blake.

"I said 'someday.' So don't go getting all cheerleader-y about it."

Zoe turns to Heidi. "I don't have a mom, either."

Heidi's face lights up. "We're twins! Did your mom die, too?"

Zoe nods. "She did."

"Mine died when I was a tiny baby. But she gave me to daddy because he loves me the best." She looks up at Blake and grins at him with a smile smeared with ketchup.

"You've got that right," Blake says.

"So a stork didn't bring you?" Zoe asks. I had forgotten that I told her that.

Heidi looks confused, then shrugs. "Charlie, you tell her. I hungry," she says, then takes a bite out of the piece of watermelon she's holding.

Charlie looks to Blake with an eyebrow raised, and he nods his head. It's his story, not mine, so I'd never tell it without his permission, either. Then Charlie turns to Zoe. "Blake went on a date with Heidi's mom once. He didn't know she had a baby until she showed up with Heidi. He and Heidi's mom weren't a good match, so they never went on a second date, but my brother here," Charlie says, clapping him on the shoulder, "was apparently adorable with Heidi.

"So, a couple of months later when she needed help and had no one to turn to, she showed up at his door and asked if he could take her for a week. And because Blake is a good guy under all that gruff exterior, he said yes. She didn't come back for six weeks, though, and by then, we'd all fallen in love with Heidi."

"Cuz I'm lovable," Heidi says as she goes in for another bite of watermelon.

"That you are," Charlie says.

Blake clears his throat. "When she came back, it was with paperwork to give me full custody of her. She found out she had terminal cancer, and the doctors thought she might only have days to live. She didn't have any family and didn't want Heidi to go into foster care. I didn't want her to, either."

I glance at Zoe and see her looking at Blake with curiosity and admiration. Like she's seeing him differently.

"None of us did," my mom says.

"So we all rallied together to help," Charlie says, "and now we get to love Heidi forever."

My eyes are still on Zoe, and I can see that the story is making her emotional and that she isn't okay with everyone seeing her get emotional. My mom is watching Zoe closely, too, and it hits me that she probably understands so much more about how Zoe grew up than I do.

I'm trying to think of a way to change the subject but come up empty. My mom doesn't, though. She says, "If it's not Blake, maybe Emerson."

"He is the nicest and most adult of us all," Jace says.

"Or Charlie could fall for someone at any time," my mom says. "You never know."

"Well, there is someone I kinda have a crush on," Charlie says, dragging out the word "kinda."

Everyone is whooping and Charlie is blushing and I'm pretty sure Charlie never would have made that announcement in front of everyone if she hadn't also noticed that Zoe was uncomfortable and was looking to take the attention off her. Charlie's amazing about things like that.

"Tell us more about him!" Mackenzie says, "What's his name? What's he like? What does he do for a living? How did you meet him?"

"His name is Owen. I don't know his last name. He's got dark hair, some scruff, kind eyes, a happy smile, and… I really don't know much more about him— he just moved into the townhome attached to mine in the middle of last week. I don't know what he does for a living. I've seen him on three different days so far. On one of the days, he was wearing a suit. Another day, he was wearing construction clothes— work boots, jeans, a t-shirt, all covered in dust. And the third time, he was wearing gym clothes."

"His job has a very confusing dress code," Mackenzie says.

"So," Miles says, "either he is a member of a *Village People* cover band and sings *YMCA* on the weekends, or he's moonlighting as a superhero with the worst disguise ever."

Charlie laughs. "I'm sure it's one of those. To answer how we met… Um, do you remember how the washer went out in my place last week? Well, I came home from the laundromat with two garbage bags full of wet laundry—"

"—because your dryer still works—" Jace cut in.

"—yep, and they were heavy and awkward. One of the bags caught on a thorn from the rose bush, and I left a trail, all Hansel-and-Gretel-like, of clothes from the roses all the way to my front door. I didn't notice until I got to my door just as Owen was pulling in."

"Oh, no," Mackenzie says. "Please tell me that bag didn't have your 'delicates' in it."

Charlie nods. "They were right where the bag tore open. Okay, we don't need more of that story because I've already done a pretty good job repressing it and I'd like to keep it that way. Let's just say that I only know him well enough to have a tiny crush on him."

I sit up a little straighter. "But do you know him well enough to know if he's good enough for you?"

"You won't go out with him if he's not, right?" Emerson says.

"Do you want me to question him for you?" Blake asks. "Because I will. I'll find out what he's really like. See if he's good enough."

Charlie raises her hands, palms out. "*Everyone*. Thank you. But no— I don't need that. I don't even know him well enough for that yet."

"It sounds like you need to do some recon," Zoe says.

Charlie practically chokes. "Like *spy* on him?"

"You literally grew up in a family of spies," Zoe says looking around at everyone. "Does it really seem strange to you?"

"I can't use agency resources for that. It's illegal."

"No, but you can do your own recon, like go through his garbage. Once it's out on the street, it's fair game. You can learn a lot by going through someone's garbage."

"I'll keep that in mind," Charlie says.

Mackenzie has been on her phone since she asked Charlie for the guy's name. She turns the screen toward Charlie. "Is this him?"

Charlie leans in close, then takes the phone. "It is! How did you find him?"

"I'm really good at social media," Mackenzie says. "That's his Instagram."

Everyone, even my mom and Heidi, gets up and crowds around Charlie, looking at the phone. He's a decent-looking guy from his profile picture. But that doesn't tell much of the story, of course.

Zoe points at his short bio. "He's an architectural restoration specialist. He 'restores historical buildings to their former glory.'"

"Oh!" Charlie says as she taps on the first picture, which shows him wearing construction clothes, including a hard hat, in front of a building. "He's restoring the historic theater downtown! So when I saw him in the suit, maybe he was addressing the city council or at a fund-raising gala or something."

"He's cute," Mackenzie says. "And this picture was posted just twenty-seven minutes ago." She gasps. "We should go see if he's still there."

Charlie hands the phone back to Mackenzie. "And do what? Because I'm not ready to bump into him and have a conversation."

"You could just observe," Miles suggests. "Try to get a sense of what he's like."

Charlie pauses a moment, then nods slowly. "Okay."

"Yes!" Mackenzie pumps her fist. "We are going on a recon mission. Who's in? Zoe? Will you come with us?"

Zoe looks shocked that they are asking her to join in. If she knew my family at all, she wouldn't be. I love the smile that spreads across her face right before she nods.

"And if Zoe is in," I say, "I'm in."

My mom says that she and Heidi are going to stay back and have a treasure hunt, if Blake wants to join in on Operation: Spy on Charlie's Crush.

Twenty-five minutes later, dinner is cleaned up, Charlie is wearing a mic and a button camera, and Blake, Emerson, Miles, and Jace are in Blake's Honda CR-V half a block away. All of us are wearing comms units. They aren't as nice as the ones the agency has, but they're plenty good enough for this kind of range.

Zoe, Charlie, Mackenzie, and I are sneaking from where we parked at an ice cream shop next to the theater to a couple of pallets of bricks that we plan to hide behind. We've got a separate video camera to place on the bricks, and we've got a tablet both here and with my brothers in the SUV, both showing feeds from the brick camera and Charlie's button cam.

On our front-line team, we've got two field operatives, one handler (who is very experienced in setting up successful ops), and one physical therapy tech. Which, granted, isn't a skill particularly needed for this op, but I remember how good Mackenzie was at evading her FBI tail not long after I saw her for the first time.

Our backup team contains two field operatives, a brilliant analyst, and a dentist. Also not a helpful skill in this situation, but if we ever needed to disarm a bomb, he does have some impressively steady and precise hands.

For the amount of skill crouched behind these bricks

and in the compact SUV half a block away, you'd think nothing could possibly go wrong.

My gut tells me, though, that it will. Zoe gives me a look that tells me she thinks there is a high chance of that, too, and that she's going to wish she had a big bucket of popcorn to eat as it does.

CHAPTER 26
CROUCHING SPIES, HIDDEN CRUSH

We've surveilled the area, and Owen, the guy Charlie is interested in, isn't outside at the historic theater. He isn't gone, though, because the front door to the theater is propped open, and Charlie recognizes the truck out front as his. So he must be inside. Which, honestly, isn't surprising. Almost all time on any stakeout is spent staring at a building, so this is completely normal.

What isn't normal is being on a stakeout with civilians. Especially when those civilians you are crouched with behind a couple of pallets of bricks are the sister and the future sister-in-law of the guy you've been falling in love with.

At least I assume that's what this is— I've never actually been in love before to know how it feels. All I know is that a year and a half ago, in Moldova, I didn't think it was real, and now it feels very real. Everything about now is different. My feelings toward Ledger are stronger. Deeper. And even when I'm focusing on something else entirely, he's on my mind. I even dream about him.

I keep imagining the two of us doing regular things together. Sharing a place, giving each other a kiss before heading off to work in the mornings— even if work is taking us to two very different parts of the world, going to the grocery store, practicing counter-surveillance techniques during date nights, decrypting coded messages over breakfast, conducting threat assessments on our neighbors. Regular, everyday stuff.

The strangest thing about this past week is that I've spent it away from work but near Ledger. And if I was given the choice of which of the two I had to give up while recovering, I would give up work. Not Ledger. It has never even been fathomable to me that I would *ever* choose a person over my job.

Yet here I am.

Maybe it's just me, though. Because even though Ledger has been at my side this entire week I've been off work, he hasn't tried to kiss me. Not once. We were only in Moldova for three days. It felt like eons longer, but that was how long it was. *Three days.* He kissed me on Day Two.

Yet he's been at my side in my hotel for seven days and nothing. Since leaving for Dublin on the Ambassador's plane, Ledger and I have gone from being practically enemies to becoming friends to becoming something well beyond friends. At least I want it to be more than friends. But the fact that he hasn't kissed me yet makes me wonder if he doesn't. Maybe he's fine with the way things are now.

But what do I know? I don't have any real relationship experience. Every relationship I've had has been fake on some level. I don't have enough familiarity with any of this to know.

And I definitely don't have enough familiarity when it comes to hanging out with family. I've met Evelyn, Charlie, Emerson, and Jace all as Intelligence Operative Zoe Steele. I've worked with them on a mission now. I was starting to get a little comfortable around them, almost like coworkers.

But here, I am not Intelligence Operative Zoe Steele. I'm just Zoe. Or Ledger's Girlfriend Zoe. Right? Is that what I'm called at this point in the relationship? Does it automatically happen at a certain point, or is it something you have to agree to in words? I have no idea.

And I'm not quite sure how to act. Operative Zoe knows how to act in any situation. Girlfriend Zoe? Not so much. All my knowledge and experience should translate to this situation, yet I feel a bit out of place. Like an outsider. As if Ledger's family is a rugby team that was down a player and pulled me in from the sidelines to play for their side, assuming I know all the rules, yet I don't actually know any of them.

Not knowing is like having your bra clasp break while undercover at a black tie event—uncomfortable and embarrassing when all eyes are on you.

Thankfully, they're not. Charlie is peeking around the corner, even though we have a surveillance camera on top of the bricks, aimed in that direction, that is broadcasting to the tablet in Mackenzie's hands and to the one in the SUV with Ledger's brothers. Everyone else's eyes are on the screen.

I'm crouched on my left leg with my right leg and its cumbersome boot awkwardly stretched out to the side. Ledger is crouched next to me. His leg is brushing up against mine, and it feels like it's electric, sending thrilling currents up my leg. My upper arm is brushing against his, and his face is only about fifteen inches from mine. All I want to do right now is turn forty-five degrees, wrap my arms around his neck, and kiss him good and hard on the lips. Even if it knocks us both over onto the dirt-covered asphalt and compromises the mission. Even if it hurts my broken rib and bruised spleen.

Of course, I *do* care about this mission. I care about Charlie and Mackenzie, even though I barely know them. I know that Ledger cares about this mission, too. And if this thing between us is real for him, too, I don't want to mess it up.

But I have to know if he wants our relationship to be something more, and I don't want to wait any longer to find out. Ledger's arm is at his side, in the small space between our bodies. My hand is on my knee, but I drop it to the space where Ledger's is, causing our arms to touch from nearly shoulder to wrist. The sensation sends a buzzing up my arm and right into my chest. I'm barely breathing as I bump the back of my hand ever so gently against his. It's subtle enough that he could act like he thought the touch was accidental and not respond at all.

Almost immediately, he responds by brushing my knuckles with his before moving his hand to the other side of mine, sliding his fingers into mine. I nearly whimper at the touch. It means he, too, wants our relationship to be something more than the friends we've become.

It's not like we haven't touched before— the man even carried me when I was injured— but this touch carries so much more weight. He would carry any injured person because that's the kind of guy he is. But this? Hand holding? It feels like he's choosing *me*. Only me. It makes my chest feel like it's soaring.

"So do you live in town, too?" Mackenzie has turned her head to look at me over her shoulder.

I've been so deep in my own world that her question catches me off-guard and I drop Ledger's hand. "Oh. Um, no— I usually live in McLean, close to CIA headquarters."

Charlie turns toward me, too, her eyebrows drawn together. "*Usually?* Do you not always live in the same place?"

I shake my head. "I live in a hotel and don't always choose the same one."

"You *live* there?" Charlie says. "Like, temporarily?"

"No, permanently. I'm not home much, so it doesn't feel like it matters where I am."

"So," Mackenzie says, "you just moved in all your stuff?"

"Everything I own fits into two suitcases— a carry-on size and a check-in size." Both Mackenzie and Charlie are just looking at me, seeming baffled. So I explain more. "I can check out whenever I go on an away mission and just leave my extra suitcase in the trunk of my car. Then I check back in when I get home. I never have to worry about watering a plant, feeding a pet, or cleaning. I'm good to go at any moment. It's perfect for a field operative."

"Doesn't that get expensive?" Mackenzie asks.

"I mean, I don't stay in nice hotels— I only need a place to sleep. And I am away on missions *a lot*, so there are many nights every month where I'm not paying for a place at all. Plus, I rack up a lot of points."

"But you don't even have one hotel that you call home?" Mackenzie asks.

I shake my head.

Charlie's eyebrows are still drawn together. "How do you cook food?"

"Oh," Mackenzie says. "Do you have a waffle maker? Because I can show you how to make the best cornbread ever in a waffle maker."

Now, my eyebrows are the ones drawn together. "I... don't have a waffle maker. I don't cook food. A lot of times I have a mini microwave, though."

They're both quiet for a moment before Charlie says, "You grew up in foster care, right? Have you ever been able to pick your own comforter, curtains, furniture, anything?"

I shift my feet. "No."

"Don't you want to be able to?"

The answer I always tell myself is *No. I don't care about any of those things.* But deep down, truthfully, I do. So I nod. But I'm twenty-six years old, and I don't have the first clue how to pick out home things for myself because

I've never done it before. It's embarrassing. Admitting it would feel like admitting that I don't know how to cook toast or boil water. Sure, I bought my own bedding when I first left foster care. But I found it at a thrift store, and the gray and blue plaid comforter was the only option they had.

"We should take you shopping, then!" Mackenzie says. "Me, you, Charlie, and my friend, Livi, because she's really good at stuff like that."

Charlie nods. "Everyone deserves to have a place where they get to choose at least one thing there. Something that makes them happy."

I cock my head and try to swallow down the rising emotion. Would they really just accept me into their circle this easily? They hardly know me.

Charlie peeks around the corner and gives a quiet yelp. "He's coming out!"

Ledger and I both lean forward to see the tablet in Mackenzie's hands. He's walking out of the building with a little boy who is probably five years old and a woman who I'm guessing is the boy's mom.

"He's married?" I'm pretty sure it's Blake's voice coming through our comms.

"He's not married," Charlie says.

"Yeah, he's not paying any attention to the woman," Emerson says in our earpieces. "His entire focus is on the kid."

I know exactly what is happening because something similar happened to me as a child plenty of times. It was one of the few perks of being a foster kid. "The kid is fascinated with construction stuff. Owen is giving him a tour. Showing him all the cool equipment."

"Aww," Charlie says. "That is so cute."

We don't have sound wired where Owen is, so we all just watch the screen as Owen talks to the kid, crouched down, so he's at his height. Then he hands him something that looks like it was either a piece of the original brick or tile or maybe even a piece of trim. The kid looks at him with wide eyes and a face full of wonder. Then the kid hugs Owen, and there's a chorus of *Aww*s from everyone, including the guys in the SUV. Although theirs sound not quite as genuine.

The kid and his mom wave goodbye and head away, and Owen starts walking in our direction. He pulls a tool from his belt— a pair of pliers, maybe?— and tosses it in the air, spinning, catching it, and repeating, all while whistling a jaunty tune.

"Oh my gosh," Mackenzie says, "he's as cheerful as you are."

"If you're both in the same room," Ledger says, "we might need to install some solar panels to harness all the sunshine."

Charlie just turns to us and flashes a grin. "Okay, we can go now."

"Don't you want to go talk to him?" Mackenzie asks.

Charlie looks horrified. "No! I'm not prepared for that. We came to get a sense of what kind of a guy he is. We got that. Now let's go."

We all look at the tablet in Mackenzie's hands to watch for an opening so we can leave undetected. But instead of turning his back to us so we can leave, Owen misses catching the pliers he's tossing. He tries to recover, though, and instead hits the pliers in a way that sends them sailing out in front of him, and they skid to a stop just past the pallets of bricks, right next to Charlie. Owen immediately looks around, probably self-conscious as to whether anyone witnessed it.

For a beat, we all just stare at the tool.

In our ears, Jace says, "Charlie. Pick them up and go give them to him."

"I can't!" she hisses. "What am I supposed to do, just pop up from hiding? That would be so awkward!"

"I don't know," Blake says. "It doesn't sound as awkward as him coming to pick them up himself and seeing the four of you hunkered down behind the bricks."

"It's okay," Emerson says in our ears. "We've got your back. You can do this."

Charlie takes a deep breath and then turns partially toward us. "Okay, fine. Stay on alert for an emergency extraction, though. Listen for me to say the phrase 'Mango Tango' in our conversation." She reaches forward, picks up the pliers, and stands up as Owen gets within five feet of us. Then she says, "Hi, neighbor."

Owen startles at seeing Charlie suddenly appear, and I am glued to the screen in Mackenzie's hands, right along with Ledger.

"Sorry," Charlie says, "I was just walking along and had to tie my shoe, and then I saw your pliers, or whatever these are."

Owen glances down at Charlie's shoes, which don't have laces. He doesn't say anything, though.

I whisper to Ledger, "She could never be a field operative, could she?"

"She's a brilliant handler. Actually, she's pretty brilliant in general. But no. She doesn't like to be seen, which is why she's always on comms and never in the field."

Charlie keeps talking, a million miles a minute, a nervous smile never leaving her face. "Anyway, I figured that you picked up my dropped, uh, clothes and brought them to me, so I thought I would return the favor and pick up your dropped pliers."

"Thanks," he says, taking them from her, playing with them a moment, and then putting them back in his tool belt.

"So, you're fixing this building?" I'm hearing Charlie double— in real life and through the mic she's got hidden in her necklace.

"Yep! I'm restoring her to her former elegance. With modern amenities, of course. I just gave a little boy a 'before' tour. Would you like one, too?"

For a moment, I think Charlie will respond with, "Mango Tango! Mango Tango!" but then Jace says in our ears, "Tell him yes!"

"I'd love that," Charlie says.

They turn to head back toward the building, and Ledger whispers, "Maybe we should go back to the car to wait for her."

"Good idea," Mackenzie says. "Then we can get Zoe off

that broken leg. Charlie is wearing the camera and mic so we can watch from anywhere."

A loud squeak sounds from Charlie.

"Okay," Mackenzie says into her mic. "We won't watch. You just get your flirt on, girl!"

"Take as long as you want," Ledger says. "We'll be waiting at the car."

Then Ledger slides his hand into mine like it's the most natural thing in the world. I never thought this could feel so right. And so nice.

We watch the screen until Charlie and Owen have their backs to us and are far enough away that we can leave without them seeing us, and then we stand and stroll back to the car. Well, Mackenzie and Ledger stroll. I do more of a step, clomp, step, clomp. But Ledger's hand is in mine, so I could have boots on both feet and I wouldn't care.

CHAPTER 27
COMPETITIVE KISSING
LEDGER

Zoe and I are leaning against the railing of the deck at my mom's house after everyone else left. It's dark, the stars are out, crickets are chirping, and it's the perfect temperature outside. I point toward a tall maple in the backyard. "See that tree? When I was about ten, Charlie got a Frisbee stuck in it. So, she did what any self-respecting kid would do and took off her shoe and threw it up to knock the Frisbee free."

"Let me guess. Then the shoe was stuck, too."

"Yep. And then her other shoe. And then a soccer ball, a water bottle, a tennis racket, and a stuffed pig with wings. I tell you, *nothing* was falling down from that tree. So I figured I'd climb up and rescue all the items." I chuckle. "It turned out that something *could* fall down from that tree. Broke my leg right here."

"Did you get a boot as cool as this one?" Zoe asks, holding up her booted foot like she's modeling footwear.

"Cooler. Mine was pink, and I put Ben Ten stickers all over it."

Zoe laughs, and I soak in the sound. I soak in just being with her. "I remember that show." She glances over at me, then looks at the back yard again. "You all seem pretty protective of Charlie. Is that an older brother thing? Since she's the youngest?"

"Yeah," I say. "It probably is. But it's probably also because she was kidnapped as a kid."

"What?" Zoe says. "When?"

"She was three. My dad was director of the CSA, our personal information was leaked, and some bozo thought it would be smart to kidnap Charlie to use as leverage to get their demands met." I swear, I can almost feel Zoe's confirmation that having people you care about makes you vulnerable. I continue so she'll understand why it doesn't. "But what it really did was made every intelligence and law enforcement agency in the US band together to go after them."

"I can't believe I don't know anything about this. How did it happen?" She pauses for a second, then asks, "Are you okay to talk about it?"

"Of course," I tell her. "It was a long time ago— I mean, I was five at the time. Charlie was three, and Blake was eight. We were at a park, and the three of us were kind of off to the side of the playground equipment, playing with tractors in the wood chips. Our nanny was there, too, and she was by where Miles, Emerson, and Jace were climbing on the equipment.

"So, me, Charlie, and Blake were all scooping up wood

chips and making big piles with them when a woman walked by with a dog on a leash, headed toward a walking path by some trees. Blake was obsessed with dogs back then, so he got up to ask the woman if he could pet the dog, and Charlie went with him. The woman was already near the trees, and there were a lot of bushes around there, too, so I couldn't really see them.

"And then after a moment, something made me get up to go see the dog, too. So I left the tractors behind and walked over there. As soon as I rounded the bushes, I could see the woman and the dog and Blake petting it. Charlie was maybe twenty feet away, looking at something on the ground by a shrub. Probably a bug.

"Then I noticed two men step out from the trees nearby. The taller guy reached down, wrapped one arm around Charlie's middle, put the other hand over her mouth, and just picked her up.

"He just *picked her up*. I remember the shock and horror I felt. That anyone could just come and lift her up and she had no choice in the matter. I was stunned and frozen for a moment. The road wasn't too far away on that side, and the men were running with her right toward a van. I started screaming and chasing after them."

I shake my head just remembering it again. "But they were so fast. And my legs were so short. I ran with all my energy, but they were so much quicker.

"And then they were gone. I remember whirling around and saw that Blake was right on my heels, and the nanny and my other brothers weren't far behind. No one else was at the park that day. I didn't even see the woman with the dog again. But we all saw the van pull away, taking Charlie away with it."

My arms are on the railing of the deck, and Zoe places a hand on my forearm. The comfort from that touch might be the only thing that makes me continue. "I had nightmares every night for months after and less frequently for a lot more years. Every time, the bad guys were there, so easily picking Charlie up. Or sometimes it was me. Or one of my brothers. The location sometimes changed, but always, someone was picked up just as easily as I could pick up one of the little toy tractors I'd been playing with."

I'm surprised that all the emotions of the moment came flooding back. I haven't told this story often, and it's been a good long while since I last did. And I've definitely never shared the part about the nightmares or how it made me feel.

It hits me how comfortable I am talking to Zoe about stuff I normally wouldn't talk to anyone about. In the past year and a half, I wouldn't have guessed that would ever be the case, but things have changed between us. We'll likely always be competitive, but only about stupid things. Not about the things that matter.

I clear my throat. "Anyway, spoiler alert, we got her back and she was unharmed. But she'd been gone for a full twenty-four hours, and we had all felt pretty helpless during that entire day. I'm pretty sure we'll be overprotective of Charlie until the day we die."

"That's beautiful."

I turn toward her, leaning my side against the railing.

"Beautiful? That isn't a word I've heard used before in relation to Charlie's kidnapping."

She turns to face me. "Well, not the shared family trauma, obviously. But how bonded you all are. You all know without a doubt that your family has your back and that a lot of other people do, too. It's beautiful."

I gaze at Zoe for a long moment, knowing that she has maybe never experienced that. It's hard to imagine what it would be like to grow up in a world where that wasn't a given. Yet, that is her reality, and it sends every protective instinct I have in me into overdrive. I want to be that for her. The person who she knows, without a doubt, has her back no matter the situation. The person who will always be there for her.

"Plus," she says, "it explains a lot."

I cock my head. "Like what?"

She lifts a shoulder in a shrug. "Like your need to be strong."

"No, it doesn't."

"Ledger, she was kidnapped when you were at an age where you could've been picked up and carted off, too. You can't tell me that didn't affect the choices you've made. For one thing, I mean, look at you. You're the least pick-me-up-and-cart-me-off person I've ever met."

My biceps flex involuntarily.

"It's probably also why you try so hard to never be in a situation where someone could take advantage of you. Why you make sure you're always strong enough to fight back. Maybe it's also what drives you to be competitive.

Why you like being the one to save the day, not the one who needs saving."

"Is that such a bad thing?"

She shakes her head slowly. "I think that is also a very beautiful thing."

Her eyes rove over the muscles in my arms and then my shoulders. When they get to my chest, my pecs are now the muscles flexing involuntarily. She is standing so close. The moon and the stars bathe her in a silvery light, her eyelashes casting a shadow on her smooth cheekbones. She is so beautifully perfect.

The rise and fall of her chest tells me that her breathing has picked up. She reaches up and runs her fingers along the side of my neck, across my shoulder, and comes to a rest on my chest. The slight touch is making all my nerve endings fire, sending a cascade of electricity and heat through me. She is intoxicating. When we left for Dublin, I thought I was an impenetrable vault. It turns out that she is the safecracker.

Her eyes come back up to meet mine, flick to my lips for a moment, and then are back on my eyes, searching. One side of her lips pulls up in a sly smile. "Speaking of competitiveness, why haven't you kissed me already? I'd think you'd want to claim the win for being the first to initiate."

I shake my head and reach out to brush a lock of hair off her cheek with my fingertips, then skim my knuckles from the base of her ear down, along her jaw, feeling her smooth skin beneath mine. "That's a win I've wanted you to claim. No matter how long it takes. No matter how many days we spend together without you making a move. No matter how much I'm dying to kiss you every second I'm around you. This one is your—"

My sentence is cut off by her lips pressing against mine. A slight moan escapes me at how good it feels to finally have her kissing me. She had blown my mind with the kiss she gave me in the hall of Savović's mansion when we were trying to not get caught by security. That kiss had felt like it was a need we'd had for ages. She had brushed that one off as being fake, just born of necessity, but I had felt then that her emotions had been mirroring mine.

This one has that same need, that urgency behind it. But it is so much more because we have become so much more. This kiss is filling a well inside me that I hadn't realized had been so empty since that first day in Moldova. Her lips are moving against mine in a rhythm that feels like it's matching our heartbeats.

There is so much longing and passion and connection and bliss being poured into this kiss, and I can't tell how much of it is coming from me and how much is coming from Zoe. All I know is that everything feels so perfect and so right.

I wrap my arms around her, holding her close as we're kissing and she's tickling the hair at the back of my neck, sending the best kind of shivers up my back. My lips leave hers long enough to place a soft kiss just below her ear before I plant a trail of kisses down her neck.

Then my lips are back on hers. I don't want this to ever end.

CHAPTER 28
HEARTSTRINGS AND HOME THINGS

ZOE

ife is good, I think as I plop onto my couch. *My couch*. In *my* apartment. Four days ago, after having dinner with Ledger's family and doing surveillance on Charlie's love interest, I couldn't stop thinking about how great it would be to actually have my own place. A place I could call "home."

I spend money on almost nothing, so I have a good amount saved up. I started searching online for apartments to rent, and each one got me more excited than the last. Then I found one that was currently unoccupied and ready to move into immediately. It had a month-to-month contract, too, so it didn't require a huge commitment, and the rent was less than I'd paid in hotel costs over the past month. It's not far from work, either. I didn't think finding one this perfect was even possible.

I contacted the owner right then and signed the

contract the next day. I've never had the universe align for me like that before.

So, I've had a pretty monumental week. I kissed Ledger, met all his family, went back to work (finally), saw Ledger every night, checked out this apartment, signed the contract, got my keys, ordered a bed that was delivered last night, and went shopping with Charlie, Mackenzie, and Mackenzie's friend Livi today, buying so many of the things I needed for this place.

There's a knock at the door— *my* apartment door— and I would skip over and answer it if *skipping* and *this boot* weren't incompatible, even though I was probably five the last time I actually skipped. I throw open the door, and Ledger is standing there, holding a large gift bag by the handles with one hand, a bag with food in the other, and a smile on his face that has to be one of the most beautiful things on the planet.

I step over the threshold and plant a kiss on those perfect lips of his, and he wraps his arms around me, pulling me close, the bags he's holding bumping into my backside. I take a quick moment to soak in how great it feels before I step back into my apartment, throw an arm out wide, and say, "Welcome to my humble home."

We are standing in my living room— *my* living room— and he takes it all in, smiling as much as I am. It's all open to the kitchen, on the left, and the bedroom and bathroom are down a hall to the right. He walks over to the small kitchen table which, along with my couch, was delivered less than an hour ago. He holds up one bag and says, "I brought soup and rolls." Then he holds up the bag in his other hand. "And a housewarming gift."

"For me?" I ask, taking the bag from him.

He nods, and I pull out the coziest throw blanket in a deep purple color. It is so soft that I can't resist the urge to hold it up to my cheek, letting it feel how soft it is, too. I wrap it around both of us, cocooning us together for a moment as I tell him thank you and how much I love it.

And kiss. Obviously.

I've seen plenty of pictures where people artfully drape a throw blanket on their couch, and it always looks nice. I think it makes it feel like it's a place for people to actually live in, not just look at. I can't say I get it right— it mostly looks like I tried to put a blanket on a sleeping pig— but I love it.

Ledger sits down on my couch, stretching his arms out along the back of it. I have to admit, as I was shopping for a couch, I looked at each one, trying to imagine exactly this — how it would look with Ledger relaxing in it. I think I chose perfectly. "How was shopping?" he asks.

I sit on the couch next to him but with my good leg bent and resting on the couch so I can look right at him. "At first, I thought it was going to go horribly. I didn't know Livi at all, I barely know Mackenzie, and only know Charlie a bit more than I know Mackenzie. And I was just so clueless about everything."

I shake my head just thinking back on the whole thing. I was embarrassed, yet I'm somehow not embarrassed at all to tell the whole story to Ledger. "I mean, the skills that I have are pretty impressive, but they're all related to being an intelligence operative. I've got no skills that make me good at shopping. I was such a fish out of water there. A fish out of water wearing a gigantic boot. The one who didn't know anything and was completely unskilled. Which is a pretty uncomfortable feeling, by the way.

"Anyway, the entire time, I didn't show that I was good at one single thing, yet they all still seemed to enjoy being around me and liked me and wanted to spend time with me."

Ledger is cocking his head with his eyebrows drawn together, like he's confused, which tells me we are on the same page. So I continue. "When we first meet, they ask what kinds of things I need. It's not like I have a list, so I was trying to think about what I use at a typical hotel that actually belongs to the hotel. I start by saying that I had a bed delivered last night, but I couldn't sleep here because I didn't have any bedding yet.

"So they take me to a store to pick out bedding. And the place we went to— Ledger, you wouldn't have believed how many choices they had. Comforters, duvets, duvet covers, and sets that also included sheets, bed skirts, and pillow shams— it was a little overwhelming."

I run my hands over my face. "I can drop everything at a moment's notice, travel to another country, manage multiple identities, and handle high-pressure situations, all while doing risk assessment, navigating sophisticated technology, blending into my surroundings, communicating covertly, adapting to changing situations rapidly, and negotiating high-stakes outcomes." Ledger's smiling at me now. Kind of an amused smile, and I really like it. "But, standing there in that store, I realized I had *no idea at all* what I liked. I couldn't even seem to narrow down my choices, and I felt so stupid about it. I was seriously about to bolt.

"But they were so sweet. Charlie said that sometimes choosing is really hard, especially if you haven't had enough experience lately choosing what you want. And that it was okay because we could get it figured out. I looked at all three of them, and there was zero judgment. I'm not even kidding. *Zero judgment.*

"They told me that when I wake up in the morning, my bedding will be the first thing I see. So I should imagine that no one else would see it ever, and just think about which one would make my soul the happiest. They told me that I could take as long as I needed to decide how I feel, and they never acted impatient."

"So what did you end up choosing?"

"Come see," I say as I stand, grab his hand, and pull him down the hall toward my new bedroom, my boot clomping on my hardwood floors as we go. Then I Vanna White the room. I watch his face as he sees it— just long enough to notice that his pupils widen, so he likes it as much as I do— then I look back at it, too. It's a deep purple with a light gray skirt and sheets. I've got sleeping pillows, pillow shams, decorative pillows, and the works. No more plain white hotel bedding for me.

But I'm not done showing him things, so I pull him back out into the hall. I feel like a little kid taking him by the hand to show him all my "cool stuff," but I can't help it — I have cool stuff now. "They also helped me to think about things like towels for my bathroom, a shower curtain, and garbage cans. I never would've thought of garbage cans! And curtains. Do you know Livi? That woman knows where to shop for everything. And the three of them have an insane amount of shopping endurance."

"I am really digging this side of you," Ledger says.

I look at him, trying to tell if he is being serious or sarcastic.

"I really do," Ledger says, seeming to sense my skepticism. "I like seeing you this happy and excited about having your own place."

He looks like he really means it, so I keep showing him things. When we finally end up back at my little table and sit to eat the soup and rolls, I keep talking, telling him more about our marathon shopping day. Things we looked at. Things we talked about. I put his stellar listening skills and endurance to the test, and he still claims victory. It's such a Ledger thing to do, and I am taking full advantage of it because apparently, I have a lot to say about today.

After we eat, we head over to the couch, and I snuggle up next to Ledger and sneak a couple of kisses. Okay, a couple dozen kisses. Each one of them is sweet and caps off a perfect day.

"Thanks for listening to me nonstop. I thought shopping was going to be awful, but it was amazing. It was so… different and nice to have friends who are women."

He's looking at my face and reaches out to brush a lock of hair away from my eye. "I'm so glad you had such a good experience today. And I'm gathering that you aren't having renter's remorse over getting your own place?"

I shake my head, chuckling. "Not even a little bit. I am loving it so much more than I thought I would. I know 'home sweet home' and 'there's no place like home' and 'home is where the heart is' and all that, but I figured it was just hype. Something that other people might need, but not something that *I* needed. I mean, I've lived most of my life without one, and I'm just fine. But I don't know. After hanging out with you and your family, it just… made me crave it."

Ledger gives me a sweet kiss on the forehead, and I close my eyes and soak it in. I soak in the feeling of his arm around my shoulders, too, the feel of his shoulder against my cheek. Then he says, "So, what was growing up like for you? Are all foster parents just awful people?"

"Oh. No. Not at all. There are a lot of really great ones who make a huge difference in a lot of kids' lives." I shrug. "But there are some not-so-great ones, too, and I think I got more of those than most foster kids do. I also got some who were decent people but were overwhelmed or over-worked or who just didn't really get me.

"And regardless of how great the foster parents are, I think that it's normal for every foster kid— at least the ones who moved around a lot— to feel like they never really had a home. I think it only feels like you have a home if you connect with a family and stay with them for a while. And I did get one of those— that very first foster family I stayed with was like that."

"Oh, yeah?" Ledger asks.

I nod. "It was a larger lady with blue glasses who came to our apartment to get me and take me to my first foster home. I was scared to death because she was taking me from everything I knew. But she was nice.

"I loved my mom, and I kind of missed her, but living with that family— the Jensens— opened up a whole new world for me. There was stability, and everyone treated each other well. I had siblings, a mom and a dad who worked together, regular mealtimes, eating together as a family— so many things that I just hadn't experienced before.

"I craved it all. I *thrived* there. It wasn't my life, but I sure liked living in it. I was even starting to believe that I was worthy of living in it.

"And then, about five months in, right as the school year was ending, all six of us were sitting around the dining room table, eating roast beef with mashed potatoes and gravy and those little carrots. My foster dad was telling a story about his favorite place to go camping with his dad when he was a boy, and he told us that he was going to take all of us there that summer.

"I couldn't believe that I was actually going to be able to go on a vacation. I was going to get to go camping! I was so excited. I sat at that table and thought about how I hadn't been lucky enough or good enough to be sent to a family like that at birth, but I was so grateful to finally get it."

"So, did you go camping with them?" Ledger asks.

I shake my head. "Later that week, the lady with the blue glasses came and said that I could go back home to my mom. There were tears from my foster family and from me.

"When the woman with the blue glasses came to get me that second time, I was actually excited. I would get to live that ideal life again, and I'd get to go camping. But the woman said I'd be going to stay with a different family— the Jensens had moved to a different state.

"I was so devastated. I felt betrayed and lost and so alone. I was six when I left the Jensens— it wasn't like I had a cell phone or an email address so I could stay in touch with them. They were just gone forever, and it was *so* hard. But I'll always be grateful for them because they showed me that love was possible."

Of course, the experience also showed me that love is temporary. That it could easily get taken away with no notice. That it couldn't be trusted to be there for me, and that it would be painful when it wasn't.

I clear my throat. "When I lived with the Jensens, my foster mom had a necklace that she always wore. It was a little heart locket with a picture of her and her husband in it. I loved it so much and asked every day if I could open the locket and look at the picture. When we said our good-byes before I went back to live with my mom, she said she wanted me to have the necklace. That way, I'd always remember her and remember that she cared about me."

I reach up to touch the locket, even though I know that it's gone, then I drop my hand back to my lap. "It was one of only two things that I took with me from foster family to foster family. It got me through a lot of really hard times. I mean, I was little when I lived with the Jensens, so the experience often felt like it was a dream— that I had just let hope make up the 'memory.' That necklace was a confirmation that it was real. That it happened. That I was loved once."

I swallow hard. I wish I had put it in my pocket that night I fell off the roof. A sharp pain in my ribs reminds me that they still hurt at the memory, too.

I turn to look at Ledger. This is the most real and vulnerable I've ever been with another human. Possibly even including myself. I probably told classmates or foster siblings that I missed living with the Jensens that first year or so, but I've definitely never told anyone the full story. And just like with Charlie earlier, I see zero judgment in his eyes. Just caring concern. Somehow, I just know that the story, my emotions about it, my raw and open heart— they're safe with him.

"That sounds really tough. Thank you for sharing it with me." He's quiet for a long moment, just holding me. I kind of hope he doesn't want to keep talking about my childhood because I've only got so much emotional energy that I can spend on that particular subject in a day, and I'm pretty sure I just spent it all. I hope he can sense that.

Ledger shifts how he is sitting, and I know he wants to be able to see my face, so I turn, too. "I want to go back to something you said earlier," he says. "You said you were surprised that Charlie, Mackenzie, and Livi liked you even though you were injured and didn't have a clue about shopping or about what you liked."

I nod.

His eyes shift to my hair. It's not often that I have it

loose like this and not in a ponytail or a braid. With the lightest touch, he brushes his fingertips across my cheek as he tucks part of my hair behind an ear. "You are so beautiful."

I blush. I've heard this before, but it's always different when it comes from Ledger.

"Your beauty is not what draws people to you, though." He lifts one shoulder in a shrug. "In fact, some people might say that you are 'intimidatingly beautiful.'"

I try to hold back a smile. "*Intimidatingly*?"

"Yep. That's the exact phrase Emerson used to describe you. What draws people to you isn't what they're seeing on the outside. They're drawn to you because you have a deep inner beauty."

"What?" I say. "What does that even mean?" I'm pretty sure he's messing with me.

"Okay, for example," he says, "let's talk about what you do for a living. Being an intelligence operative in the field takes a lot of courage, commitment, training, skill, conviction, resilience, adaptability, creativity, discipline, grit, patience, and a whole lot of other things, right? And you're one of the best there is, so obviously, you've got all those things in abundance.

"Not only that but all of those things could be combined to be helpful in a lot of different careers. You chose to utilize them in a career that helps people. Keeps them safe. Looks out for those in danger. Me? I just do it for the adventure and the challenge.

"But I know you do it to help people. I know, because I saw you stop in the middle of a mission to help that little girl." He taps two fingers on my chest. "Your heart? Everything about you? *That's* what draws people to you. Not your knowledge about or experience in a specific subject. Not how helpful you are to someone at any given time.

"But who you are in here. *That's* what shines through. That deep inner beauty is what makes Charlie and Mackenzie and Livi and everyone else want to be around you. It's what has made me fall in love with you."

My heart is so full of emotion right now that I worry it can't contain it. I just gaze at Ledger with watery eyes, taking him in. I wish I had everything that Ledger just said recorded so I could listen to it again, over and over. I want it to be in a physical object that I can hold, just like that necklace from my foster mom. Then I could hold onto this moment forever. Remember that it is real. That it happened. That I am loved.

I know from experience that this is ephemeral, and I want to soak in every bit of it while I can. I want to hold his words tight. I want to bathe in them. I want them to surround me every moment.

So I snuggle back into Ledger's side and soak in every bit of how incredible it feels to be loved by him.

CHAPTER 29
CANOE CONFESSIONS
LEDGER

step into the elevator from the parking garage at work a few minutes late after dropping Zoe's necklace off at a jeweler to be repaired. Between Zoe falling off that roof, the stress of the hospital, making sure her recovery was going well, and wanting to spend every moment I could spare with her, I had somehow forgotten about her necklace that I'd slid into my pocket right before picking her up in that skinny alley.

Still, it's baffling to me that I managed to forget about the necklace. Up until that point, I'd never seen Zoe without it. I guess I was just focusing too much on her amazing eyes. Or how much she makes me laugh. Or her lips. It could've been her lips.

It took me a minute to even remember what I'd been wearing that night. Well, it took me until I remembered that I had been soaked by the rain— those wet pants made me very aware of what I was wearing for long enough that I had no question.

Of course, they've been laundered since then. All my clothes from that trip have been. I panicked for a moment until I remembered that once Zoe had been doing well enough in that hospital that I could go out to the rental car and get our bags, I'd found a restroom and changed. I had checked my pockets first, found the necklace, and put it in a zippered part of my bag that I rarely used, worried that I'd lose it otherwise.

So I went to my bag, and there it was. Right where I left it. I hadn't brought it up to Zoe when she told me the story behind the necklace because I worried that it might have fallen out of my pocket somewhere along the way, and I didn't want to give her false hope that it wasn't lost. The jeweler said they'd have it fixed by tomorrow afternoon, so I decided to just wait and surprise Zoe with it then.

Zoe has been on my mind nonstop, and I get to take her to see one of my favorite places tonight. I'm floating as the elevator takes me up. As soon as I step out onto the floor, Emerson catches my attention and taps the watch on his wrist. I roll my eyes and head over to him. "Sorry I'm late, Mr. Punctuality. I had to drop something off to be repaired and had to wait for them to open."

"Dropping something off, huh? If it was your sense of urgency, I'm not sure they can fix that."

I chuckle. "Maybe not, but I figured while I was at it, I'd see if they could fix your sense of fashion. Turns out that's beyond repair, too."

Emerson looks down at his neatly-pressed light blue

shirt, his tie with a subtle pattern of mathematical symbols, and his gray sweater vest like he's trying to see what issue I might have with his outfit.

"Relax, bro. I was kidding." I make eye contact with Kella and wave her over. "What do you have for me?"

He picks up his tablet and the three of us head into one of the conference rooms at the back. "Not too much new, unfortunately. There still have been no attempts made to steal the Trust pieces with the trackers in either Dublin or Belgrade.

"We've also been monitoring everything we are getting from our contacts close to Aragundi. It seems that his business, nefarious as it is, has been running along as usual. We are still looking for ways to capture him, since that would be optimal, but you know how slippery he is.

"Of course, our second best scenario is capturing the two men who have been stealing the Trust pieces, since they are currently looking like they're the strongest contenders for Aragundi's fortune and his network. Now that we know who they are, we've been working to figure out who their network of people are. These are some bad men, and we do *not* want them adding Aragundi's resources to their own.

"Still no sign of them?" I ask. They've been ghosts ever since stealing the Trust piece in Ankara. In the nearly two weeks since we've been back, I've been in touch with every contact I have in Europe and in the Middle East but every lead has come up empty.

Emerson shakes his head. "Nothing." It's seeming more and more likely that they were able to get the number off the Trust piece from that case before we got it in our possession.

Kella taps her pen on the conference table. "Maybe one of the brothers was injured and they're waiting for him to heal. Or maybe they had their own internal catastrophes that had to be dealt with before they could spare a trip to either of the locations of Trust pieces."

"Or," I add, "they could suspect we're onto them and figured we placed trackers on the final two pieces. They could be trying to finish whatever challenge Aragundi set up without the numbers from them."

"Could be any of that," Emerson says. "As far as information we can get from here, we might be at an end unless they make a move."

———

Zoe and I head over to my childhood home, hitch up the trailer, and load on the canoe I used so much as a kid. Then we take the twenty-minute drive from my mom's house to Piney Run Lake, where my dad had taken us so many times.

"Wow, it is beautiful here," Zoe says as we lower the canoe from the trailer into the water.

The last of the sunset is reflecting across the smooth water and makes it look rather incredible. "It's one of my favorite places in the world," I tell her. "It's just as amazing in the middle of the day, too, when you can see all the trees lining the curves and bends of the shore and the sun glinting off the water. Or in the early morning, when you can see mists rising from the water. You really can't go wrong anytime of day, but I'm excited for the stars to come out, because seeing them reflected on the water is the best."

A few minutes later, the trailer is parked, we're wearing our life jackets, and I've stepped into the boat. I hold out a hand for Zoe, and she steps in, careful to get her booted foot positioned on the curved floor of the canoe. I can tell that the thing still annoys her, but she hasn't complained about it much lately, and she hasn't tossed it into the nearest Dumpster. If her doctor doesn't give her some kind of award for that, I will.

We sit on the two benches, facing each other, and I pull an oar from the floor of the canoe. There's two oars, but I'm worried that Zoe rowing might prolong the recovery of that broken rib and bruised spleen. But I also know that she'd rather act like she's not injured. I say what I'd want her to say to me if our roles were reversed. "I know that in a rowing competition, you'd win, hands down. But, I really want you cleared to go on a mission with me soon. Plus, I kind of just want to show off my mad skill with an oar, so do you mind if I paddle?"

She tries to hide a smile, like she knows exactly what I'm doing. "Go ahead," she says. "I wouldn't dream of denying you a chance to show off those arm muscles of yours. I'll just sit back and enjoy the show."

I grin. "Speaking of going on a mission with you, has the CIA found anything on our art thieves?"

"No, but I've been thinking about the Trust piece I acquired."

I flinch. My mind immediately goes back to that moment where I was running toward the handoff of the case from one bad actor to another when Zoe stepped out of a building and got to it first.

"Now that we know who the men are who have been stealing the trust pieces…"

My eyes go wide. "They were the ones who were *receiving* the handoff, not *giving* it!"

Zoe nods, a satisfied smile on her face. "I had the same realization this morning. Which means they likely didn't already get the secret number from the chip on that piece before we intercepted it."

"So they're down by at least one. There's no way they'll be successful with only seven of the numbers. They *have* to go for at least one more of the Trust pieces."

We are both grinning. We will get a chance to go on another mission together.

I pull the oar through the water, first on one side, then on the other, guiding us along the meandering shoreline of the lake, not far from the shore. The night is still, the crickets are chirping, an owl is hooting, a few frogs are croaking, and the paddle is making a swishing sound as it enters the water. Every once in a while, a fish breaks the surface of the water, making a splashing sound, and occasionally, we hear distant laughter from the one other couple who is on the lake tonight. The night is the most relaxing I've had in a while.

I've been pointing out all my favorite spots to Zoe. When I show her my favorite fishing spot, she says, "Huh. I can't really picture you as the fishing type."

"No?"

"Not even a little bit. You, sitting in a lawn chair at the edge of the lake, hat pulled down over your eyes, a fishing pole in your hand. I'm just not seeing it."

"Oh, yeah, that's not how we fished. My dad tried to teach us that way once, but it didn't stick. We all just dove into the water, and it became a competition of who could catch one with their bare hands. They're slippery little things— it isn't as easy as it sounds."

"Ahh," Zoe says. "*That* I can picture. Speaking of favorites, that's what we should play."

My eyebrows draw together. "Oh, that game where one of us asks something like, 'What's your favorite spy movie?' And by the way, if you say anything other than *True Lies*, we're turning this canoe around."

"Nope. It's got to be *Spy Kids*. It's the ultimate classic. And exactly. Except the questions aren't limited to favorites."

"*Spy Kids* doesn't have Arnold, but it does have jet packs, so I'll give that one to you. Who asks first?"

"I will. Um…. Oh. What's your favorite embarrassing story from growing up? You know, just in case I need to know for teasing purposes later."

"Okay, I'll tell you," I say, "but only if you tell yours first. I need to know how high to set the bar."

"Fine," Zoe says as I paddle the boat along an inlet. "There are so many… What to choose? Oh, got one. Okay, so when I was a teenager, I looked young. When I say young, I mean *young*. And, I've got to tell you, at an age when you want people to treat you as if you're older, it's the worst time to look younger. Especially when you're doing things like getting your driver's license and applying for your first job.

"Anyway, I had been in the same foster home with two foster brothers for about a year, so we knew each other pretty well. I was fifteen— a sophomore— and my foster brother, Justice, was a junior. We were both in the same biology class.

"One day, we had a substitute teacher, and I remember Justice referring to me as his sister at one point. At the end of class, the sub asked us to stay after and come talk to her. So we did, except she mostly talked to Justice. She said in a super kind, trying-to-be-helpful-and-understanding voice, 'I think it's sweet that you brought your sister to class. I'm impressed with how well-behaved and surprisingly knowledgeable she is.'"

"Well-behaved?" I say, mostly because it feels so odd.

"Yep. Then she says, 'But this isn't the place for her, and it's not really appropriate to bring her with you. If it's a matter of having a single parent at home with no babysitter, there are resources available.' Okay, that look of confusion on your face right now? That's exactly how our faces looked at this point. Then she says, 'And don't you think her elementary school teacher and her friends are missing her not being in her own class right now?' She thought I was in *elementary school*."

I give a hearty laugh. It's ridiculous how happy it makes me just being with her. "Oh, wow— that is young!"

She's laughing, too. "I swear to you, I didn't look elementary-school young. I looked more like fourteen instead of fifteen. And, of course, the most gossipy jock was also waiting to see the teacher, so he started a whole rash of people saying things like 'Did you get permission from your mom?' And 'Does your mom know you're here?' anytime I did anything, and it lasted for the rest of the school year."

"Well, if it's any consolation, you totally outgrew it in the most beautiful way possible."

Zoe smiles and lifts her boot a bit. "It's because I accessorize well, isn't it?"

"That is a factor." The doctor told her to keep the boot on for six weeks. I didn't think she would make it past two weeks. At times, I didn't think she'd make it past two days. But it's been three weeks, and she's still going strong.

"Okay, your turn."

"All right," I say. "I'll stick with your substitute teacher theme. I think we've already covered that it was important to me to do well in school. And I did. But when people would look at me, what they saw was 'Dumb jock.' And, well, let's just say that sometimes I played it up for a laugh. Like in my junior year math class when we had a sub.

"It was clear from the beginning of class that was exactly how she saw me, so I decided to mess with her. Every time she asked a question, I'd raise my hand and give an answer, showing I clearly didn't even know basic arithmetic. She called me up in front of the class to do a problem on the white board. I'm pretty sure it was so she could stress the importance of doing our homework.

"So I did the math, in the most wrong way possible,

giving my reasoning behind what I was doing for each step out loud. Some of my reasoning wasn't even math-related— it had to do with things witnessed in nature, or things I overheard while at a movie theater or something. All of it was ridiculous. And, of course, my answer wasn't even in the ballpark. It wasn't even in the same state as the ballpark."

Zoe starts laughing, and I continue, hoping I can make that laughing continue.

"Everyone in the class was loving it. It was early in the school year. Probably half of them knew me well enough to know that I wasn't that dumb, but the other half probably had their suspicions. My plan was to eventually blow the sub's mind by correctly solving the other problem that was on the board, which was much more complex, thereby proving that she— along with anyone else who had been judging the book by its cover— had been wrong about me.

"Just as I was about to reveal my true genius, the principal came in and asked if he could take a minute to tell us about… I don't even remember. New school safety procedures or about the standardized testing schedule or something. And then he talked until the bell rang to end class, leaving me looking like I couldn't tell a mathematical variable from a pirate's booty, thereby solidifying my reputation as a dumb jock."

"Oh, I will definitely be teasing you about this later." Zoe's laughing enough now that she's wiping a tear from her eye, and getting that kind of reaction from her makes my chest puff up just a bit.

"Okay, my turn," I say. "If we got stranded and had to

camp out here, which of us do you think would survive the longest and why?"

"Me, for sure, because my bag has a secret stash of chocolate. Survival of the sweetest."

"And you're just going to live off chocolate?"

"I'm pretty sure it can be done. Why? Do you think you would last the longest? What do you think you'll survive off of?"

"Oh, I'll have plenty of food. I can fish with my hands, remember?"

"As vital as chocolate is, protein would be nice. I'll give that to you. Okay, what would you do if that bird that has been following us is a spy bird, trained to eavesdrop on us?"

"Easy. I'd recruit it. Turn it into an asset. How about you?"

"I'd feed it false info. Make up a good story."

I grin. "I bet we could come up with a good one." I glance at the oak, maple, and pine trees that are lining the shore, thinking. "Okay, I've got one. What's the first extreme sport you tried?"

Zoe looks upward for a moment, thinking, before her eyes come back to me. "I think it was motocross. At one place I lived, there was an empty field nearby that some kids had turned into a dirt bike course. One time, they made a big jump because they wanted to recreate the jumping over cars thing. But since we were young, we all lined up our bikes instead. I talked one of the kids into letting me try making the jump with his dirt bike, even though I was young enough that I probably shouldn't have been trusted with a motorized vehicle.

"I summoned all the courage I needed, and I'm pretty sure all the speed I needed, too. But it was getting late and a storm was rolling in. Just as I was going up the ramp, lightning struck and startled me enough that I jerked the handlebars to the side and instead of soaring over the line of bikes, I soared up and over to the right, managing to land in the lone tree in the field. Somehow, neither the motorbike nor I was injured, although it took seven of the older boys to get it out of the tree.

"They never let me get on the dirt bike again, but it did earn me the nickname 'Lightning Bolt.'"

"And I will definitely be teasing you about that later."

"Go ahead. It's a nickname I'd still wear with pride. Okay, yours."

"Wind skateboarding," I say as I start paddling us toward the south end of the lake.

"Is that even a thing?"

"Land windsurfing is, but we didn't know about that yet— it's a much better idea than what a friend and I had come up with as ten-year-olds. We had seen a couple of videos one summer— one with windsurfing and one with hang gliders— and thought they looked like so much fun. We knew we couldn't do either. We checked. Both needed waivers to be signed by someone over eighteen, and we knew our parents wouldn't.

"So we decided to make our own version— a big hang gliding-shaped frame covered in fabric to strap to our backs and a skateboard at our feet. Then we took it to the top of a street at one end of town that, at the time, had felt really steep."

I can tell that Zoe can already see where this is going, because her hand is over her mouth and her eyes are wide.

"We envisioned the wind catching us, blowing us really fast, and being able to skate all the way to the other side of town just with our momentum. What we hadn't thought through was that when you're skateboarding downhill, the wind blows *against* you, not at your back.

"I went first. I got the frame strapped to my back like a giant backpack, got on my skateboard, and gave myself the biggest push-off to start down the hill. You know, to give the wind a really good chance to catch my wings. I realized our conceptual error not too far into my trip down the hill, but like I said— biggest push-off, so it was too late to just stop.

"A few seconds after that, the wind caught my wings enough that it sent me sailing backward while gravity took my skateboard forward."

"Did you get injured?"

"Not enough to keep us from trying again but that time with the skateboard strapped to our feet. Spoiler alert: neither that, nor starting at the bottom of the hill to have the wind push us up worked."

Zoe laughs. "I wish I could've seen that."

This lake has so many twists and bends along the shoreline, and I lead us through a part that opens up into a wider area that feels almost like a hidden lagoon. It's one of the most peaceful places on the lake. Lily pads are growing at the edge of the shore, trees are lining the lake all around, the water is still, and the sky is clear.

I move from sitting on the bench to the floor of the canoe, and Zoe comes to sit in front of me, leaning back against my chest. Her outstretched legs are against mine, and her forehead is against my cheek, so I turn slightly and give it a kiss. I wrap my arms around her, and we both look up at the stars, taking in the perfect surroundings.

I can't imagine a night more perfect than this— being with Zoe in one of my favorite places, talking, laughing, kissing, holding her in my arms, and just relaxing together after a few challenging weeks. I wish I could stay in this moment forever.

CHAPTER 30
PERMANENT
ZOE

I love Ledger. And it scares me more than anything has in my life. More than jumping out of an airplane. More than going up against a terrorist. More than failure.

The problem is that I also love him more than anything. More than my new apartment. More than my job. Even more than I loved my first foster family. And that one was the one that taught me just how much it can hurt to have it taken away.

Logic tells me to back away.

I thought I was a logical person. Apparently, though, I run on emotion, because I don't ever want to give up nights like last night with Ledger. He's the best person I've ever known, and I want it all with him.

After work, I step-clomp out to my car. I've gotten pretty used to the boot, but it's still annoying. Under normal circumstances, I would probably be walking without the boot right now— my leg is feeling that much better. I want to be back in the field as quickly as possible, though, and I know that it's healing much more quickly by keeping it on.

I do take it off once I get into my car, though, because it's too difficult to drive with it on, and I can't handle taking Ubers to work any longer. I need the sense of freedom I get from my car. During my drive home, Ledger calls and asks if he can come over with dinner. The man is so thoughtful. He's always doing things like this for me, and I'm never the one who thinks of doing it for him. So I tell him no— that I am coming to *his* apartment and bringing *him* food.

As much as I like to be the best of the best as an intelligence operative (and beat Ledger at everything), when it comes to navigating a relationship and being good at it, I am *not* the best of the best. I'm not even the best of the worst. I have not figured it out any more than I had figured out how to be an intelligence operative as an eight-year-old.

Ledger grew up knowing how to do all of it. He probably didn't even realize he was learning it. He probably doesn't even know how good he is at it. And I'm scared he'll find out how bad I am at it. He has been at my hotel and my apartment so many times, yet this is the first time I am going to his apartment. I'm not even sure I knew that he lives in Cloakwood.

He opens the door before I get close enough to knock— probably because he heard my clomping steps coming up to the door, and I think the view of him when he opens the door will be forever burned in my mind. He just looks so elated to see me. I don't think I've ever had someone so deep-down thrilled at my presence. He's got me smiling right back, feeling that same happiness.

He welcomes me in, wrapping an arm around my waist and giving me a kiss that I savor. Then he smiles into the kiss and whispers, "Welcome to my home."

"Where do you want this?" I say, holding up the bag that contains the pesto chicken salad sandwiches and strawberry lemonade pie that I got from a little café I found in his town. He sets it on a countertop that doubles as a breakfast bar and a half-wall separating the kitchen from the living area, and I take a look around.

This place is exactly how I expected it would be. Open and instantly welcoming. A big, comfortable-looking, modern sectional sits in his living room, and it isn't hard to imagine it filled with Ledger's friends, all playing games, laughing, having a good time. It isn't hard to imagine the two of us cozied up together on the couch, either.

The walls have colorful artwork interspersed with photos of Ledger with people that I'm sure mean a lot to him, as well as photos of him skydiving, in scuba gear underwater with colorful marine life, windsurfing, ice climbing, high lining, you name it. There's even a few, like kite skiing and steep creeking that I haven't even tried. There would never be a dull moment around Ledger, that's for sure.

Ledger just holds back as I look around at everything, including his bookshelves and sound system. When I turn back to him after looking at everything, he puts his arms around me again and, now that I'm no longer holding the bag with dinner, I wrap my arms around his neck and keep him close as we kiss. It feels so good to be like this that I memorize the way it feels to be in his arms. To have his lips against mine. I want to be able to remember this forever.

As we eat side by side at his breakfast bar, we talk about our day and about any progress we each made in our search for Aragundi or the Barno Brothers.

I am just finishing eating my strawberry lemonade pie — which is incredible— and I can practically feel the excitement that seems like it's been building in Ledger for the entire meal. I turn to him, "Okay, what is it? You're killing me, here."

It was as if all he needed was permission to end the meal early, because he practically bounds off his chair and into his bedroom. He emerges a few seconds later with a small, flat box in his hand. "I've got something for you."

I spin on my barstool to face him, a question on my face as he nears and holds it out to me. The box is from a jewelry store. It's not even close to my birthday and it's not Christmas, so I don't have any idea why he's giving this to me. I remove the lid, and so much is going through my mind that it takes a second to process what I'm seeing.

It's a necklace with two pendants on it. The chain and the heart look exactly like my necklace that I lost. *Exactly.* Did he find one online and recognize it as similar to the one that I lost? No, this is the real one. Mine. I would recognize it anywhere.

I touch the pendant, then place the box back in

Ledger's hand and, fingers shaking, work to open the locket. I know this is the necklace I lost. The one I've worn around my neck for the past twenty years. But the part of me that knows it can't possibly be the real thing is telling me that the locket is likely empty, and that it's going to feel like a stab to the heart to open it and see. But I do it anyway.

I gasp and a hand flies to my mouth. It has the picture of my first foster parents in it. It *is* my necklace. The very same necklace that I lost. My eyes are filling with tears as I look at Ledger. "What? How? Where did this…"

He gives me a smile that shows he's seeing all of me. All the emotion that's filling me. "It broke when you fell in Ankara. I found it on the ground next to you and put it in my pocket before carrying you to the car. I still can't believe I even saw it in the darkness and rain. I guess it wanted to be found.

"The clasp was broken, so I had to take it to a jeweler to have it fixed, but it should be as good as new now. I know it means a lot to you and reminds you that your first foster family loved you."

"I can't believe you found it," I say, my voice coming out as barely a whisper.

He reaches out and touches the second pendant, the one that is hanging right next to the locket. It's a lock, and it's gold, too, just like the rest of the necklace. They go well enough together that it looks like they were always meant to be together. "I had them add this. I hope it will remind you that you are loved by more than just your first foster family— you're loved by a lot of people. Especially me.

The lock represents that it's not temporary. You will always be loved."

I am so overcome with emotion that I can't even talk. I'm glad that Ledger is holding the box now, because my hands are shaking. Ledger sets the box on the countertop and removes the card that the necklace is displayed on, carefully pulling the chain out from the slits at the top. I hold up my braid as he fastens it at the base of my neck.

As soon as I feel its familiar weight against my skin after going so long without it, everything immediately feels right again. The thing most precious to me is back where it goes after I thought it was gone forever. I reach up and touch the locket, like I've done thousands of times before. And this time, my fingers also touch the lock.

You are loved by a lot of people. Especially me. Ledger's words echo in my mind, and I want them to stay there forever. To always be tied to the lock in the same way that my first foster parents' love is tied to the locket.

I look at Ledger, overwhelmed with gratitude for him, and can't even begin to express a thank you big enough to encompass this. So instead, I just kiss him. I pour all of it— all the emotion I'm feeling— into the kiss. My fingers grasp his hair at the base of his skull, and I hold him close, kissing him as tears stream down my face, making our kiss taste salty. The tears are streaming so much that they are even falling off my face and onto us.

Eventually, I pull back just enough to gaze into Ledger's beautiful gray-blue eyes. I smile and shake my head a bit. "I don't deserve someone as amazing and as thoughtful as you," I say, meaning every word.

I collapse back onto the barstool I'd been sitting on before, feeling incredibly spent from experiencing so many emotions. I pull the necklace forward as much as it can, looking down at it. I can't believe I have it back. And back even better than it was.

But I really don't deserve Ledger. I am not worthy of the kind of love he is showing me. As I look down at the necklace, I start to feel it more intensely. This represents a deep kind of love for someone who is worthy of that kind of love. I am not. As much as I am enamored by everything it represents, I feel like a fraud having it bestowed upon me.

It would be like really *really* wanting to win the school spelling bee, and working so hard to learn the words. In the end, though, being awful at spelling and not even coming close to actually winning. But then they crown you "Spelling Bee Champion" anyway and hand you the trophy as if you did. And everyone acts like it rightfully belongs to you even when you *know* it doesn't.

I didn't earn this kind of love. I don't deserve it. And one day, Ledger is going to realize that.

My own mom realized it. For so long as a kid, I had wondered if something was fundamentally wrong with me: if I was unlovable. Then, in living with my first foster family, I had started to feel differently. Like maybe I had been mistaken. But after the next couple of foster homes, I started to realize that feeling lovable with my first foster family was the anomaly. Actually not being lovable was the reality.

When I was about nine, I was in a foster home where I

tried so hard to get that same kind of love I had felt with the Jensens. I would spend hours cleaning the kitchen, making it sparkle. When my foster mom saw it, she would say things like, "This looks amazing. Thank you." And it kind of felt like it was enough. At least, I told myself it was.

But then, one day, my after-school young detectives club meeting was canceled, so I got home earlier than my foster parents were expecting me. I was walking to the kitchen as one of my foster siblings was presenting my foster mom with a bouquet of dandelions that she had picked in the back yard. My foster mom accepted them, gave the girl a tight hug, and said, "I just love you so much."

I had never been treated that way. I had never heard the words, "I love you" outside of my first foster family. It was my confirmation that I am not worthy of love no matter how hard I try. Ledger just doesn't know it yet.

The tears start again, but this time, it's not because of the love and gratitude I felt moments ago. It's the tears of the lost, lonely little girl I used to be. The lost, lonely little girl who still lives inside me.

I remind myself that I figured out long ago that I don't need love. I was built to be an intelligence operative. Intelligence operatives aren't lovable. You can't be both an operative and be lovable. They can't coexist. I accepted that a long time ago.

So Ledger showing me this kind of love feels like a knife to the heart. I want it so badly, and I know that the lock is supposed to represent that it isn't temporary, but I know that it is. If he knew the real me, deep down, he'd know that I'm not worthy of his love. Which makes it not real. It's a spelling bee trophy that I didn't actually win.

And I want to hold onto it so desperately, but I know that it'll only make it harder. It'll make the wound deeper.

Ledger's face is so full of love. He reaches out and wipes at my tears first with his thumb and then with his knuckles. "I love you, Zoe," he whispers.

I know he does. And I realize that this pain I'm going to feel, the pain that's going to just keep getting worse the longer this goes on— this pain is not only going to take down me. The blast radius will take down Ledger, too.

My heart starts to race and I can't seem to take in enough air. I'm breathing fast, but not deep, because I can't seem to get my tight chest to let in more air. And it's just so hot in here. The heat is suffocating, making it even more difficult to breathe.

"Are you okay?" Ledger asks, concern all over his face.

No, I am not. I stand and shake out my hands, trying to shake away the heat, repeatedly tugging at my shirt to get more air flowing, but I still can't get enough oxygen, and I'm starting to get dizzy.

Ledger's looking alarmed now. His arms are moving like they want to do something— anything— to help. "Zoe, are you okay? What is wrong?"

"What is wrong," I say, feeling like I'm shouting the words, except that I don't have enough oxygen for shouting, "is that we don't get to live normal lives, Ledger! Operatives don't get normal lives! Operatives don't get to fall in love!"

Instead of just agreeing, or even letting me push him away, he steps closer to me, then envelops me in a hug, pulling me tight to him. One arm is across my back and he's running the other hand down my hair. Over and over, he says, "Shh. It's okay. Everything is okay."

It is not okay. It's not.

But feeling his strong, protective arms around me, his low voice repeating that it's going to be okay, calms me anyway. It isn't long before my lungs let me breathe again and it doesn't feel so stifling hot.

When my heart rate starts to return to something edging closer to normal, I pull back. He lets one hand slide down my arm until he's got his fingers entwined with mine. Then he reaches up and tucks a lock of hair back into my braid. When his eyes meet mine again, he says, "'Operatives don't get normal lives?' Or you don't feel like you can?"

He seems to have it figured out, so I guess it is just me.

In a voice that's so calm and sweet and loving that it makes my heart ache with longing, he says, "You said you don't think you deserve me. If anything, it's the other way around. You, Zoe, deserve so much more than I could ever give you."

I look into his eyes, scanning them for a long moment, seeing the full depth of which he believes those words.

Then, with my clomping boot, I turn and run.

CHAPTER 31
LET ME BE BRIEF
LEDGER

still don't understand what happened last night. Things seemed to be going so well, then suddenly, they weren't. I chased after Zoe to find out what was wrong, but she had just said, "Ledger, please. I need to go." And I could tell by the look on her face that she really did— what she most needed was space.

As much as I wanted to go to her and make things better if I could, I gave her space. But knowing that she was distressed made it so hard. I'm proud of myself for not giving in until this morning when I texted to ask if she was okay. I just need to know that she's okay.

I haven't gotten a text back yet, and I can't concentrate on anything at work. Even though we got word this morning that the Trust piece in Dublin has been stolen and has been making its way across Europe.

We've been watching its movement all day. Just after lunch, we were unsure whether the men vying for

Aragundi's empire were heading straight to Serbia to get the Trust piece in Belgrade or if they were heading back to their base. There has been a flurry of activity here, planning for all possibilities.

Then, moments ago, we found out that they are heading back to their base, which we now know is somewhere in Montenegro. So the directors of both the CSA and the CIA have called a joint briefing late this afternoon.

The moment we get the alert that the team from the CIA has arrived— something I will never get used to, and from the looks of it, neither will anyone else in my department— we all stand up from our desks. I barely breathe as I wait for them to come around the corner from the hallway leading to the lobby.

The moment I see Zoe, relief washes over me. She is beautiful, as usual. She's even smiling, which makes me finally able to take a full breath. She walks toward me, along with Director Sullivan, Kenneth, the CIA's analyst, and a guy with curly blonde hair that I am guessing is her tech op, Packston. Her eyes are taking in everything, and it reminds me of the first time she walked into our offices weeks ago.

This is going to be a bigger mission, so we're meeting in the large conference room. I head over to it, and Zoe meets me as her team, along with Miles, Jace, Charlie, and Kella all start filing inside.

I am so happy to see Zoe that I'm grinning like a fool. I nod at the smaller brace she's wearing that doesn't look nearly as cumbersome as the boot. "I see you ditched the boot. You must be thrilled."

"As much as I hated to give up the fashion accessory, the doctor said this morning that I'm healed enough for the mission, and that I just need to wear this as a precaution. It's a bit more stealthy, so they won't be able to hear me coming."

She's talking in words that sound a lot like our normal flirty bantering, but her tone is way off. Whatever upset her last night is still bothering her. I've asked myself a million times if it could've been because I added the extra charm to her necklace. I can see she's wearing the necklace tucked into her shirt, though, and when she moves a bit, I catch a glimpse of the lock. If it had been the source of what upset her, I think she would've removed it.

Even though I don't have any direct evidence, only a sense of the vibe, it feels like she's in the same state of mind as she was when we last met here for a briefing—before everything between us happened. Like she's trying to put distance between us. Between me and loving her. I give a little shrug. "This boot might not be as cute, but it will better match our tactical uniforms."

"And I'm all about aesthetics in the field."

I study her for a moment, then ask, "Is everything okay?"

"Yep. Doing great."

I might have been able to take that answer at face value a few weeks ago, but now I know her deeply enough to see past what she's showing on the surface.

As Director Lancaster comes down the aisle behind Zoe, a tablet and some papers in her hands, Zoe's eyes flick to the wall that holds the tally board showing how many missions each of us has won. "I see that you've added two tally marks to each of our columns since I was last here."

"Well, you know, Dublin and Belgrade, joint missions, and all."

She nods, thoughtful. Then her eyes meet mine, and there's conviction in them. "I'm going to win this mission."

She turns and walks into the conference room to join everyone else.

"Oh... kay," I say to no one, then I walk in, too, and take a seat at the conference table.

My mom reaches the head of the table and sets her papers down but doesn't take a seat. "It's been a busy day for all of us and there's still a lot to do, so I'll make this quick. The men vying for Aragundi's empire— the Barno Brothers— along with their group, have made their base at the Fortress of Dormitor in the forested mountains of Montenegro."

She taps on her tablet and an image comes up on the big screen of the fortress. It's... well, "formidable" is a good word for it. But so is "awe-inspiring." The structure is built into the mountain itself, and it's a thing of beauty. The whole area is. It's all surrounded by a dense forest, rocky terrain, green grasses, low shrubs, and many stone outcroppings.

"We want to capture them and take down their network before they combine it with Aragundi's," the director says, "so you'll be headed to Montenegro and traveling to this fortress.

"There will be four teams going out into the field. The

CIA sent out a surveillance team in the past hour. Since they'll arrive ahead of everyone else, they'll monitor the perimeter and provide us with real-time intel on enemy movements. We will also have a distraction team and an extraction team, and they each consist of operatives from both the CIA and the CSA. They will be briefed separately." She nods in the direction of Zoe, Jace, Miles, and me. "The four of you will be the infiltration team."

I look to my right at my brothers and grin, and they grin back. Jace holds out his fist and I bump it with mine. Then Jace shakes out his hand. They might not be in it for the adventure as much as I am, but they can't deny that the adventure excites them, too.

I look to my left and grin at Zoe. I'm so glad that she was able to talk her director into assigning her to this mission even though she isn't fully recovered yet— I know how important it is to her to finish it. The two of them must have a good working relationship and he has a lot of faith in her abilities even while injured, or he likely would've selected a different operative. Her eyes are on the image, not on me, but I can see the excitement there. This is going to be an adventure, for sure.

Director Sullivan of the CIA stands and says, "The distraction team will, obviously, create a distraction that will pull as many of the enemy forces away from the main entry points of the fortress as possible, making it easier for you and later, the extraction team, to enter. The extraction team will round up any enemy forces inside as well as secure the stolen Trust pieces.

"Your job, as the infiltration team, will be to penetrate

the fortress and disrupt communications. We believe they have a server room in the fortress. You'll need to get to it, download everything onto a drive, and gather every bit of intel you can find before the guys inside know there's a problem so they don't just burn all the data to keep it out of our hands. Getting that data might be the most important part. We're hoping it'll contain info that will lead us to a takedown of Aragundi, as well."

Zoe raises a hand. "I will get the drive."

I nod. If Zoe wanted to "win" a mission where we all have the same goal, securing that drive would be the way. After her comments outside this room, it doesn't surprise me at all.

"I just got off the phone with Montenegro's Minister of Defense," Director Lancaster says. "They were not too pleased to find out that they'd drawn the short straw as to where these guys decided to set up base, and they are more than happy to help us get them out of their country. So they will be supporting the Distraction and Extraction teams."

Director Sullivan is standing with his arms crossed. "We're going to get these guys, and hopefully get Aragundi, too. It'll make the whole world a safer place."

All of us nod. I can see Zoe from the corner of my eye. I can't wait until this meeting is over so I can talk to her. I want to find out how she's really doing and what freaked her out so much yesterday.

Director Lancaster starts talking again. "You'll leave at oh-six-hundred tomorrow from Washington-Dulles. You'll be flying on one of the CIA's jets with the other two teams.

We'll have as much information as we can get about the layout of the fortress on the plane waiting for you tomorrow morning. Whatever we can't get by then, we'll send during your flight. Analysts, you'll need to arrive at oh-six-hundred as well, since the surveillance team should be on site by then, sending you information.

"It's a ten hour flight, and there is a six-hour time difference. By the time you make it with all your gear from the airport to just outside of the Fortress of Dormitor, it'll be just after one a.m., local time. You should be able to infiltrate by two a.m., which will be optimal for catching them by surprise. Packston, Charlie, and Kella, you'll start supporting them in the field at that point, which will be about seven p.m. our time."

The director looks at each of us for confirmation that we got all the info and don't have questions. Once we all nod, she says, "Finish up what you need to, and then get home and get some rest. You've got a big day tomorrow."

Everyone stands and starts filing out of the room, including Director Sullivan, Kenneth, and Packston. Zoe's turning to leave, too, but I say, "Hey, can I talk to you for a minute?"

She glances at the door. "I can't. My ride is leaving."

"How about later tonight, then?"

She shakes her head. "I've got to get ready. Mission to make the world a safer place, you know. I'll catch you tomorrow at the airport."

I just nod and watch, hands in my pockets, as she walks out of the conference room. I'm still standing there when I realize that my mom is in the room, turning off the big screen and gathering her things, and she witnessed the exchange.

"Do you want to talk about it?" she asks.

I plop down into a chair, which rolls backward. Apparently I do, or I would've just shook my head and left quickly. I take a breath, and then meet my mom's eyes as she sits down in a chair, too. "I love her."

"I know you do."

I look at her for a moment. "At first, I thought she just didn't feel the same. Or that it… I don't know, scared her." I pause, trying to put into words what I've seen on Zoe's face. "I love her, and I don't think she believes that I do."

And I thought that maybe, just maybe, I might be more important to her than the mission now. But I think as far as she's concerned, she's still willing to sacrifice anything, including me, for the mission.

My mom nods like she gets it. "And do you believe that she loves you?"

"Yeah. I mean, most of the time. She's pretty good at faking things, so there's always a part of me that wonders." That line of thinking instantly exhausts me and I say, "Do you know what? Whatever." I look toward the wall of the conference room that separates us from the rest of the department, not really seeing anything past the glass. "It's not like I want a relationship anyway. Relationships make people boring. I don't want to be tied down."

My mom stays quiet for a beat. Then she says, "That used to be true."

I look back at her.

"But is it still true?" She asks. "Because from what I've seen, Zoe came along and changed everything."

She really did. I exhale a huge breath. "It hasn't been true in a long time. I think it's just what I like to tell myself to get over Moldova."

"Moldova?" She looks confused, and for good reason.

"Do you remember the mission I was on a year-and-a-half ago when I was trying to get that laptop from that scientist, and it took me deep into the forest there, and communications went down?"

She nods. "We lost contact with you for three days."

"That's when I first met Zoe. It was our actual first mission together. She was after the laptop, too, so we teamed up. At least, I thought we were working as a team. I also thought she liked me as much as I liked her. Turned out she was faking both."

"I see. Why didn't you report that she was on the mission with you in your debrief?"

Because I was embarrassed that I let her pull one over on me? Because I was embarrassed to be rejected? Because I was embarrassed not to bring back the laptop myself? I don't say any of that, though. Instead, I shrug.

My mom nods, like she can tell by my expression exactly what my reason is. She spares me the lecture about disclosing it— and I absolutely should've disclosed it. I'll probably get the lecture later, actually, but right now she's being my mom, not my director.

"Maybe Zoe wasn't actually faking it in Moldova," she says. "Maybe she had just as hard of a time believing that you could love her back then as she does now."

"That makes no sense. How can she not believe that I love her? She has to know that. I mean, she's perfect in every way— if you told me that everyone who knew her loved her, I would believe it."

"Maybe she doesn't feel that way."

I rub my forehead with my fingertips. "And the worst part is, when I was trying to tell her how loved she is, I think I made things so much worse. I might have really hurt her. I don't even know what I did, so I have absolutely no idea how to repair the damage."

My mom stays silent for a long moment. Then she says, "Would you mind if I talked to her this evening? Not as the Director of the CSA. And not as your wing-man. Just as someone who understands what she's going through. I might be able to help her."

Sometimes I forget how much my mom has experienced. "Please do," I say.

This is an important mission, and I'll need to have my head fully in the game. I can compartmentalize other things going on in my life with the best of them. I can compartmentalize my feelings about Zoe and get the job done, just like I did in Dublin and Serbia.

But let's just say that I would rather not have to compartmentalize my worries about Zoe and whether or not she's okay while being on a mission with Zoe.

CHAPTER 32
SMOKE AND MIRRORS
ZOE

When I went shopping with Charlie, Mackenzie, and Livi, they thought I should buy some kitchen items. I reminded them that I don't know how to cook. They convinced me that it will be helpful to be able to, because it's not always convenient to go get food. I thought that was why Door Dash was invented, but I just nodded.

"Start out making easy things," Mackenzie had said. "Like spaghetti! All you have to do is boil the pasta and warm up a jar of sauce. Easiest thing in the world."

I took her word on it and got a package of spaghetti noodles, a jar of marinara, and a loaf of pre-sliced, pre-garlic-buttered bread. Today was taxing and spaghetti is comfort food, so I figure it's a good time to try out my new pots. So I've got sauce heating in one pot, spaghetti boiling in another, and two slices of the bread toasting in the oven.

Seeing Ledger today was hard. He was just so happy to

see me. I know he thinks he loves me, and I want him to love me so badly. But I also know that it can't last, so wanting it and being around it is just a painful reminder that it is an impossible dream.

I've climbed up onto a tall pedestal with him, and I know that falling from that kind of height will be too painful. So I've started climbing back down the ladder. But I can see that me climbing down is hurting Ledger. It makes everything worse because I love and care about him so much, too.

I just need to focus on work. Focus on this mission— it might be the most important one of my career. It could lead to the takedown of some global bad guys, and I'm sure the Montenegrins will be very happy to no longer have them operating out of their beautiful country.

If I focus on work, I feel confident. Amazing. Like I am the best.

I never feel so completely incompetent and like I have nothing together as I do when I focus on my personal life. So I focus on what I am good at. I grab my tablet so once I start eating, I can look up everything there is to know about the Fortress of Dormitor.

Then I start to smell something burning.

I drop my tablet onto my table as I rush back to the oven. As soon as I open the oven door, smoke starts to billow out of it. I grab a hot pad, pull out the baking sheet, and put it on top of the two free burners. I shut the oven door, hoping to trap some of the smoke in there, but it's still filling the room.

Then the smoke detector goes off. I don't know if it's

connected to building security or everyone else's apartments, and I really don't want to find out by drawing anyone— including firefighters— to my apartment. So I grab the hand towel and start waving the smoke away from the detector as I cough repeatedly from breathing it all in. I stop for a moment to open a window, then go back to fanning the air.

Finally, gloriously, the fire alarm stops it's wailing *Beep, beep, beep*ing, which allows me to hear a different sound. A hissing one. I look over at the oven to see that the boiling of my pasta is no longer confined to the pot, and it's now going over onto my stove. And the pasta sauce is bubbling like it's an angry volcano, spewing its hot lava everywhere. I hurry to shut off both burners and put both pots on top of the baking sheet, just squishing them right in there with my blackened garlic bread.

I run my hands over my face and just stare at the destruction on my stove through the still smoke-filled air.

Then I hear a knock at the door. It has to be a neighbor in my building who is wondering if I simply don't know how to use an oven or if I am in the process of burning the place down. Not exactly the way I want to meet the neighbors. I grab the hand towel again and wave it as I head to the door, figuring I can at least clear a path. Like the smoke is just going to stay where I tell it to go.

I open the door, ready to tell my new neighbor that everything is fine, and see Director Lancaster. She's wearing the same navy pantsuit and mint blouse that she was for our briefing earlier today. Her hair is no longer in the loose bun of earlier— it's in waves at her shoulders.

I stand stunned for a moment. *The* Evelyn Lancaster is at my apartment. *My* apartment.

My eyes go wide. My apartment that is currently filled with smoke, marinara splatters, and starchy pasta water burned to my stove. For the first time since I got my apartment, I wish I was back at a hotel.

"May I come in?"

"Oh, yes. Of course." I open the door the rest of the way as I step to the side, letting her in. I motion to the kitchen with the hand holding the towel, which just flops like a dead fish. "Sorry about all of this. I didn't know that cooking spaghetti could be so problematic."

She glances toward my kitchen and says, "It's not nearly as bad as the time I burned canned chicken noodle soup. I had to throw away the pot and the curtains over my kitchen window." She doesn't so much as get judgmental eyes or squinch her nose at the smell. Her eyes just come back to me, and she says, "I was hoping we could talk for a few minutes. Are you free?"

I nod and lead her to my couch, where we both sit down. The air is clearing, so either the smoke is escaping out the window or my apartment's ventilation system's filter is doing its thing. Not in time to keep the woman I've admired my entire career from witnessing it, sadly, but at least she's in less danger of lung damage.

"I read your file before Sully and I decided on having you and Ledger do a joint mission."

How do I respond to that? By saying "I read your file, too?" No, probably not. That sounds creepy. Instead, I just nod.

"But even if I hadn't," she says, "I would've recognized a fellow foster kid."

My eyes fly to hers. "You were in foster care, too?" I haven't ever had clearance high enough to know that detail.

She nods. "My parents were happily married, and my mom meant everything to my dad. Then, she passed away very suddenly when I was six. My dad didn't handle his grief well, and we had no support system, so I spent the next five years in and out of foster care. Honestly, I thought my dad had sent me to foster care because he utterly despised me. Every interaction I had with him from age six until I moved out at eighteen supported that theory."

I can't take my eyes off Director Lancaster as she's telling me this. She might have seen a fellow foster kid in me, but I have never seen it in her.

"I moved out with plans to never look back. I figured both of us would be happier if I wasn't ever around. The older I got, though, and more distance from when my mom passed, I guess, my dad started reaching out to me, and we were able to rebuild at least a small part of our relationship.

"I eventually found out that his reactions to me and sending me to foster care hadn't been because he despised me. It had been because I reminded him too much of my mom, and he was too grief-stricken to deal with that reminder. And it definitely made it hard for him to show any love to me. In fact, for most of those years, I don't think he was even capable of showing love to me."

This is all so personal, and I don't know how I feel about having the Director of the Clandestine Services Agency sitting in my apartment, telling me about something that must have been so difficult for her. I didn't do anything to earn this level of familiarity and closeness and vulnerability from her.

But I have wanted to know more about this woman for the past four years. Things beyond what my clearance level got me access to, and I am soaking it all in. I just don't know why she is here telling me these things, beyond simply the camaraderie that growing up not being loved by a parent gave us.

Then, as if she can tell that I'm wondering, she says, "I'm sharing this with you because I realized that my dad's lack of love was not because I was unlovable. It had nothing at all to do with me and everything to do with him."

Emotion is starting to well up in my chest, and I clear my throat, trying to free some of it.

"Once I was recruited by the CIA, I realized that my childhood experiences made me a really good operative. I suspect that you have noticed the same."

I just nod. It's no wonder this woman has fascinated me for so many years. We are so much alike.

"Navigating a dad who couldn't move forward again after tragedy and not having anyone close to me was an asset. I figured I was a good operative because I had nothing to lose. That was the key— that was what made me strong."

I nod. That's why I'm strong, too. That's how I got to be the best. I need to get back to that.

"Then, I met Rick and fell in love." She smiles. "That was when I found out that having a lot to lose actually made me a better operative."

My eyes flash to hers.

"It made me try harder. Want to be better. Become more. Part of what made the difference was knowing that he loved me, and knowing there was that kind of love in the world helped me to remember what I was fighting for. It reminded me why trying so hard as an operative was important.

"The way it made me better was knowing that I had his undying support. No matter how bad things got in the field, I knew I could go home to someone who loved me and had my back no matter what. That got me through some of the toughest assignments I've had. Ones that I'm not sure I would've gotten through otherwise."

"Really? It made you stronger? Better?"

She nods. "It really did. And together we decided we wanted to raise kids with that same undying love and support. Kids who knew without a doubt that we had their backs, and that we would no matter what profession they chose. If they wanted to grow up to be intelligence operatives, they could. We would prove that the best operatives didn't have to come from the worst backgrounds. Maybe they could come from the best. Maybe that would make them the best they could be. Just like it did for me."

I'm silent as everything she is telling me is pushing its way around my head, making room for itself, moving the parts out of the way that no longer fit. She patiently sits as I think, not making me feel rushed. So I do. I give it time and permission to work its way in and find a place to stay.

I've got a question that I don't quite know how to ask, but it's burning a hole inside me, so I ask it in the unelegant way it just happens to come out. "How did you manage to fall in love?"

She lets out a short laugh. "When Rick first started showing that he loved me, I had such a hard time believing it was true."

"You did?"

"Yep. I kept pushing him away. Over and over. We actually broke up at one point, but I had pushed him away quite a bit before then, too. I just couldn't accept that he knew what he was talking about when he said he loved me, because all evidence I had pointed to me not being worthy of love. I was fine with him thinking I was a great operative, because I was. But I couldn't seem to open myself up to him loving me."

Suddenly, something Sully told me pops into my head. It was along the lines of *If you're not going to open yourself up to love, you crave the next best thing— admiration?* It had felt like an attack at the time. Maybe because I had felt the truth in it, even if I hadn't been willing to admit it. And now that I know what love feels like, I know that admiration isn't even a close substitute. Somehow, it's easier to accept Sully's words as truth knowing that Director Lancaster had felt the same way herself.

"So, how'd you get past it?" My voice comes out shaky as I ask.

"I had been working on an operation at the CIA when I ended things with Rick. We had been tracking a slippery arms dealer who had evaded us for years. But we knew we were close to getting him and he knew it, too.

"We finally caught a break in the form of a lot of evidence that showed he was in an abandoned factory on the outskirts of a remote village in Eastern Europe. I'm talking satellite images, intercepted communications, on-the-ground intel, all of it. We planned a high-stakes raid with a full team.

"But when we got there, the factory was empty. No signs at all that they had *ever* been there. He had planted the evidence, all while he worked out of a bunker miles away. He'd known we would believe the evidence without question.

"That mission taught me that sometimes, no matter how compelling it seems, evidence can be wrong. I had thought I had all the evidence I needed to believe that I was unlovable. But it was a false trail. It wasn't the truth.

"I suspect you've had those same doubts, and you've had the same experience of believing evidence that isn't true." Her eyes have been on me through the whole story, but her gaze turns fierce as she says, "But I'm here to tell you that those doubts aren't the truth. You were worthy of unfathomable love as a child, and you are worthy of unfathomable love right now. For who you are. For who you were. For who you will be. All of it. For all of you."

Tears are streaming down my face, falling off my cheeks onto my lap. Then Evelyn Lancaster, my role model and idol, wraps her arms around me in a hug. She holds me tight and doesn't let go even as my tears are wetting her shirt.

So many emotions are running through me that I can't even make sense of all of them. All I really know is that right now, I'm being hugged by a mother figure. And that she believes I'm worthy of unfathomable love. My sobs are quiet, but they've turned audible, and still, she holds me tight. I soak it all in.

She continues to hold me until she can tell I'm okay.

I thank her. She tells me that she's glad she's gotten a chance to work with me, and that she's proud of me. I cry some more. I'm not sure I've cried a single other time in my adult life, and now I've cried twice in two days. Both times because of what a Lancaster that I fiercely admire has said to me.

As the director is getting ready to leave, I realize there's one more question I need to ask her. She's told me I'm worthy of love. But she hasn't told me if, when Ledger says that he loves me, that he's right. And I can't think of the words to use to ask that in a way that doesn't sound like I'm actually asking, *So... Do you think your son might be lying about being in love with me?* But I have to know before she leaves. The words that end up coming out are simply, "And Ledger?"

She looks at me in a way that tells me that she understands what I'm really asking. Then she smiles. She pauses a beat before saying, "That is a beautiful necklace. I've noticed that you wear it almost all the time."

I reach up to touch it, and instead of just feeling the locket between my thumb and finger, like I used to, I am already in the habit of touching it with two fingers, one on each pendant. "Always," I say.

"I bet it's so familiar to you that if it was on a table with a few others that looked very similar, you'd have no problem recognizing the real one."

I nod. "Easily."

"Ledger has spent his entire life being surrounded by love. It's a familiar enough emotion to him that he can easily recognize when what he is feeling is the real thing. If he says he loves you, you can trust that he does."

CHAPTER 33
HIGH-STAKES HIDE AND SEEK
LEDGER

Miles, Jace, and I drive to the airport together. I don't know what it is, exactly, but there's more of a buzz of excitement in the air when leaving on a trip while it's still dark. Maybe it's because most of the rest of the world is still asleep, so it feels more like something big and secret is about to go down.

Not that any of our missions *aren't* a secret.

Like the other operatives, we step onto the plane thirty minutes early. "If you're not early, you're late" is pretty much the motto of every intelligence agency. I've never done a big operation like this with the CIA, so this is my first time on a CIA jet. It's not the luxury jet of the ambassador's that we flew to Dublin on but it's not exactly coach, either. It's more what I imagine professional sports teams fly to games in. Not that I have any idea what kind of jets sports teams fly on. But the seats are bigger, and so are the aisles and storage space.

I stow my gear and start chatting with the eight operatives on the extraction team and the six on the distraction team as they are doing the same. We might not be working directly together, but we're all working the same mission. What we do will directly affect one another, so it's good to get to know each other. Besides, you never know when you might cross paths again. It's good to have friends everywhere. I make friends with the crew of the plane, too.

I had hoped to talk to Zoe before takeoff. She is here, but somehow in this small space, I can't seem to cross paths with her, strange as it seems. Everyone starts taking their seats while I'm distracted by a conversation with someone from the (aptly named) distraction team about the best way to create diversions, which means that I don't get a chance to sit right next to Zoe. We are on the same row, at least, but there is an aisle and another operative separating us. We barely get a chance to say "Hi" before the flight attendant gets on the intercom.

She's dressed in a pantsuit, and says, "Good morning and welcome aboard this flight to Montenegro. If we let you on the plane, then, well, you're on the right flight. Fasten your seatbelts and use this time to review your mission briefings, which should be hitting your in-boxes right about now."

I pull out my tablet, connect to the wifi, and sure enough, the mission briefing is waiting for me. It mostly has information about the Fortress of Dormitor that is public knowledge, along with a detailed list of our objectives. Nothing too exciting yet.

I keep hoping to get a moment to chat with Zoe across the aisle, but she sleeps when everyone else sleeps and looks out the window, deep in thought, when she isn't.

Sleep doesn't come easy, but on a ten-hour flight when the people around you sleep, there aren't a lot of other things to do. By the time we land, I'm awake, alert, and ready to get this party started.

As we step off the plane, a new briefing package lands in our in-boxes with information that the surveillance team on the ground here sent to the analysts back home. This one contains things like schematics, where the entrances to the fortress are, which ones are most feasible for entry, where guards are stationed, and guard movements.

The guys already on the ground here got us four SUVs — silver, white, and dark blue ones, not FBI black, thank heavens. My team got a silver one, and I joke that they should've given us gold because we are going to do a gold-medal job on this operation. The drivers are all part of the surveillance team, too, which means that not only do they know the way from here to the forest and from the forest to the staging area near the fortress, but they know about all the obstacles along the way.

I take a seat right next to Zoe in the SUV. She smells and looks great, even after traveling so many hours. I want to tell her how amazing she is, how much I love every second I'm around her, and how much I love her. I want to cup her face with my hands and kiss her until both of us are gasping for air. All of which would probably be pretty inappropriate right now.

Okay, it would definitely be inappropriate. And ever since she ran out of my apartment, I haven't been able to get a good sense of how she feels about us. I really want to talk to her and find out how she's doing. I know my mom went to her apartment yesterday, but when I asked, all my mom told me was, "We just talked." So I'm still every bit as clueless as I have been since I gave Zoe her repaired necklace with its extra pendant.

We all go through our expanded briefing memos as we travel, and our driver, Andre, is throwing in lots of helpful details. So we figure out which entrance we should sneak into the fortress through and which direction each of us is going to head as we place our portable surveillance devices that will map out the fortress for the extraction team and give our handlers eyes everywhere.

We also figure out which of the four of us is going to disable the radio transmitters, the satellite uplinks, the internet routers, and the internal communication networks, and what needs to happen when Zoe gets to their command center. The entire drive ends up being about planning the mission. Which fair enough, should be all about the mission.

And normally, I'd be all about focusing on the op. I'm just having a hard time not focusing on Zoe. Trying to read all of her facial expressions. Wishing I understood as much about body language as she does.

Once we arrive at the staging area, we check our backpacks again to make sure we have all the equipment we need and load our cargo pockets up with everything we might have to access quickly. Then we begin the hike. The other teams are hiking in, too, taking different routes to better avoid detection. Each team is using dedicated frequencies for communication with encrypted channels so the enemy can't easily take them out.

It's a little chilly out, but with our gear and the hiking, it's the temperature I'd pick. The night is clear, and we're far enough away from civilization that there's no light pollution at all, and the sky is incredible. Even the Milky Way is visible from here. I glance at Zoe, wondering if when she looks at the stars, she also thinks about lying against my chest in the canoe on the lake as we both looked up at the night sky.

The forest is beautiful, too. We each have lights strapped to our foreheads so we can hike to the fortress in the dark, but they're pretty dim so we won't be seen from a distance. We keep our voices quiet, too, so they won't travel. Not that they really could in the dense part we're in right now, or over the sounds of the forest. Besides the cacophony of insects doing their thing, we've heard the howling of wolves and a few yowls that we think might be lynxes.

"How's your leg?" I ask Zoe as we hike.

"It's not one hundred percent," she says. "That's become abundantly clear. But I've had worse. I'll be fine."

I nod and fight the urge to offer to give her a piggyback ride because I know Zoe wouldn't go for that in a million years.

We reach a clearing and can see the fortress on the

other side of it. The picture we saw yesterday in the briefing room didn't do it justice at all. The thing is majestic. It's built right into the mountain, and it's as if you can feel how ancient it is. How many people have come here before. The stone is weathered, and moss and ivy are creeping up the sides in some places, and honestly, it kind of makes it feel mystical.

There is a narrow, winding path I'm pretty sure was made by animals that cuts through the trees, shrubs, and rocky terrain and looks like it emerges near the fortress, so we take that. Once we get close, we stick to the forest but head in the direction of an entrance on the side instead of toward the main entrance with the massive wooden and iron gate that's flanked by guard towers. That's near where the distraction team will do their magic.

We stay hidden in the trees, not far from the small door inset in the fortress that, if I hadn't known it was there, would be invisible to me. I'm glad the surveillance team did their job well. We all put in our earpieces and make sure our cameras are on and strapped to the fronts of our vests. Then we each take turns saying "testing" in a low voice to make sure they're working. Through my earpiece, I can hear Zoe, Jace, and Miles here, and Charlie, Kella, and Packston back home.

"Abraham is here, too," Charlie says. "He told me to tell you all 'Good luck, have fun, and don't die.'"

"Will do," I say.

Our handlers are coordinating with the other three teams and their handlers so we don't have to have everyone in our ears. We sit back and wait silently for the go-ahead once the distraction is in play.

It's nearly two-thirty in the morning, local time, when we hear an explosion. Based on the way it lights up the whole area without causing the ground to shake as much as I'd expect with an explosion that size, I suspect that the distraction guys might have added some fireworks to the mix. Some of those booming loud ones. The guys are all making quite the ruckus themselves, too.

It does what it's supposed to, and moments later, we see ten guards running out of the fortress, armed, ready to take on whatever threat has presented itself. If only they knew that the threat was here to arrest them.

"You are cleared for entry," Kella says.

"Go, go, go!" Packston adds. Like we need the extra prodding. I've been bouncing on my toes for a good fifty minutes.

Jace, Miles, Zoe, and I quietly run the rest of the distance across the rocky ground from the trees we were taking cover under to the side door. It has a modern electronic lock, and Jace places the disruptor device on it. A moment later, it clicks, and we all hold our dart guns at the ready and go inside.

We figure that most of the people were drawn out of the fortress by the distraction team, but we will likely run into a few more. We're only here to arrest people, and we can't exactly have sounds of a fight carrying through the fortress walls if we're going to stay stealthy and get the information on that server.

A long hallway runs parallel to the fortress wall, so Jace

and Miles go right, and Zoe and I go left. The hallways have cold stone walls and flagstone floors worn smooth by centuries of use. The air's a bit musty-smelling, which fits.

There are torch sconces on the walls, but they aren't in use— instead, the corridors are lit by LED lights strung along the walls. The guys who set up base here didn't make the installation of the modern lights pretty, or even permanent-looking, which tells me that they probably haven't been here for long. And they're emitting kind of a bluish light, which doesn't go with the fortress at all.

At the end of the hallway, just before it makes a right turn, Zoe places one of the surveillance devices just below the wall torch sconce, hidden in its shadow. It'll scan the area and send live video feed back to our base and on to our handlers. The device also contains signal boosters that will amplify our communications as we take out theirs. I can see that Jace is doing the same thing at the opposite end of the hallway.

The next hallway is short before it splits into two. As I'm placing the surveillance device at the corner, Zoe says, "I guess this is where we split up."

I know we are in the most active part of an active mission, and now is not the time to bring up anything relationship-related. I also know that the camera and the comms are going to catch every bit of this, but still, I reach for Zoe's hand. She meets me halfway, and I give it a squeeze. In the bluish light, I scan her eyes for a moment, wishing I could tell her everything I want her to know. Instead, in a voice that betrays the emotions I'm feeling, I simply say, "Let's go make history."

She nods, seeming to not want to pull her eyes or her hand away from mine, either, and says, her own voice affected by emotion, "I'll bring the pen."

"Splitting off," I hear Miles say through my earpiece.

"Us, too," I reply as I let go of Zoe's hand and head down the corridor away from her.

I quickly make my way through the dimly-lit corridors, dart gun raised, placing surveillance trackers at every corner and in every room I find, confirming into my comms as I place each surveillance device. Every room I've come across so far has been small and feels like it hasn't had a human inside it in decades. As I go, I hear everyone sounding off in low voices about their progress.

"I just found a big storage area," Miles says.

"Tagged the entrance hall," Jace says. "I'm going to find a way around the backside to avoid walking through it."

"Oh," I hear Zoe say. "I think this is a chapel. It has stained glass windows and benches. Tagged."

All three handlers are giving instructions, too, updating us as to how things are going outside.

"I just found the base of the left observation tower," Miles says. "I took out a guard, tagged it, and am heading up."

A moment later, Jace says, "And I just took out a guard at the base of the right tower. Heading up."

Each of my brothers take out a second guard up on the observation deck. Miles fries the electronics in his tower, and after taking out a guard on his side, Jace disables the radio equipment they were using in that tower. Then he heads onto the roof as Miles heads back down to the main level. We hear Jace through the comms as he uses a jammer and a pair of cable cutters to take out the satellite uplinks and communication antennas on the roof.

"I just found the barracks," I tell the team. "No surprise that no one is here sleeping, still. Tagged."

"I found the armory," Zoe said. "Not a single guard here."

Miles says he found the stairs leading down to the holding cells and tagged it, but is still heading toward the center of this level. I peek around the next door opening to find the command center, which houses all of the high-tech equipment, computer terminals and servers, screens showing surveillance feeds, and maps. And two guards, trying to figure out why their cameras went out. I use my dart gun on both of them, and they fall to the ground.

"Found the command center. Zoe, how close are you?" This is exactly where she needs to be to download all their data, then upload a virus to take out their system, and I'd like to hang around to watch her back while she does. Especially because while she does it, she'll be using a localized jammer to disrupt radio frequencies. It'll disrupt the rest of their communications, but it'll also disrupt hers, and I'm not a fan of not knowing what's going on while she's in there.

I hear some grunting, then she says, "I just found the tactical planning room. Three guards. One jumped me." My heart leaps into my throat in the breath between that sentence and her next, "All three are now down."

I grin. Of course they are.

Charlie says, "Zoe, the command center is not far from

your current position. When you get your surveillance device planted, just head into the south corridor. That should lead you toward Ledger."

While she's still in the tactical planning room, I head out into the corridor to watch for her. In my comms, Kella shouts, "Ledger! Behind you!"

But I don't have time to turn before two men grab me.

CHAPTER 34
LOVE, LOCKS, AND AWKWARD CONFESSIONS
ZOE

breathe heavy as I look at the three unconscious men on the ground. I recognize one as one of the Barno Brothers who has been stealing the Trust pieces. Hopefully the second one is somewhere here, too.

Charlie comes on my comms to tell me that the command center isn't far. I put my hand on my healing rib and spleen and step over one of the men on my way to the east wall. It's moments like this that make me realize that I'm not operating at one hundred percent. My leg's a little sore, too, so I shake it out, then place the surveillance device on the wall, just below a map. Then I head to the opposite wall. There's enough stuff in this room that I want to make sure the cameras can pick it all up.

Just like this whole mission, I'm constantly thinking about the three devices in the side pocket of my utility pants. The device that will jam communications in the command center as I work so no one can stop me remotely, the drive I'll plug into their server to download all their data, and the drive with the virus that will take down their system, making it unusable to anyone else once I release the communications jam.

And I try to not think about Ledger and everything that Director Lancaster said when she showed up in my kitchen-disaster apartment. But since that has been running on a loop in my head non-stop, it's been a bit difficult.

I place the second surveillance device and am catching my breath a bit as I head over to a big planning table in the middle of the room. It's filled with so many plans, and I know from past missions to not just assume that all the information can be gathered later just because that's the plan. So I aim my body camera at it so it'll go straight to the agencies now. I hear a bunch of *Whoa*s and gasps from all three handlers.

The Barno Brothers weren't just a couple of guys who were good at scavenger hunts and that was why they were almost set to be gifted Aragundi's empire. They're not just good at being art thieves, either. These guys have plans to sow chaos and destruction across the world that would make even Aragundi proud. It's amazing that they've been able to fly under the radar for so long.

Through my earpiece, I hear Kella shout, "Ledger! Behind you!" and I freeze for the briefest of moments, then I start to run. I race around tables and leap over one of the downed men as I'm heading toward the door. Someone near Ledger growls something in a language that I can't understand.

There's grunts, then the buzzing sound that I know is a stun gun. Then I hear Ledger scream. It goes straight to my heart, and I know it'll be burned there forever. I shout, "Ledger! Ledger!" as I run, slamming into the door that doesn't open as fast as I'm running and head out into the corridor, racing in Ledger's direction. As soon as I round the bend to where Ledger is, I see the bottom half of Ledger's legs quite a distance down the corridor just as they drag him around a corner.

"Zoe!" I hear Ledger's voice in my comms, but it's strained, cracking. "Finish the mission!" And then I hear a high-pitched squeal that tells me someone just pulled out his comms unit and stomped on it.

I run faster. As I pass a panel in the wall, I glance long enough to see that it leads to a secret passage where I'm sure the men were hiding before they grabbed Ledger. "Miles!" I shout. "How close are you?"

"I'm close. I'll go after him."

"No. I need you to get the devices from me to download the data and finish the mission. I'm going after Ledger."

"Are you sure?" he asks.

"Yes!" I can tell my leg isn't liking this punishment, but I've got adrenaline on my side. And a very intense need to get to Ledger. To keep him from harm.

"Okay," Charlie says. "Zoe, keep heading in that direction. Miles, take your next left. Yeah, that one. Okay, about halfway down this corridor, there should be an opening. Go right, and you should intercept Zoe."

I pull the three devices out of my side pocket. Miles

emerges from a corridor to my left just before I get there, and I slow just long enough to get them into his hands without dropping them. Then I run. I round a corner, thinking I should be catching up to them, but don't see them anywhere.

"Back!" Packston calls out in my earpiece. "There was a corridor you missed. It's hidden in a kind of alcove."

I head back in the direction I just came from, slowing just a bit as my spleen makes its displeasure at my activities known. I breathe through the pain, trying to calm my body when it wants nothing even close to calmness.

"A little further. Do you see it?" Packston asks.

"Found it!" I say and hurry down that corridor. This time, I don't run blindly. Our tech ops have the surveillance cameras we placed on their screens and they have the one on Ledger's chest, so they are seeing so much more than I do. I just need to trust that listening to them will get me to him more quickly than I can on my own.

Packston directs me to a door that leads down to holding cells, and I can hear the slam of a prison door closing echo up to me. I stop and take two measured breaths in an attempt to calm my body before I head down. Normally, I'm good at calming myself as needed. But when the man I love is in danger, apparently none of that works.

I still manage to walk quietly down the winding stone staircase, my stun gun raised, as the sounds of the men talking carry toward me. Even if it's not as supportive, I have never been so grateful for my new boot as I am while sneaking down the stairs. With my previous boot, the sounds of me clomping down these stairs would've been bouncing off the walls, alerting the entire fortress to my actions. With this one, I'm almost silent.

I slow as I reach the bottom of the stairs and peek around the last corner. I see both guards, talking and gesturing to each other and the cell where they've put Ledger. I lift my stun gun higher, take aim, and then tag both guards, one right after the other. They both drop to the ground, unconscious.

I run toward the cell. The area has stone walls, floors, and ceiling. Rusted metal bars run from the floor to a low ceiling, separating Ledger from me and the guards. My eyes rove all over his perfect body. "Are you okay? Did they hurt you?"

He's standing. Well, leaning against the bars for support, but standing, which gives me immense relief. I can't stop scanning him for damage.

"I'm just Tased." His voice is still cracking, so he clears his throat. It doesn't help much. "I'll be sore for a day, but I'm fine. You didn't get the data? Plant the virus?"

"No," I say as I step over one of the guards.

"You didn't finish the mission? You weren't supposed to sacrifice the mission for me!"

I shake my head. "I passed it off to Miles. Did you really expect me to stay when they were hauling you off?"

"Yes! That's exactly what I expected!" It's the smile he's trying to hide through his electrocuted-moments-ago exhaustion that makes me realize that he's saying to me almost exactly the same things I said to him when I found out he sacrificed the mission in Ankara to save me.

So I give my own little smile back as I shuffle sideways in the small space between the guards, shaking my head, and say what I remember he said to me. "Never going to happen. I will choose to save you every time."

He lifts an eyebrow. "Oh, yeah?"

I nod and step over the second guard so I can be right next to the cell's bars. Over my comms, I hear Miles say, "I'm activating the localized signal jammer, so I'll be dark until the download is complete, then I'll check in."

Then Jace says, "I'm almost to Miles. I'll watch his back."

I remember that Ledger no longer has an earpiece, so I tell him, "Miles is in the command center now, downloading the data. Jace is watching his back."

"So," Ledger says, "you're saying you sacrificed getting the most credit for the mission for me? You sacrificed the win?"

I grab hold of the bars separating us. "I think I would sacrifice pretty much anything for you."

He had asked the question in almost a teasing, flirty way, but I can see how much my response is affecting him. It tells me that until this moment, he wasn't really sure that I would. Maybe I wasn't sure I would myself.

No. I knew. If I'm being honest with myself, I've known I'd sacrifice anything for him for quite a while now. There is so much I want to say to him. So much I've figured out over the past couple of days that I want to share with him. I just don't even know how to start. I wish I was better at this kind of thing. "Your mom came over to my apartment last night."

"Yeah?"

"You knew she did?"

He nods. "But she wouldn't tell me what you two talked about."

"She told me that if you say you love me, I can trust that it's true."

"And here she said she wasn't going to be my wing-man."

"In all fairness to her, she didn't bring you up. I did."

He reaches between the bars and brushes his knuckles lightly across my cheek before tucking a lock of hair behind my ear and into my braid, just like he had after giving me my repaired necklace. I close my eyes as the touch sends shivers through my whole body. When I open them, he's looking deep into my eyes, like he knows me. All of me. Then he says, "I love you, Zoe Steele. More than I ever knew I could love someone."

Emotion wells in me, and I can feel the truth of his words soaking into me. Filling me to every corner. Settling in my core. Nourishing every part of me. Even the parts of me that I thought had withered and died long ago. It's all coming back to life. I can feel all of it.

"I know," I whisper. And I feel the conviction in my own words deeply. I can trust all of it. For the first time, I *know* that I am loved. All of me. Not just the parts Ledger has seen. He loves even the parts of me he hasn't seen yet. The parts of me that maybe neither of us knows exist yet.

I'm not sure how to even tell him what I'm feeling. Just like with shopping for house things, I am not skilled in this department. But I open my mouth and speak from my heart anyway.

"And I love you. I have loved you for a long time— I'm pretty sure I've loved you since Moldova. It's just grown so much since we left on that plane for Dublin. A lot. More than I thought I was capable of loving someone. I didn't realize, though, how many things were holding me back. Even though I didn't truly believe that I could be loved, I didn't think I'd been limiting how much *I* could love *you*."

I shake my head in frustration. "I don't even know how to put into words how I'm feeling." I look up at nothing, searching for a way to explain, because Ledger deserves to know. This man has given me so much of himself; he should know how much I love him.

I grab hold of the only metaphor I can find. "It's like my heart was a hotel room. It had everything I needed— a place to sleep, a mini fridge and microwave, a little table, a bathroom, a closet. I pretty much kept the door shut tight for most of my life, but I still had it, you know? Then you came along, and I opened the door, and I loved you with my whole hotel room heart.

"And then my heart became an apartment, and I suddenly had a kitchen and a living room, too, with a couch, and pots and pans—"

"And even garbage cans," Ledger says.

"And even garbage cans," I say, letting out a little laugh as I dab a knuckle under my eyelid. "And suddenly, my heart was so much more open. I had so much more capacity to love you. More than I ever thought was possible. And I loved you with my whole apartment heart."

I'm not even sure I'm making sense at this point, but it's the only way I've got to explain, so I press forward. "But I didn't know that my heart was bigger than my apartment. I still didn't believe that you could love me because I didn't know I was actually lovable. I knew that what you were offering me was unconditional, but I thought that it was only because you didn't know yet that I wasn't worthy of your love. And once you found out I wasn't, that would be it for us.

"But now I know. Now I get it. I know that you love all of me. Now that I finally understand, it's like you came along and opened all the doors to places I didn't even know were there. Ledger, my heart is a freaking mansion! And I had no idea that it was. But now that it's all open, I know that I love you with all of it. My whole mansion heart."

My sinuses are swelling and my eyes are getting watery, but still, I chuckle at how ridiculous this must sound. I shake my head and look up, hoping that will help with my eyes and my sinuses and my emotions. "Gah. I am so bad at relationships. I think I'm getting this all wrong."

I meet Ledger's eyes. They're soft. Sweet. Full of emotion. Full of love. In a choked voice, he says, "You're doing so much better than you think you are."

He puts his arms through the bars and wraps them around me, pulling me as close as we can with this prison wall between us. Then, with both of our faces in the space between two bars, he plants the sweetest kiss on my lips. It feels like trust and a promise, and like the lock pendant on my necklace represents, it feels like it's anything but temporary. It feels like it's a kiss promising forever.

Through my earpiece, I hear a throat clear, then Miles says, "I really hate to interrupt this love fest, because, honestly, it's the greatest thing I've heard in a good, long while. But I just need to report in that I've got everything copied over to the drive, and I've uploaded the virus. It has finished its thing, and we have what we need."

"Copy that," Packston says. "I'm clearing the extraction team to go in."

My face instantly heats to the temperature of the sun, and I cover it with my hands to cool it and block out everything.

All of that. I just said *all of that* with two of Ledger's brothers listening. And his sister. And both our tech ops. I had completely forgotten that I had my mic on. I uncover my face and my eyes go wide as it hits me that with a mission as large and involved as this one, we are up on the big screens at both the CIA and the CSA. Our directors heard all of that. Our coworkers heard it.

And not only did they hear it back home, but they saw it. Both of our body cams are on. I shut off my mic and my camera, and Ledger shuts off his camera. "I can't believe I did that," I say, pulling at my collar. It's suddenly so much warmer in here. "I didn't mean to embarrass you like that."

He smiles at me and tugs me closer. "It didn't embarrass me." A smile spreads across his face, then he turns my mic on and says, "In case any of you were wondering, I love Zoe Steele with my whole mansion heart, too." Then he turns it back off.

I swat at his arm. Then I grab him by the collar, pull him close, and press my lips against his.

There is only so much kissing you can do when your cheeks are hitting prison bars, though, so even though I don't want to let go of this amazing man, I do so I can start searching the guards for the keys.

I'm looking through the pockets in the first one's vest when Ledger says, "So… funny story. I don't think they've been at this fortress for long. The guards and I don't exactly speak the same language, and you got down here really quickly— impressively quickly— so there wasn't exactly a verbal conversation going on. But from what I gathered, I'm their first lockup. I think they realized after they shut the cell door that no one has the keys."

I turn in my crouch to look at Ledger. "Are you serious? No keys?"

He nods. "No keys."

I turn back on my mic. There's been a lot of action on the comms as the extraction team moves from room to room, guided by our surveillance mapping, clearing any of the Barno Brothers' people, gathering all physical evidence as they go. I wait for a break in the conversation and say, "Um, it looks like we've got a problem here. There are no keys to Ledger's prison cell."

He leans closer to my mic and says, "I'm hoping that the extraction team brought lock picks. Or maybe the distraction team has some kind of explosive? Or, you know, maybe someone has a master key that works on ancient fortresses."

"We're on it," Charlie says. "It could be a bit, though. We have to clear everywhere on the main level and in the towers before we can get someone down there. Just hang tight."

CHAPTER 35
A PRISON CELL BUILT FOR TWO
LEDGER

oe stands from where she's crouched next to one of the guards who brought me down here and looks intently at the bars that separate us, starting from one end and going to the other. She must see something in the last one, because she walks over to it. She glances at the spaces between it and the stone wall and then it and the next one.

She must decide that the space between the last one and the wall is greater, because she tests it by putting her head between the bars.

"Zoe... What are you doing?"

She turns her mic off again and checks to make sure her camera is still off, puts her head between the bars all the way to the other side, and then she turns sideways and squishes her entire body between the bars. Like a cat, she somehow manages to get through it. When she gets to the inside of the cell, she grins and says, "I'm going to be captured with you."

I point at the iron bars as she's walking toward me. "Did you really just—"

"I couldn't kiss you like I wanted to from out there," she says as she comes up close to me and puts her hands on my chest.

"Okay, this… This I can get on board with."

She runs her hands up over my shoulders and to the back of my neck, leaving a trail of something tingly and wonderful. My muscles no longer care at all that 1200 volts of electricity just went through them, causing them to seize. All they care about is Zoe's touch. She plays with the hair at the nape of my neck, and it sends shivers across my shoulders and down my back. A moan escapes me at the touch.

Then her lips are on mine, hard and urgent, and it's like she's trying to show me through a kiss all of the things she just told me, almost like a confirmation, and I am all for it. I cup her face with my hands, caressing her cheek with my thumb, and our kisses slow. Soft and purposeful, sweet. Our lips are moving together like this is what they were always meant to do. Her body is pressed against mine, and nothing has ever felt more right.

I release her face and wrap one arm around her waist, the other at her back, and I turn us so that she's against the wall. With one hand on the wall, bracing myself, I move the other to cup the back of her head and brush soft kisses down the side of her neck. This time, she's the one to let out a moan, and the sound of it sends a thrill through me.

My muscles haven't quite recovered from being tased yet, and I need to sit before I collapse. I place a kiss on her forehead, then touch my forehead to hers. "I love you, Zoe." Her smile lights me up because now, I know she believes my words.

"And I love you right back, Ledger."

Before long, we're both sitting on the stone floor. My back is against the wall, and her back is against my chest, just like we were in the canoe. My arms are around her, my hands resting on her stomach, and she's got her arms over mine, running her fingers lazily along the backs of my hands. I don't care how hard this cell floor is— I could stay like this forever.

Zoe shifts her position so she can see my face a bit, and says, "For real, though. I've never been in a long-term relationship before. Of *any* kind. Well, I guess you could say I've had a relationship with the CIA for four years. But I don't have any experience or know-how. Are you really okay with that?"

I shake my head. "Zoe, you don't need any of that. You are enough." I pause a moment. "Besides, since when have you ever let a lack of experience or know-how stop you from becoming an expert at something?"

Zoe blinks.

"If you ever want something, I have one hundred percent faith that you can figure out how to get it. There is nothing out of your reach. No matter what it is that you're reaching for— whether it has to do with our relationship, some life goal, or anything else at all, just know that I will be there with you, supporting you in whatever way you need, cheering you on."

"Someday," she says. "Someday I'll be as good at this as you are." I chuckle, and she turns back around, resting her back against me again, her head at my shoulder. "So, have you ever been captured and kept in a dungeon cell before?"

"Yep. When I was tracking a weapons smuggler in Sudan, I was captured by local rebels." I look around. "The stone was a warmer color. Less silver and gray, more golden brown. And the bars weren't far enough apart for you to sneak in. I snuck out through an old drainage tunnel. How about you?"

"Once, when I was on an undercover operation in Colombia and captured by a drug cartel. I snuck out by disguising myself as one of the guards."

"Oh, nice," I say. "Have you ever escaped from somewhere using something the bad guy left you with because they thought it was harmless?"

She nods. "I got out of a handcuff situation using a broken sunglasses arm. How about you?"

"I escaped from a zip tie restraint using a plastic straw from a juice box."

"Wow. Really?" she asks. "You'll have to show me what you did sometime. Have you ever sweet-talked your way out of captivity?"

"Of course. Once, I talked a particularly vain guard into not actually locking my restraints before leaving the room by complimenting his shoes and asking where he got them."

"I should've known better than to ask you such an easy one."

"How about you?"

"I was in a mansion, tied to a chair, when someone came in to bring me food. I flirted with them and convinced them to 'adjust' my bindings. Once they left, it was easy to slip out."

"Impressive. I wish I could've witnessed that one."

We continue to swap stories, with Zoe occasionally updating me about the situation above from what she hears on her earpiece. A few times, she turns her mic back on and responds to a question or two. But mostly, we just sit there, holding each other, and I soak in every bit of bliss.

Eventually, Zoe hears that they have cleared the main floor and will be sending people down. A moment later, we hear voices and footsteps on the winding staircase, and then three guys from the extraction team come into view. They take a look at the two guys still unconscious on the floor, then the two of us in the cell.

One of the guys, Oscar, points between the two of us, his brows drawn together. "I thought it was just one of you in the cell."

Zoe lifts a shoulder in a shrug. "It got boring on the other side of the cell, so I joined Ledger."

The guy doesn't look any less confused, but he pulls out a lock pick set while the other two lift one of the unconscious men and carry him up the stairs.

"How did it go up there?" I ask him.

"Better than expected, actually. A good number of their

guys were drawn out by the distraction team's very effective distraction. It helped that we did it in the middle of the night— I think it kept them from making good tactical decisions on that front. So we got all those guys captured before heading inside. It took us a bit longer on the inside because that secret passage those two guys came out of when they grabbed you actually wove throughout the fortress."

Oscar glances up from the lock for a second. "Zoe, you took down one of the Barno Brothers in the tactical planning room, right?" Zoe nods. "When we cleared out the main floor and the towers and got all those guys out with the others, the other Barno Brother was still MIA. But we eventually found him weaseling through the secret passages."

A smile spreads across my face. "So we got them both."

An audible click sounds, and Oscar smiles as he pulls the lever and swings open the cell door. "We did. Between us, we accomplished all of the mission objectives. We also got a lot more information on Aragundi and the Barno Brothers' contacts than we ever thought we'd get."

I give Zoe a high five, then high-five Oscar. Zoe and I both walk out of the cell, and I shake the man's hand and say, "Hey thanks for letting us out."

"I never miss a chance to pick a lock." He glances at the two of us. "I hope you weren't in here too long. They said to get everything wrapped upstairs first— that you two wouldn't mind waiting."

I look over at Zoe and smile.

"We didn't mind waiting," she says, and smiles back at me.

Even though my muscles are still protesting, Oscar and I pick up the second guard and haul him up the stairs. I got to hang out and kiss Zoe while all the action was going on— it's the least I could do.

When we make it back outside, the sun is coming up, lighting the mist rising from the forest, and it's one of the most beautiful things I've ever seen. Then my eyes fall on Zoe, and I think, *But it doesn't even come close to comparing with her.* "Well, we made history," I say. "Should we head home?"

She grins and nods. "Yep. Let's go home."

EPILOGUE 1
METAPHOR IN REAL LIFE

ZOE

I just got back from a six-day mission in Morocco and Ledger just got back from five days in Finland. Neither were comms blackout missions, so we were able to talk every night. Still, though, we've been dying to see each other. And it's my turn to pick the date, so right now, we are on the top of a cliff overlooking a valley.

"Okay," I say as we both drop our bags of paragliding equipment on the ground. "For today's challenge, we have to get our equipment set up and strapped on." I point out across the valley toward a small lake in the distance. "See that outcropping of rocks just before the lake?"

Ledger steps up behind me, and he nuzzles my neck before saying, "The ones with the tall grasses by it?"

I nod, leaning my head into his. "Yep. That's our target destination."

Ledger puts the tip of his finger in his mouth, then holds it up in the air. "Wind is going the right direction."

"It is." I know, because I checked wind maps when I chose this location and again an hour ago.

Ledger and I have had just as many of our individual missions cross over and found ourselves at the same place at the same time just as much over the past six months as we did in the year and a half before our joint mission. We've even gone on a second joint mission with both our agencies.

Ledger's tally board at the CSA has changed, though. Instead of listing which one of us "wins" each mission, it has morphed into a list of which one of us wins our "date night challenges."

And right now, Ledger is up by one. I'm hoping that changes by the end of this date.

I turn around to face Ledger and grin. "And we've got ten minutes to jump off that cliff, starting now."

"Ten minutes, huh?" Ledger says, wrapping an arm around my waist and pulling me in close. "That means we have time to spare."

He brushes his knuckles along my jaw, which always drives me crazy. Then he cups his hand on the side of my face, cradling it, like I am more precious to him than anything. I accepted long ago that his feelings are true, but it still takes my breath away to know that I am so fully loved by this man.

I rise up on my toes, put my arms around his neck, and press my lips to his. He moves both hands to my back as we kiss, and I soak in the feeling of being held by Ledger. I will never tire of this. I don't think Ledger will, either— we are both just as crazy for each other as we've always been.

I once thought that if we were in this exact scenario except with a real mission on the line, Ledger would spend the entire ten minutes talking to whoever was on the cliff with him about something other than the mission, right up until it was time to jump off the cliff, not even getting his paragliding equipment ready. Just jumping with the hope that he can get his equipment on and ready during his fall. It had annoyed me.

Now, though, I get it. I understand how he works and why he prioritizes relationships with people— it's one of the things I love about him. And I have to say, I'm okay with him spending ten minutes not preparing for the mission if it means kissing him this much.

Well, mostly. I do still want us both to survive this.

But we can definitely take kissing time, too. Of course, I'll always say yes to any time with Ledger. Or with Ledger and any of his family.

Over the past six months, I've gotten to go to so many of his family dinners. I had forgotten how great it feels to experience that feeling of family. I've even gotten to meet more of his family. Like his dad's parents— his grandpar-ents— who are the nicest people. They're like TV show grandparents. The kind who show up to spoil their grand-kids, have a great time, enjoy lots of laughs, and make cookies. I'm talking real, made-from-scratch cookies. I've even met a couple of aunts and uncles on his dad's side, too.

And I've met Reese, who is Miles's best friend. I've

even met her bees, which is a whole thing. I've gotten to be good friends with Charlie, Ledger's almost sister-in-law, Mackenzie, and Mackenzie's friend, Livi, who I now consider to be my own friend. And I've made friends with so many other people through Ledger. I even got to play a game of hurling with Evan, the ambassador's aide friend that Ledger made on our plane trip to Dublin. Our life will never be void of people because Ledger is so good at making friends with everyone.

I care greatly about all the relationships I've formed. Especially my relationship with Ledger. He has added more to my life than I ever thought one person possibly could.

I've also had more "family" in my life than I ever imagined. I love them all, and I know they love me, too. I hope that one day they will officially be my family. When Ledger and I are ready. Which isn't something I ever really thought I'd be hoping for.

I sigh into our kiss and pull back just a bit, even though I leave my arms around his neck. "As much as I would love to continue kissing you until long after the sun goes down, we better get moving if we're going to jump off this cliff before neither of us can win a point for this challenge."

"True," Ledger says, then gives me one more kiss. "We better get moving."

We both race to strap on our harnesses, making sure each other's is secure, then put on our gloves and helmets. Then we each lay out our own canopy and connect it to our harness.

As we are doing our last-minute checks, I look at my watch. "Thirty seconds."

Ledger grins. "One thing I know for sure is that our life is never going to be boring."

I shake my head. "No, no it is not."

Then Ledger whoops loudly as we run toward the small clearing, and then we both leap off the cliff.

EPILOGUE 2
OPERATION HONEY POT

CHARLIE

Livi, my almost-sister-in-law's BFF and the woman with whom I'm sharing Maid of Honor duties, stands up in front of the guests, who are all seated in chairs in a big circle on the grass behind the row of townhomes where I live. She says, "Okay, and now we're going to play a game I like to call, 'How well do you know Mackenzie and Jace?'"

Mackenzie is seated right next to where Livi stands, and she's practically glowing with happiness. My brother, Jace, has had the same look as her for quite a while. I am so excited for the wedding coming up!

Everyone's here. Mackenzie's mom, her three sisters, my mom, some people from Mackenzie's work, my roommate Reese, who is also my brother Miles's best friend (and he makes sure I remember that she was his best friend first), two of my aunts, and three of Mackenzie's, and my future sister-in-law, Zoe.

Well, she's not *officially* my future sister-in-law, yet— Ledger isn't the type to rush into something as big as an engagement, and I don't think Zoe is, either. But I'm calling it right now that they *will* get engaged.

Just like I called that they were going to have their enemies-to-lovers arc on that mission. I'm rather good at noticing all the little things that show when someone likes someone else, but I'm not the only one who sees it with Ledger and Zoe. It's plain as day to see that the two of them got in a car together, put the top down, turned onto *It Will Only Ever Be You* boulevard, and are currently driving, music blaring, hands in the air (except for the one on the steering wheel), straight toward *Wedded Bliss and Babies* town.

It may take a while to get there, but they'll get there eventually. Those two look at each other like skydiving, sunsets, and fireworks didn't even exist until the other stepped into their lives.

Ledger and Zoe can take as long as they want to make things official, but I'm not waiting to claim Zoe as my sister-in-law. She's one of us, now. I've spent my whole life as the only sister in a family with five brothers— it's about time we started evening out the numbers.

While Livi explains the game, I hand out the cutest papers to each person in the circle for them to mark their answers on. They've even got a little honeycomb and the words *Bride to Bee* at the top to match the theme.

Mackenzie was smart to name Livi and me as co-

Maids-of-Honor. The details of things sometimes… go wrong for Livi. The details are where I shine. Plus, there is no way that *I'm* getting up in front of everyone to run this game, yet Livi doesn't even mind having all eyes on her. I'll gladly take hostess duties any day of the week, and Livi will gladly take the reins for interactive fun.

"Okay," Livi says, "Question number one: where did Jace and Mackenzie first meet? Was it *A*, in an escape room where they accidentally got paired together and couldn't escape. Was it *B*, at a restaurant while Mackenzie was on a bad date, and Jace pretended to know her. Or was it *C*, at a sidewalk sale at an outdoor mall, when Jace tackled the guy who stole Mackenzie's purse and returned it to her? Write down your answer."

It was *B*! Of all my brothers, I am closest to Jace. And although he does tell me a good amount about Mackenzie, I doubt I get as many details as Livi gets from Mackenzie. I am one hundred percent sure that Mackenzie shared the details with Livi all along the way of her and Jace meeting, dating, and falling in love.

But also, I had tapped into the cameras inside that restaurant and had been on comms with Jace, so I was present for the whole glorious date interruption where Jace and Mackenzie came up with a story together about how they knew each other. I was also on comms and cameras during the sidewalk sale with the purse snatching, so I know that happened the second time they met.

The escape room, though? Total fiction, unless Jace is holding out on me. I walk over to the refreshments table to check on everything as Livi runs this game.

People should hire me to come up with the food for any bridal shower they are planning because this spread is next-level. Jace and Mackenzie seem to have some kind of inside story related to honey, and since my roommate, Reese, is a beekeeper, I did everything honey-themed. I even got Mackenzie a sash to wear that reads *Bride to Bee*.

Everything is in yellow and white and spread out beautifully, if I do say so myself. The table holds all of the refreshments and also glass jars of lemon drops, butter mints, and yellow flowers. Mackenzie has taken a picture of every date that she and Jace have gone on, so I printed out their favorites and have each one stuck in a place card holder and spread throughout.

I've got cupcakes that look like they're each part of a honeycomb, sugar cookies each frosted with two bees and the words *I found my honey*. I've got cute little honey mascarpone cheesecakes, honey hummus with veggies, blackberry and honey tarts, and a fruit board with honey-spiked cream cheese. Oh, and grilled pear, brie, and honey crostinis.

People should *not* hire me to do the actual baking, though, because that never goes well. But, I mean, who hasn't had a batch of potato chip cookies in the oven when they get an emergency call to support the intelligence operative who's intercepting a rogue agent in Berlin? I am an excellent planner, though. Top notch. I'm good at searching for the best bakery, picking out the best items, and presenting it all in a way that is beautiful and matches the bride's personality.

And based on the looks on everyone's faces, it tastes every bit as good as it looks.

Which I already know, of course, because I taste-tested one of everything before I brought it out here. What? I had to make sure I was serving high-quality refreshments.

"Okay, question two," Livi says. "What did Jace and Mackenzie do on their first date? Did they *A*, have a picnic in the park and then play miniature golf, where Jace protected Mackenzie from a rogue golf ball. *B*, go to a black tie fundraising event where they both tangoed, or *C*, attempted to build the world's largest pizza at a make-your-own pizza restaurant?"

A! Man, I am killing it. It's too bad I can't play. Okay, even if I wasn't hosting this, I would have an unfair advantage. I was also present (remotely) for the picnic/panic at the golf ball incident and at the black tie event. It's too bad Jace stopped letting me tag along on his dates via comms. I miss out on so much.

Movement at the side of my townhome catches my eye and I glance over. My heart kicks up a notch at seeing that it's my neighbor, Owen. Our units share a wall and he's got another unit on the other side of his, so he has to come around to the space between buildings on my side to get to the garbage bins. He's tossing in a big bag, probably from his kitchen. The man is just so cute!

He either hears or sees our group in the backyard, so he looks in our direction, curious. Our eyes meet, and he smiles. He's got such a great smile, and I find myself smiling back with my whole face. He gives me a nod before he turns to go back to his house.

It's been a few weeks since I hid behind the bricks for that reconnaissance mission. We didn't talk too long that day, but I really liked getting to know him a teeny bit and seeing what he was working on. Neither of us has made any kind of move since then. I've mostly been admiring him from afar.

And daydreaming. Lots of daydreaming. He's just got a face that makes me all… I don't know. Fluttery. It's a kind face. A happy face. But also an intriguing face. Like there is so much more about him that I don't know. And so much that maybe he doesn't share with anyone. It all makes me unbelievably curious about him.

And suddenly, I'm right back behind those pallets of bricks when Zoe was saying that I could learn a lot about someone by going through their garbage.

Oh, look. We are running low on honey mascarpone cheesecakes. I better go back inside and get some more. I pick up the platter and motion to Livi that I'll be right back, just as she starts asking the next question.

"Where did Mackenzie and Jace have their first kiss? Was it *A*, when they bumped into each other while Mackenzie was going on her never-miss-a-day walk and Jace was walking a dog that wasn't his when they got caught in a downpour. Was it *B*, in an elevator that got stuck between two floors. Or was it *C*, behind the stage at the concert on Main Street while the cover band sang *Man! I Feel Like a Woman*?"

It was totally *C*. I wasn't on comms at all for that one, but I did manage to get a few details about the night from Jace. I knew that he danced (on stage, even!), and I knew that they kissed. I didn't know that it happened behind the stage or to a song about unleashing your girl power.

As I reach the end of the grass, I pick up a stick with the hand not holding the platter and head toward the garbage cans. The bag I saw Owen bring out is right on top, practically screaming *I hold so many answers!* It's one of those translucent bags where you can kind of see things inside but not super well.

And really, all I can see are some banana and orange peels, Chinese food boxes, used paper towels, and eggshells. I hold the platter away from the garbage and poke at it with my stick. Then I kind of tip it up with the stick, trying to see if there's anything visible from the side that might be more telling than what things he probably has now added to his grocery list.

I spy some food wrappers, an empty spice bottle, and an old candle almost completely melted down. If anything is interesting in there, it's not on the surface, and the bag is too clouded to see it. I sigh and toss the stick in the garbage with everything else. I've learned nothing, and I really need to refill this platter. I spin toward my apartment, taking a step in that direction as I do, and crash right into Owen. I let out a squeaking sound as the force of our collision knocks the platter from my hand.

Owen drops what he is holding, twists, and manages to catch the platter without a single little cheesecake falling off.

"We've got to stop running into each other like this," he says, an amused smile on his face.

I swear, he was completely out of sight when I started looking at his trash! How did he even know I was here?

It suddenly feels very hot. And I have a strong urge to hurry back to the party. Or into my apartment. Whichever is faster. Instead of trying to gracefully exit this awkward moment, I make it more awkward.

"At least this time, what I dropped isn't spread across the front yard." I cannot believe I just reminded him of the incident with the tear in my wet laundry bag and the trail of tush covers and booby traps I left strewn for all to see. I nod at the cheesecakes. "Thanks for saving the day for these."

"Glad I could help," he says, handing the platter back to me. "Now, if I could just keep from dropping things."

I glance down to see that what he'd been holding until he decided to go all superhero and catch a flying cheesecake-laden platter in mid-air was a second garbage bag. This one is much smaller— maybe something he forgot the first time around. That's why he saw me here. I crouch down to pick it up for him at the same time he bends to pick it up, and we bonk heads.

Seriously, we *bonk heads*. Like toddlers do in situations like this. I swear, I am not this inept normally! Something about being around Owen just makes me forget how to work my body. And my brain. Which is immediately evident in the fact that I still grab hold of the bag, even though he's grabbing hold of it, too. We both stand with the bag between us like it's a baton in the world's slowest relay race.

And I just look at him, like I'm trying to memorize the

way his eyes crinkle at the corners or the way his cheek dimples as he smiles. Or the way his scruff looks perfectly touchable. Thankfully, I do manage to let go before it starts to feel like we're in a standoff, and he tosses it into the bin. Then he nods at his bigger garbage bag that's lying right on top and raises an eyebrow. "Find anything interesting?"

My face flames with heat. So he definitely witnessed that. "I, uh," I say, trying to quickly come up with a reason why I had been poking his garbage bag with a stick. "When I saw you over here, I thought that your hair looked like it smelled great. I was wondering what kind of shampoo you used, and I thought I saw a bottle in your bag."

His eyes shift to his garbage bag so mine do, too. There is nothing visible that looks even remotely like it could be a bottle of anything. My face is not cooling down anytime soon.

Then, his eyes come back to mine and he seems to be trying to suppress a smile as he says, "If there's anything you want to know about me, you can ask."

"Thanks," I say. "I will." The smart thing to do right now would be to ask him something I've been curious about. Or to say something witty. Or to get my flirt on. Be a honey pot. But I just told the man I was searching his garbage for a shampoo bottle because, from a distance, his hair looks as if it *smells nice*. I think it's best if I don't ask right now. It's like the quote that says something like, *It's better to not talk and be thought a fool than to speak and remove all doubt.*

I figure that from this point onward, I have two options.

One: I can avoid Owen. Avoiding Owen will avoid the whole "body and mind forgetting how to work in his presence" thing. This will, in turn, keep my face from harnessing the heat of the sun.

Or two: I can do exposure therapy. Maybe if I'm around Owen enough, his power to incapacitate my brain will lessen.

Option one sounds safe. I like safe. Option two makes my heart race just thinking about it. A bad kind of race, in the way that only thoughts of future awkward embarrassment can cause.

But also a good kind of race, like maybe I'll be able to find out more about this man. I can tell that he's one of those people who are happy as their default state, but no one is as perennially happy as Owen seems to be. Everyone has something going on under the surface. Some people just like to hide their something behind an ever-present smile. And this racing heart of mine? It wants to discover what's behind that ever-present smile of his.

But, since I already decided that I shouldn't ask any questions and risk showing just how disconnected my brain is around him, I just lift the tray a bit and say, "Well, I better go... get this refilled so I can get back to the party."

Then, instead of heading toward the front of my place so I can go inside and actually refill the tray, I prove how disconnected my brain is around him and head toward the party.

It's too late to turn back, though. So I just put a hand on

my face to cool it. Just before I reach the refreshments table, though, I have to know that he's gone. I take a glance back and see him standing by the trash bins still, giving me an amused smile.

———

Want more of Charlie's and Owen's story? Pre-order your copy of Spies Don't Fall for Their Neighbor.

And of course, it'll have more of the Lancaster family!

ACKNOWLEDGMENTS

I want to give a huge shoutout to all the Bookstagrammers, BookTokers, reviewers, and early readers who do so much to get the word out about my books. I am so grateful to you!

Many of those readers graciously contributed names I used for characters in this book. A big thank you goes out to Shauna Douglass, Kaila Willardson, Holly Carol, Mandy Biesinger, Allie S., Mark Brandwein, Nati Hurtado, Jessica, Lisa Bell, Nikki Scheuermann, Stephanie Price, Shanna Johnson, Gmaw, Traci H, Jennifer Kelley, Rosie M, Marilee Merrell, Alissha Wilhelm, Kelli Moffett, Tiffany Thompson, and Angie Bourdages.

Another huge thank you goes to my brilliant editor extraordinaire, Rebecca Rode, who helped me to see things I couldn't and helped me to make this book so much better, and to all the early readers who scoured this book for any typos that managed to make their way through.

I owe big thanks to body language experts, especially Joe Navarro, who have been willing to share their expertise with so many. Their help was invaluable for Zoe's scenes.

@milliebrookeslivesbooks— The dead drop in a diaper was for you. :):) Thank you for the suggestion.

A massive thank you and much love always goes out to my husband and my ultra-supportive family. You are my everything.

And a very heartfelt thank you to you, the reader. Your enthusiasm for books means the world to me and is what keeps me writing.

ABOUT MEG EASTON

Meg Easton is the *USA Today* bestselling author of contemporary romances and romantic comedies with fun, memorable, swoon-worthy characters, and settings you'll want to pack up and move to. She lives at the foot of a mountain with her name on it (or at least one letter of her name) in Utah. She loves gardening, bike riding, baking, swimming before the sun rises, and spending time with her husband and three kids.

She can be found online at www.megeaston.com

Sign up to receive her newsletter and stay up to date with new releases, get exclusive bonus content, and more.

If you liked this book please leave a review. Your review can help other readers find books they might fall in love with.

youtube.com / @megeastonauthor
bookbub.com / authors / meg-easton
instagram.com / megeaston_author
facebook.com / MegEastonBooks
tiktok.com / @megeaston_author